Julia Wherlock is the
historical romances,
United States. Origi
near Cambridge wit
her first historical sa

Also by Julia Wherlock in Futura:

THE BELOVED

JULIA WHERLOCK

Bridge of Dreams

Futura

A Futura Book

First published in Great Britain in 1990
by Macdonald & Co (Publishers) Ltd
London & Sydney
This Futura edition published in 1991

Reproduced, printed and bound in Great Britain by
BPCC Hazell Books
Aylesbury, Bucks, England
Member of BPCC Ltd.

ISBN 0 7088 4888 5

Futura Publications
A Division of
Macdonald & Co (Publishers) Ltd
Orbit House
1 New Fetter Lane
London EC4A 1AR

A member of Maxwell Macmillan Pergamon Publishing Corporation

Acknowledgements

My wholehearted thanks to Mr Michael William
able Secretary of the Brunel Society. Also a gra
you to the Vicar of Eton, Berkshire for Brunel fa
dates (the dear fellow scoured the graveyard m
me). And a mention for Reece Winstone who
records of my home city, Bristol, have captivated
was old enough to read the captions.

Part 1
The Waif

CHAPTER 1

Early Summer in Bristol, 1843

Teddy Bird was not a bad man. He didn't want to sell his daughters. It was the only way out – as far as his mind was capable of figuring – and the sensible thing to do.

He was a poor, ignorant man fallen on hard times, a labourer on the land with too many mouths to feed. Other men had wives who were barren, or sterile from female maladies that thankfully put paid to their childbearing days. It was his hard luck that he had a wife who was rude of health and bred like a doe-rabbit.

True, he could have denied himself the pleasures of the marriage bed, but it was his *only* pleasure, he had excused himself, and nothing would stop him indulging himself, not even unwanted brats. So he solved the problem with the same consummate selfishness with which he had caused it and, paradoxically, shed a tear or two in the process, for even when ruthless he could still feel sadness at his approaching loss.

May, born in the month of the same name eight years before, and her sister, Jane, the senior by a year, were bemused by the proceedings: May gazed around in blank-faced puzzlement while Jane snivelled and wiped her nose on her sleeve, distressed by the sea of adult faces before her.

They were not placed upon an auction block. Nay,

nothing as uncivilized as that. Such would have smacked of slavery and trading practices long past in Bristol's history. Those things had died with Wilberforce's campaigning and resulting anti-slavery Bill, continued now only in foreign lands through backwardness or economic necessity. England – smugly superior in her humanitarian guise – no longer dealt in slaves. However, that didn't stop her selling her own children in servitude, and in a society where the poor were kept poor at the bidding of the wealthy, such occurrences were not uncommon, no matter how unsavoury.

The Llandoger Trow – named after a coastal vessel which had transported coal across the River Severn from Wales to Bristol – was a riverside tavern frequented by every type and class, from lowly matelot to informed, wealthy merchant searching for a new line in trading cargo.

A lowly-born writer of periodic articles and pamphlets who had signed his work D Foe, Dan Foe, Dan D Foe and finally – having found fame – Daniel Defoe, had, in the previous century, met and talked to a sailor who had made it home miraculously to Bristol after an adventure that almost seemed too far-fetched to be true. The sailor, Alexander Selkirk, had been shipwrecked and lived alone on the uninhabited Juan Fernandez Island, furnishing Defoe with the background and inspiration he needed to write *Robinson Crusoe*. Selkirk understandably put off the idea of going back to sea after so unimaginable an experience, and spent the remainder of his days, so the story goes, recounting his tale for a price in the Llandoger's public bar and allowing his avid listeners to keep his tongue loosened with endless tankards of ale.

With leaded windows and half-timbered walls, the Llandoger Trow faced out upon a cobbled street wet with rain and full of nautical clutter. Hampering the progress of traffic were barrels and bales, trunks, crates and rigging blocks, mooring ropes and sail canvas.

Beyond, at the end of the street and so close that May felt she could have reached out and touched them, rode the brigs and barques at their berths, masts and rigging undulating noticeably against the stationary, solid structure of buildings. She'd never seen a ship before, and fell under their odd spell immediately, forgetting the unhappy Jane and her stony-faced father who, with such words as 'clean', 'honest' and 'hard-working', was attracting a small, interested crowd willing to give a minute or two of their time as they arrived at or left the Llandoger Trow.

May wasn't even halfway towards understanding what was happening, unlike Jane who'd overheard the terrible words at the cottage the night before. She had heard their mother crying and knew that Teddy had hit her to put an end to the argument once and for all. May had slept through it, saw this day as a great adventure – even if it was raining and Ma hadn't been able to come with them – and couldn't understand Jane's behaviour at all.

She smiled, humming along as a bawdy sailor's song came to her on the warm breeze. While she watched the men work on the decks she tapped her toe in time to whistle and squeezebox. 'The boys'll be murd'rous jealous when they find out what fun they missed,' she told her sister cheerfully.

'No they won't!' came the doom-laden reply. 'They'll be glad they was left home to work in fields. They'll be countin' their blessins.'

'Whatcha mean, Jane? Ain't they missed out on seein' the sights o' Bristol? Din't Ned always say he wanted to visit the city?'

'This ain't no visit, May. Don't you see? We ain't goin' home again, *ever*. Da is goin' to sell us as servants. We'll never see Ma again!'

May's arched eyebrows drew together, puckering her forehead. Could that be why Ma had cried so long and hard that morning when she said good-bye? May had thought it was a bit overdone when they'd only be gone for a day. Never going home again? She couldn't imagine that. Jane must be making it up. She did that sometimes – told tales, big fanciful stories that no one believed but everyone found entertaining.

'Don't be silly.'

11

'I ain't. It's the bleedin' truth.'

'Shut it, Jane!' barked Teddy Bird as the crowd thickened and impressions became all-important. 'You two be on yer best behaviour. Don't speak lest youm spoken to and then be mindful of yer words.'

But if they were never going home again, where *were* they going? How would she ever see Ma, Ned and Jim again? And there was her doll. It had been Jane's before it was handed down to her, but it was all she had. Da, impatient to leave for the city that morning, had refused to let her go back and get it when she realized – a hundred yards from home – that she had left it behind. Did this mean she would never see her doll again? Her lip began to tremble. 'But, Jane, we don't belong nowhere else, 'cept with Ma and Da.'

'They can't afford us no longer. Girls costs too much to look after, needs money for marrying, don't pull their weight.'

May looked at her father, but he seemed to be making a point of avoiding the picture his frail, tattered daughters made, touching his conscience and causing guilt to rise. Her eyes travelled on, past the snivelling Jane to the gathered crowd; to the bare-footed sailors in canvas trousers and knitted pullovers with bobble-hats to match, or peaked caps pulled down low over one side of the face; and over the gentlemen in black patent leather shoes, crisp white linens, pressed trousers, frock-coats and tall top hats.

The thought struck her suddenly that within a short while she might be taken by the hand and led away to the house of one of them. Fear lurched within her, alive and growing larger out of the numbness of disbelief. Who was going to take her away? The man with the bad teeth standing apart from the others beside an alley, where a woman sat on a barrel feeding her baby? The man taking snuff, with a sniff, from the back of his hand? The woman who'd just ordered her carriage to stop so that she could witness the proceedings? She at least looked kindly, nice, and clean, in dark clothes and bonnet with just a trimming of lace to soften her face. May wished silently that if she had to go with someone then it be that lady.

12

But she'd have rather gone home – home with Jane and Da, and back to Ma who was soft and simple, who couldn't cook very well and sewed just as badly, but that didn't matter. 'I want Ma,' she wailed suddenly, joining Jane in a spate of high-pitched, discordant weeping.

Teddy Bird had also noted the presence of the kindly-looking woman, and a naive hope and trust in mankind prevailed. There, surely, was a woman who could offer his daughters a good home.

'I be a-askin' twenty guineas each for my girls. And I'd be a-wantin' it in writin', mind you, so as none could argue the terms of sale. They'd be legal property of who-so-ever did buy 'em until the age of twenty-one. Then they'd be free to suit their selves as to their future. Or they might be 'appy to stay on in their post for as long as it did suit 'em, though o' course t'would be only fitting that they'd get paid a decent wage in that case.'

She shook her head, dismissing the sum contemptuously. 'I'll give you twenty pounds for the pair of them. In truth I'd be doing you a favour by taking them off your hands. They're too young and lacking in muscle to give a decent day's work. But I've a Christian heart and would offer them a good home and the basic necessities of life, provide for them selflessly until they were old enough to repay the kindness with good, hard work.'

'Well . . . ' Teddy's forehead creased as his bushy eyebrows met above uncertain, shifting pale grey eyes. Disappointingly, she seemed the only one to show much interest. 'Twenty-five guineas, the pair,' he compromised.

'Twenty-five *pounds*,' she quibbled.

Momentarily he gnawed the dirty nail of his index finger, eyes focused upwards in deep thought so that little save the whites were visible. His wife was going to be mighty mad when he went home with just twenty-five pounds. After all, she hadn't wanted him to sell the girls. And to have got so *little* for them . . . ! She'd probably throw the rolling pin at him. 'I can't rightly go no lower'n twenty-five guineas.'

'Oh, all right then,' agreed the woman waspishly. 'I'll write you out an IOU.'

13

'An IOU! What good'll that be to me? I want *real* money, woman.'

'Sir,' she said, as if there was an obnoxious smell under her nose, from her superior vantage point in her carriage, 'I am not in the habit of carrying around such large sums of cash with me. If you do not trust me to have the money delivered to wherever it pleases you within the day, you are at liberty to ride with your girls and I to my place of abode, and there you will be the recipient of the *real* money.'

Teddy's mouth twisted. He didn't care for her attitude. What gave her the right to think she was any better than him? Just because she had a carriage, decent clothes . . . If his wife had spoken to him like that he would have taken his belt to her. He would almost have liked to be able to tell her what she could do with her mean offer, but he needed the money. Twenty-five guineas, although not as much as he had hoped for, was still a larger sum than had ever come into his hands to date.

Business seemingly almost at a conclusion, the crowd began to disperse into the pub, or down the street to be lost amongst the everyday crowd. May, through streaming tears – not to mention nose which she wiped instinctively on her sleeve – watched her new owner in trepidation, clinging to the terrified Jane who had gone quiet with fear. They were being cast off by a father they had always assumed loved them, shunned in grand biblical manner, and May – with the clear and simple thought to match her years – decided that she would never forgive him, especially when he hadn't even let her take her doll along to give comfort. She would hate him until the day she died.

'Man, would you dispose of your own flesh and blood so lightly? Have you no interest in the fate of these innocents, blinded as you are by the promise of twenty-five miserable guineas?' The question came from one of the stragglers of the dispersing crowd.

The woman in the carriage, Teddy and the girls looked his way, finding a short, *very* portly man to claim the gentle tenor of his voice. At a glance they knew him to be wealthy,

14

and moderated their manners somewhat in deference, the woman was instantly subdued and Teddy, at his obsequious worst, shuffling uncomfortably and stooping, chin almost settling onto his chest, muttered, 'I can't see as how it be any business of yours, sir.'

''Tis my Christian duty, man, to see that the innocent are not used to further the evil desires of others. I could not sleep easy in my bed this night knowing that I had stood back and done nothing to save them from a life of immorality in that woman's charge!'

Both Teddy and the woman denied the possibility vehemently, their expressions hostile.

Obediah Goodbody shook his head at them, indignant on behalf of the children. He knew Ruth Mead, madam at the notorious Dolls' House, and guessed that her anger was at his interference. Two potential fresh and pretty whores were slipping through her fingers. As for the man, Obediah believed him to be without true blackness in his heart; he was just ignorant. Desperate. Such men did diabolical things. But the man should have checked upon the intentions of the woman concerning his children. It was his duty not to be so trusting, so naive. Obediah was angry with him because of that and felt his heart wrenching when he looked at the two wretched daughters, very nearly gone like lambs to the slaughter. He had a daughter too, a gentle, prim miss, fourteen years old, and as he visualized her in the same situation, his indignation surfaced again and his blood reached boiling point.

'Sir, you cannot permit this. I *know* that woman, of her dealings in the flesh of womankind. Be not persuaded by any glibness of her tongue.'

'Is what he says true?' Teddy demanded, treating the woman instantly like a pariah.

'So what if it is? They'd be getting food and a bed to sleep in. It's more than a lot can boast. The docklands are full of beggars, homeless, streetwalkers . . . ' said the woman, defensively.

'Bleedin' 'ell,' mouthed Teddy disgustedly.

'Take your daughters home, man,' urged Obediah.

15

'I cannot. I ain't got the means to keep 'em fed,' moaned Teddy.

'Then,' decided the man on the spur of the moment – something he felt certain he'd regret later, 'I'll buy one of them for twenty-five guineas – your original asking price. You take the other home and look after her, as you would your sons, from now on.'

One might have supposed that Teddy would be pleased. And he was – concerning the money. The man was willing to pay the full sum just for one daughter. But that still left him with the other on his hands. And *which* daughter should he let go? There was nothing to choose between them. He liked them both equally in an indifferent kind of way.

Obediah Goodbody allowed himself a small smile of victory. He'd thwarted Ruth Mead right enough and felt a certain amount of satisfaction at the thought of having saved a couple of souls. But *what* was he going to do with the girl, whichever she might be? She would be unschooled, unclean, uncouth . . . He couldn't take her home as a companion for his darling Anne. Anne would be horrified. Maybe he'd see her placed below stairs for the time being, watch her and see what developed. Perhaps she'd show enough aptitude to be a scullery or parlour maid.

He almost laughed out loud, being a jolly man by nature. He had come to the Llandoger Trow that midday dinner hour to meet some of his fellow members of the Merchant Venturers, discussions to be held on Mr Brunel's latest proposed engineering feats. He had never envisaged missing the meeting and using the time to indulge in the buying of child labour. It all seemed ludicrous – melodrama of the type Mr Dickens turned out in order to make his middle-class readership more aware of the poverty and degradation in the seedier districts of the cities in which they lived.

'Done!' agreed Teddy, causing the madam to snarl and order her rough and ready driver to move on. The father's eye settled on Jane. 'Ye may take the eldest.'

Immediately she burst into tears, howling like a wounded animal. 'I don't wanna go! I don't wanna go! I wanna go home!'

16

Obediah had expected a few such awkward moments, but that didn't prepare him for them any the better. 'Poor child. It does seem such a shame . . . '

'She's young; she'll get over it soon enough.'

May – clutched and hugged desperately by Jane as if she were a rock that might save a drowning soul – wriggled free and pushed her elder sister away from her. 'I'll take her place.'

'You would?' Obediah looked her over in surprise. She was smaller, more fragile, yet there was something in her face – in the eyes especially – that interested him. *She* wouldn't cry, not in front of them at any rate. Nay, not that one. She was sad and frightened, like her elder sister, but more than that she was angry. As her gaze settled coldly on Teddy, Obediah realized her anger was for him, the man who had betrayed his own family. She would never forgive him.

'Yes, I'll go with you,' she said in a small voice, sealing her own fate.

17

CHAPTER 2

Early Summer in New York, 1843

'Have you a comb I can borrow, Cap'n Mitchell, sir?'
wondered Jude Somerton, pulling grey wool stockings up
over legs that were still wet and turning blue now with the
cold.

'Aye, here you are,' said Captain Jack, obligingly, taking
one from his trouser pocket and tossing it to the lad, his lazy
gaze never straying from the busy doings on the Hudson.

Jude turned it over in his hand, curious.

'Fine, ain't it? Whale bone that is, fashioned by some
sailor from up Cape Cod way. Precious little else to do on
the voyages once the whales had been caught and butchered,
so he carved these to pass the time and used to sell them on
his return to port.'

'Hum . . . ' murmured Jude, appreciative of the crafts-
manship, dressed again now after his dip in the dark waters
of the Hudson, and very nearly tidy as he dragged the comb
through his hair, lounging on the deck of Captain Mitchell's
ship, *The Celestial Piper*. She was a barque, old but sea-
worthy, and a sight to behold when in full sail with the wind
behind her.

'You've no time for lying there day-dreaming. Best be
getting yourself home. Your being late for supper don't
bear thinking about,' reminded Jack, talking around the
pipe in his mouth.

'Yes,' agreed Jude, picturing his father and the fist that could strike with only the slightest provocation. Morgan Somerton was not a tolerant man. The length of Manhattan's westside shore, where wharves and berths crammed the water's edge, the name of Somerton was met with an answering frown. Everyone had had dealings with the man at one time or another, for Somerton had a finger in every pie. He was fair, they wouldn't deny, and honest, but there was *something* about him – a kind of menacing cantankerousness was perhaps the nearest one could come to describing it – that made him virtually impossible to like. Add to that the fact that he was a man whose drinking habit was fast becoming a problem – making him anti-social, even violent – and the lack of social life in and around the family was better explained.

Mama had long since given up entertaining the wives of her husband's contemporaries who worked on Wall Street. Her nerves hadn't been able to take it in the end – wondering if and dreading that Morgan might come home early from his offices and interrupt her teas with one of his icy stares or blunt, even downright unfriendly remarks. Neither did the children invite home their friends, though they were both popular at the schools they attended. Morgan Somerton had a way of frightening children which Jude had never thought fair to inflict on any of his friends. Thirza, his sister, had taken her class mate, Mary Montgomery, home once for tea, but his father had made her tremble with his loud voice and dictatorial manner and eventually Mary succumbed to tears and had had to leave earlier than expected, never to return.

Jude got to his feet, collecting up his school books and handing back Jack Mitchell's hair comb. 'Where you heading this time, cap'n? The China Sea? Tom Brannigan told me they still got pirates in the east. Said they weren't above cutting off people's heads when they captured a luckless ship. Didn't believe in taking prisoners. Is that right?'

'That bosun of mine's got a runaway mouth and imagination to match,' scoffed the captain. He could have told tales that would turn hair prematurely grey with fright, and they'd all be true, but to relate them to others gave him – unlike Tom Brannigan – no pleasure at all. 'Rest easy, Jude, my lad. This trip is unlikely to prove anything more than a month or so of routine hard work and boredom. We're going to Wexford then on to Le Havre. I'll be back before you know it, having met not a single pirate on the way. Still got a hankering after the sea, have you?'

'Sure, cap'n. I like Manhattan, don't get me wrong . . . . It's a swell place. But I kinda feel penned up. Shucks, in history class last week when Mrs Egan was teaching us about Peter Stuyvesant and all that, she told us that Manhattan is only thirteen and a half miles long and two miles wide. I know it like the back of my hand already, couldn't imagine living just in this one place for ever. I see the ships sailing and steaming out into the Atlantic and I get a powerful urge to go with them,' sighed Jude, dodging aside as a sailor absailed down out of the rigging and landed agilely beside him.

'Maybe one day you will,' soothed Jack Mitchell, keeping the boy's dream alive. He'd always taken an interest in Jude, though there was no special reason why. Jude was just one of many kids who hung around the docks, swimming in summer or listening to the embellished tales of the sailors around braziers in the winter. There was something about the jet-haired, blue-eyed child that cast a spell over adults. He was the opposite of Morgan; everyone liked Jude, and he never had to try, never ingratiate himself. There were other children who were more polite, intelligent, fetching of looks and sweet of nature, but Jude had that certain something else. Charm, Captain Jack supposed it must be, a charm that guaranteed him a welcome almost any place.

'My father won't allow it. He says I have to go to Columbia University same as he did, then join the family business,' muttered Jude, his gaze following one bare-footed sailor who climbed like a monkey up through the barque's rigging to make last minute repairs to one of the sails. 'I'll be the fifth generation of American Somertons to join the merchant trading firm of Somerton, Somerton and Van Hann. It's expected of me. Since Uncle Dudley died two years ago without a son to carry on, his *Somerton* has been just a name, left for the sake of tradition, his interests taken over by my father and Van Hann. Both of them are against outsiders joining the firm.'

'That puts a lot of pressure on you though, doesn't it, Jude,' commiserated Jack. 'Do you really see yourself working beside your father in an office all day long?'

Jude rolled his eyes at the prospect. '*This* is what I like, cap'n . . . the waterfront. The smells, sounds, watching the ships, even the changing colours of the Hudson. I see things the same as you. I'd like to just sit aboard here for ever and ever and draw and paint everything I saw, everywhere we went. But . . . ' – and the light went out of his eyes – ' . . . I have to do as my father tells me.'

Jack nodded sadly at the fact. 'And now you'd best be going, lad, or he'll be angry at your being late for the evening meal. Is there anything you'd like from Ireland or France? Anything I can bring you back?'

'No, thanks, cap'n. There's nothing I can think of. I just wish I was going with you. That's all I've ever wanted.'

'One day maybe. Perhaps your father could be persuaded in the future to let you take a trip to Europe. Lots of families send their sons on 'Grand Tours'. Seeing life in other countries is supposed to help them mature and give them character, I do believe.'

'Father would think such an extravagant indulgence without creditable point. His line would be that hard work builds character and that I'll get plenty of that at Somerton, Somerton and Van Hann. Besides, Cap'n Jack, I'd have to be of age before I could do such a thing – even supposing he'd allow me – and twenty-one seems a darned long way into the future to me. Shucks – I'm only *thirteen*!'

'Aw, Jude, stop looking on the black side. The future looks bleak, I know, but things change, and fortune and circumstance hold surprises for everyone. Bide your time. Patience, lad,' Jack instructed.

'How can I be patient for *eight* years?'

Jack didn't have an answer to that, so he turned his attention to the loading of his ship, preparing for her sailing on the morrow's early tide.

Thirza had sat for a long time at the window in her bedroom, anxiously scanning the street below where Broadway met Wall Street in a vain search for her brother. She did so worry on Jude's behalf, hidden away in her room, out of sight and out of mind, she hoped, of her papa. Often lately, her brother – four years her senior yet none the wiser for that, she thought – had taken to wandering after school was out, across town to the Hudson where the ships had an irresistible pull. Each time he came home later, cutting things too fine, and if papa were to find out . . . ! Her insides knotted at the thought.

The fact that she didn't love him, not even half as much as she loved her mother and brother, left her riddled with guilt. But it was difficult to love someone when you knew youself to be an irritant to him, a person he'd rather not have to share the company of if it was at all avoidable. Thirza and her papa only met at meal times lately, and then he wouldn't make any effort to be polite, but instead scorned her ever-plumpening figure.

It had been a beautiful day, but the pleasure of it was cancelled when papa arrived home from work. He'd stopped at some watering hole on the way, doubtless knocking back half-a-dozen Bourbons in quick succession, and had begun shouting orders the moment he slammed the front door of their Federal Adam style house. All gaiety vanished, everyone made themselves scarce and poor mama quivered and trembled, apologizing for the fact that the meal wasn't already on the table but she hadn't expected him home half-an-hour early.

'Pathetic excuses!' papa had snarled, his eyes glaring and his heavy features twisting unpleasantly, as he shoved her aside and headed for the liquor cupboard in the drawing room. 'I want my meal on the table in five minutes, or else . . . '

'Yes, Morgan,' promised mama, fleeing in terror to the

22

kitchens where she mobilized everyone, infecting them all with her fear.

Thirza left her haven reluctantly and went down to supper, hardly speaking during the meal, where the sounds of awkward coughing, swallowing and the clatter of cutlery in nervous fingers dominated.

Having cowed wife and daughter into silence, Morgan Somerton was still not satisfied. The sound of his wife Mary-Anne masticating her food irritated him just as much as her hesitant, tentative attempts at chatter usually did. 'What have I done to deserve such tedious company? Well, woman, will you answer?'

In grey taffeta and with her salt and pepper locks pulled back into an unattractive bun on the top of her head, mama looked like a mouse and acted like one as she stiffened in her chair, then shrank before him. 'You did not seem to want to talk during the meal, Morgan. I was only trying to comply . . . '

'Bah! And where is that son of mine? He knows the rule about being here promptly at meal times. His increasing bouts of absence are beginning to displease me.'

Thirza quaked, fearful for her brother, her movements slow and careful as she ate, so that – she hoped – she wouldn't draw attention to herself and have to suffer papa addressing himself to her in some menacing fashion calculated to ensure that she left the table with indigestion.

Bravely, Mary-Anne defended her son. 'He is growing up fast, Morgan, dear. It's natural at that age for boys to begin to stray. Manhattan offers a great many diversions for young, inquisitive minds.'

'Madam, do not presume to tell me the nature of my own sex! *I* was never like that.'

'No,' agreed mama readily. Morgan had never been like that. He'd been born demanding and dictatorial and had never changed.

'And what do you mean by that tone of voice?' he demanded to know.

'Uh . . . I . . . nothing, dear. I just meant that everyone is different. You and Jude have little in common.'

'I'll not deny that. I never misspent my formative years mingling with the riffraff around the docks. I worked, *damned hard,* so that my father would be proud of me when eventually I joined him in the firm of Somerton, Somerton and Van Hann. I took duty more seriously, was very much aware of the honour entailed in working for such a long-standing, well-established and respected financial concern. My son is a disappointment. He needs a sense of duty knocked in to him. And if I catch him drawing again, so help me I'll take my belt to him. I'll not have anyone in this family fancying themselves as artists,' he spat. 'It's low . . . shameful . . . calls his masculinity into question.'

Mary-Anne frowned, confused by what she deemed to be words without sense.

'Pass the decanter,' ordered Morgan, his manners absent.

Mary-Anne poured him a small measure instead, and that proved to be a mistake.

'What are you about, woman? Do you think to control my drinking by serving me half measures? Or is it that you don't think me capable of pouring myself a drink without spilling it?' he hissed, head down and gaze directed at her from beneath thick grey eyebrows, the intense eyes as cold and pale as Sheffield steel. He got ponderously to his feet, the better to dominate proceedings.

'No, of course not, Morgan. I never thought . . . just wanted to be helpful. Here, take the decanter. Help yourself,' she pleaded.

'Snivelling bitch!' He threw the whisky in his glass directly at her, the liquid hitting her in the face and taking her breath away.

Mary-Anne spluttered, bursting into tears and groping blindly for a napkin with which to mop herself. Thirza sat like a statue, frozen with a horrified expression, watching the scene.

And then Jude walked in smiling, with his school books under his arm, about to greet them all in his usual politely casual manner, when he noted their expressions. His smile faded.

24

CHAPTER 3

Morgan Somerton, austere in black frock-coat and trousers, with crisp white linen showing at neck and cuffs, drew himself up to his most impressive full height, a tic pulsing at the corner of his eye as his violent gaze fastened on Jude, his words coming in a roar. 'And *where* have you been?'

Jude was looking at his mother, indignant on her behalf as she sat there mopping away at herself, embarrassed and fearful, her coiffure and gown ruined. So *much* fear all the time, he thought in despair. It was never right and fair that one house be visited with such cold, continuous hostility. Never right that one man should be able to make so many others so miserable. God forgive him, but he wished his father dead. What joy it would have been to wake just *one* morning and anticipate a day ahead when there would be no trembling with fear, no hiding away to avoid the man's brutality, no standing by in impotent anger while his mother got a black eye or bleeding nose.

Jude took a handkerchief from his pocket and wiped the whisky drips from her hair, only to have his arm grabbed and twisted by Morgan.

'An answer, if you please.'

'I've been down by the docks.'

'I thought as much,' said Morgan with satisfaction, being right giving him childish pleasure. 'Mixing with the water-front scum when you should have been home here taking supper with your family.'

'I'm no later than normal, sir,' Jude said, defensively. 'I think it's rather that you are having supper early.'

'Don't dare to get smart with me!' shouted his father, grabbing Jude by an earlobe and dragging the wincing boy close so that they were almost nose to nose. 'There'll be no supper for you tonight for being late. Perhaps that will ensure that in future you get yourself home at a reasonable hour, in plenty of time to sit down with the rest of the family.'

'Very well, sir,' Jude conceded quietly. His father doubtless was itching for an argument, but he wasn't. If going without supper meant that the outburst would be over and done with, then so be it. It was a small price to pay to spare mama and Thirza further distress.

That should, therefore, have been the end of the matter, and the females were, by small degrees, beginning to relax once more, but Morgan wasn't satisfied, didn't take kindly to the clever way the child had extricated himself so smoothly from the fraught situation.

'And what have you there? Don't think you're going to sneak off to your bedroom and sit there reading Walter Scott or the like. *Oh no.* That would suit you just fine, *wouldn't* it?' hissed his father.

'I've nought but my school books here, sir.'

'Indeed? Then what about the sketch book I can see?' demanded Morgan.

'It's for my drawing lessons at school, sir.'

'I think I'd like to see it.' He said it in such a way that it sounded like a command, then stood there imperiously.

Jude, infuriated by the shaking of his own limbs, and having intercepted looks from mother and sister which urged him to greater courageousness, set down his books and presented his father with the sketch book tied up with an old piece of Thirza's hair ribbon. Then the two of them stood at the head of the table and for a while there wasn't a sound.

Morgan snatched off the ribbon then turned the pages in a rough, uncaring fashion, drawing in his breath wrathfully when he found what he'd been looking for amongst the still-lives and botanical studies. 'Ah-ha!'

26

Jude held his breath.

Mary-Anne gripped the arms of her chair so tightly that her knuckles showed white, and Thirza put an arm up in front of her face to shield herself from the indiscriminate blows that must surely follow.

'Just as I suspected!' spat the master of them all. 'He's been drawing *everything*, going far beyond anything that he's been called on to do at school. Look at these, wife. Ships, sailors, the Hudson. I can recognize these places easy enough, even one or two of the people. Don't tell me this is school work!'

'No, sir,' admitted Jude.

'And what have I told you about drawing and the like?'

'That you don't like it, sir,' supplied Jude, voice cracking up as terror made his mouth go dry.

'That I *don't like it*! Correct. So why do you persist in it? Art is for idle females and males of a Bohemian disposition. You will cease it immediately, do you hear, confining yourself solely to the work set for you at school, and when you go on to Columbia and the subject of art is no longer compulsory, you will drop it altogether from your studies. As for these drawings . . . '

The three of them held their breath, aghast as Morgan snatched up the sheets of heavy paper and rent them in half, then quarters.

'Don't do that,' cried Jude, hurling himself at his father and momentarily enjoying the advantage of surprise. Never before had he retaliated. Morgan lost his balance and Jude grabbed the papers, father and son fighting like two dogs claiming the same bone.

'Oh, stop it, please,' squeaked Mary-Anne, trying to get between them, frightened though she was, and protect Jude from the inevitable rage that must soon overpower them all. 'Please, Morgan, don't hurt him. He's only a boy.'

Morgan clouted her about the head and his wife staggered forward, slamming into the sideboard. A stuffed bird under a glass dome went crashing to the floor and she followed it, sliding down in semi-consciousness and cutting herself amongst the splinters.

27

'Mama! Mama!' sobbed Thirza, wanting to go to help her, yet too frightened of getting past her father to do so.

By this time Morgan had gained the upper hand with his son, holding on to him by the belted waist of his knee-breeches and loosening his own belt with a menacing, pleasurable look in his crazy grey eyes.

Jude screamed with horror as he remembered the last belting he'd endured at the man's hands, and twisted feebly to try and escape. The buckle ripped through his breeches, scratched skin, then ripped through flesh when there was no longer fabric to afford him protection. Jude howled, going limp in his father's grip, and the last thing he saw was poor Thirza looking around frantically for help then being sick all over the white starched table cloth.

The house was black and quiet when Jude rose from his bed and turned up the gaslamp slightly to give himself enough light to dress by. He moved slowly, in pain as he pulled on breeches and stockings and buckled shoes. Morgan Somerton had taken his belt to him for the last time, the boy decided adamantly. He was going, tonight. And he would *never* come home again.

Fully dressed and with his best black woollen jacket with red velvet collar fastened against the night chill, the matching peaked cap having slipped carelessly to one side of his head, Jude placed some of his smaller, favourite things into an old canvas travelling bag, turned the lamp down low again and let himself out of the room.

He was taking nothing of real worth, as he would be starting a new life, with few reminders of this unhappy time to cloud what must surely be a bright future. He didn't want anything from this place, not even the memories of a privileged childhood. Gladly he was giving up his warm, well-fed, carpeted and cushioned past with a cold, brutal tyrant, for an uncertain future where he could laugh and breathe easy, no longer flinching at the sound of a certain voice.

He crept on tiptoe along the landing where low burning lamps played on the scarlets and golds in the carpet under

28

foot, and very carefully – the doorknob making a barely audible whine and click – let himself into Thirza's room.

She wasn't asleep, just as he had expected, but lay hidden beneath her eiderdowns and pillows, sobbing wretchedly.

'Thirza,' he called softly, lifting the pillow aside. She almost squealed with terror, assuming it was her father come to reprimand her about her noisy crying, then let out a noisy, heart-rending sigh when she saw Jude in the gloom. 'Thank God, it's *you*! Oh Jude, I've been so worried about you, and so sad. Did he hurt you real bad?'

'Yes. But this'll be the last time. I'm going, Thirza. Tonight. I'm running just as far away from this place as I can get. I've come to say goodbye and tell you not to worry about me any more. From now on I'll be fine,' he told her brightly.

'Running away?' She gaped at him, her deep blue eyes, so like his own, wide in awed wonder.

'Yep.'

'What if he finds you?'

'He won't. I intend getting away quick. I'll change my name. Disguise myself,' Jude assured her confidently.

'Oh, you *are* brave,' she praised, drying her eyes and smoothing the jet ringlets back from her tear-wet face with podgy fingers. 'I wish I had your courage, Jude. Maybe I *would* if you took me along.'

He shook his head, sadly. 'You're too young, Thirza. And where I'm going there's no place for a girl. I'm sorry.'

'I understand, really,' she said, miserably resigned. 'I'll stay here with mama, and try to protect her as best I can. But promise me, Jude . . . '

'What?'

'That when you're able you'll come back and rescue me, please,' she pressed.

'On my honour, sister.'

They hugged, Thirza crying again softly, and Jude slipped out of the room and further along the corridor to the stairs, passing his parents' room from which his father's inebriated snores resounded. Maybe his mama lay in there even now beside the ogre, not daring to cry the tears within her for fear of waking him and causing his wrath to fall.

Jude would have liked to say good-bye to her too, but he couldn't take unnecessary chances. With him, instead, he would carry a reminder of Mary-Anne the way she had looked the last time he saw her; crumpled defeatedly into her voluminous skirts and crinoline hoops, her palms bleeding where she'd saved herself from falling heavily to the floor by putting out her hands, blood smears on her clothing merging with the whisky splashes so that they spread quickly like ink on blotting paper. She hadn't deserved *that* and she had *always* deserved better than Morgan Somerton. The man was obscene. But what was most disturbing of all was the fact that he was Jude's father, thereby passing on something of himself in the body of his child. He owed his existence to that very man he most despised. He just prayed that none of Morgan's character proved hereditary.

30

CHAPTER 4

Midsummer in Bristol, 1843

Bristol City was an inland port second only to London in trading importance, its heart given over to warehouses and docklands broken up geographically by the natural loops and bends of two converging rivers, the Avon and the Frome. Dredgers worked constantly keeping the estuary clear of mud so that shipping could be piloted down-river through the magnificent cut of the ancient gorge, out of the Avon's mouth and into the strong tidal waters of the Severn and Bristol Channel.

Bristol traded in tobacco and cotton from North America, coffee and mahogany from South America, and imported a good percentage of Portugal's sherry. She also had a reputation as a leading manufacturer of fine azure blue glass, which looked unusually striking when turned into stemmed goblets for the local merchants' tables, or decanters and fruit bowls that served as table centrepieces.

Once Bristol had had a great castle not unlike London's White Tower in structure and size, but the parliamentarians had knocked it about considerably during the Civil War and by the reign of Charles II it was demolished, much of its stone disappearing to be used in local building. Houses and shops were built on the site and eventually no hint of the fortress remained, its existence remembered only in the place name, Castle Street.

Bristol abounded with bridges, city gates and enough medieval churches to satisfy worshippers and students of architecture alike. It also had a cathedral, once an Augustinian abbey founded by the great saint himself, and, according to Good Queen Bess, 'The fairest Parish church in the whole of England'. Unfortunately, St Mary Redcliffe had suffered from the ravages of time and acts of God even before the Virgin Queen's visit, and by 1843 it was in need of much restoration. Still grand of proportion, its perpendicular tracery, buttresses and stained glass had had to endure centuries of smoking chimneys coating it black, and since 1446 it had been facing the world with a truncated stump, for its spire had tumbled down after being struck by lightning.

Sweeping up and away from the docks, past the cathedral and College Green, was Park Street, which in the seventeenth century had indeed led to the Bishop's park at the top of the steep hill. By 1843 the top of the hill, overlooking the picturesque gorge, had become a cliff town, the dwelling place of merchants and shippers, engineers and bankers. The rich lived in Clifton, their houses Georgian, Regency and Victorian terraces of three or more storeys with basement kitchens below ground level. Most were built in sandstone or Cotswold limestone, roofed in grey slate and fenced off with ornately wrought railings that ran up beside the front steps.

Obediah Goodbody lived at Number 8 Beaufort Rise, his front door painted a cheery pillar-box red and window frames a sedate mushroom, while his footscraper – for practical reasons – was of black wrought iron which his charge, May Bird, cleaned every morning with strong soda water, her routine well established now, her work satisfactory.

Next door at Number 6, where the front door was mustard yellow like the mail coach livery, the facade was much the same, the Georgian pillars bordering the door bearing the brass house number and a knob which a caller pulled to summon a maid to answer the door. Avon Midwinter lived here, virtually alone since the death of his parents in the freak accident at Weston-Super-Mare the summer before.

Swimming was all the rage and his mama and papa had ever been mindful of staying at the top socially, which meant keeping their names on everyone's invitation lists. It took a great deal of stamina to stay in demand. They'd made it their life's work to appear gay and charming, witty and clever whenever they were in public. Only Avon and his elder sister, Aurelia, had seen the other side of them – the tired, irritable reality of the perfect pair; dyeing their hair to maintain the illusion of youth, corseting their thickening figures ever tighter so as to always look trim and fit, and indulging in madcap escapades the likes of which Avon had grown out of at grammar school. He'd become impatient with them long ago and by the time of their death, had scant regard for either, his grief quickly overcome.

One day they were home entertaining all their middle-class cronies at tea, the next day they were dead, swept out into the Bristol Channel after drinking too much champagne on the sandy beach to wash down the buffet they'd enjoyed for lunch. Neither had been very good swimmers and it appeared – from what witnesses told Avon on bringing home the two black-bathing-suited corpses – they went out further than was prudent considering the treacherous tides that dragged and pulled fools out to sea before they knew what was happening.

Showing off, Avon had decided. They'd been doing their utmost to impress and overdid it. He was only surprised that their friends had managed to recover the bodies. By all accounts a dinghy had been pushed out the moment the alarm was raised and the floating bodies found in calm, deceptive waters.

Avon – pronounced in Bristolian manner like the river, A-vun – was sixteen now, a wealthy orphan who, having suffered parents to whom appearances had been all important, decided that he was *never* going to worry about what others might think. He could, because his father had bequeathed almost all to him, do precisely what he wanted, and would never have to please anyone unless it pleased him also.

33

It had been arranged between his father, the late John Dagwood Midwinter and the firm of family solicitors, Craddock, Mountjoy and Dyce, that Master Avon should receive a conservative sum to take care of expenses on a monthly basis. All major transactions, however, would be dealt with by his trustees, who – it went without saying – had his interests uppermost in mind until he reached his twenty-first birthday and could take charge of his own affairs.

The way of things suited Avon fine. He had money to pay his bills, freedom from parental dictate and whim, a housekeeper to see that he lacked neither for food on his table nor creature comforts and an elder sister who, although she didn't reside at Beaufort Rise, was to all intents and purposes – especially those irritatingly detailed ones in the Last Will and Testament – the boy's closest living relative and therefore, on paper, his guardian.

By mutual agreement Aurelia trusted him to behave in a gentlemanly manner without having to resort to constant surveillance and supervision. It was a situation which suited them both. Aurelia would much rather have spent her time in the pursuit of her own interests, and Avon had no wish to share his home with her again. There had never been any bond between them and when she had married Sir Courtney Spicer, no one had been happier than Avon to see the back of her. He wouldn't countenance her moving back in.

So he behaved, as much as it was necessary for a gentleman to do so, and enjoyed his life, eventually taking no interest in the business his father had bequeathed him. Where was the point? He had trustees to act and think in his best interests, employees to see that his business ticked over profitably, and a housekeeper to see to the smooth running of his home. In the years when his future character was most susceptible to influence, Avon Midwinter was spoilt and pampered, served without question, and was left without doubt that everyone was there solely to serve him. Whatever he wanted he got. No one ever said 'No' to him. Such was his outlook on life as he sat back and anticipated his coming of age with relish. Life promised much and he'd already

34

decided to have it all and grab anything else which came along and took his fancy.

The gothic country mansion at Long Ashton in the southerly outskirts of the city, with its twelve bedrooms and two bathrooms – which actually had hot and cold water plumbed in! – was grand indeed, but Aurelia was unappreciative of her good fortune in marrying well. She hated the place, resenting greatly the fact that Courtney didn't have a house in the city proper where most of her friends and acquaintances resided. All the visiting to and fro wore at the nerves and patience, and the solitude of the park in which her home was set was driving her crazy. It was too removed from the hurly-burly of city life, too quiet. It made her uneasy.

She strolled along the gravel path at the rear of the house where the grounds had been terraced and stone urns placed with much forethought for the pleasure they would give the eye, spilling over with geraniums and hedera. Beyond were balustrades, separating manicured lawns from the wilder, though carefully controlled parkland where azalea and rhododendron bushes had grown as tall as trees over several decades, successive gardeners nurturing them like offspring.

A parasol shaded her pale face from the sun, its fringe fluttering gently. There was no air to speak of, the sky hazy as if a storm would hit before the day was through. The weather didn't help to soften her disposition. Aurelia made for a stone bench, lowered herself down daintily and proceeded to watch one of the younger, more appealing looking gardeners weeding a bed of scarlet roses.

He had his sleeves rolled up purposefully, big brown hands getting to grips with the weeds and throwing them into the nearby wheelbarrow. He knew she was there, she didn't doubt, but he didn't dare to look up, remembering well his position and place, and her overwhelming superiority.

People envied her, she knew, having a young, wealthy husband and a beautiful home. She would appear to have been blessed. She had health, beauty, everything, and a

35

whole lifetime ahead to enjoy. But apart from her beauty Aurelia didn't feel that she had anything, certainly nothing she cared for very much.

Things had been promising; marriage to Courtney had seemed ideal, a match to make all others envious of her. But she hadn't expected him to be so set in his ways, so stubborn. She'd thought a man so besotted with desire for her (and he had been prior to the marriage, because she'd employed her seductress's artistry on him wholeheartedly) would be like putty in her supple fingers. But Courtney had proven irritatingly unmovable on one subject, *the* subject that held the key to Aurelia's imagined happiness.

He would not move back to the city, not even for her, having a deep love for his country home complete with carved lions on the pillars at either side of the main gates, and griffins and fork-tongued lizard-like creatures upon the rooftop parapets. The place was pretentious, a statement of advancement and social climbing not to be ignored, and it went well with his recent knighthood, bestowed by a monarch on behalf of those appreciative of his services to industry.

She was allowed to visit friends in Bristol whenever she desired, but she would not live there again whilst Courtney, her lord and master, ruled the roost. She was tempted to stay with Avon for a while, to give herself a short respite from the tedium of Long Ashton, but Avon irritated her too of late. Her father had had no right to leave virtually everything to her brother, fobbing her off with a miserly allowance each month that kept her for ever dependent on that husband of hers. If she'd received a decent lump sum things would have been so much fairer. Then, at least, she would have had the means to support herself should life with Courtney prove just too awful to be endured any longer. But her father had seen to it that she wasn't rich in her own right and would have a permanent need for a husband.

Mean bastard! she decided, putting the subject from her mind and concentrating once again on the gardener, crossing her legs in such a fashion that the multi-layered

36

petticoats lifted in front displaying her silk-stockinged legs almost up to the knees.

The gardener's head was down and his gaze lowered in an obsequious manner, but Aurelia could tell that her tantalizing display hadn't gone unnoticed. The gardener faltered in his work, stealing furtive glances at the slim, shapely calves, trim ankles and pale pink kid ankle boots, believing all the while that his perusal went undetected. Her pretty lips twisted in a smile, for although it pleased her to know herself desired, she also despised the man because of his unruly show of base hunger. Courtney was like that – swelling in his trousers at the least sign of encouragement, panting after her. So weak, so lacking in pride as he all but begged for favours, sweetening her up with trinkets, craving a few minutes between her legs. And with Courtney it was only a few minutes. As a lover he was a dismal failure. She guessed she overwhelmed him, excited too much and too quickly, for his sexual forays were nearly always over before they'd begun, and she was left unsatisfied, her frustration building.

That was why she wanted to live in Bristol again. She wanted things the way they had been before her marriage. Enticing the gardener was but a cruel diversion to amuse herself, for never would she have succumbed to illicit fornication with him or anyone else in her employ, no matter how great her need of a good man. The thought of him on top of her, in her, made her breathe heavily, her eyes looking at the bulge in his trousers with longing, but to have weakened, become transparent in her desires like the despised opposite sex, could have proven dangerous. Men talked, boasted . . . That was dangerous.

Whereas before, when she was young, unwed and *very* eager to become initiated into the world of sexual delights, she had very cleverly seen to it, by stealth and deception, that no one would ever guess at her true nature. When she had been in the mood to play temptress and longed to be treated like a whore, Aurelia would become someone else, someone so physically removed from herself in appearance that not even Courtney – in the absurdly unlikely event of him frequenting the whore house where she took her pleasure – would have recognized her.

Such clandestine escapades had kept her happy during those years before her marriage when her parents were too wrapped up in themselves to keep too close an eye on her, and, a consummate actress, Courtney had never doubted her virginity on their wedding night. This blasted marriage and Courtney, especially, had spoilt everything! It would be better if she'd stayed unwed; gay and free to do as she pleased for always. But no. Aurelia had been worried about getting pregnant, had married Courtney so that she might convince him he was the father if such an accident happened. Whichever way she looked at it nothing had worked out according to plan, and she felt she'd got a raw deal.

She'd forgotten about the gardener, so deep had her thoughts become, and now she looked his way, glowering as she found him licking his lips and actually winking at her, his erection bowing out the front of his corduroy trousers. Such audacity! Yes, she had been right. Entanglement with one's employees was not worth the risk. Aurelia rose imperiously, her skirts covering her legs again, and with a frown calculated to strike fear into any heart. 'How dare you stare at me so insolently, young man! Get back about your work instantly or I shall see that you are dismissed from my husband's employ!' she told him icily, striding off with her head held high and expression haughty, while inwardly she laughed, finding the suddenly fearful look on his face terribly amusing.

CHAPTER 5

With the approach of the 1830s a gentleman in his early twenties had come to Bristol and been adopted by – and had adopted – the city in a mutual spate of regard that had neither reason nor rhyme. In the future it would be the place of his greatest engineering triumphs, but also his most frequent frustrations at the hands of his fellow man.

After completing his education in France, Isambard Kingdom Brunel joined his father as Assistant Engineer on the Thames Tunnel project at Rotherhithe, a would-be first as never before had a tunnel been built beneath the soft bed of a river.

In January 1828, and by then Resident Engineer subordinate only to his father, he missed death by a hair's breadth when the Thames broke through and flooded the half-finished tunnel. The Brunels, worrying for their son who recovered slowly from internal injuries, sent him first to Brighton for the sea air, then on to the Bristol suburb of Clifton where he was to meet for the first time that city's mercantile elite.

The following year he was back again, showing no traces by then of having been almost buried alive and half-drowned under the Thames. He was drawn to Bristol by the announcement, by the Bristol Society of Merchant Venturers, that a decision had been made to bridge the mighty Avon Gorge, connecting Leigh Woods, on the Somerset side of the river, with Clifton on the Bristol side.

A design competition was held and on the closing day, 19 November 1829, Brunel submitted four sets of beautifully drawn plans for the delectation of the judges. Aged twenty-three, his designs, along with those of four others, were put on a short list. The eminent Thomas Telford was called upon to judge, but the veteran canal and bridge builder dismissed, for reasons known best to himself, all the plans before him on technical grounds. Telford was then invited to submit a design of his own, but this one was rejected because its convolutions of engineering and building costs would have been astronomical, and the Merchant Venturers were relying upon the limited monies of a legacy to fund the project.

The resulting stalemate brought about another competition the following year, to which Brunel submitted altered plans that shortened his suspended span to 630 feet, with a large abutment on the Leigh Woods side of the gorge. This was the design that the judges were to accept.

To most men such a project would have been as much as they'd care to handle, considering the headaches of organization, supervision and execution. But Brunel's interests were always many and diverse. This was just as well, perhaps, because although work started enthusiastically enough in July 1831, it quickly came to a halt again. There were legal difficulties regarding the approaches to the planned bridge on the Leigh Woods side, only half the estimated £52,000 cost was readily available, and Bristol was at that time suffering civil unrest with riots erupting on the city streets.

A new start was made in 1836 and the Marquis of Northampton, President of the Bristol Association, laid the foundation stone for the Leigh Woods abutment. Work went on slowly thereafter, until in 1840 the piers which would take the suspension chains had been completed, standing on opposing edges of the mountainous limestone gorge; two Egyptian style squat stone pillars as tall as a house and with arched access through the middle of some two carriage widths, to take the eventual traffic when the wonder was completed.

But then the money ran out again and regretfully the Bristol Association informed their extremely patient Engineer Extraordinaire that the estimated £30,000 needed to complete the bridge couldn't be raised until some fifteen – – maybe even twenty – years into the future! Brunel was not pleased but he took it with good grace, allowing his mind to travel other paths of interest he seemed to have in abundance.

When the locks needed to be brought up to date, there was Brunel, designs at the ready, the estimated cost already calculated. The price was high, but the Dock Authorities knew there to be no real alternative. If they were to continue to compete with that growing giant, Liverpool, they had to make their port easily accessible to shipping, and modernization at the dock entrance loosely known as the Cumberland Basin was the logical way to begin.

While Brunel built bridges, dredged harbours and constructed locks some 260 feet long, he also had time to plan and propose to his friends of the Merchant Venturers the building of a broad gauge railway which would mean travel between the two major cities of Bristol and London taking hours rather than days. How could they resist him?

By 1840 the line was running between Bristol and Bath, the residents of that fair Georgian city giving their consent to the railway passing through such fashionable surroundings so long as it was done tastefully. Brunel promised it would be so, building footbridges and balustrades at Sydney Gardens so that his railway's path through the park would not be an eye-sore. Thereafter the idle gentility, ever eager for diversions, sauntered there in greater numbers to admire the dark green locomotives pulling carriages of mushroom yellow and chocolate brown.

By 1841 Brunel had reached Paddington, London, each bridge sympathetic to its surroundings, each tunnel fanciful, whether its style happened to be Gothic, Tudor or Italianate as in the case of the famous Box Tunnel near Bath.

The Bristol terminus at Temple Meads was built to resemble a Tudor palace rather than a station, its booking offices turreted and towered in the manner of Hampton

Court or Lambeth Palace, its gatehouse bearing a roman-faced clock where passengers could check on punctuality. Its platforms were colonnaded in Tudor style, the vast roof constructed in steel with mock hammer-beams.

This then was the Great Western Railway, its board members made up from several close friends of Brunel's who had shown confidence in him since his first Bristolian endeavour, the postponed suspension bridge back in 1831, and many of them were also of the Society of Merchant Venturers.

While Brunel built his railways – sixty miles a year on average including viaducts, bridges and tunnels – from Bristol to Bridgwater on the Exeter line (Gloucester, Wiltshire, Somerset and Weymouth were already in his mind) the GWR Company mulled over his other proposal, which was to extend steam travel from London to New York, with Bristol no longer merely as the end of the line, but an important pause. Brunel's idea was to build ships for a Great Western Steamship Company, its Board to be made up of those philanthropic merchants who had involved themselves in all his other projects.

Passengers would travel from London by train in relative comfort, sample the luxury of a hotel built specifically for them in Bristol's city, then transfer to the newly built, highly efficient and tastefully fitted steamships for the final leg of their journey. It was to be travel with style.

With an eye to profit, Brunel's idea was adopted with haste and the new company formed, Brunel being instructed to design the steamship and collaborate with R S Pope on the Royal Western Hotel where the travellers were to rest in transit.

The *SS Great Western* was launched in July 1837, a timber-hulled paddle steamer designed by Brunel and built by his friend William Patterson at his Wapping Yard in Bristol's Floating Harbour. She was some 230 feet in length, 50 feet broad in the beam and could carry 148 passengers. Her maiden voyage to New York in April 1838 meant that she was just narrowly beaten for the honour of achieving the first westward steam-powered crossing of the Atlantic

42

by the Irish steam ferry *Sirius*, hastily adapted in Liverpool for the crossing, that city's fathers determined that the prestige of the honoured 'first' should be theirs.

Despite detractors and critics the *SS Great Western* gave good service and enjoyed a successful career, convincing all and sundry that steam ships could be reliable, even at sea. She also enhanced Brunel's reputation as an engineer of great merit.

Eventually it became apparent to all, however, that the *SS Great Western* couldn't cope any longer with the volume of traffic wishing to avail itself of GWSC facilities. A sister ship was needed.

In July 1839 work started on the building of a second ship, Brunel's design this time revolutionary compared to anything that had gone before. She, he had decided, would be iron-hulled, the paddle wheels abandoned in favour of something he called screw propulsion. She was eventually named the *SS Great Britain*; a sleek, black coated ship with white trim at passenger deck level, sporting one funnel and six masts. The first iron built ship driven by screw propeller, she was 322 feet in length, 51 feet broad in the beam and able to carry 360 passengers.

In the first months May Bird spent at the Goodbodys' home she was able, from her attic window, to look down from Clifton to the docks and see that majestic ship nearing completion, she felt as if she and *Great Britain* shared this summer as their time of creation, that nothing had come before and *everything* lay ahead.

CHAPTER 6

Bertha Veysey, the housekeeper, jabbed May in the ribs with her elbow, bringing the girl – who seemed to be nodding back off to sleep on her feet as she dried the dishes – back to reality with a jolt. 'Front door bell's a-ringing, May. Go see who tis. I be floured up t'elbows an' gotta get this bread int the oven.'

'Yes, Bertha.' May yawned and took to the stairs. She found little pleasure in such early rising, unless, of course, you happened to be partial to bird song. There was a blackbird in the lilac tree in the back garden which seemed determined to out-sing every other bird in the district.

Who was calling at this hour in the morning? Only the servants were about, cooking breakfast loaves and simmering porridge, laying tables and trays or polishing shoes. May glanced at the imposing, mahogany-cased grandfather clock in the hall. It wasn't far off the Westminster chimes that would announce seven o'clock. The milkman maybe, his cart loaded with churns of fresh, still warm milk from the farms at Redland and Bedminster? Or the water seller?

May turned the heavy key and struggled with the bolts, pulling them back and then opened the door to find Mr Brunel on the chequer tiled step of the porch.

'Mr Brunel, sir? No one told me you was expected before the formal dinner tonight. If youm 'ere fer breakfast, youm too bleedin' early!' May told him, frowning. No one had given her guidance on how to deal with unexpected guests, so she trusted to instinct.

'I haven't come for breakfast,' Isambard informed her, chuckling at her lingering lack of manners and still evident lapses into less than ladylike language. Obediah was having difficulty in schooling her, and in the meantime she was proving an unintended amusement to most callers at the house, though of course some ladies took exception to the strong language.

'Then what *are* you wantin', sir, at this un-Godly hour of the mornin'? I'da thought you'da been down the dock givin' that ship of yers a final lookin' over, for ain't it 'er launch day today?'

'Indeed it is, Birdy, and I *have* been down there – since first light in fact, supervising the flooding of her dry dock so that she floats out without a hiccup for his Royal Highness this afternoon. Besides, I couldn't sleep very well.'

'I ain't surprised. There ain't nowt natural about sleepin' in a gert wheeled carriage no matter how posh the GWR might have done it out fer ya. I'd be frightened silly that they'd fix me up to a train while I was sleepin' and I'd land up in some bleedin' city next morning that I dint even know!'

'I was on a siding and quite safe.'

May gave him a look which told him she was unconvinced, then gave his clothes a disparaging look up and down. 'Lookin' at ya I can see now that you've been down t'the dock. You'll have to change before the launchin' ceremony. Tut! Look at yer trousers all spattered wiv mud and them shoes . . . ! Do yer want me ta clean 'em fer ya?'

'No, no need. I'll do them when I get back to Temple Meads.'

'Better 'ave a shave then too, sir, cus ya got a black shadder around yer chin.'

Isambard knew only too well what sort of picture he must be presenting. He looked like a navvies' foreman rather than the celebrated engineer, but that was his way, what suited him. The three-piece suit of black wool mixture had seen better days; it looked permanently crumpled and baggy at the knees. Hands that spent too much time in his

45

pockets, while his admirable brain worked, had creased and dragged the trousers out of shape. Hours of work on construction sites and at the bottom of dry docks had left his heavy duty and much cobbled work boots without the slightest evidence of a shine. His shirt was clean enough but it was clear Isambard had tied his cravat that morning without bothering to check it in the mirror, and on his head was that old top hat which the sun had faded in places from black to charcoal grey, its small brim serving as a handy ledge on which all manner of dust and dirt landed and made itself at home. The only thing that sparkled brightly amongst the homely drabness was his fob watch chain which hung suspended between buttonholes and pocket.

At thirty-five years old Isambard Kingdom Brunel was, to all intents and purposes, at his peak both mentally and physically, and there was much about him that others found appealing. He was neither overly tall nor devastatingly handsome, but there was something, when all the points in his favour were weighed, that made him immensely likeable.

He was dark of hair and eyes, betraying his French blood, though his hairline crept back at the temples with each year that passed, and just maybe accounted for his liking, especially in public, for that favourite top hat. The regular features, particularly his rather handsome bow of a mouth, were touched with a youthful plumpness and clarity of complexion that many women envied.

To May he was the most wonderful man in the world, *after* Obediah Goodbody, of course. He called her Birdy, hugged and cuddled her often, and laughed when she lapsed into slang, unlike Bertha who was in the habit of hitting her over the head with a wooden spoon for such unconscious reversals. She wanted to speak *proper*, of course she did, but it was such hard work, and such a temptation to take the easy way out and say 'ain't' and 'bleedin'.'

Mr Brunel knew hero worship when he saw it and was careful of how he handled it, stealing himself against spoiling Birdy more than any of the other children in the house. She should not think herself exceptionally special to him, even if she was. Children who were constantly over-

46

indulged became, to Isambard's mind, insufferable. He didn't like to think of Birdy turning into a demanding termagent, the archetypal brat that he shied away from. He wanted her – whilst presenting gob-stoppers and humbugs, prettily dressed dolls from the Arcade and bottles of scent (about which she'd expressed delight after smelling lavender water on his newly shaven chin one day) – to remain as she was: wide-eyed, grateful and totally unspoilt. But loving her, just as Obediah did, because of what and who she was, he couldn't help but want to lavish upon her all the things his own family took for granted, the very things that might change her.

He looked at her, a tiny, frail-looking child standing against the gigantic proportioned doorway to her house, her summer-weight grey cotton dress hemmed at the calves to show off the frills of petticoats and pantalettes beneath and a white starched and frilled pinafore buttoned on over the top to try to keep her clean.

'You coming to see my ship get its royal launch today?' he quizzed, though he already knew the answer, for her excitement at the prospect was common knowledge.

'*Of course* I am! Mr Goodbody said I can keep Anne's company in the landau by the quayside. Said we'd have a good view from there,' May informed. She'd woken that morning with a great sense of anticipation, her stomach all a-tremble. Nothing would have stopped her watching that ship take to the waters of the Floating Harbour properly for the first time. Nothing! She'd watched it being built, piece by piece, until she felt she knew its layout intimately, if not better than Mr Brunel did himself.

'And what are you going to wear? It's a special occasion, remember. Everyone'll be decked in their finery.'

'Huh? Why . . . *this*, I suppose,' said May, holding out the full skirts to inspect them and hopefully gain his approval. 'It's clean.'

'Yes,' said Mr Brunel, frowning theatrically.

He didn't like it, May could tell, and felt panic rise lest he should think her too plain to attend the launch. 'I've got my Sunday best,' she told him, thinking perhaps that the severe black tafetta kept for church and any possible funeral in the future might find more favour with the man.

He shook his head. 'No, not black. That would never do, Birdy. This is a happy day. And that is why I got your measurements off Mrs Veysey and had a Park Street modiste make up a dress specially for you. She's been run off her feet; it seems that everyone wants new gowns for the occasion, but I told her she had to find the time to fashion a gown and bonnet for you, otherwise I, Isambard Kingdom Brunel, would simply stop the launch. And you know as well as I that I *could* do it. After all, I'm the one who saw to the building of the ship in the first place.'

'Mr Brunel, you didn't!' gasped May in delighted awe and wonder. He'd threatened to stop the launch unless *she* got her dress! *Crikey*! May was in a state of bliss.

From behind his back, nestling against the large box of cigars he always kept strapped there, Mr Brunel produced a large, shallow box tied with string and papered in a pink and white candy stripe bearing the modiste's name, and another, deep and round, that looked suspiciously like a hat box. 'For you, Miss Bird, so that you match the brightness of my spirit on this occasion. Now though, I really must be gone. I'd not be here at all this morning save that I forgot to have the dress delivered yesterday. I hope it fits.'

'I'm sure it will. Ooh!' May didn't know what else to say, so great was her surprise and joy. She launched herself at the laughing man instead, crushing the boxes between them as she kissed him noisily all over his face.

The milkman, doing his deliveries, squeezed past them on the porch step with his quart jug, quirking an eyebrow at the pair.

Cedric Goodbody was eighteen now, a man of the world and scholar at Oxford where he was reading Classical History and English Literature. Like all the Goodbodys he was a chestnut-maned, hazel-eyed offspring who enjoyed moderately good health, good fortune and bore no malice to any of his fellow men. Asked for an opinion on May Bird, he would have had to think long and hard, for in truth his opinion was as abstract as his feelings. He supposed he pitied her for her former misfortune, could quite see the logic of his father who had set her among them, first as servant, then, as her popularity in the household grew, as family member, the affection she commanded putting her on the same level in their regard as some likeable, though unfortunately poverty-stricken, socially lacking cousin. By and large Cedric didn't waste too much time thinking about May Bird, and saw her as his father's charitable indulgence, a kind of living proof of Obediah's Christian beliefs. Cedric was much more interested these days in girls nearer his own age, and found the constantly giggling May worthy of nought but an occasional patronizing pat on the head.

Beside Cedric in the family landau sat the younger brother, Jasper, who, at eight – the same age as May herself – found her as distasteful as any girl seen through a typical boy's eyes. Her only saving grace was her liking for his masculine toys, and sometimes, especially on rainy afternoons when he was desperate for a playmate, he'd condescend to have her play guard to his engine driver when he set up his clock-work train set on the velvet smooth pile of the Wilton in the back parlour.

The boys were scrubbed and starched, their high, white collars unmercifully stiff at the necks of formal black suits, their hair washed and combed back and under smoothly *à la Prince Albert*.

In the seat facing them were the girls; one demure and much aware of what was right and proper behaviour in a young lady, the other fidgeting as if the seat burnt her behind, her head swivelling and mouth babbling with excitement. Anne, feeling quite grown up at fourteen, smiled mildly with indulgence, making mental excuses for the lacking behaviour of the child. May was young, untutored in the ways of middle-class society. It would take kindness and patience from all, but they'd be ultimately rewarded – Obediah often voiced his certainty of this – with the satisfaction of knowing that they had changed the course of one child's life undoubtedly for the better. So Anne and her brothers treated the situation with an adult, benevolent attitude, glad to please their papa and feeling in their hearts that it would have made their mama proud.

The fourth Goodbody child remained home at Beaufort Rise. He was the baby, Jon, whose first birthday was only a matter of weeks away, but who had never slept a whole night through, who cried more than was natural or good for him and never seemed to thrive. A nurse was employed to care for him in the stead of his natural mother who had died bringing him into the world.

To May, Jessica Goodbody might never have been anything but a name and a portrait above a mantlepiece, an unfortunate woman who had died the year before May went to live with the Goodbodys. But Jessica lived on in all of them; in their attitude towards others, their lack of ill will and abundance of mild manners and understated kindness. Jessica had left her mark upon them all, the mere mention of her name enough to bring a sparkle of love to their eyes and drag a shuddering sigh of pained loss from Obediah. He could have resented the baby, Jon, hated him even, for depriving him of the woman he had adored – a woman who had overlooked his grossness of physique as if she were blinded to it by the goodness of the man beneath – but it wasn't in the man to hate. God had willed it and his Jessie had been taken. He had questioned it at first while anguished by grief, but now he told himself that it was not for him to try to fathom the will of God, but to live with it, accept and go on, his faith shaken but still basically intact.

Obediah cherished Jon, loved him the more, if that were possible, because Jessie had died delivering him, and worried about him constantly, too, because his grasp on life always seemed so tentative and frail. Jon was ethereal, a will-o-the-wisp.

Anne wasn't yet permitted to wear a full-length dress, but the creation in white tafetta layered over in tulle and lace, and cinched at waist with a wide sash of crimson satin, was certainly more sophisticated than anything she had worn before. She felt quite elegant, sure enough of her blossoming regular good looks not to take exception to the exquisiteness of the peach and apple green frilled and flounced moppet beside her.

Mr Brunel's dress and matching bonnet had been the talk of the house ever since May had snatched them, with squeals of delight, from their tissue-paper lined boxes. And they were beautiful indeed, several yards of peach silk going into the elaborate knee-length skirts, the sash and bows of velvet ranging in colour from apple green to *eau-de-nil*. The straw bonnet was lined inside with ruched silk and fastened beneath the chin with a monstrous bow that complimented the sash on the dress, its exterior decorated profusely with artificial flowers, ribbons and even a feather dyed bright green.

Anne could not have imagined herself in anything so bold, so bright and frothy. She would never have chosen such a gown, would have felt uncomfortable in the extreme in such a colour. But it suited May admirably, even though, contrarily, it clashed with the brilliant russet of her hair falling in wild ringlets down her back and curling unbidden from the brim of her bonnet to ruin the tidy, smooth coiffure which Victorian society approved of. Everything about May was unruly, Anne couldn't help but think. But that did not detract in the least from the girl's unquestionable charm, in fact it proabably had much to do with it. She was untidy, noisy, exuberant and often loud in appearance too, and when she was around all eyes invariably settled upon her and people smiled and were amused.

Anne envied her that easy grace and the deliberate self-deprecating humour which endeared her to others. Anne had never felt easy with anyone, not even her immediate family, being by nature quiet, prim and rather – she hated to admit it – prickly, adhering to matters of etiquette with rigidity. Not to have existed by those rules would have terrified her.

May giggled and jumped up from her seat once more, dragging off a white cotton glove and waving it at Isambard as he – upon a platform with the others of the Great Western Steamship Company, and His Royal Highness, Albert the Prince Consort – signalled for the dry dock gates to be opened and the *Great Britain*, already afloat, towed before them.

A cheer went up from the wharves and cobbled jetties, the crowd raising top hats or waving flags with enthusiasm, as the ship emerged from her place of birth, splendid in black and white livery, her funnel and six great masts dripping with different maritime flags which carried a nautical message to suit the occasion, though the coded greeting was lost on most of the land-lubbing middle-classes drawn to the waterfront of the Floating Harbour by the promised spectacle and a chance of glimpsing the queen's husband, Albert.

Anne rolled her eyes and hid her discomfiture behind her fan, wishing that May would calm down and sit beside her once more, thereby ceasing to unwittingly show off her numerous petticoats and pantalettes to all and sundry as she jumped up and down, carried away by the occasion, the carriage springs taking a great deal of punishment from her violent movements.

The crowd was dense, only the rearing heads of the matched pair of horses coupled to their carriage was visible amidst the sea of top hats and bonnets, black suits and full-skirted gowns. Anne and the other members of her family had a good vantage point, and were able to see clearly the slim elegance of the Saxe-Coburg prince, who had stolen Victoria's heart until, infatuated, she had insisted upon marrying him. Dark and handsome, Prince Albert would have turned any female head. But May hardly spared him a glance. Her cheers and enthusiastic waves were for Obediah and Isambard, and for the awesome, sleek-lined *SS Great Britain*, which had no ungainly protruding side paddles like the *SS Great Western*, and whose means of propulsion was hidden below the water level so that the ship would always maintain an outward facade of effortless grace like a swan.

The sight of her cutting through the water with slow majesty that first time made May's spine tingle with pleasure. The man who had bought her this dress, choosing the colour and instructing the modiste as to the style he wanted, was also the man who had created that beauty in

52

the water with a calculating mind that took precision drawings and mathematics confidently in its stride, his genius enough to boggle the minds of lesser mortals. Oh, how she loved him! This day was theirs. They were in the midst of a multitude with a prince and members of the GWSC attending. Even Mr Brunel's 'family' – as they would ever be distantly referred to – had come down from their London home to enjoy the patriarchal glory, but May felt sure that only the two of them, Isambard and herself, had experienced so wondrous a depth of pleasure, were part of the general celebration yet separate and superior of feeling.

May took pleasure in it all, surrounded by her family; Anne clapping politely, Jasper whistling and Cedric ignoring the event entirely and concentrating instead on flirting with the pretty young misses in the crowd. She loved the dress, the ship, and the glorious day. She couldn't envisage there being such a high point in her life ever again.

It was only after the royalty left and the crowds had gone home that the *Great Britain* was moved to the entrance of the harbour and it was found that her fifty-one feet breadth was too wide for the lock gates to accommodate! To all intents and purposes she was stranded with no way of entering the Avon and reaching the sea.

It was to be eighteen months before the engineer sorted out his differences with the dock authorities, with whom he'd had altercations concerning the *Great Western*'s berthing fees in the previous year, and could carry out work on the south entrance lock at the Cumberland Basin, so freeing his great ship from her inland prison.

It was an eighteen months in which May took all opportunities to talk Obediah and Isambard into taking her aboard to investigate every elegant nook and cranny of the upper deck's saloons and state rooms. It was a time of happiness for her, but not for the members of the GWSC who had financed the building of the ship and saw her prolonged period of idleness as a time of lost profit. Mr Fox Talbot – the local photography pioneer – even came and took one of his magical pictures of the great lady alongside Mardyke Wharf in Hotwells, and Obediah acquired a copy, hanging it, protected by glass and frames – at May's insistence – above the mahogany sideboard in the dining room.

On the high tide of 11 December 1844, Brunel – with great difficulty even after all his modifications to the lock – managed to squeeze the mighty ship out of the Bristol dock and into the river between the faces of the gorge, but all knew that such problems meant that she was never likely to use Bristol at her home port again, and might even have to operate – as the SS *Great Western* was doing in order to pay her way – out of the rival port of Liverpool.

CHAPTER 7

The crew forced Jude's first ever drink upon him in Wexford, Ireland. The dark brew, with a half inch of head as thick as whipped cream, tasted disappointingly bad to his childish palate. Used to lemonade and gingerbeer, real ale, especially the Irish variety, would take some getting used to.

By the time he'd taken his first trip around that notorious point of land, the Horn, aboard Jack Mitchell's *Celestial Piper*, Jude Somerton had learnt a dozen of the choicest swearwords used in nautical circles, how to help the cook in a galley that hadn't enough room to swing a cat, and how to bear the practical jokes that the rest of the crew seemed to feel duty bound to play on him, Jude being the youngest and most naive of the ship's company.

There was little about him now to hint at the well-heeled student of Columbia University he might have been, but for a pleasant twist of fate.

He'd found Captain Mitchell at a waterfront tavern the night he stole away from the house, and, close to tears, had begged the man to let him leave with him in the morning. Jack was against it, telling Jude he had no place getting involved in the lives of others and liked to mind his own business, but Jude only had to mention the belting he had received and the veteran salt relented; he even had to be restrained by Bosun Brannigan so that he wouldn't go after Morgan Somerton in a white hot rage. If there was one thing Jack couldn't abide it was violence against children,

55

and, like Jude, he worried about Thirza who was left behind.

In time Jude's knee breeches had worn thin and shiny in the seat and his shoes grown too small. New ones were bought in Amsterdam, heavy duty leather boots with wooden soles and a mass of nails that struck sparks on the cobbles when he went ashore. He forgot his starchy manners and lived by the sailor's almost unconscious code of conduct, gained a tan that made his azure blue eyes all the more striking, and added some muscle to a slim, ever upward growing frame that had never known true physical hard work until then.

Jack, who had never married – there being the legendary girl in every port and no good reason that he could see to choose between them – acted like a father to the boy but never molly-coddled him. Pure single-mindedness of purpose and hard work had got Jack his ship and, if Jude was to eventually take over as her skipper – which was Jack's unspoken dream – then he had to learn the hard way, and *only* way, to Jack's mind. Being worthy of a captaincy wouldn't come easy.

Life at sea wasn't all hanging on to life-lines during raging storms or cursing the limpness of sail when they found themselves in the doldrums. When the weather was with them the *Celestial Piper* pretty much sailed herself, scudding along majestically under sail with the hands always busy but never worked to the point of exhaustion. There was leisure time when their hobbies could be indulged, when the squeezebox came out and the popular sea shanties were given an airing verse by verse, masculine voices thick with different accents. They knitted themselves sweaters, read, kept journals of sorts, or, as in Jude's case, turned the sketches executed at the last port of call into works in oil upon canvas.

He'd sold several by the time his fifteenth birthday had come and gone, his mind quick in noting the number of ships' masters who took pride in possession of an oil painting of their particular brig, barque or schooner. He sketched the ships, showed the captains the results and, if they found them pleasing, often went on to negotiate the price of a prestigiously generous sized canvas. Thus it was that every spare moment at sea was used in the fulfilment of commissions, the paintings delivered and payment made the next time he was in an agreed upon port at a particular time to meet the eagerly awaiting buyer.

Marseilles in the autumn of 1845

They ran just ahead of the storm for the nearest port, tacking across a Mediterranean that was wild and dark, thunder clouds blackening the sky and rain lashing down in slate hued cascades which reduced visibility to a matter of yards beyond the bowsprit. Even at Marseilles their troubles weren't over. The gales that struck were such that the *Celestial Piper* crashed against the quay at her moorings and had to undergo repairs so extensive that they were forced to remain in port for nine days, idle and increasingly bored, with nothing to do save loiter about the waterfront, trying occasionally to communicate with the local French fishermen, but more often indulging in brawls over idiotic matters of patriotism. When it came to national pride and jingoism it seemed that the Americans were outdone only by the British!

The ship's barber had trimmed them to look more respectable ashore, treating all to the same style. Thereafter, the ship's company was easily picked out around Marseilles because none of them sported a hair more than half an inch long upon their heads, looking disquietingly like a group of convict labour.

Jude, severely shorn like the rest and concealing most of the barber's atrocity beneath a knitted woollen hat, sat in a light linen shirt and canvas trousers amongst the fish-heads and scavenging gulls upon the quayside, drawing any vessel moored there that looked ship-shape enough to be owned or sailed by a reasonably wealthy captain. He was doing well, but a little extra wouldn't go amiss because he wanted to buy something for Thirza which he could secretly see she received when they next reached home port. There were ways and means of speaking to her without placing her in unnecessary danger. Usually he waited for her at the steps of her school, laughing and joking, cuddling as they exchanged news, then fighting desperately to keep his tears in check when he let her go so that she wouldn't be late home and cause Morgan's ire to be raised against her. He liked to be able to give her small things; handkerchiefs trimmed with Belgian lace, Japanese fans, bracelets of Indian silver, all of which she kept safely hidden at the back of the bottom drawer of the tallboy in her bedroom on the corner of Wall Street and Broadway.

Besides his presents for Thirza, Jude also made the effort once a year – though he was anything but fashion-conscious at the age of fifteen – to buy himself a full set of sensible clothes and pay one of the hands who knitted to make him a roomy pullover that could keep him snug beneath his oil-skins when the weather proved to be a swine. There was also the continuous expense of brushes, turpentine, linseed oil and pigments. Canvas was free, as there were always plenty of offcuts when the sails were replaced or patched, and the ship's carpenter (who also knocked up the coffins out of pine planks when there was a death at sea; such as had happened off the north coast of Algeria only a month before when one man lost his footing aloft and crashed to the deck, the impact killing him outright) supplied the wooden stretchers over which the canvas was pulled and nailed taut prior to priming and finally painting with oil.

After expenses and allowing for the occasional treat for himself – like a jim-dandy silver cased penknife he'd seen in Deauville the last time they'd dropped anchor there – Jude was still very much in profit and, after seeking the advice of the worldly-wise Jack Mitchell, Jude decided he would open a bank account with the First National on Wall Street, thereby earning interest on the savings he amassed. This he had done, using the name which, for caution's sake, he also signed at the bottom of his paintings, Mariner. He thought that was pretty clever. A painting by Somerton might arouse his father's curiosity, and who could say that some captains of Jude's acquaintance might not go about showing off their artistic acquisitions on returning to New York? Better to be safe than sorry, and he rather liked being called Mariner; it was appropriate to say the least, considering his occupation, and somehow, to his mind, rather romantic.

Eventually the light faded and, packing up sketch pad and tins of charcoal, Jude ambled back to the ship, praying as he went that the stew he'd helped to prepare that morning would turn out when cooked to be better than that awful steak and kidney pudding he'd been responsible for concocting the day before.

Jude lit the lamps hanging over the scratched and scarred, soda bleached table in the wardroom, the supper in the cauldron above the old fashioned Brodie stove of the galley very nearly ready. He set a pile of tin plates and cutlery at the head of the table, then placed thickly sliced loaves on wooden boards at carefully calculated intervals down the centre of the table. The hands could be touchy, to say the least, if they thought even for a moment that anyone had conspired to do them out of their fair share. Any slight – real or imaginary – or difference of opinion, was a good excuse to roll up sleeves and start fighting.

'What we got tonight then, Jude, my boy?' enquired Bosun Brannigan, already seated at table, his pipe filling the wardroom with heavy, aromatic grey smoke. Smoking, especially pipes, was a major occupation of nearly all the crew. It amazed Jude that the ship had so far survived without suffering a fire either minor or serious. He – the willing but clumsy cook's assistant – was in all probability much more likely to cause such an accident.

'It's stew, bosun.'

'Better than yer pie is it?'

'I hope so, sir.'

'So do I, lad, or you'll likely get yourself keel-hauled,' joked Mr Brannigan.

'Yes, sir,' mumbled Jude, making himself scarce as soon as he was able, Mr Brannigan's jokes rarely making him laugh but often causing him unease. He never could quite decide whether the man was entirely joking when he made such foul threats. Jude felt almost certain that Mr Brannigan was one of those men who took delight in frightening children. Not a physical abuser like Morgan Somerton, but a mental one; fear in the mind satisfying the warped workings of Mr Brannigan much as flesh suffering pain brought Morgan short moments of contentment. Fortunately for Jude there was always Captain Mitchell to curb the zealously nasty tongue of the other, to cut off with an icy stare or barked order the words that weren't suitable for so young and impressionable a mind.

The crew filtered in, each taking a chunk of bread and finding his own particular three-legged stool, and the cook and Jude transferred part of the stew to a more manageable vessel and transported it to the wardroom, the cook then ladelled out the fare which thankfully looked wholesome and actually permeated the room with a vaguely appetizing smell!

Jude went to fetch the captain, who had been ensconced in his cabin ever since the boy's return to ship, thinking it best if the stew was eaten whilst still piping hot. There was enough familiarity and friendship between them that he never bothered to knock, just opened the door in his usual jaunty manner, the call to supper dying on his lips. He choked, mouth turning into a shocked 'O'.

Things happened very quickly thereafter, but to Jude they were slow to the point of painfulness, the scene before him on the cramped cabin bed played out as if in slow motion, every detail vivid and terrible.

Captain Jack, his hero, the man he most admired in the world, was as naked as the day of his birth, his rear staring Jude in the face as he thrust and bashed at some hapless *mademoiselle* sprawled beneath him, her limbs outflung as if she had been beaten beyond the point where she could retaliate further against her attacker. They were oblivious to him and Jude couldn't see their faces, only the back of Jack's platinum and, nowadays, increasingly white head. But he could hear and was revolted by the animal grunts of his friend and the soft whimperings of the female who now, it would appear, had found some reserves of strength and

60

was putting up a fight again, her nails scratching Jack's back and neck, leaving angry red streaks across the tanned muscles.

Such savagery must surely kill her? Certainly her cries grew louder, her squirmings beneath Jack and attempts – it appeared – to wrestle free, more frantic.

Jude came alive, his mouth closing and face losing its stupefied gawp as he launched himself at Jack's back.

The *mademoiselle* saw Jude's attack, screamed with surprise and fear, 'Jack!', and clung the tighter to her lover who thrust into her at the height of pleasure. Jack performed all the surer, gratified by what he assumed was her appreciation of a good lover, taking her and himself to the point of climax as Jude grabbed him about the neck in an arm lock and tried to prise him off. His essence flowed and he groaned with delight even as he spluttered with vexation, his female companion of the hour squealing with ecstasy and terror combined as she contracted with waves of passion, yet had to suffer added weight and the possibility of Jack engaging in a brawl whilst still joined with her.

'Get off her, you devil!' shouted Jude, holding on to the dumbfounded Jack like a terrier, a knee in the small of his back. 'Foul beast! Murderer!'

'What in God's name! *Jude*!' Jack disengaged himself clumsily from the sated woman beneath him and got to grips with Jude, capturing the offending arm and shoving the boy aside. By the time Jude gained his feet again, snarling and taking the pose of one about to box by Queensberry rules, Jack had got himself free of bedclothes and female limbs and gained his feet, brows drawn together in a frown of angry puzzlement. 'Whatever has come over you?'

'You were hurting her. You're no better than my father!' Jude accused.

'Don't be so damned insulting! Does she look as if I've hurt her? Well? Have a good look; she won't pay you any heed, it being in the interest of putting your mind at rest.'

Jude's eyebrows knit, thoughts in a quandary as he glimpsed her way, going crimson with embarrassment. She was smiling, all pink and unabashed on top of the crumpled sheets, breasts wobbling as she stretched like a kitten in the sun sleeping off a full meal. No she didn't look hurt at all, he had to admit, shaking his head in confusion.

Jack laughed, clapping him understandingly about the shoulders with an arm, his air now one of condescending amusement. 'I think you got the wrong end of the stick, lad, need to learn a few basic facts of life. What the sweet Marie and I were up to is what life is all about. I was making love to her, Jude. Didn't you realize that?'

Jude cringed with embarrassment, wishing that the ground would open up and swallow him as the truth was put to him and his own ignorance and innocence became apparent. He shook his head, averting his eyes from the bed where the willing, happily satisfied Marie rose to her knees and sat back on her heels, watching him as she deliberately displayed herself and enjoyed immensely his reaction.

'No, I didn't know . . . Nobody ever told me . . . ' he tried to excuse himself lamely, believing the humiliation of this would be the end of him.

'That father of yours has got a lot to answer for. Remind me sometime to teach you the basics, if, that is, there's any need after what you've seen here today. I ain't never been interrupted before. It was kinda novel, I suppose, and certainly made the finale one I shan't easily forget.'

Jude mumbled something unintelligible beneath his breath and Jack took pity on him, dismissing him forthwith. 'Go get your supper. I'll be along just as soon as I've seen this bunch of tricks off my ship. And rest assured this'll go no further than the three of us.'

Mademoiselle Marie said something to Jack in her native tongue, giggling as she did so, her eyes on Jude, but his grasp of the language was poor and he had to wait for the captain to translate. Jack chuckled, slapping one of her pink buttocks as he threw a sheet her way and she carelessly draped it about herself to hide her more intimate delights, his French faltering in return.

Then he turned to Jude. 'Marie was willing to give you your first lesson. Said she liked the look of you very much,

62

saw potential, but I told her you'd suffered enough shocks for one day and will lose your virginity some other time.'

When Jude found himself out in the companionway he paused, unable to face the wardroom and supper just then, certain that the ever-observant crew would see the blush on his cheeks, badger him into finding out what had put it there. But most disquieting of all was the fact that for the first time ever that Jude could recall, his manhood – which he'd always been able to overlook, forget about even – had become a problem, growing alarmingly stiff and pushing at the material of his canvas trousers as if it wanted to escape. The throbbing expansion and lengthening bewildered him, increasing, he realized, every time his mind went back and dwelled upon the memory of Mademoiselle Marie kneeling before him offering to be his teacher. He'd never seen a woman's body until that day, had never even had cause or inclination to speculate on what one would look like. But after the unscheduled calling in at the port of Marseilles that year Jude was to spend a great deal of time remembering and maybe even regretting that Jack had decreed that he remain a virgin.

CHAPTER 8

The Society of Merchant Venturers, this time exchanging their GWR and GWSC hats for that of the Clifton Water Works, consulted with Mr Brunel on the possibility of giving the gentility of lofty Clifton the new sanitary wonder and convenience of clean water on tap. He thought about it, made drawings and calculations and broke gently to them the estimated cost of such a grandiose scheme; £1,364.

They consulted and finally agreed. Brunel immediately put to work builders at the foot of a part of the gorge not far from where his bridge piers dominated the skyline. At this particular spot, known locally as Black Rock, a natural spring had been discovered back in 1836 and Brunel envisaged no problem in building a housed pump to carry the natural abundance of piped water up the face of the gorge some 250 feet to Clifton. Thereafter clean running water was available to the maids of the mansions from conveniently situated standpipes, and some houses immediately indulged in the luxury of plumbing actually in the home!

But it was to be Isambard Kingdom Brunel's last project of real note in the city he had adopted and so loved. Railways in the south and Wales beckoned; daily he received letters, begging technical advice, assistance, offering new posts further afield. His private car on the GWR network travelled more frequently along the broad gauge rails until eventually he was rarely seen in Bristol, his base becoming 18 Duke Street, London, overlooking St James' Park, amongst his family, his leisure spent in readying his country home at Marychurch, near Torquay in Devon, in anticipation of future retirement.

When Obediah Goodbody shook hands with the man – jokingly saying that if he and his fellow Venturers could come up with some new scheme to suit Isambard then they would be in touch – May was beside him, looking sad and knowledgeable far beyond her years. She knew a good-bye when she saw one, even if it was disguised simply as just another small, friendly dinner party for a handful of members with close commercial and social ties. There was no talk of good luck or *bon voyage*, no speeches of gratitude for what he had done to bring their city forward with the times. Such things would have smacked of finality, something which no one wanted to admit to.

Brunel and the Merchant Venturers had been well matched for a long while but now they had outgrown each other, the city ran out of problems worthy of being solved by such a man of brilliance. The dreams had been wonderful, but turning them into realities had seldom proved an easy task. No one's fault; just fate really, fate and matters of money. But then all projects are the same, with someone keeping a tight hold of the purse strings. That was only prudent. But sometimes, just once in a blue moon, to be too frugal ultimately meant strangling the baby – the products of his genius – at birth.

May had had to beg the use of Obediah's handkerchief, blowing noisily, and not the least bit daintily, into it. 'When shall we see you again, Mr Brunel?' she asked, her appearance surprising no one. Brunel's magnetism worked on all. She fetched his top hat and overcoat, delaying him for as long as possible in the hall of their home at Beaufort Rise, determined to wring some truth about his plans out of the man before she allowed him to leave.

'Mr Brunel is very busy, Birdy. He's got contracts for bridges, railways . . . ' Obediah explained, but not to her satisfaction.

'When will you visit us again?'

Isambard smiled, putting his head through the custom

built strap that made transportation of his cigars all the easier, the fine leather crossing his chest like a medieval sword harness, while the boxed cigars nestled down his back. 'When next I'm in Bristol you can be sure I'll invite myself up here to take tea or supper with you and Obediah.'

'And when will that be?' pressed Birdy, ignoring Obediah's frown. She knew it was ill-mannered to persist but she couldn't stop herself.

'Truly I cannot say, my pretty child,' Isambard soothed, tapping on his hat and opening the door himself. 'I've detained you long enough, Mr Goodbody. You should return to your other guests.'

'Aye, just as soon as I've sent this young miss off to bed,' agreed Obediah.

He was going, the door about to shut on him, perhaps for ever. May jumped forward and grabbed it in panic. 'Write to me, please, so I know you fare well . . . what you're doing.'

'But you cannot read, Birdy,' Obediah reminded her, laughing.

'*I'll learn*,' she vowed adamantly. If she could master the speech of a lady, which she had nearly done now, she didn't see the written word proving any great difficulty.

'I believe she would,' chuckled Isambard, impressed, cupping her chin in a hand and kissing the high, shiny-clean forehead over which the russet curls rambled. 'If hearing from me means so much to you, Birdy, then I *shall* make the effort, say monthly, to sit down and set on paper the things of interest that may have happened to me, and forward them on to you.'

'That would be wonderful,' she breathed with relief. She wouldn't lose him, not entirely. He was to be hers exclusively on paper. A joyous thrill ran through her at the thought and when he went down the steps at the front of the house, raising his hat in brief salute, May wasn't in tears as she had anticipated, but smiling.

Two years of marriage had not mellowed Aurelia into a more placid wife for Sir Courtney Spicer. She hated him, hated the mansion at Long Ashton, hated the isolation and simply *loathed* the fat baby Lawrence, whom she had borne some eight months before. She avoided him, leaving him to the charge of his nurse, and concentrated all her energies on trying to figure out a way of escaping from her awfully dull life.

To Courtney's face she remained, for prudence's sake, a caring, polite wife, ever deferring to his wants and wishes. Behind his back she thought the pale, insipid creature the most contemptuous excuse for a man. Oh, how she needed . . . craved a real man.

Things had come to a head recently, after months of enduring Courtney's own particular brand of bedroom games. They could hardly be called sex, and certainly weren't love-making. Courtney dabbled timidly in matters of the marriage bed, and not very satisfactorily. It still made Aurelia shake her head with wonder that he had actually managed to get her pregnant. He had no control, found release from his basic cravings almost the instant he mounted his unenthusiastic, barely tolerant wife, and never saw reason to enquire as to her feelings on the matter, her desires, her cravings. Maybe he thought – it being a widely held view – that no female of gentle birth could possibly be interested in something so base as sex except as a means of doing her duty and bearing her husband a continual stream of children. Only low women, *abnormal* women enjoyed sex.

Well, Aurelia couldn't care less what Courtney thought, not any more. She had been neglected long enough and was determined to be appreciated once again by a lover worthy of her, a man who would use her, *thoroughly*.

So Aurelia had formulated a plan, sketchy at first until one or two things happened by coincidence to help enormously. She had decided on stealing away during the night and indulging herself, then getting herself safely back home before the maid came at the usual time to wake her for breakfast. Her first problem was Courtney, who just might decide to come and share her bed that particular night and find it empty. The other problem was transport. The city lay not far away, a matter of a few miles as the crow flew, but Aurelia frowned at the thought of covering it on foot. Yet to take a horse would necessitate one of the grooms being privy to at least part of her plan. She frowned at that too.

Then Courtney contracted chicken pox and confined himself to bed for the two weeks recommended by his doctor, quite understanding when Aurelia explained her fears for herself and little Larry, should they come into contact. No, of course he wouldn't hear of them being put at such a risk. He would isolate himself. With plenty of books to read, meals brought in and his chamber pot emptied regularly, Courtney didn't believe the solitude would be too unbearable, even though, of course, he would miss his dear wife and darling son.

She had two weeks in which to think of something, come up with the means to taste freedom for one night. It wasn't asking a lot. She deserved a bit of fun.

Fate was kind. The very same day that she saw Courtney off to his self-imposed exile, his itching arms plastered with calamine lotion and piled high with books, she was on her way back from a stroll in the park when she happened upon two of her employees at the back of the laundry house.

She stopped, startled, and found cover behind a rhododendron, never thinking to intervene, her nature such that she watched instead with mounting excitement.

There against the wall, one of her laundry maids was being ravished; a burly labourer, his corduroys down about his ankles, thrusting up into her mercilessly. Maybe the girl *had* been willing to begin with when his kisses were tender and words sweetly persuasive, but now she squirmed, pinned against the hard brick with her legs spread and face grimacing, her moans one of discomfort rather than pleasure.

Aurelia sighed, her connoisseur's gaze travelling over his taut, pale buttocks and strong, hairy legs, her depths fluttering as lewd thoughts and erotic images assaulted her eyes and brain.

The man finished, towering over and sneering down at the crumpled girl. 'Don't say ye didn't ask fer it, Iris. Yuv been teasing me since Satday last,' he told her sternly, as if

68

excusing his actions, before he walked away, straightening his shirt and raking fingers through his hair.

Aurelia dismissed the girl from her mind as unimportant, but hurried after the man, catching up with him at the side of the stables and halting him with a snarled command, 'A word with you, rapist!'

The man turned, recognizing her and blanching, the brutal arrogance of moments before deserting him. He stumbled over his words, trying to find a way out, an excuse. 'She were willing, ma'am, been showing off 'er ankles an' too much of what she do keep in 'er blouse fer weeks. I be only 'uman, did but take up the challenge.'

'When you speak to me address me as "my lady". As to what took place behind the laundry, I have eyes, neither am I a fool to be persuaded by your talk of enticement. What I saw was rape.'

'My lady, I beg ye, please don't fetch int police. I'll never do nowt like this again, I swear, ull keep me lust fer me wife only. But please don't fetch the police.'

'Why?' Aurelia wanted to know, his fear amusing her greatly.

'Cus I already been 'ad up fer this kinda thing afore. Only last time there weren't no witnesses, only girl's say so, and they let me off. You 'and me over they'll find me guilty without doubt an' then there'll be no one to look after the missus and the kids an' they'll be evicted from their cottage. *Please*, my lady, I ain't a wicken man really. I jus' gets carried away by the sight of a pretty girl now and then.'

Aurelia looked down her nose at him, contemptuous of the cringing, sycophantic wreck he had become. She would have liked to make him crawl and beg a while longer, kept wondering as to his fate, but already the germ of an idea had formed with this vulnerable brute figuring heavily. If she could but get organized, then this night she could be in Bristol enjoying herself as she hadn't for *so long*! The thought was too tempting to be resisted.

'Very well,' she told him, certain of his compliance, 'I shall take you at your word and not bring in the police. But I want something in return . . . services.'

His eyebrows quirked. He misunderstood and his gaze immediately raked her body with possession in mind. 'You'd be wantin' me to do fer you the same?' he asked, seeking clarification.

Aurelia laughed acidly. 'You conceited dimwit! Nay, I want not *that* sort of service. You will, when I require it on the occasional night, leave my horse saddled for me in the rhododendrons behind the laundry. I shall expect your silence and tolerate no questions, but I think that a small price to pay for the freedom in which to go on indulging your base instincts.'

'Oh yes, my lady,' the man was quick to agree.

'Tonight you shall commence this new duty, remembering to collect the horse at dawn from the same location and rub him down before returning him to his stable.'

'Anything, my lady.'

'And in future he is to be ready for me whenever you receive my signal. I'm not certain what it will be yet, but I'll let you know. Do we understand each other?'

'Very well, my lady. I be grateful to ye an' more 'n 'appy to serve,' gushed the obsequious labourer with infinite relief.

So it was that Aurelia gained her freedom, stealing from the house by the unused side door, to which she had conveniently taken possession of the only key. The horse, as demanded, was ready and waiting and, after walking it gently from the park for caution's sake, she mounted up and took off joyously into the blackness of night, tingling with anticipation.

70

CHAPTER 9

The back gardens at Beaufort Rise were all similar in lay-out, with the area nearest the house given over to pavings and a balustrade and, lying beyond, a series of terraced levels. Some gardeners had made this part of the garden more colourful by positioning pots of geraniums or marigolds in spots pleasing to the eye. Others had constructed goldfish ponds or ornamental fountains. In good weather wrought iron garden furniture appeared, painted a gay white or more serviceable black, with screening trellis work giving some privacy from neighbours when honeysuckle or climbing rose was in full bloom.

The Goodbodys had a well-kept garden in which Obediah took personal delight, taking himself off there on Sundays to dig and weed, and producing enough vegetables for the household's need so that Bertha Veysey, the cook-house-keeper, never had to go haggling at the market in Broadmead. They had potatoes and cabbage, spring onions and shallots for pickling, and runner beans that always reminded May of Jack and the Beanstalk as the tendrils wound their way upwards around a network of bamboo canes, their flowers like giant red cowslips.

May loved the garden, particularly when spring was fast changing to summer and the lawn and shrubs were at their freshest green. Summer was too hot, sometimes making things wilt, autumn was just plain sad as leaves dropped and the flowers shed their blooms, but spring she loved. Spring was the beginning.

But this day, as she sat outside with Jon keeping him amused with a jigsaw while his overworked nurse saw to his dirty laundry, autumn was on the way, the geraniums already taken off to the safety of the potting shed at the bottom of the garden so that the frost shouldn't have them, the delphiniums and foxgloves past their best.

Jon was three years old, with brown hair and hazel eyes like his brothers and sister, but frail and sickly to the same degree that they were healthy and robust. Like a small bag of bones he sat beside his beloved Birdy, taking the pieces she held out for him whilst hinting at the places she thought they might just fit into. He loved her because she was always quiet and calm with him and didn't shout or lose her patience as Nurse sometimes did. She even gave him the gobstoppers and aniseed balls – while they were alone – which Nurse forbade him. With her his cough had a habit of subsiding and his shallow breathing became somehow less laboured. He wouldn't choke; Birdy had told him so. And if he did she would simply take him by the legs, hold him upside down and slap him on the back until the offending gobstopper had been dislodged and popped out! He believed her, was never afraid when in her charge. Papa trusted him in her care and that was confirmation enough for Jon of his own convictions. Birdy was his guardian angel. Why, she even looked like one. They'd stopped in the cemetery of their parish church, St Andrew's, one Sunday morning to lay flowers on Jessie's grave before going in to hear morning service, and Jon had watched Birdy beneath the walk where lime trees had been pleached over it to form an arbour. She wore her Sunday best, the black tafetta so severe that somehow it contrived to turn her peaches and cream complexion to the starkest magnolia. Only her mouth and eyes had colour, lips cherry red and eyes wine-bottle green. And, framing her face and taking away Jon's breath with pleasure, as it often did, was her shock of hair, infernal perhaps rather than angelic in its fiery beauty. She should have been wearing her black bonnet, should have conducted herself quietly with cast-down eyes like the dignified Anne, but Birdy hated bonnets and would wait right until the last

72

moment, until they entered the porch of the church itself, before she would cram that hated black monstrosity on her head, flattening her abundance of unruly curls. She loathed her fresh washed hair to be confined so, knowing that by the time they reached home again its lustre would be lost to dampness caused by the heat of the sun striking on and being absorbed by the black ruchings and bows plonked on it.

Even before that day, Jon had adored her. Birdy was bright and beautiful, just like the line from that children's hymn, infecting him with her vitality. She laughed, smiled, could never keep still, possessing life in full measure; that sense of being – of joy – somehow touching him, making Jon feel alive also, though his body, alas, couldn't convert the longings of his mind into physical energy.

While Jon put the puzzle together, May read again the post-card which had come from Exeter, labouring over the italic script Isambard employed in his correspondence, and frowning at the scant words on the back. He wrote – dutifully she sensed – every month as promised, keeping his brief diary-like disclosures simple, for although May was ten years old and quick witted, it was only recently that she had begun to acquire the skills of reading and writing, Anne and Jasper having patiently taught her the rudiments and the brother now carrying on, with patience, to bring May up to a level of competence somewhere eventully, he hoped, near his own.

'My dear-est Birdy,' May read falteringly aloud, Jon paying her no heed as, with tongue poised between lips with concentration, he slotted a wooden piece of jigsaw into place, eyes brightening with delight at the feat. 'Am in the West Country, as you can see by the postmark, the GWR's railcar acting as my home while I o-ver-see work on this new sec-tion of railway. Rest assured I am well, but nothing has happ-ened of in-ter-est that I might write you of, save maybe to tell you that my son does well at his schooling and I am proud of him. Your writing grows more pleas-ing each time you write, Birdy. Good girl. Mr Brer-eton sends his regards. Fond greet-ings, I K Brunel.'

73

May gave a disdainful 'huh' and read again, this time in silence, and commented when she'd finished, 'And why should *I* want to know about Mr Brereton? Or Isambard's son, come to that? I want him to write about himself, not *Brereton*. *He* is a frightening fellow for all his politeness. Do you know, Jon, he wears a black patch over his left eye.'

Jon's picture of an Hussar was growing quicker now that he had put most of the outside pieces in their proper places, but his attention was all Birdy's as he digested that piece of information. 'Caw!'

'Yes. It makes him look like a pirate.'

'Who is he?'

'Mr Brunel's assistant. Very important,' enlightened May knowingly.

'So he's not really a pirate then,' concluded Jon, disappointed.

'No,' admitted May. 'He's got mutton chop sideburns like your papa and *kiss curls*.' They giggled. 'Last time he was here in Bristol with Mr Brunel he brought me a yard of ribbon for my dolls' dresses and a hairbrush with tortoise-shell on the back.'

'Everyone likes your hair, Birdy. So do I.'

'Do you, Jon?' pressed May, fishing for compliments. She loved it when he talked to her that way. And he often did.

'Yes. I sit thinking sometimes when I'm with you, trying to make up my mind what it looks like. I think mostly it reminds me of a glass of sherry. Jasper reckons it's like carrots.'

'Jasper would,' said May, with a superior sniff.

Jon chuckled, then coughed weakly, taking several moments to calm before he could speak again. 'And Anne reckons it's like marigolds. The bright orange ones.'

May smiled and nodded agreeably, finding that comparison to her liking.

They finished the puzzle leisurely, just as most things that involved Jon always were, Jon hiding the last piece in his trousers pocket so that May was obliged to get down on her hands and knees searching for it, only to rise again without

74

success and find that he'd set it into place and was grinning like a Cheshire cat.

'That was sneaky!' she said, disgustedly.

'I know,' Jon agreed, going red in the face and doubling over as his giggles gave way once more to a hacking cough.

'And that serves you right,' she told him, observing the coughing fit as his just desserts, though, as it went on seemingly without end, May held Jon close and gentled him with words and hands, her soothing presence having the power to calm him eventually.

'Maybe we should go back inside now. Your papa will soon be home from the office and we have to wash ready for tea,' she wondered out loud, smoothing his hair.

His pathetic grasp on her arm tightened. 'Not yet, Birdy. Let's stay here until the sun goes. That'll be soon enough.'

She nodded. 'You put the jigsaw back in its box then, and I'll water the roses in the tubs.'

As she watered, May looked up and found herself observed by the occupants of Number 6 Beaufort Rise, at leisure in their back garden. She smiled politely as was expected and greeted them. 'Good afternoon, Lady Spicer . . . Master Avon.'

'Good afternoon, May Bird,' said Avon, looking at her down the arrogant length of his thin, straight nose.

Aurelia – who was pouring tea for them both – managed a slight uplifting of the corners of her mouth, but didn't put herself out enough to reply.

May moved on to the next rose requiring water, thereby doing away with the necessity of attempting to hold one of those polite, yet stilted conversations which the Midwinter household habitually indulged in.

'Shh!' Aurelia told the tiny occupant of the perambulator, reaching out from the table and pushing the contraption (which was heavy and plush, its black lacquered sides and leather hood as fine an example of coach building as you'd find on a duchess's landau) with movements almost violent in their irritation, '*Quiet*, Larry. God, I hate snivelling brats.'

75

Avon sneered with amusement, to Aurelia's deepening displeasure.

'Perhaps *you'd* like to hold your nephew for a while,' she asked, smiling as she wiped all trace of amusement from his features.

His brain working feverishly, Avon took on a look of disappointment. 'I'd love to, Relia, believe me, but I've been having a spot of trouble with this wrist,' he lied, holding forth his left hand and moving it gingerly, a suitably uncomfortable look upon his face. 'Dashed painful, you know. I think I sprained it yesterday when I was out riding.'

'Huh.' She gave a sceptical snort, then turned to the house and ordered at the top of her voice, 'Nanny, come take your charge away.'

Avon drank his tea, observing her in the same uncaring, familiar fashion that she did him. They were brother and sister, the blood ties strong, yet neither gave a jot for the other and were as cold and detached as they had been about their parents. Aurelia, Avon believed, experienced only two true emotions; indifference and contempt. She loved no one, least of all Courtney, save maybe herself, he corrected, his amusement hidden. Physically he was much like his twenty-three-year-old sister, sharing her tendency towards being thin, her pale hair and the rather gaunt bone structure of her face. Mentally he had to admit to similarities also, though he'd vehemently reject any talk about two peas in a pod. He never saw himself as a vicious schemer. He thought he was grey, rather than black like she was. He blamed his disposition on his parents, believing it was nigh on impossible to be loving and caring when, however much spoilt materially, one was neglected emotionally. He couldn't love because he'd never experienced it himself, didn't understand it, or for that matter, truly believe in it. Lust he understood, however, realizing that was yet another thing he had in common with the woman across the table.

Her eyes were blue like the sky on a hazy day, her hair – which in truth was sandy like his own and used to bleach naturally in the sun when they were children – was pale blonde now, almost colourless, its means bought monthly

76

from the chemist on Park Street who made it up specially for her. Her thin features were at present fetching, though in years to come he could imagine her deteriorating into a claw-handed, bony-nosed baggage. If it wasn't for the rouge on her cheeks and lips she'd be too pale, even sickly looking. Without the expensive wardrobe that encased her, she wouldn't be anything special at all. Eighty per cent of Aurelia Spicer was sham, Avon had concluded, his theory on what lay beneath the surface unflatteringly near the truth.

Was he, he wondered, as transparent as she? If he was then he took comfort from the belief that he wasn't half so artificial. He might not be totally agreeable, he summarized wryly, but at least he was genuine.

Aurelia quickly forgot about Larry, whom the nanny had taken off to the nursery to be quietened down with another feed, her gaze – rarely lacking malevolence – flitting over Avon with intense dislike. Lucky swine! She hated him. He had it all: looks, money, her much liked former home. She wished for his death almost as much as she wished for Courtney's, longing for a life where she had wealth that would bring independence, and the freedom for total self-indulgence.

Still, she mustn't despair. Even healthy men hardly out of boyhood had accidents, *fatal* accidents. There was still a chance, a glimmer of hope to cling to. At eighteen marriage was a thought he'd given no time to. Why should he, after all? Where was the need of a wife when every scullery, chamber, and kitchen maid engaged by his housekeeper fell under his undeniable spell and gave in, willingly enough in most cases, to any masterful advances. Master Avon, with his wicked silver eyes, harsh red mouth and complete arrogance, had a household crammed to the rafters with female flesh, ranging from the maidenly, eager to lose its virgin status, to the worldly-wise wanton with tastes as deviant as his own.

At eighteen he had experienced almost everything, though never liked to think that he'd tasted *all*, for if that were the case the life before him would be rather lacking. Avon liked to think that he'd gained only experience so that whatever occurred in the future he'd be equipped to handle it.

Aurelia had heard things, whisperings between the cook and housekeeper at Number 6 when they thought themselves alone. It seemed that Avon made no attempt to hide his tomcat-like habits, his sexual gymnastics in various novel parts of the house causing quite a bit of amusement amongst those more senior members of staff employed solely for the *functions* their work titles implied! And long might it continue, Aurelia hoped, for purely selfish reasons.

If Avon was content to find release between the legs of the willing lower-classes then marriage would continue to be something he didn't think about. If there was no marriage there would be no children (not legitimate ones at any rate) to inherit and therefore she would remain the sole beneficiary.

Avon replenished their teacups. 'How is Courtney, by the way?'

Aurelia smoothed back an imaginary wisp of hair from her pink powdered forehead. 'He is well . . . busy as usual.'

'None the worse then, for his bout of chicken pox?' laughed Avon.

Aurelia laughed with him, the matter of Courtney and her licence as his wife now very satisfactorily resolved. After her nights of freedom while he was laid low with his stupid ailment, Aurelia couldn't bear the thought of restrictions once more when his health improved. She'd thought hard, her devious brain eventually coming up with the answer: sleeping powders. Now, when she made her monthly visit to the chemist for her hair preparation, she also purchased the harmless powders that speeded along sleep in those already predisposed towards slumber. She put the powders, with sleight of hand, into Courtney's pre-supper sherry any evening she wished to be assured of his immobility and whereabouts, then, when his snores reverberated through the upper storeys at the Long Ashton mansion, stole off into the night. The arrangement was perfect.

Avon's thoughts drifted as did Aurelia's, neither of them seeing the point in holding a stilted conversation merely for the sake of politeness. His eye was on May Bird as she refilled her watering can from the freshwater barrel near the bottom of the garden, her dowdy grey, uniform-like dress riffled by the breeze to show the layers of starched linen petticoats beneath and the frills and ribbons of her pantalettes.

One side of his mouth lifted as he experienced something that might be humour.

Aurelia gazed in the same direction, tittering contemptuously. 'Surely you have no interest in the waif, brother? She's still very much a child.'

He smiled loftily, shaking his head in denial. 'She has potential though.'

'Obediah is hardly likely to stand by and allow you to seduce her,' Aurelia remarked acidly. 'She's his little darling; the resident angel.'

Avon laughed, sure of himself. '*If* I chose to add May Bird to my harem, which couldn't be further from my mind at present, then I think I've skill enough to do so right under Obediah's nose and he be none the wiser.'

'Such conceit!'

'I prefer to think of it as confidence,' drawled Avon, his eyes leaving their perusal of the girl dismissively, though his thoughts dwelled on her and that strangely compelling quality she had for a good while longer.

CHAPTER 10

Lightning zig-zagged across the sky and outlined the black opposing faces of the gorge, lighting up the docklands ahead of Aurelia as if, momentarily, it was day. Her horse reared and snorted, frightened as she directed it across the bridge at the Cumberland Basin lock, the sharp use of the crop on its flanks not helping at all to calm and reassure it against the terror it felt.

The dwarfing black bulk of bonded warehouses engulfed them, making it difficult to progress with confidence, then the lightning came again and the way ahead stood fleetingly illuminated. She dug her heels into the beast's ribs, shouting at it over the noise of the storm, the rain lashing her and soaking through the black hooded cloak that concealed all but a portion of her face. 'Hurry, you nag, damn it! I'm late and Ned'll be furious. He's not a patient man. Gallop, blast you, or I'll send you to the knacker's yard!'

Mention of the man she was hurrying to meet brought him vividly to mind and for a while she hardly noticed the direction she travelled, anticipating their meeting with a heady mixture of delight and dread.

She was known at The Dolls' House as Red, that mysterious alias borne of the simple fact that the full wig Aurelia wore as part of her disguise was the most unnatural shade of vermilion. With eyebrows and eyelids darkened and cheeks and lips liberally rouged she bore no lingering resemblance to Lady Spicer of Long Ashton. She performed as one of the best whores in the brothel because, quite simply, she adored using and being used by the bodies of others, and was willing even to give her services free so long as the man in question could satisfy her totally. After all, she had no real need of money, but just took it as her due and spent it on stockings or whimsical furbelows.

Ned Bland was a poor man, and a rough man from the lowest social class, who could get no job because people didn't take to him, didn't want to employ him or have him around. So he stole, his particular brand of thievery picking pockets, and his area of work centred upon the docks. But he was lazy and shiftless and barely managed to keep himself in beer money even then. Certainly he wouldn't have been able to afford Red on what he lifted from people's pockets. Red cost more than most of the other girls at The Dolls' House because of her overwhelming enthusiasm and dedication to her work! Such factors made her very popular. It was on condition that the madam, Ruth Mead, named the price charged for services rendered that she had allowed Red to indulge herself there on odd nights in the week, putting up with the whore's irregular appearances because of the increase in business when it was known that she *was* there on any one night. A hefty percentage of Red's earnings was going towards keeping Ruth Mead healthily in pocket.

Aurelia and Ned went back a long way, their relationship having been established when she'd lost her virginity to him at the outset of her illicit games. According to the other whores, he was, despite his physical imperfections, the *best* when it came to giving a performance. So Aurelia had taken their advice and offered herself unashamedly, her repugnance and fear and the subsequent physical abuse he subjected her to not dampening her ardour at all. Ned was an ugly, smelly brute and she loved him *and* all the horrible things he demanded she do for him!

He would be evil because she was late, keeping him waiting when she'd promised to be there at midnight. The devil only knew what punishment he might exact from her because of it! Her eyes grew round and bright at the thought, her thighs – gripping the horse's barrel girth as she urged him ever quicker along St Augustine's Back edging the River Frome – tingling expectantly. He would be displeased . . . rough . . . might even put her over his knee and spank her naked bottom before he . . .

She reined in the horse just in time, her lack of concentration almost sending them crashing into the over-hanging jetty of a half-timbered ironmonger's shop. 'Streuth!' she exclaimed, whipping the whinnying horse as if it were all his fault. 'You could have killed me, you stupid beast!'

The horse bolted, trying, it seemed, to outrun the hand that inflicted pain, careering along Lewins Mead, then up Magdalin Lane and past St James's church where the weather cock was lit up by a sheet of lightning that cast a stark white light over all. She was almost there.

Further down the narrow, dark passage off which the whores had their individual, though exceedingly small and spartan rooms, a high, cackling laugh and deep guttural male response rose above the general busy noises of the night at Ruth Mead's Dolls' House.

But Ned and Red were oblivious to all that went on about them, engaged as they were in their own particular brand of self-indulgence. Ned's displeasure at Red's tardiness was feigned, all part of the charade that stimulated the desires of the couple, but his brutality was real, each twist of a limb, pinch and slap genuine and calculated.

'I said I was sorry,' whimpered Red, casting down her eyes and flinching as he lashed out again, missing her, his snarling mouth scornful of her excuses.

'Cowardly, cringing bitch!'

Red got down on her knees, clinging to his leg as Ned plonked himself down in a chair. 'Please give me another chance, master. Ask anything of me. I shall obey . . . want only to serve,' she begged, tingling still from the whacking he'd administered to her rump with the giant span of his palm. *Everything* about Ned was big! Generous! She smoothed the thigh muscles that bulged from his outward thrusting legs. He slapped the delicate hands away, pinching a rouged nipple and turning his singular gaze unmercifully upon her.

Ned Bland was an ugly brute of a man, his pale face shadowed by black and grey stubble, for he hadn't felt like taking a razor to his chin that day, or the day before that, in truth. His was a nightmarish visage, the rough, heavy features worsened by a mouth full of crooked and bad teeth and by the sinister black patch that covered the empty socket from which his eye had been gouged out some twenty years before in a dockland brawl. There were few in Bristol who could recall Ned Bland with two eyes.

Red didn't flinch from him though. To her, Ned's vile ugliness was sublimely revolting, horrible to the point of fascination. Her skin crawled when his hands, tipped by dirt-filled, bitten fingernails roved her body insolently, yet whether it was from horror at the touch or pleasure, she had long since given up trying to fathom.

All Red knew was that Ned was everything the stuffy, delicate Courtney would never be. Ned used her, dominated. For someone as menacing as he she could never nurture contempt. She admired him because he could control her, make her quake with genuine fear before him.

'Kiss me,' Ned demanded, his lone mid-brown eye flitting over Red's naked body – a body that cried out for attention, for rough caresses and savage possession.

'Yes,' she breathed obligingly, raising herself and reaching out to slide her lust-dampened arms about his neck.

'Not on my mouth! Yer t'be punished for keepin' Ned awaitin'. Get yer 'ead down thur an' pleasure me until I feel like bein' forgivin'!'

'Yes, Ned. Anything you say, Ned. Only forgive me.'

'Aah,' he sighed as she unbuttoned his rag-like trousers and gently took charge of the grimy flesh that had been harboured there. 'Treat me nice, like, an' I jus' might send ya 'ome wi' a smile on yer face int' mornin'.'

Her pale blue eyes turned opaque with desire, her manicured fingers toying reverently with Ned's stalk of desire as her pretty rose pink mouth went devotedly to work.

83

Ned growled beneath his breath, reaching out occasionally to squeeze one of the breasts she thrust forward enticingly, or else run a finger down from her navel to between her thighs and extract a ragged breath from the half-crazed female.

At length her toying aroused him to the point where he knew he must take her or else lose control of the situation and shed himself there and then. So he ordered Red off and down onto her knees, thrusting himself into her without further ado and smiling as she groaned with pain and pleasure mixed inseparably into one: his possession.

CHAPTER 11

Clifton, Bristol, at the brink of spring, 1846

May fretted about Jon, somehow connecting the bad
weather with his poor state of health. When the snow went
at last and the wind-fierce months passed, she felt certain he
would rally, gain just a little colour to his tiny hollow
cheeks. She tried to cheer him, to smile a great deal as no
other in the house felt inclined to. Their ties were close,
almost as if the same blood ran through their veins, her
devotion to him poignant to such an extent that Obediah
had to avoid them on occasion for fear of bursting into
unmanly tears that might betray the truth of circumstance.

Everyone knew Jon was dying, save for Jasper and May.
Somehow nobody knew how to tell them, knew the hurt
would be intense and bewildering whichever way the news
was broken. Both were nearly eleven years of age, at that
point in their development when questions became endless
and complex, their desire to grasp the truth concerning God,
the universe, evolution and all the rest frightening Obediah.
In truth he didn't know what to tell them any longer, wasn't
even certain of God's existence himself, not now that Jon
hovered on the brink . . .

May didn't know for sure but she guessed, despairing
when Jon could no longer walk unaided, but had to be
carried down to the back parlour where they occupied the
armchairs by the French provincial style windows, watching

and waiting for the first snowdrops and crocuses to thrust up through the frost hardened soil in the ornamental stone pots just beyond the glass paned doors. But the winter seemed to have no end and Jon, without the cheery warmth of the sun and perhaps knowing, instinctively, as May did, that it was not to be, faded before her eyes, even his capacity for speech weakening, the cough without end, wracking his pathetic, tartan blanketed body.

The doctor came and went with greater frequency and Obediah became more worried and grave, prowling about the large house in a kind of resigned, black stupor, eating infrequently, drinking just a little too much and blaming himself. If they'd known what ailed the child sooner then perhaps they could have taken him to Switzerland for a cure. Obediah had heard of such things happening. It was the altitude, something to do with rarefied air. But the doctor had shaken his head with kindly compassion, putting a comforting arm about the man's shoulders as he expressed his doubts. Jon had been afflicted too severely and with such speed that taking him to a sanatorium would have been of no benefit.

Jon and May were in the parlour taking their time over tea to try to alleviate the boredom of another bleak day when the boy began the coughing fit which was to signal his end. May ran to his side of the table and held him supportively about the shoulders, then, terrified, screamed for help as the bent, tortured form in her arms gasped and choked, went blue in the face and speckled her grey woollen winter dress with bloody sputum.

Obediah and Anne, followed close behind by Mrs Veysey, burst in in alarm and immediately took stock of the situation. Obediah scooped Jon up into his arms and carried him – the tartan blanket falling aside to disclose the wasted white nightshirted boy beneath – up the oak staircase bathed in winter gloom. Anne ran behind in case she could be of help, and Mrs Veysey wandered hurriedly off, shaking her head and wringing her hands, to fetch her black bonnet and thick winter cloak, then off once more for the doctor.

May stood on the Wilton in the middle of the room

trembling, her wide green eyes transfixed by the mess on her dress. She understood fully then that Jon was going to die, felt a terrible lump grow in her throat which threatened to choke her, and clamped a tiny, plump hand over the uncertain mouth in her horror-stricken face to stop the scream that rose but mustn't be allowed to surface.

For weeks Jon lingered, drawing on everyone's reserves of strength, lasting until the first flowers appeared by bitter coincidence in the garden.

Cedric was summoned down from Oxford, all socializing came to an end, and the family at Number 8 simply waited, strong outwardly in their Christian beliefs and prepared for the inevitable, yet ever hopeful of a miracle. Jon was deserving. But beneath the surface both hope and faith had gone. Death *was* the only conclusion. Jessie had died . . . and for what? That her son, such a beloved child, would be with them for so painfully short a time? Obediah thought his heart would break and could perceive no fairness in this – no just hand of God. Henceforth he would attend church dutifully, giving every appearance of pious devotion for the sake of his children and their standing in the community; but in reality his belief was gone, shattered. For him there was no longer a God.

May stirred, looking up in bewilderment at the grief-ravaged features of Obediah, the candle he held in a silver holder weakly illuminating the two of them but little else besides. She raised herself sluggishly, rubbing her eyes as she wondered aloud, 'What is it?'

'He's asked for you, May. Wants to see you. Said something about angels,' said the man in a tremulous voice, his eyes, she noted, red and inflamed and lids puffy from weeping.

'He's not going . . . ?'

'I fear so, my lamb. It will not be long now. Come. You must be quick.'

'But . . . ' But he *can't*, May wanted to shout hotly in denial, angry because although she wanted to so much, there was nothing she could do to alter things. She had

87

control over nothing, that thought frightening her, making her realize how insignificant and small she and everyone else was in the face of the inevitable.

She hurried into her dressing gown, slipped on her slippers and followed swiftly behind Obediah, across the landing where lamps in wall sconces burnt low, too fearful of being too late to speak just once more with her sweet Jon to have time to be afraid of or even think of death.

Jon's room was dotted about with lamps, the light oak furniture scattered with his toys; lead soldiers, sturdy model ships and his favourite monkey automaton placed where he could see them. Only yesterday May had wound up the mechanical wonder for him and they had sat, smiles raised as ever, when the monkey produced a cigar from under his top hat and proceeded to smoke it between thick, garishly red painted lips. She made herself ignore it now, and Jon's other favourite – the battered rocking horse which had endured the energetic, imaginary gallops of all the Goodbody children – knowing that it would bring tears to her eyes. She mustn't cry, she knew that Jon wouldn't like it.

He lay in his too large bed, his chestnut head and feeble shoulders clad in a white nightshirt resting against snowy sheets and pillows, his drawn face worried by a frown as he watched Anne succumb to uncontrollable tears. Then his eyes flickered back to the doctor, innocently questioning and anxious, and the man, seeing May had just entered, saved any awkwardness by beckoning her forward and telling Jon with a smile, 'Here is the angel you were speaking of, my boy.'

A light came into Jon's eyes as May entered his field of vision and perched herself in the chair which Cedric had vacated, smiling at him, as she sensed she must, and stalling indefinitely the tears she wanted to shed.

He gazed over her, recognition bringing the glimmer of a smile to his face. 'Watch over me, angel,' he bade her, relaxing quietly back into the bed with that familiar hint of peace and fearlessness exhibited whenever he had May near.

She took his hand and squeezed it calmly, smoothing it thereafter with her dry, warm palm in a manner which Jon found particularly soothing. For a while, even, he drifted off to sleep, leaving everyone else in the room to watch over him fearfully, agonizing, as he did, over each breath that was laboured and falteringly taken, and then very quietly, so that no one knew precisely when, he died.

May heard Anne weeping again after the numb silence which followed the realization that Jon was indeed dead, and felt, herself, as if it were all a dream. Maybe the fact that she had been brought from her bed still half asleep had dulled her senses to the reality of events. Whatever, several moments passed before she could grasp the truth.

The doctor covered Jon up, hid him from her, deprived her of him. She turned great green eyes upon him, their anguished stare of rage perturbing him, and then the tears came, flooding her eyes to emerald, spilling over and down her face and the sobs were torn from her, wrenching her apart. She clung to the hand which held hers still, even in death, shook her head and resisted when Obediah tried gentle persuasion, quite vehement in her irrational wish to stay with Jon, until Obediah begged her, the plea in his voice breaking through her grief, 'Please, May, I need you now as he did. Will you not hold my hand and comfort me?'

She quietened, laid Jon's hand gently down and kissed it in farewell, taking the much larger, plump hand which Obediah extended. The pain of grief could be no less than the pain of dying, she knew, neither was her love for the father less than her love for the son. So May let Jon be taken from her, hoped that he would understand and would be glad that she was seeking to give solace to Obediah, like a token of love for his memory.

With death now a fact Obediah's grief intensified and he ceased to function with the logic of a sane man. Anne and Cedric took over the funeral arrangements and consulted him only for final approval of their plans. May, Jasper and Obediah could offer no practical help, trudging about the house and avoiding the black draped front parlour where Jon had been laid out in an open oak coffin with silver handles and nameplate. They saw reminders of the boy everywhere, burst into tears at the mention of his name and could not contain their grief with the genteel decorum expected of the middle-classes when people called to express their deepest sympathies.

Then the awful day of the funeral arrived and the house was filled with black clad relations, many of them County of Bristol Goodbodys, though several had also travelled from the farthest reaches of Gloucestershire, Wiltshire and Somerset, the family name nothing if not widespread.

May and Jasper kept handkerchiefs tucked up their sleeves and ready at a moment's notice to be snatched forth and used against the likelihood of tears, trying to be polite as they were asked the usual questions about age, success at school and general behaviour. May was always asked the same question: Was she a good girl for Obediah? And how else could her answer be but in the affirmative? Adults could be so silly sometimes.

May resented their presence knowing that they made this whole awful business much more of a trial for Obediah with their politely solicitous words and insistence that *they knew* how painful it all must be for him and his remaining children. How could they? Jon hadn't been *their* much loved son or brother . . . or playmate. May wanted them all gone, and quickly, so that she and the rest of the family wouldn't be forced to a politeness they were far from feeling any longer than was decently necessary.

She gritted her teeth when the lid on the coffin was screwed down and six black frock-coated, trousered and top-hatted bearers with flowing hat bands of black crepe, bore up the small box and began the solemnly slow descent down the steps from the front door to the waiting hearse bedecked with black drapery and tassles, cut glass and brass. Her dear, sweet Jon was in there, quiet for *ever* and *ever*, but she wouldn't allow herself to think about that, so she stopped the shivers which kept running down her backbone. Jon had gone to heaven, his spirit already flown to leave only his earthly body behind. Obediah had said so, his way of explaining things much less alarming than the dark imaginings of her own mind.

The hearse was pulled by four black horses in black livery and head plumes, the six bearers escorting it at a slow pace dictated by the unobtrusive yet regimental beat of a drum. The immediate family followed behind in a closed black coach hired from the funeral directors for the occasion, with the rest of the family and friends behind them in their own particular modes of procured transport, those of least importance bringing up the rear.

The sun was out, May noted bitterly, for the first time in many a month, warm on her face and glinting off the silver furnishings of Jon's coffin as the six bearers lowered him into his final earthly resting place with the vicar of St Andrew's intoning, 'Ashes to ashes, dust to dust . . .'

Then everyone returned to Beaufort Rise in a quiet, orderly fashion for egg and cress or cucumber sandwiches, Victoria sponge and tea or sherry to wash it all down. The smoothness with which the service was conducted, the vicar's oratory skill and the cooperation of the weather were the main topics of conversation.

May dutifully followed Anne's lead, handing out the fare which Mrs Veysey put on to plates, and constantly asking everyone, 'Would you like another cup of tea?' Then the plates ran out and used ones had to be taken to the kitchen and washed so that they might be used again by those who had taken a fancy to the Victoria sponge, which was sandwiched together with strawberry jam and fresh cream and did, indeed, look inviting. Mourning, to whatever degree, seemed to dull their appetites not at all, May observed as she dried the crockery Mrs Veysey was washing. And so then back to the parlour, May following behind the housekeeper, the pair of them carrying trays laden with clean, shiny Royal Worcester. There were relations everywhere, an obscure, exceedingly eccentric aunt from Chipping Sodbury carrying on a conversation in the doorway and thereby stalling their progress.

'Excuse us, please, ma'am,' coaxed Bertha Veysey politely, but the relation didn't appear to hear, and certainly took no notice, continuing her diatribe concerning the untrustworthiness of the gardener she had recently hired.

The person to whom she spoke understood Bertha's predicament but had her own attempts to butt in on the conversation forcefully talked over. There was nothing for it but to wait until the silly old woman took it into her head to move of her own volition.

May's arms began to experience the first twinges of strain and her foot began to tap beneath her black skirts with mounting impatience. She could see Obediah through the door, nodding somewhat mechanically in agreement with the words of the vicar, but looking very much – especially to May because she knew him so well – as if he wanted desperately to be rescued. She was so busy alternately watching the man and glowering at the woman who blocked the way of Bertha and herself, that at first May wasn't even aware of Avon Midwinter at her shoulder. When she sensed his presence, she turned and managed a rather wan smile, the occasion proving to be one that would leave her pale and strained for days to come. 'Master Avon.'

He inclined his head only slightly. 'Miss Bird,' then squeezed close down the length of her back as old Uncle Frederick passed by, his doddering state necessitating a wide passage. Avon's body was a shock when its contact registered with May's brain and, had she not seen the reason for his action, she might well have succumbed to an irrational bout of panic and dropped the tray. She could feel the warm play of his breath upon her bare nape from which the curls had been dragged up and severely braided in an unflattering style appropriate to the occasion, causing her to look at least three years older. And then she could feel something else as he lingered far longer than was necessary, for Uncle Frederick had passed clear by. She felt a hard lump rubbing against her buttocks, even through the many layers of petticoats. She turned abruptly, her eyes going from his secretly grinning face down to the front of his trousers where his fly buttons strained to keep the fine woollen material together over that bulging, offensively prominent part of his anatomy.

May gulped and gasped with shock, took a deep breath but couldn't get her words out. She knew what boys looked like but this was the first time she had ever been made to acknowledge maleness to such an overwhelming extent. Just the thought of the gigantic member Avon was keeping, apparently hidden, down his trousers frightened May witless, for her lack of knowledge was such that she couldn't know it was her own body so close to the young man which had caused so dramatic a reaction, and that reaction only temporary.

Bertha moved forward, the door now thankfully clear, and May bolted after her, the Worcester rattling on her tray. She didn't know what had happened, but she felt deep inside that somehow it was bad, forbidden, and that Obediah would be angry were she to tell him. But she couldn't tell him, not today when his whole world seemed to have crumbled, and probably never would. In future, though, she would be very wary of the young man from next door, and would take precautions to ensure that he never caught her unawares like that again and bestowed his alarming, most definitely uninvited attentions.

'It's a bad business next door,' opined the housekeeper, Mrs Butler, at Number 6 as she opened the front door to her employer. 'Sank the whole street into gloom, there's no denying.'

'Indeed. Indeed,' agreed Avon, removing gloves, top hat and frock-coat. 'I'll take tea in the back parlour, Mrs Butler. Have Dolly bring it for me. Then I do not wish to be further disturbed.'

Mrs Butler raised an eyebrow but refrained from making humorous comment. She was only the housekeeper, after all, and it was not her place, and if Master Avon wanted to take liberties beneath the skirts of the scullery maid she cared little either way, merely finding it amusing. It wasn't as if the buxom Dolly was an innocent virgin, though, admittedly, she had been when she'd first arrived to take up the post. Avon had quickly dispensed with that tiresome obstacle in the path of his pleasure and had been favouring the scullery maid – besides others – ever since.

Dolly – fresh and pretty in a plain dress and starched,

frilled pinafore – barely had time to deposit the tea tray on the table by the fire before Avon was upon her, his hands roving, body pressing insistently against her until the girl found her back to the wall and giggled.

'Ooh, Master Avon, sir, youm wicked,' she cooed, her breathing growing deep, her pert bosom rising and falling beneath its imprisoning bodice. Avon Midwinter was a handsome, persistent womanizer used to taking what he wanted, and Dolly adored him, feeling honoured by the interest he showed in her and loving the things he did. He knew just how to pleasure a woman when in the mood and often transported Dolly to the farthest bounds of ecstasy.

But not today.

Today Avon wanted quick release – an end to the torturous throbbing at his loins which the naive May Bird had caused with her tiny delicate waif's body draped in the black weeds of mourning.

Having pinned Dolly against the wall and kissed her deeply to make certain of her arousal and willingness, Avon hoisted her skirts and petticoats, exposing white thighs and black woollen stockings gartered just above the knees, his hand delving straight between naked thighs as a knee nudged her apart, for Dolly – wanton and ever willing to oblige – never wore pantelettes.

He stabbed up and into her, robbing Dolly momentarily of breath, her moans soft and delighted against his ear as she clung desperately about his neck, her legs buckling with the overwhelming thrill of passion.

His silver eyes were closed, his thoughts of May Bird and her delicious buttocks smooth against his love-thickened manhood. His harsh red mouth tightened determinedly as he thrust on, relief within his grasp, thinking of hair like a sunburst and a mouth which looked, and must surely taste, like alpine strawberries. He was oblivious to Dolly and her squeals of pleasure, mind chanting in time with the final strokes of fulfilment. *One Day . . . one day . . .* Yes, one day, he decided, as release came and the agony of wanting ebbed, leaving him relaxed and inwardly calm, one day he would make her his own. It just seemed to him to be inevitable, like the sun's rising and setting with each day.

Cool of thought and manner again, Avon dropped Dolly's skirts and gave her rump a dismissive slap, pouring himself tea as he motioned her to the door with a wave of his hand. 'Thank you, Dolly. *That* will be all.'

CHAPTER 12

Eighteen forty-six would ever be remembered by May Bird
as a bad year, so full of ill-fated events that it was best
quickly pushed aside, conveniently forgotten. First the
spring had brought the death of her dearest Jon and then, in
the autumn, and almost too much for the unhappy May to
bear, her beloved Isambard's *SS Great Britain*, on her fifth
voyage went aground on the coast of Ireland, her captain
mistakenly believing he'd suffered a collision with the Isle of
Man. *The Illustrated London News* carried the story, and
the elegant ship seemed doomed to break up on the shore, a
salvage team unable to refloat her.

May laboured over the details in print but relied on
Obediah ultimately to simplify the facts so that she might
understand. He tried not to alarm her, to sound hopeful for
the liner's future, but May was devastated, knew the pain
that Brunel must be feeling. The ship's captain should be
whipped for allowing such a disaster to befall their pride
and joy, and the fact that none of the 180 passengers were
injured in the accident did little to mollify her. She hated not
knowing the ship's fate. Ireland was so far away. But surely
someone must be trying to help her, fighting to save so
grand a vessel from breaking up in the seasonally worsening
weather? Surely Isambard had been informed? Then why
wasn't he doing anything? Or maybe he was, May prayed,
suffering an agony of uncertainty.

Obediah hoped and prayed too, though his concerns were
financial in nature, the pending loss of the *SS Great Britain*

spelling disaster for the GWSC, already in difficulties with the banks and other major creditors. Ruination for many seemed probable, bankruptcy a certainty. Obediah could survive such a loss, but there were other shareholders who had put their last penny into the venture, would be nearly beggared by the experience.

Brunel took the news of the SS Great Britain's grounding like a father informed of some serious accident befalling a favoured child. His patience was non-existent and immediately he wrote to those concerned in heated terms, furious that his creation, 'the finest ship in the world', should be left lying, 'like a useless saucepan kicking about on the most exposed shore you can imagine'. He commandeered a locomotive, had his private car – nick-named 'The Hearse' because of its sombre black hue – connected up, and charged the engine driver to get him to the west coast with all possible speed. From there he took a boat and descended upon Dundrum Bay to take personal charge of his beloved vessel's rescue from the ravages of the Irish Sea, finding comfort in the fact that her hull of iron offered protection against the furies which no wooden hull could have withstood.

Isambard snarled and strutted on the beach, furious at the indignity inflicted upon the ship by, as he saw it, an incompetent captain who should be stripped of his office. Listing and stuck, she made – on days when the weather permitted excursions – a tourist attraction of sorts and he had the added irritation of a beach cluttered with curious folk as he tried to formulate plans to extricate her from the greedy clutches of the sand.

Finally he decided there was nothing for it other than to protect her from the sea's onslaught until the high tides of spring when she might be refloated. Brunel ordered the Great Britain to be protected by, 'a mass of large, strong faggots lashed together, skewered together with iron-rods, weighted down with iron, sandbags etc, the whole wrapped around with chains, just like a huge poultice'.

Satisfied that he had done all within his power to save

her, Isambard retreated to his hotel to await the next ferry back to England, thinking that perhaps he might write to his wife to explain the situation. He had time on his hands and was quick to grow bored unless occupation was found for his brain. But no. Mary would doubtless read of his Irish endeavours in *The Times* and would need no more detailed explanation than that to satisfy her. She was a good wife and she pleased him, not bothering him and bringing up their three children with a competence that made him proud. But his regard – love, some would say – for her was, and ever would be, superficial. Work would always remain the consuming passion of his life.

He sat at the dressing table where stationery with the hotel's name headed the water-marked paper, and decided to write to May instead. Doubtless she would be worried about *her* ship, he surmised, setting down his colossus of a cigar box and bringing forth one of the fat tobacco creations that he had rolled specially for him. He lit it, drew deeply and coughed, then set the smoking article to the side of his mouth as quill dipped into Indian ink and began scratching. His writing, like his technical drawings, was always executed with an eye to perfection.

'Dear May,

She is safe though still aground, my plan to see her off this accursed shoreline come next spring. Then the tides should be high enough to float her free. I feared for her, as I know you would have, but am confident now that the worst shall not occur. It will take more than the lacking seamanship of one captain to destroy her, and how pleased I am that her hull is of iron, for I'm certain she'll not break because of it. My sympathies are with Obediah and others of the GWSC. This accident, for them especially, is a disaster and will surely wind up what could have been a powerful company. Selling the *Great Britain*, I think, will be the only sensible course of action left for them to take *if* they are to salvage anything at all. I feel responsible in no small measure for some of the gloom which has doubtless affected those about you. Knowing you though, May, I sense I am forgiven. Yet to more fully make amends might I bring you back something from Ireland? Yes, I shall see to it before I leave on the morrow. Perhaps a shawl or a dainty piece in crystal for your bedside table. After all, we can't be unhappy when saving *her* becomes a possibility most probable rather than just a desperate wish between kindred spirits.

Ever affectionately,
I K Brunel'

Aurelia gave the possibility of encountering Courtney during one of her nocturnal escapades scant thought. The likelihood of it happening was almost nil, the odds against thousands-to-one. But it happened, and on a night when she had thought herself indulging without the least risk, for Courtney was supposed to be in London discussing India rubber with someone who was interested in the proposed manufacture of waterproof footwear. He was supposed to catch the early train home the next morning, but evidently had changed his plans, and came within a hair's breadth of catching her out.

She had left the Dolls' House after fornicating with her last customer of the night who was too drunk to give a memorable performance, stealing out into the dark before dawn feeling less than wholly satisfied. Pulling her cloak about her to ward off the winter chill, Aurelia had gained the saddle of her horse and departed at a leisurely trot, wending down through steeply sloping alleyways until she had reached Canon's Marsh where she pointed the horse down Anchor Road and yawned, knowing that he would, from familiarity of the route, find his way home from there.

It was then that she heard that scratchy voice which always jarred her nerves, and reined back the horse beneath her cautiously, eyes scanning the dark street ahead.

All the public houses and taverns were closed by then and there were few people still on the street, those that were falling into two general categories; drunkards and thieves, for all God-fearing, law-abiding folk were in bed and slumbering lest they had some powerfully good reason to be abroad.

Aurelia followed behind the voices at a distance, enjoying the feeling of danger, yet never truly believing that her husband would spot her, or suffer a dawning of recognition. Lamplight occasionally touched him, turning him and his equally inebriated companion into black, top-hatted silhouettes.

They were laughing and jovial, and Aurelia concluded that their business in London had been settled to their satisfaction in a speedier manner than had been expected. She squinted at Courtney's companion, almost certain that he was that up-and-coming colleague in the Spicer company. He was unimportant, to her mind, and she dismissed him forthwith, finding Courtney's whisky induced observations on life much more entertaining.

She would listen for a while, she decided, and, when it looked as if they were about to part company and Courtney find himself a cab, she would put heels to her horse's belly and speed him home, thus assuring herself that she could be changed in appearance and in bed before his homecoming. She would greet him with a drowsy smile as though he had woken her but she didn't mind, and she would enquire about his journey and business and ring for a servant to warm him milk before he went to bed. Her sweet disposition would be so pleasurable to him that the stupid Courtney wouldn't even notice or comment on her slightly dishevelled appearance. And if he did? Then Aurelia was confident of plucking an excuse from thin air plausible enough to satisfy him.

'I'shad one too many,' Courtney slurred, his mouth lax and tongue out of control.

'Sho 'ave I,' chuckled his friend, 'but we had to shelly-brate, din't we?'

'O'corsh. That contract'll make ush both ex . . . exsh-treemly rich, Crawford, old boy.'

'Yesh,' breathed his staggering companion with unashamed glee.

100

They swayed and clutched at each other, calling out as a hackney passed by, and swearing when it didn't stop.

'I musht shay Shur Courtney, that I *have* enjoyed myshelf tonight. Those shluts we picked up in The Rummer weresh pretty damned well obliging for half-a-crown, weren't they?'

Courtney made a noise which implied masculine prowess, sticking out his feeble chest and all but swaggering. 'She'll not forget the pleasure I gave ta 'er this night in a hurry. Moaned with delight she did when I took her down that dark alley an' 'ad hersh against a wall. But we mushn't e'er talk about thish again, ja undershtand? If my wife wush to get to 'ear 'bout thish . . . ' Courtney rolled his eyes in horror. 'Sh'wouldn't undershtand. I've never been able to . . . not with her . . . not the shway I'd like to. She'sh too delicate. You can't go ramming at a woman like that, a gentshell woman . . . You hash to be tendersh, conshiderate . . . '

'Shur Courtney, there ish no need to exshplain. I can quite shee your point an' my lipsh are shealed,' vowed Mr Crawford.

It was as much as Aurelia could do not to start laughing at the absurd idiot she'd been lumbered with for a husband and thereby give herself away.

Another hackney approached, its side lamps lit to offer some comfort against the hostile darkness of night and Mr Crawford bellowed at it, bringing the conveyance to an obedient halt on the cobbles beside them.

'And where would you two gentlemen be wantin' to go?' asked the driver, breathing on his cold fingers which peeped out from fingerless mittens and grasped the horse's reins.

'Take thish fellow to Newfoundland Road,' instructed Courtney.

'I coulshunt 'ear of it,' argued Mr Crawford. 'Take thish gentleman home to Long Ashton.'

'No, no, I inshist. I'd like to walk for a while an' shmoke a shigar. I'll find a cab when I getsh to the Cum'erlan' Bashin,' said Courtney, firmly, his head nodding emphatically with determination.

Between them they got the door open, argued some more,

then Mr Crawford was assisted into the coach, though he still managed to half fall and flounder on his knees between the seats. Courtney slammed the door, paid the driver in advance and staggered off in the opposite direction as the coach pulled away and built up speed, Mr Crawford leaning out of the window and calling a cheery, barely coherent 'Goodnight'.

Aurelia nudged the horse into motion again, thoroughly enjoying this unknown side to Courtney's character. The man – her puny, passive spouse – had a liking on the sly for drink and whores! She would never have believed him capable of anything so base or *daring*, and armed with such information from his own loose lips, she would have to think long and hard about how best to use it against him. She might tell him that she knew about his escapades, that someone at his place of work had talked carelessly and the truth reached *her* ears, his dear, wronged wife, Aurelia. She would never forgive him unless he consented to move back to Bristol, only that would be enough to erase from her mind the painful thought of him with another woman, and worse still a creature of the night! Perhaps. She'd mull it over later, safely tucked up in her warm, comfortable bed.

Meanwhile, Aurelia cast her eyes into the gloom ahead of her and suffered several moments of panic as her gaze failed to find that excuse for a husband of hers. Then there he was again, evidently having made a quick detour down an alley to answer a call of nature in the dark. He began to sing, a tuneless rendition of some Penny Ballad, and resumed his walk in the correct direction.

Aurelia followed behind.

He strayed again, the lapping of the waters in the Floating Harbour reaching his ears, a lamp on the far embankment, near the dock from which *SS Great Britain* was launched, creating a thousand murky water ripples with silver light. He was lost, and paused, twirling to try spot some landmark in the uncertain darkness, the violence of the movement making him totter like a baby and keel over.

Aurelia laughed, her amusement making her careless so that she had allowed her mount to trot closer than was

102

perhaps wise, the gap between husband and wife dangerously closing.

Courtney became aware of rider and horse for the first time and immediately reached to assure himself that his wallet was safe in the inner pocket of his coat. 'Who are you? Are you following me?' he wondered aloud, fear sobering him very slightly.

Prudently, Aurelia thought it best to make a speedy withdrawal from the scene and tried to back her mount out of the narrow alleyway between a chandler's shop and a sailmaker's. The horse didn't want to go backwards into the unknown, though, and began to fidget and snort. She dug her heels in and hissed at it, aware that Courtney was watching closely, intrigued by the fleeting glimpses of her and the horse afforded by the various scattered lamps about the harbour.

That horse looked dashed familiar. In fact if Courtney hadn't been the worse for drink he would have sworn it was the one he had bought last year at an auction on Blackboy Hill.

'Where didsha get that 'orse?' he asked the shadowy female with a dark, almost black-looking mouth in a face greyed by lamplight, her hair escaping from the hood of a cloak in long, wild tendrils that seemed the most unnatural shade of scarlet in the purple, lanterned night.

He squinted at her, the thoughts in his head mirrored clearly in his face where his expression changed with alarming speed. Courtney had the strangest feeling . . . was very uneasy . . .

'The horse is mine. Let me pass to go unmolested about my business,' demanded Aurelia, forcing her voice down several octaves so that it bore no semblance to her own, deciding that if the horse refused to retreat then there was nothing for it but to get past Courtney and gallop for her life.

As she came abreast of her husband, freeing her foot from the stirrup and trying to ward him off with a kick, he caught the reins and held fast with a drunkard's penchant for irritating stubbornness.

103

'That *is* my horse!' he declared, staring from steed to rider in consternation, determined to get to the bottom of this mystery.

Aurelia experienced no small measure of disquiet. She could see difficulties in extricating herself from this dilemma. Even if she escaped Courtney and reached home, he was liable to demand to see this particular horse almost immediately, and how could she explain away a hot, sweaty, exercised animal? She could blame it on one of the grooms, say he must have taken the horse without permission for a nocturnal ride. But somehow she didn't think that even the gullible Courtney would be satisfied with that explanation. After all, what would one of his lads be doing galloping around Bristol docks dressed as a woman? His suspicion, therefore, was bound to fall on her. She was going to be found out. Unless . . .

There was nothing for it. Aurelia jabbed her heels into the horse's belly and he jumped forward, his barrel chest connecting with Courtney and sending him crashing against the door of the chandler's shop.

Winded, Courtney staggered up and backed off, sensing of a sudden that events had taken on a whole new quality of menace. Horse and rider advanced, threatening to trample him beneath hooves if he didn't scamper out of the way quickly enough. He looked up into Aurelia's face again, saw something familiar, and was about to put his thoughts and the terrible realization into words when he stumbled over an iron mooring ring set into the flagstones of the quay. He saw the water only two steps behind him, black and frightful, and let out a squeal of fear, jumping away only to come up against the equally intimidating and unpredictable horse being manipulated by a deadly rider.

He knew who it was now, though he would never know why she was there, disguised and abroad in the dead of night. He had sealed his own fate, Courtney realized with an hysterical sob, crouching and clinging to the mooring ring, his hold determining life or death.

She hit the horse, goading him to rear and kick out to catch Courtney a blow to the temple with a steel-shod hoof, her face fixed with a cold-blooded look of divine purpose.

Courtney groaned but held on, knowing that the waters waited, cold and lethal to him, a drunken non-swimmer, shrieking her name in astonished terror, 'Aurelia!'

She was furious, his desperate hold upon life forcing her to dismount the horse and use physical force against the crouching bundle clutching the iron ring on the edge of the quay. He reminded her of a hedgehog rolling himself into a ball at sight of trouble and hoping that fate would be kind. She kicked him, her dainty boot of black leather, fastened up to the calf with criss-crossed laces, catching him under the chin and stunning the unfortunate man so that his grasp slackened.

He toppled over the side, clinging frantically there for a while by his fingertips until Aurelia stepped forward and ground her heel down upon the clawing flesh, then he fell, his half conscious wail giving way to watery splutterings and frantic splashings from ineffective moving limbs. Incapacitated by drink, weighted with clothes and nearly swooning from the pain inflicted upon him by Aurelia, Courtney disappeared beneath the black waters almost immediately, air bubbles exploding on the surface. His wife turned away smiling, confident that he would not be yielded up again until thoroughly dead and quite harmless.

CHAPTER 13

Aurelia took care over the next couple of days to act as any wife would whose husband had apparently been delayed abroad on business. She made a point of frowning worriedly in front of the servants when his prolonged absence became apparent, sent a message to his place of work to enquire whether they had received notice of his imminent return, then, when the reply came that he had returned to Bristol two days past, acted like a truly alarmed wife fearful of an accident or criminal act perpetrated against his person, and called in the police.

She dressed with subdued care, went easy with her make-up – leaving off the rouge so that she would look touchingly wan – and indulged in much dabbing of eyes and nose with a lacy handkerchief whenever the Inspector called, asking questions and trying to piece together the scant information on her husband's last known movements and make sense of them. Then a contrite Mr Crawford came forward and admitted that, on their return from London, he and Courtney had been drinking heavily in celebration of a business deal which had almost been finalized. He had left his superior near the docks and taken a cab home, and he feared, though of course he prayed he was wrong, that the unfortunate man must have strayed and fallen into the Floating Harbour and been drowned.

Aurelia showed herself to be a convincing actress and went into hysterics, then a swoon for good measure, the upstairs servants reviving her while police inspector and a wretchedly guilt-ridden Mr Crawford looked on, only for her to declare with a spine-tingling wail of despair that she wanted to die, to be sucked down a silt and water filled subterranean conduit like her poor lost and lamented husband.

'Life will cease to have meaning for me,' she had babbled, hiding behind her handkerchief, 'for Courtney meant everything . . . *everything*!'

All at Long Ashton went into deep mourning, the mansion quiet and Courtney's portrait hanging bedecked with crepe drapery and laurel in the blue drawing room.

In the absence of a body there was a memorial service instead of a funeral, and Aurelia cried loudly throughout, leaning on a frowning, hardly comforting Avon for support. She told all and sundry afterwards that she thanked the Almighty for having given her a son who would bring her comfort in her bleakest hour of despair. Avon couldn't altogether swallow that. Mr Crawford attended the service but kept a low profile, crying into his hymn book and shaking his head in woe. He would never forgive himself for being persuaded to take the hackney that fearful night in Sir Courtney's stead.

Careful not to appear hasty, the widow mourned deeply and when possible in public by day – declining invitations to tea and visiting church instead for comfort of the spirit – and frolicking as usual at night. When a suitable period had elapsed she let it be known that the mansion held too many painful memories of her beloved Courtney and that she was going to sell it and move back to the city with Larry to be near her sole living kin, her brother Avon.

Avon heard and digested news of her plans and the way she worded them with a cynic's scepticism. Maybe he was being unkind to Relia when she most needed his support, but Avon couldn't bring himself to believe her.

And so it was that before Christmas 1846 Lady Aurelia Spicer, grieving widow, with her son Lawrence and his nurse, moved into a newly built pale stone mansion 'just around the corner' from brother Avon Midwinter, their close proximity having more to do with her mindfulness of outward appearance than genuine sisterly fondness. She felt no guilt or remorse at having committed murder, worried not about divine retribution for the sin and suffered not even one sleepless night because of it. Getting rid of Courtney in a spur-of-the-moment attack had been a master stroke and in no way did she regret it.

The house on the corner of Wall Street and Broadway, Christmas Day, 1846

Morgan Somerton wouldn't hear of having a decorated tree in his parlour, despite the fact that Mary-Anne said that half the other families in the district had taken up the custom, and that it would also be such a delight for Thirza. No, let the British suck up to Victoria's Germanic consort Albert, and adopt his customs if they pleased, but Morgan was American and not given to seasonal fads. They would have a quiet day as usual without out-of-place frivolity, would celebrate the holy day as it was meant to be remembered. They would go to worship at Trinity Church, lunch at home, then perhaps take a coach ride about the city in order to gain the benefit of some fresh air.

To console herself during the afternoon when their coach ride was done and the most that Thirza had to look forward to was her bed when it grew dark, she kept taking the peppermint creams from the cut glass dish on the table while she sewed, the lingering pleasure of the taste compelling her to have just one more, then another . . . Pretty soon they were all gone and guilt came in pleasure's stead, Morgan scowling and slanting his grey eyes at her with distaste. He sipped his sherry and came up with the hurtful remark, 'You're a fat, greedy disappointment, daughter. Get yourself off to bed and out of my sight. Being forced to look continually upon your pudginess does not please me.'

'Please, Morgan,' interceded Mary-Anne, 'try and be kind. It *is* Christmas. Such words hurt.'

'They were meant to! A stern line is needed, madam, to shake her out of these disgusting bouts of gluttony. She is weak, lacks self-control. She ought to pull herself together. But instead she merely continues to eat, to be a disappointment to me . . . a failure. Never was a man cursed with such unworthy children. My son was wilful and contemptuous even of his father's authority, and my daughter is making herself so obese and ugly that no man will ever want to marry her and she'll be on my hands for evermore relying on my benevolence.'

Thirza rose, indigo eyes overspilling with tears. It was true . . . *true*. She was everything he said, and, knowing that she couldn't even console herself by citing his injustice and inaccuracy, only served to make Thirza more wretched than ever. She gathered her needlework and bent to plant a goodnight kiss on her mama's forehead, but when she would have done the same to her father he turned away, making it plain that not even her kisses were welcome.

For a while after reaching her room Thirza sat and wept in the dark, sniffing and wiping with a handkerchief, then she remembered Jude's Christmas present for her, hidden carefully away at the back of the bottom drawer in her tallboy.

They had met last month under the walls of Castle Clinton in Battery Park, had given each other news and gifts and cried a great deal on parting. Every time Thirza saw Jude he seemed to have grown taller, rougher and wilder and every time he told her of his voyages with smiles of enthusiasm, she wanted to go with him all the more. But she was sensible now, as was only natural she liked to think for a maturing girl of twelve, and she could see that his freedom would never be hers. She had not his means of escape, was held prisoner by dint of her gender. And he had gone again, off on another voyage with Jack Mitchell, his festive celebrations maybe taking place on the high seas.

For a moment Thirza dreamt of such a possibility, then, with a deep breath of anticipation, she tore the brown paper from the object in her hands and gasped low beneath her breath with secretive delight. Tied with a silken pink bow and in a *papier-mâché* container with lid decorated in the red Japanese manner, was powder and a fluffy pom-pom puff just crying out to be dabbed here, there and everywhere.

Thirza sat at her dressing-table and postured, delighting in the reflection that had clouds of headily perfumed dust wafting about her throat and cheeks. Trust Jude to think of such a present for her. He was so thoughtful, his present appealing greatly to the twelve-year-old as embroidery accoutrements never could.

Her delight blotted from mind her father's stinging remarks of earlier, until, from nowhere his voice and that of her mama came to Thirza's ears, loud in argument, and she froze in horror, gaping in fright at the illicit gift in her hands.

They were evidently on their way up to bed and if her father should come in and catch her with it . . . ! He was drunk, very much so as the festive occasion gave him a plausible excuse, and in such a state he could be terrifyingly unpredictable.

Swiftly Thirza pulled open a drawer and pushed the gift beneath piles of neatly folded camisoles, closing it rather too violently in her agitation and holding her breath in dread. But her parents arguing, as they came up the stairs, had fortunately made them oblivious to her and the harmless fun she'd found for herself.

She hated it when her mother faced the brunt of his displeasure in order to defend her daughter, and wished that mama wouldn't take such risks, that she would be quiet so that he had no cause or justification for the violence he was apt to indulge in. But Thirza knew that wouldn't work. If Mary-Anne wouldn't rise to the bait and try reason with him in heated argument, then Morgan was quite capable of picking a quarrel instead. No one could win against him.

Thirza willed the pair of them to calm and the potentially volatile situation fizzle out on its own, but Morgan's voice rose higher as he reached the landing and came ever nearer to Thirza's door, and mama shrieked, the sound dying away until it was little save an echo of its original self. There was a loud thud, then several softer ones that sent a chill down the child's spine and then, for an eternity, came silence so frightening that Thirza rose from her dressing table, hardly breathing, and went to the door.

Something had happened. She could feel it, hear it, and had to open the door and find out what it was, even though terror kept her continually on the brink of a scream.

Papa was on the landing as Thirza came out of her room but he didn't see her, disappearing almost immediately down the stairs in a slow, drunkenly weaving manner, and Thirza had reached the balustrade of the landing long before he gained the lower floor.

Her mama was lying there, where the carpeted stairs gave way to the marble hall, her eyes staring askew, her body without movement.

'Mama!' Thirza screamed, taking the stairs perilously fast, her trailing dressing-gown threatening to trip her at any moment.

Morgan was kneeling over Mary-Anne by then, and had her by the shoulders and was shaking the unconscious woman with violent urgency, the harm that this might do not registering in his sotted brain at all. 'Wake up, woman, damn you!'

'Papa, *don't*!' the child beseeched, wresting her mother's lolling form bravely from him and lying her gently down again on the cold floor.

'Why you insolent . . . ' Morgan snarled, only to be stalled by his daughter's frantically spluttered words.

'She cannot hear you, papa. She is bleeding. See? There is a head-wound. We must get her to a hospital or I think she might die. Shall I rouse the servants, or will you?'

'Die? Nah, she's faking,' he declared, with bravura to hide his fear. He lent low, breathing alcohol fumes in the unconscious woman's face, as he hissed, 'Stop acting, Mary-Anne. It was only a little push I gave you. It doesn't warrant so melodramatic a show from you.'

Thirza shivered with horror, his words telling her the truth of what had happened though he was too drunk to realize it.

Sitting beside Mary-Anne on the way to Bellevue Hospital

111

in the horse-drawn ambulance, Thirza avoided her father's slightly drink-clouded gaze, frightened of him as if he were the very devil himself. Her mother's hand was still and warm within her own concerned grasp and occasionally her limbs twitched of their own volition.

Her father was sobering, though Thirza had come to realize long ago that to casual acquaintances he probably seemed that way most of the time. Morgan was such an accomplished drunk that only the smell of spirit and unusually glassy eyes gave him away. He was never too unsteady on his feet unless required to move at speed and his speech never deteriorated into comical slurrings. He spoke slowly when under the influence and with care, hiding well from any who didn't know him closely the fact that he wasn't in complete control of his faculties. He was a clever, wicked man.

Bellevue Hospital, on the banks of the East River, had initially been built as a treatment centre for contagious diseases after New York's 1795 outbreak of yellow fever, and not until 1826 did it become a fully fledged hospital.

They bore Mary-Anne out of the ambulance on a stretcher and took her to a pale green painted room where glazed tiles of an olive hue skirted the walls to shoulder height. A stark white mantled gaslamp cast exposed light over spotless white sheets and the blooded patient waiting for the doctor on night duty. He arrived soon after, ignoring Morgan and Thirza and hitching back the sleeves of his frockcoat the better to examine the woman.

At length he drew himself up self-importantly and gestured for the relatives to accompany him out into the corridor.

'How, might one ask, did this happen?'

'She fell,' supplied Morgan, quickly, his head nodding emphatically as if he expected his daughter to contradict him.

As if she would! She feared Morgan above all else and wouldn't speak the truth. Who would believe her anyhow? The doctor was not the sympathetic type to whom she could have unloaded the torment of her soul. He looked eager to be rid of them, to have the orderlies come and take care of mama so that he might the sooner get back to his bed, book, game of cards or whatever else he might care to entertain himself with on this Christmas night. Mama was just another patient to him, a nuisance that interrupted him.

'Yes, she fell,' repeated Morgan, more confidently this time as the possibility of a challenge faded.

'Well, sir, I can detect no fracture, though that is still a possibility not to be dismissed. Your wife has a great deal of swelling, contusion and laceration. We will not know how serious the injury is until she regains consciousness though. We shall keep her under observation. There is nothing you can do; you might just as well take your daughter home.'

'I'd rather stay,' said Morgan, shaking his head. 'I want to be here when my wife awakes.'

'As you wish,' replied the doctor without interest, 'though you may well have a lengthy wait ahead of you.'

'I'll wait.'

He sounded so concerned about mama, as if he couldn't bear to leave the place where she was while she remained in any danger. But Thirza knew better, knew the truth of the matter to be that Morgan was determined to be at Mary-Anne's bedside as soon after she came to as possible so that he could coerce her into adopting his story concerning the events that had resulted in her injury this night. Mary-Anne would tell everyone that she had been clumsy and fallen, because of her fear of her husband. And that would be that and thus things would continue, Thirza surmised, until the day when either mama or herself didn't survive his brutality, until, in all probability, he murdered one of them.

CHAPTER 14

For years the British had been dropping anchor at the ports of Canton and Macao to fill their holds, not totally with tea as might have been expected, but leaving ample space for the most widely harvested crop of those regions – opium. But relations between China and Victoria's merchant fleet were not always good. Recently the Opium Wars had erupted, confrontations between naval warships and fleets of armed junks the climax of growing resentment brought about by the unruly behaviour of her Britannic Majesty's subjects on foreign soil. British sailors were notorious for their drinking and brawling in ports of call and the natives' smouldering hostility became actual physical violence when one of their number was killed in just such a brawl.

Seeing things turning decidedly ugly, Britain, rather than tactfully adopt a low profile and wait for ill feeling to wane, brought her might to bear in the shape of the Royal Navy, and eventually the Manchu Emperor backed down, the threat of coastal bombardment too fearful a prospect. His was an ancient nation, and against so modern and disciplined an adversary he knew his only real strength to be in the number of able-bodied he could have called upon to fight in his name; but he doubted that even that advantage would have been enough. Britain's power was surprisingly awesome considering her geographical shortcomings. Maybe she was best described as a terrier whose loud bark had the ability to fool larger dogs into thinking her more ferocious than she truly was.

The Treaty of Nanking was signed and thereafter the Orient was truly opened to Western venturers for the first time. Britain, far from being an innocent party in the troubles, came out of them even better off than before. China opened four ports of trade to Britain as well as Canton, and handed them the island of Hong Kong as a naval base. The opium trade was made legal, relations were established between the government in Peking and London, and other western governments, including America, Russia and Portugal began to press for similiar concessions.

Thus it was that in the summer of 1848 the eighteen-year-old Jude Mariner, aboard the *Celestial Piper*, crossed the Pacific after a nerve-racking passage around The Horn, and entered the shark infested China Sea. They called at Shanghai, where he drank too much and allowed himself to be persuaded into having a tattoo, sailed down to Foochow where they took on tea, then further south again, to the teeming island port of Hong Kong where foreigners of all nationalities abounded and the natives had become westernized and, sadly, showed signs of corruption in many cases. Their aim, it appeared to Jude, was to squeeze the foreigners dry of the wealth that they had stolen from China by one means or another.

Masonry was scarce, save on the official buildings of the British Consulate and the like and, instead, most buildings were wooden, their roofs sloping down to eaves which curled curiously – much as the native's black shoes curled at the toes. There were no stout walls or thick oak doors to shut out the outside world. Structures were flimsy and open, lending an airy feel which seemed to breed noise and activity. Everywhere there was bustle, with people trying to sell you their wares or cooking over ferociously flaming ranges set out in the open, the food cooked on the spot in oil and aromatic spices that set the ship's company's mouths drooling after several weeks of less than commendable fare.

They ate until pleasantly full on chicken, prawns, bean sprouts, bamboo shoots, water chestnuts and the like, forsaking chopsticks the quicker to down the food with their fingers. Then, with much belching, beaming smiles and nods of appreciation for the cook's artistry, the sailors moved on, searching out an equivalent of the western tavern amongst the confusion of streets and alleys hung with character signs in red and black, green and gold, where houses were decorated with carved dragons or dogs above their thresholds.

The wealthy natives wore silks quite breathtakingly beautiful in the embroidery that smothered them, while the more humble citizens seemed to favour dull, lightweight breeches and shirts with mandarin collars in greys, browns or black, their hair in pigtails and heads covered by black, strangely upstanding four-cornered hats. For the women breeches were replaced by plain, full length skirts, the volume of which was dictated by the wearer's capacity to afford the necessary yardage. Their jet, waveless hair was pulled back and up into a practical bun-type knot which was held in place with wooden or sometimes ivory skewers. They were docile and obedient to their husbands, but in the market place when they wanted to outsell their neighbours, the Chinese women could be quite overpowering with their squawking cacophony.

Jude had seen Chinese before, for they had made quite a community for themselves in down-town New York, but he couldn't recall ever having seen the women back home going about with their feet purposefully crippled in adherence to ancient custom. To the old order small feet were beautiful feet, and those old ways still lingered, not yet totally outlawed by public opinion and the foreign rulers of the island. Jude could only think that it spoilt what were otherwise very fetching creatures, and found himself grimacing imagining their discomfort whenever he spotted the hobbling forms moving slowly along with their balance seemingly impaired.

Slightly the worse for drink, the group by darkness had found its way into a back street den where opium was the narcotic commodity for sale and adolescent girls – sold into prostitution by desperate, or more often unscrupulously exploitive parents – acted as servants to the tables, their duties sketchy, their willingness to cooperate with the customers dependent on the colour of his money. Their smiles were few and cynicism great. With acid wit they set out to fleece their prey with the minimum of effort and concession, usually succeeding because the opium made the men docile and pleasantly willing victims of their own foolishness.

Jude stayed on the sidelines, shaking his head steadfastly at everything which the bevy of woman-flesh offered him, wary of the place and the dark corners.

Jack was not so cautious and flopped down onto a couch, willing to be seduced by such wickedness, two girls then squabbling over him because he was indeed the most handsome of men, his bronzed face and short, wiry platinum hair forever setting him apart from the rest.

The bosun and the others followed suit raucously, taking up the hookahs proffered and sucking with expectant expressions.

They were fools at times, Jude thought, sitting stiffly on a couch and asking a passing girl if she'd ever heard of sarsaparilla and, if so, whether she could fetch him one. She shook her head vaguely, the few words she spoke in her native tongue a mystery to him. Yes, fools. They got so carried away sometimes in the pursuit of their own pleasures that they left themselves open to all kinds of dangers. Not that Jude could see any here especially; but that didn't mean they weren't there. This was a foreign land with strange customs, alien ways. It was so easy to offend without even knowing it, and then there could follow a bloodbath with Chinamen coming at them brandishing hatchets and knives, hacking off heads and limbs! He'd heard tales, many of them from Mr Brannigan, who now lolled upon a cushioned bamboo couch with a squat little table beside him to carry his opium pot, from which came the tube on which he sucked and puffed so energetically, his eyes no longer focusing. Yes, fools.

Jude sat stiff and upright beside a chuckling Jack who was having his ear played with by his companion of the moment, the young man's eyes occupying themselves with the line drawings upon the walls of exotic birds perching amongst bamboo. He took out his notebook and began to draw, getting down on paper the intricacies of the fretwork screens that lent a secretive air to the already unwholesome place.

A serving-girl paused to watch him, though her expression gave nothing away, and Jude could only think that she was unimpressed. She was pretty and her feet thankfully unbound and naturally petite. Slight of figure beneath a brown skirt and loose fitting, badly cut tunic which was sashed with padded black silk beneath her breasts, she eyed Jude critically and then asked, 'You want to go back room and have much pleasure?'

Jude blushed, refusing quickly. He'd never been with a woman, although Jack had threatened laughingly to take him to a brothel on more than one occasion since that ludicrous episode in Marseilles. The young man was tremulous at the thought, wanting to and yet dreading, imagining with longing yet fearing that the reality would be a farce. It certainly would have been with the girl before him now. She was pretty, yes, but of so sour and apathetic a disposition that he doubted he could have performed adequately or even have wanted to. *When* he went with a woman it would be because she wanted him as much as he wanted her. He knew it wasn't so with these whores, and could guess well enough what was in their minds when they spread their legs and took pleasure only in the payment which would follow. Such thoughts killed passion, slight as it was to begin with.

'No, I don't want to go out the back, but I would like to draw you. Will you sit down, just for a while?' he wondered aloud.

'You have to pay,' she told him firmly, determined to get paid no matter what the service.

'Yes, of course,' agreed Jude.

'Same as if we went out back and had fun.'

He sighed, disappointed by her mercenary attitude, yet taking satisfaction from having so accurately guessed at her character. 'It's a deal.'

And so Jude scribbled away as the ship's company lost

themselves all about him in a weird land of dreams, only their earthly husks present as their minds drifted elsewhere. He finished one sketch and started another, concentrating this time upon the plump and pretty though thoroughly bored face before him.

'What's your name?'

'Mai-Yin Chow.' She seemed reluctant even to volunteer that much, as if she resented sharing anything so private with him.

'Mine is Jude. It's from the New Testament of the Christian Bible.'

She shrugged her shoulders with a dismissive lack of interest, her eyes going beyond him as the door to the den opened and more sailors entered – Jack Tars of the British Royal Navy without a doubt, and all of them drunk already and looking for fun or a fight and not fussy about which.

The Chinaman who owned the den and his subordinates bowed low and tried to look pleased by the appearance of so many potential customers, but in truth their insides were quaking, their knack of smelling trouble infallible. American seamen okay. British seamen okay. But together they pretty bad news!

The proprietor encompassed them all with a big, friendly grin. 'So sorry, my friends, but couches all full. You come back later maybe?'

They all answered back at about the same time, brows knitting and jaws jutting with bruisers' determination. 'No.' 'Not on yer Nelly.' 'I'm staying put.' 'Try throwing me out if yuh dare, matey!'

Jude listened to them with growing disquiet, turning back from a wary glimpse of them to find that his subject matter had prudently vanished into thin air. There was only himself, three nervous Chinamen and a lolling heap of immobilized crewmen and feminine playmates to repulse the might of the Queen's Navy.

Jude tried nudging and pinching Jack but it did no good. All the response that Jack was capable of was a quick, lethargic chuckle. The girl – who had been playing with his

119

ear and trying to persuade him out to the back room with her before the opiate incapacitated him completely – now stood up and tried to make herself invisible too, but one of, *HMS Dorencourt*'s able-seamen had spotted her and lumbered drunkenly forward, those behind following in his wake as if on an invisible signal.

The *Celestial Piper*'s crew came laboriously back to life as each of their serving girls stopped their tempting toying and began squealing as new hands and arms touched and encircled, laying claim to them.

'Ger off wiv yuh, yanks! Shove off why don't yuh?' shouted one particularly mouthy tar who put his foot to Mr Brannigan's rump and pushed him from the couch without seeming to use any effort.

There were roars of laughter, more squeals from the girls and more of Jack's crew tried desperately to regain their senses as they were ousted, none too gently, from their former relaxed positions.

'Oi! What's going on?' 'What the . . . !' 'Of all the bleedin' nerve!'

The drugged and the drunk came together in a heaving, ponderous mass of regulation summer uniforms, canvas trousers and chunky knit sweaters, hats and caps flying as they tried to floor each other and often missed.

The proprietor stepped in, fearful of the damage that might be done, and one of his girls snatched her arm free of the sailor who had claimed her arrogantly, and punched him on the nose, thus scoring the first true hit of the night.

The Chinaman pleaded lugubriously, held up his hands in desperation and howled as if in pain when the first bamboo table collapsed under the weight of a felled opponent. Thereafter he resigned himself to his and his property's fate and stepped out of the way of physical harm, wringing his hands and mentally counting the cost.

Jude patted his shoulder consolingly. 'I'm sorry. They're shameful at times. You send the bill for damage to Captain Mitchell aboard the *Celestial Piper* and I'll see to it that he coughs up.'

The man's distress was incredibly quick to lessen and he

wrote down that useful piece of information upon a scrap of paper.

'Uh, excuse me,' said a calm voice behind the pair of spectators, 'Her Britannic Majesty's Navy will also pay their share if you'll but present your bill to Petty Officer Blyton aboard *HMS Dorencourt* at the Haun-Lai Dock tomorrow.'

'Thanks. That's decent of you,' opined Jude, turning to smile at the young man behind him, who wore an officer's uniform immaculate in its cut and in pristine condition.

'Only fair, yank. After all, I do believe my men started it,' admitted the officer with a gleam to his blue-grey eyes.

'Your men? Are you a captain, then?' asked Jude in awed surprise.

'No,' laughed the man. 'I'm only senior to this rabble and a few others besides. I'm a midshipman, a non-commissioned officer in Her Majesty's Navy. It's my lot to try and keep them out of too much trouble while ashore, be an acting figure of authority. But, as you can see, they don't take too much notice of me after the second tankard of ale starts to affect their brain cells.'

Jude's smile was wry, enjoying the casual conversation with the Englishman. 'I suppose seeing as how we've been placed on opposing sides in this dispute, that we two should also be fighting. Though in truth I can see no sensible reason and hardly feel inclined.'

'My thoughts entirely, yank. What say you that we just settle ourselves at a table and have the Chinaman bring us a beverage?'

'That sounds mighty civilized.'

'My name's James Benedict, yank. Jim if you like. What's yours, so's I can stop using that term? I know some of you fellows take exception to it, especially those from the south who have a whole different way of speaking and such and think themselves a cut above the run-o'-the-mill northerners.'

'I *am* a yankee and take no offence at being called one, Jim. My name's Jude Mariner and I hail from New York.'

'Hum.' Jim's brows raised, expressing interest. 'I come from Hampshire . . . Bucklers Hard, to be more precise.

'Tis the place where many a ship of the line was built during the Napoleonic Wars.'

Jude absorbed that whilst watching the idiotic antics of his friends as they fought the lumbering, drunken British. Jack was on his feet and striking out in the reflexive manner of one who has no idea of where he is.

The Chinaman brought rice wine and bent their sympathetic ears with several minutes of complaints about the behaviour of their companions, before shuffling off again in black floppy slippers to fulfil their next order for drinks.

Glass shattered, someone shouted abuse and then another howled in pain after toppling into the red hot bowl of a hookah and accidently burning himself. One or two inert bodies further littered the debris-strewn floor and Jack stood amongst it all swaying, evidently having suffered a blow to the head and Jude surmised, only staying on his feet through sheer willpower.

'I think we ought to try and get them outside onto the street for some fresh air when we've finished these drinks,' suggested Jim Benedict, lifting his china drinking bowl and disposing of the liquid, with an appreciative smack of lips, at the precise moment that two brawlers, locked in mindless combat, careered backwards out of control and landed square in the middle of the table separating him and his drinking partner.

Jude and Jim seized the two between them and manhandled them out into the street where lantern light was scarce. Then they went back for the others, Jim producing a navy issue whistle and blowing on it with a shrill clarity that had enough power to penetrate even the foggiest mind.

'Everybody out and back to their ships. Refusal to obey will result in a charge,' he told them, coolly confident of his authority and certain of his men.

And they moved, sluggishly and with reluctance maybe, but obeying even so, taking themselves and dragging their unconscious friends out with them. What was even more surprising to Jude was the fact that the reeling Jack Mitchell and the bosun he clung to in camaraderie followed suit and went docilely with the rest, crewmen following their lead.

The two sober young men – one bleached and tattered by the sun and the other splendid enough to go on parade – herded their respective crews before them along streets so black there were no shadows, and down steep flights of steps amongst shanties, until they could make out the waterfront and black silhouettes of ships' rigging against a purple sky and define the smaller sampans close to shore and the junks in open waters.

Jack began to sing, though thankfully nothing of a nationalistic or patriotic nature certain to raise British hackles. Others joined in in woozy fashion, the words hardly coherent, and so it was that when confrontation came in the form of two black-clad, sinister looking Orientals brandishing knives and ostensibly barring the way forward, James Benedict's threatening tones of authority in response had to be issued loudly so as to be heard above the din.

'Stand aside. That's an order. I am British and so is this island. You and your kind have no place here.'

The Chinamen didn't budge, only gripped their knives more firmly and waited, poised and snarling, to stab anything which moved against them.

Jack squinted drunkenly, turning to Jude to ask, 'What's this, lad?'

'Frankly, I don't know,' the young man replied, feeling very inadequate and vulnerable without any means of defending himself. He looked sideways to Jim Benedict, sensing that the young Englishman – not much older than himself but seemingly so much wiser – would know what was taking place and why, and how to deal with it.

'They are T'ai P'ing,' Jim supplied, drawing his navy pistol from the holster at his belt. 'Religious maniacs who adhere to the teachings of Hsiu-ch'uan. It's a hotch-potch of Christian and Chinese religion. All rather fanatical. Mostly they aim to rid the mainland in the south of banditry. But they've also got a burning desire to see the British off, too. Stay back, Captain Mitchell, and caution your men to do likewise. This is not your fight,' instructed midshipman Benedict.

'I've never run from a fight and I ain't about to start

123

now,' vowed Jack heatedly, reaching for the knife he sometimes wore but didn't on this particular occasion. 'Curses! Damn and blast it all! Jude, why did you let me come out improperly dressed?'

Jude didn't have time to think of an answer to that absurd question, for one of Jack's crew *did* have a knife and, fancying his chances and too drunk to be cautious, had made to the front of the halted, uncertain crowd.

The two Chinamen saw him and, with spine-tingling yells, pounced immediately, knives arcing overhead momentarily before plunging into the foolhardy seaman. He fell, but then they followed, brought down by fire from Jim Benedict's pistol before they could strike again.

A crowd gathered around the three bodies, most men staring down with surprise on their faces and babbled questions on their lips. The natives who came out of curiosity to stare, whispered the name T'ai P'ing in fearful awe and disappeared swiftly into the night again.

'I'm sorry about your man,' Jim commiserated.

'Aye . . . well . . . ' sighed Jack, stunned by events and lost for words.

'Let's go back to our ships quickly before we court further disaster.'

'I'm all for that,' agreed Jack, 'but what about the bodies?'

'Their own will come and take them away, no doubt.'

'Aye, I suppose. Lend a hand, men, with the remains of poor Vinny Pollard. He was a good man, though a mite inclined towards acting without thought. It's our duty to see him buried decent,' urged Jack, his words as solemn as an epitaph.

And so, for the main part drowsy and subdued by drink and foul play, the crews trudged the waterfront, parting company at the gangplank of Jack Mitchell's ship. He paused and shook hands with Jim Benedict while his crew struggled to carry their dead companion aboard. 'My thanks, Mr Midshipman, sir. Without your quick thoughts and action I fear we would have had our numbers further depleted.'

'No man of principles would have done less,' said Jim, playing down the importance of his actions. 'And goodbye to you, Jude Mariner, and a safe voyage. It's unlikely we shall meet again, but then fate is a strange thing, so I won't swear to it. Goodnight to you all.'

'Goodbye,' Jude said in parting, grasping the other's hand firmly and shaking it with formal politeness, greatly impressed by James Benedict.

Part 2
Three Days One Summer

CHAPTER 15

Atop the gorge on the Bristol side of the River Avon, and only a stone's throw from the piers of Isambard Kingdom Brunel's ill-fated suspension bridge, stood the observatory tower on St Vincent's Rock which housed the Camera Obscura. When the weather was fine and the hour a decent one, the Victorians of Clifton took time, during their promenading, to climb the spiral to the top and watch the city panorama projected before them onto a large, round and crisp white table top. Then, when they'd seen enough, they descended, strolling on along the cliff top and watching the ships manoeuvring the muddy quirks of the river below as the tides bore their vessels along to the port. Further on, where the building of fine houses had not yet encroached, were the green open spaces of tree-covered common land set aside for public recreation, individually named but collectively known by the people of Bristol as the Downs. There kites could be flown, dogs exercised and human beings indulge in one or other of their favourite outdoor games or else partake of a wholesome picnic.

On one particular Sunday afternoon in June of 1849, when the sun beamed hotly and the breeze that channelled through the wide open space was therefore much appreciated, half the established families of Clifton seemed to have congregated on the Downs for a much publicized cricket match, old family rivalries resurfacing to lend much to team spirit. Every male arrived with his own personal willow cricket bat, while the females of the families descended from carriages and made themselves comfortable on travelling rugs, their skirts over the new fangled crinolines ballooning fetchingly about them, their hands encased in lace mittens and complexions protected by parasols.

Within this female boundary the gentlemen created their wicket and set up stumps and bails, everything done by unspoken code of etiquette, for the cricket pitch should personify, above all, the conduct of gentlemen, as if somehow taking the place of the medieval tourney field. The men of Clifton might be loath to lose a wicket to the opposing side from the neighbouring district of Redland, but they would never show it. Win or lose, it should be done with good grace. The game was more important than the result.

On the boundary, bedecked in essential white flannels and peaked cap, sat Obediah Goodbody waiting for his turn to bat, his considerable stomach hidden beneath a V-necked cream pullover, his eyes incapable of focusing with interest on anything save bowler and batsman out there on the well maintained, short mown grass. He loved the game, thinking there was much to commend a sport which didn't discriminate against the fat people of the world.

Nearby, lounging upon a tartan rug with a cigar clamped between his teeth, was Mr Brunel and the GWR engineer responsible for the building of most of that line's locomotives, Daniel Gooch; while behind them, sampling the delights from the picnic hamper which May and Mrs Veysey had prepared, sat Mr Patterson the shipyard owner, and Mr Guppy the industrialist. They had been assembled for some small matter of business by the great engineer himself, he finding it expedient to deal with them *en masse* and in this, the most convivial of settings. Isambard had always thought Bristol society charming and saw no reason to deny himself the pleasure of it when he was able. Besides, his doctor had begun to tut-tut, to admonish him because of the amount of cigars he enjoyed per day and the environments he frequented. Could he help it if his business usually entailed hours upon end in stale, smoky boardrooms? And tobacco never hurt anyone as far as he could recall, but had a positively calming effect. If a man couldn't enjoy a smoke – something which Isambard found helpful to his concentration – then the world was a pretty miserable place to his mind. Though he might concede that fifty cigars a day was a trifle beyond the bounds of over-indulgence!

Business and lunch done and washed down with wine or ale from stone, screw-topped bottles, Isambard felt at liberty to leave his contemporaries to amuse themselves, while he did his 'disappearing coin' trick for May and Jasper, certain that they'd be as spell-bound as his own offspring. The half-sovereign seemed to disappear into his mouth, only for him to pluck it moments later from behind his ear. 'Watch carefully,' he challenged a perplexed Jasper who stamped his foot with mounting frustration and admiration each time he guessed incorrectly the whereabouts of the coin.

'The hand is quicker than the eye,' laughed Isambard. 'One day maybe, lad, I'll show you how to do it, though of course each time I do it I put my life on the line.'

'Really?' questioned May.

'I did the trick for my children often, but one particular time I had a problem with the sleight of hand. The coin slipped and got stuck in my throat, and no matter what poor Mrs Brunel did, it would not budge. In truth, young friends, I grew alarmed myself when a doctor ordered surgery to remove the dratted object, but saw no alternative save an untimely demise.'

Jasper's brows undulated in sceptical consideration of such information and he finally felt bound to declare, 'I believe you're making it up, Mr Brunel, sir. It's another of your tall stories.'

Isambard indulged in mock affront. 'I swear it to be a fact, young master Jasper. Why, Daniel, whom I've known since we were both in our twenties, will testify to this being a genuine story.'

'Indeed I do. It is also a story which dear Isambard has told often over the years with much relish,' chuckled the engine builder.

'The operation failed and I, having suffered the indignity of two-foot long forceps being probed down my windpipe, felt most definitely that there would only be one sorry outcome to the business, for if London's finest surgeons couldn't with their skills solve the problem, who else could?'

'Who indeed?' laughed Daniel, knowingly.

'You!' supplied May, assuredly, for Mr Brunel could, as far as she was concerned, do *anything* he set his mind to.

'Quite so, Birdy,' he confirmed, patting her head, pleased to know that she had such confidence in him.

'But how?' wondered Jasper. 'Did you operate on yourself?'

'Heavens no! Nothing so gruesome. I hurriedly did some drawings for a piece of apparatus consisting of a board, to which I would be strapped, and the means of securing it to two upright pivots. I had this idea, you see, that centrifugal force was the only possibility left open to me.'

'Centri-what?'

'Centrifugal, Jasper. Think of a spinning top at the moment of release. One second it's twirling on the spot, the next it shoots off at great speed. I was the spinning top, turned as fast as was humanly possible for those assisting me, end over end, in the hope of forcing the coin out of my mouth. The first attempt ended in my coughing fit to expire, but the next time the coin popped out – ping – and I was set on my feet, dizzy yet restored to health.'

'Caw!' breathed Jasper, much impressed.

'Howzat!' cried fielders and male spectators in unison, and the umpire decided in their favour, giving Avon Midwinter his marching orders for being caught leg before wicket.

Obediah jumped to his feet, sorry that Avon was out, of course, but very eager to get into the fray and maybe, just maybe, score that dreamt of century. He passed Avon on the pitch on his way to the wicket, shaking his hand and murmuring, 'Bad luck, old boy. You were looking good up until the dismissal.'

'It was a bad decision,' was Avon's only comment. His

132

gaze was upon May, drawn to her by that usual animal hunger he felt whenever he had her within his sight; a predatory need to humble and tame her as strong as ever.

Sensing his gaze, she cast down her eyes and refused to acknowledge him either by word or gesture. Ever since Jon's funeral she had been careful, whenever required to keep his company, to make certain of friends in close proximity to act unwittingly as protection against any improper advances on his part. Mostly it had worked well, though the unrelenting need for vigilance sometimes wore at her nerves and patience, and she wished she had courage enough to go to Obediah and unload the whole embarrassing problem upon him. But if she spoke and Obediah acted in a suitably outraged fashion on her behalf and maybe voiced his displeasure man to man with Avon, life at Beaufort Rise could turn very unpleasant for them all. Hostility towards one's next door neighbour was to be avoided. May's complaint against Avon seemed almost paltry when balanced against the damage which the revelation of it would undoubtedly bring about. She preferred tolerating his subtle form of sexual harassment rather than live through the public outcry there would be were she to expose him.

May rose, deciding that a stroll around the boundary of the pitch would be the best means of avoidance on this particular occasion, her abstract smile for Isambard causing him to quirk an eyebrow at her.

She seemed, to the engineer, to be preoccupied with thoughts doubtless best kept to herself. A lot of fourteen-year-olds were like that. It was, he therefore surmised, merely the normal behaviour of a girl beginning to experience a woman's thoughts and feelings. All very complex and disturbing and so difficult for the developing woman to comprehend or even accept.

May – garbed in a dress which his wife, Mary, had grown tired of and handed down to the distantly placed waif who enjoyed something akin to her husband's patronage – looked alarmingly enticing in the indigo blue which was almost, but not quite, full-length, showing white cotton

133

stockings and frilled pantaloon trim, and feet encased in light grey leather boots up past the ankles. Graceful full-length was still a year and more away, when to all intents and purposes, May would be deemed fully grown – at least physically – a young woman. But even now, Isambard couldn't help noticing with fatherly interest, she looked grown up enough and was pretty enough to arouse men's interest and cause Obediah moments of disquiet. May would more than make up for the total lack of worry he had felt about Anne, for she, poor dear, had grown unfortunately plainer rather than handsome and aroused no great excitement in any of the eligible bachelors of Clifton, remaining, at twenty years, unwed.

May was fourteen but looked at least two years maturer, her breasts apparent as they strained against the tight bodice of the day dress which had fit more adequately the slighter, more modestly endowed Mary Brunel. And at so tender an age the future and the possibilities for marriage had taken over in May's mind as the topics most worthy of thoughtful consideration. Anne's dolls, which had been given to her on her arrival at Beaufort Rise in a kind of adoption, had long since been relegated to one of the tin trunks in the attic room at the back of the house. She was beginning to find that men, other than her adored Isambard and Obediah, could be attractive and interesting, to find that employing what had erstwhile been childishly winning charm in the new practice of flirting could be very amusing. Young men blushed and stammered, making utter fools of themselves if she so much as smiled their way and gazed in a certain manner from beneath thick lashes that shaded her eyes to woodland green. Boys were fun, more so than she had ever realized before, and May was taking delight in her first adolescent experiments, trifling with the affections of all in what an observer would call a cold-blooded fashion.

They came to tea on Sundays, bringing boxes of the local Fry's chocolates which had cost their whole week's allowance and willing Obediah, by power of thought, to leave the parlour, no matter for how meagre a time, so that they might try press the giggling beauty with dimpling chin

134

into allowing them a kiss. *On the hand*, of course! They fought and bickered amongst themselves; any who had appeared to be favoured certain to take a pasting on the way home from their jealous rivals. It mattered not to them that their parents frowned upon the girl, for ever reminding their sons of her total lack of breeding and background. To a man they vowed that such facts made no difference, that they would adore and love her until their dying breaths.

May, as if the worship and flattery were sustenance in themselves, grew ever lovelier under such a flood of attention, her gaiety seeming to fill the house and touch all within it. Anne could so easily have been jealous but, being a good Christian, wasn't; while Jasper, who had known May too long to think of her as anything other than a sister, thought them all fools and spied on them through the keyhole in the parlour door, finding their clodlike attempts at wooing and winning May's affection amusing to the same degree that she secretly did.

Avon caught up with May, deviously using the fact that Aurelia and Lawrence lay ahead as his excuse to seek her company, and hiding well his anger at her continuing, nigh on fanatical avoidance.

His greeting was formal, though its coming out of the blue and him along with it momentarily startled May. 'Is it not a pleasant afternoon, May? Probably the best Sunday so far this year.'

She was instantly on her guard, though comforted somewhat by the fact that they were in so crowded a setting, his hard body and the arrogance of stature it exuded setting alarm bells ringing in her head. 'Yes, indeed, Mr Midwinter.'

He sighed with exasperation, wanting more than just one of her usual faltering, stilted and totally inane replies. She acted like a mouse or canary protected by the flimsiest of cages, while he – like a tomcat with cruel teeth and claws honed to lethal extent upon a table leg – stalked nearby awaiting his chance and confident of the result.

'Your capacity for bearing a grudge is truly phenomenal, Miss Bird,' he snapped, patience gone. 'Will you hold that long ago moment of weakness against me for ever more? Be reasonable. Can you not understand that it was your beauty which led me to such an act, and thus forgive me?'

'It is not the past which fills me with disquiet, sir, but your continued unwanted attention. Have I not made it plain by attitude alone that I care not for your stalking me?' breathed May, in high dudgeon, her pace quickening and the parasol she carried stabbing the ground with mounting ferocity.

'Stalking?' He looked at her with eyebrows raised, as if her words were ludicrously untrue, their unfairness astonishing him. 'Isn't that rather an exaggeration? I prefer to think of it as "admiring from afar" and have never, since that day of succumbing to the temptation to touch you, harboured any thought of impropriety liable to cause you distress.'

'You are glib, sir. Do not think that I, because of my lowly background – of which you are knowledgeable and I unashamed – will be either awed or intimidated by your ungentlemanly overtures,' she told him bravely, finding infinite relief in the fact that they were almost upon the seemly, mourning-clad Aurelia and her son with attending nurse, and Avon was, therefore, obliged to let her go. 'Good afternoon, Lady Spicer and good day to you, Mr Midwinter.'

As ever, Aurelia inclined her head but didn't care to converse with one so obviously beneath her in station.

Frustrated, Avon thrust his hands into the pockets of his white flannel trousers and watched the girl's stiff back as she strode on with dignity, a malevolent eye seering his sister for daring to show something akin to contempt for the one he so possessively craved, his concealed hands balling into hard fists.

May sighed, feeling her body grow less tense away from the wolf in gentleman's clothing, her gaze wandering to the pitch where Obediah had just hit a four and now stood at his wicket acknowledging the polite and delicate hand-clapping of the scattered crowd around the oval boundary. Like a dark cloud on a bright day, Avon's obscuring of the

136

sun was only temporary; soon he was gone, dismissed from her mind resolutely.

She let her thoughts wander, coming back to reality only when the noise on the field from jubilant fielders told her that Obediah was out for twenty-three runs, caught by the fielder at silly mid off, that man throwing the hard, red leather ball up into the air victoriously and catching it with already smarting fingers. May called out her commiserations, smiling all the while, and paused beneath some beech trees while all changed upon the pitch; batsmen coming on now as fielders and the Redland team deciding upon their order of batting.

'Could it be, miss, that you actually *know* what is going on?' asked a youthful male voice in amused surprise.

May turned her head, smiling at the speaker as she replied in a light, conversational manner. 'It is the duty of all good British people, and the peoples of their empire, to know and understand the rules of cricket, sir. Your accent and apparent ignorance lead me to deduce that you must be from foreign places.'

Her words came easily, she hardly aware that she spoke them as she covered his physique and arresting face with her eyes, finding him an unknown and wholly intriguing quantity.

His eyes gazed back into hers, binding her as if with a spell, their colour unlike anything she had encountered before. She didn't know of anyone with eyes *that* blue, and thought, after consideration, that only Mrs Appleton's Persian cat at Number 4 had eyes that might compare.

'Foreign indeed, miss. I am Jude Mariner from New York City, America. How do you do?'

'I . . . why . . . I do very well, thank you, sir,' said May, clumsy of a sudden, as if the beauty of him had hit her by delayed action.

Aurelia had seen him, too, thinking him quite the most delicious young morsel to catch her eye in quite some time, and, shining the cricket ball against his groin in preparation for bowling and thus staining red his spotless white trousers, Avon Midwinter saw the young man also and the

137

smiling, pink-cheeked May, and frowned, the first delivery he sent thundering down the wicket towards the batsman a no ball. Which pleased him least he couldn't say, his ill grace growing throughout the over and causing the captain, eventually, to change the bowler for a spell.

CHAPTER 16

Jack Mitchell had brought the *Celestial Piper* into the mouth of the Avon with his eyes on the tricky river and a promise on his lips for Jude.

'I think you'll be filling that sketch book of yours while we're at Bristol,' he had said, manoeuvring them alongside the quay at Shirehampton where they would take aboard the river pilot and – to while away half an hour until the incoming tide was just right for safe passage inland – have a jug of beer at the public house ashore used by the lamplighters. 'She's a city unlike any other. She's got ancient gates and churches. Timber houses from Tudor times and the best of each century's building traits. Even I, who never did have more than the most basic of schooling, can appreciate the vast differences and squalid charm. She's different from London because she's in the *shires*, as these people call them. They don't have States like you and me, Jude. Here there is a relief from the dirt unknown in the bigger cities, a comforting abundance of greenery only a stone's throw from busy market places. I never forgot my first visit here and it always pleasures me to make return trips.'

And Jude had been impressed, his book coming out even before they had reached the awesomeness of the gorge to sketch the notorious horseshoe bend in the river ahead where the pilot's skills were much appreciated. Many a ship had misjudged things at that point and gone aground without dignity upon the mudbanks, there to unwillingly entertain the locals who'd come to sightsee from the hamlets.

The *Celestial Piper* sailed through without a hitch however, most of the ship's compliment atop deck to take in the unique scenery, those in the rigging calling down their appreciation of the sheer rock, so smooth it looked as if it was coated in glass plate, and ferns and shrubs which had managed over the last centuries to take hold and root in the crevices. They saw chalets, seemingly perching precariously amongst densely overgrown parts of the cliff face, looking as if they'd tumble at any moment, down into the brown churning waters of high tide. They saw Brunel's abutment and piers, cast a glance over the lowly ferryman at Hotwells and promised themselves a hot bath when they read the hoardings at the Spa entrance on the riverside offering such a service. But mostly they looked forward to getting ashore and heading for the portals of the numerous dockland pubs. While the *Celestial Piper* was divested of her cargo of mahogany from South America, her crew would be loading themselves with as much brown ale and rum as their senses would allow, stopping, doubtless, only when gravity won and they fell down.

Jude still did not, and likely never would, share their appreciation of alcohol and, sketchbook in hand and pockets carrying all the lead and charcoal he might conceivably need, the young man had set about exploring a city of rivers, hills, dockland and fashionable thoroughfares. Many were the times that he sat down with a subject in mind only to spot a distant spire, tower or gable *more* appealing. There was the cathedral, a Broad Quay, a Narrow Quay, Floating Harbour, St Mary Redcliffe Parish Church, coffee houses, ale houses, corn exchanges, Temple Meads Station, assembly rooms, Turkish baths, discreet brothels, seamen's missions . . .

Overwhelmed, Jude found himself climbing Park Street, stopping on the way to purchase a piece of Bristol Blue glass for Thirza, his feet then plodding on until he came to a place called Brandon Hill, where he stopped, aching and out of breath, to turn and survey the city sprawling below him, its heart given over to the shipping on the river. Enchanted, he had sat and drawn until his fingers and brain no longer functioned as one, weary with fatigue. Then, ravenous with hunger, he had entered a shop advertising SUCCULENT WEST COUNTRY FAGGOTS and GENUINE WILTSHIRE SAUSAGES and allowed himself to be talked into the fare recommended by an enormous cook behind the counter. Apparently she had taken a liking to Jude on sight, thinking it novel to be serving an American, and set before him a meal he'd not quickly forget. When the last mushy pea and fork-load of mashed potatoes dipped in onion gravy hit his belly, he sat back with a pleasurable groan of contentment and cradled his belted girth which, to his mind, felt twice as large as before and uncomfortably confined.

'Was it to yer likin', me lad?' asked the cook as he paid for his meal and took a sliced faggot, sandwiched between two pieces of coarse-grained brown bread and wrapped in greaseproof paper, at her insistence. 'Jus' in case youm peckish later on s'afternoon.'

'Never in my life have I felt so full,' he declared, and that seemed to please her ears for she smiled and waved him goodbye until he was lost over the brow of the next rise.

Soon Jude was at the top of the hill and the imposing, beige stone houses thinned out and green open spaces took their place. Faggots, sausages and everything else seemed to sap at him, demanding he be still while his digestion tried to cope. So he had found a tree under which to shade himself against the sun, put down his coat and lain atop it so that he wouldn't become a meal for the ants while he slept. He had awoken to find his tree lying on the indefinite perimeter of a game, which seemed quite absurd to his foreign eye, and, as he had sat up, shaking his coat and donning it again, he had seen a young girl pass by with hair like burnished copper spilling from her blue bonnet. A girl whose face was so disconcerting in its loveliness that he had felt compelled to get quickly to his feet and take off after her, neither knowing what he would say nor caring, just so long as he *did* engage her in some kind of conversation and didn't let her pass by and out of, heaven forbid, his life.

'Would it be all right for me to accompany you on your walk? I mean, I don't want to presume . . . intrude . . . Maybe your parents wouldn't like it, would find it forward,' he fired at her, hardly stopping for breath, sincere and guileless and unashamedly eager.

'My guardian is too busy concentrating on fielding to pay us much heed, Mr Mariner. And your company would please me greatly. New York is just a name to me, mentioned some times in regard to family business, but I've no idea what it's like. Perhaps we could talk about that? I'd find it very interesting.'

'Would you? Well, I'd be delighted to try and build a kind of picture for you, in your mind.'

'Do all the people from New York talk that way?' she wondered, amused.

'Why, yes,' he laughed.

'It's a strange accent; English, and yet, not. Mr Brunel laughs at my accent because it's so heavily Bristolian despite all Mr Goodbody's efforts to refine it.'

'Could it be that the Mr Brunel you're talking about is the same one who's famous, even on our side of the Atlantic, for his engineering feats?'

'Yes. In fact he's over there, wearing the top hat and smoking a cigar while he watches the match.'

'You don't say?'

'I do,' May insisted, quirking a confused eyebrow at the odd term of expression. 'He's half French, was educated mostly over there but spent his bachelor years in London and then Bristol. *His* accent has to be heard to be believed!'

'I'll bet.'

'So tell me about New York, *and* yourself . . . What brings you here. What you do for a living. Or maybe you're at university? I presume they have them in America? The eldest in our family, Cedric, went to Oxford, but that's all finished now and he's off on his Grand Tour of Europe.'

'I didn't go to university. In fact I ran away to sea instead; became a sailor.'

'How marvellous!' imagined May. 'That sounds really exciting. So you're here in Bristol with your ship?'

142

'Yes. We're docked on Broad Quay, just in past the drawbridge.'

'I know it. And do you see your parents or not? I mean, have the differences that made you want to leave home in the first place been resolved?'

'No, nor are they likely to be,' said Jude, quietly.

May waited for more but there was none, so she didn't press, hardly expecting, after all, to be made privy to his darker family secrets after an acquaintance of mere minutes. She wasn't about to become too clear about her own background, either, forever feeling that the shame of having been sold should remain a secret known only to those who had learnt it at the time the awful deed was perpetrated.

'But New York is your home port?'

'Oh yes. I share lodgings with the skipper whenever we're there. It's a busy place with bits of everything going on. People from all over the world live there.'

'Yet it wasn't exciting enough to keep you from leaving,' stated May.

'The call of the sea was too powerful then and still is even now.'

'And where shall you be sailing to next?'

'We unload the mahogany then sail up the coast around Wales to Liverpool, to take aboard a consignment of pottery from Derby and Staffordshire. Then it's back to New York.'

'I can't imagine you ever having to endure a dull moment. Your life seems so full. Shore leave must mean the only lull into boredom.'

'This leave ashore is proving to be very exciting,' vowed Jude, his eyes glittering with merriment and something else as they swept May's pinkening face. He could only guess at her feelings, but his own were quite alien and alarming in their intensity. He wanted to touch her, hug her, feel that glorious hair and breathe the smell of her up close. But most of all he wanted to kiss her. Not in the gently affectionate manner that he would have mama or Thirza, but with verve, like Jack and one of those generous females at their ports

143

of call, unleashing passion like some kind of sweet attack upon her, so that she'd be overwhelmed with sensation herself and succumb to him as a male. For her, a girl with orange hair and rosy lips, whose name he hadn't yet had time to find out, Jude felt all the longing and arousal of male instinct that no others had been able to stimulate, save for fleeting moments. He didn't know why but he could no longer think of anything except her.

'Lovely . . . ' he murmured, thoughts voicing themselves reverently without his awareness.

'I beg your pardon?' May queried, his dreamy whisper barely audible.

He came back to reality with a start, then flushed with embarrassment, faltering through a lame excuse. 'I said "it's a lovely day".'

'Oh, yes.'

Avon had been put back in to bowl by the captain, who deemed his lack of success earlier to be due to nothing more than an attack of nerves. Given the chance, it was the captain's belief that Avon would soon be bowling maiden overs with his more familiar ease and expertise. But Avon left the slips almost reluctantly and took charge of the ball, his eyes not appraising the wicket as one might have expected, but scowling across the pitch to where May and that tatty specimen who'd appeared out of the blue earlier still walked and talked, evidently enjoying each other's company. Who the blazes was he? Avon wanted to know, half of a mind to stamp across there and demand such without delay, but knowing, too, that that would make him look an utter fool.

He bowled, thoughts barely on the task, and heard willow bat and heavy ball connect with a meaty clacking noise which was likely to result in a six unless somebody was fortunate enough to catch it. Avon scowled at the batsman and a laughing May, then, finally, swore beneath his breath, and didn't watch the ball's course, for the first time ever totally uninterested in the game.

May paused and so, too, did her companion, watching the flight of that ball, which must surely go over the

144

boundary for six runs unless caught by Obediah who was positioned at long off. But her guardian wasn't too brilliant at deep fielding and had told everyone as much earlier, obliging them only because the alternatives – namely a weedy clerk called Billows and the captain's father, who was seventy-two and gouty – were even less likely to wreak havoc with the opposition than himself.

Obediah did his best, running backwards with urgency as the ball, hard and lethal like an ancient projectile slung from a trebuchet, came his way. For a moment there were even some in his team who thought that a miracle might just happen and Obediah catch it. But it wasn't to be. He got a hand to it but was already off balance, the ball slipping elusively from his fingers to bounce just inside the boundary, but then roll out.

'Bad luck, Mr Goodbody,' called May, even as he made contact with the ground, his stomach juddering like a jelly as the shock waves from the collision with the earth passed through him. 'At least you stopped them getting six.'

'How come?' Jude wondered, having watched the gentleman's action with complete confusion.

'Well,' May recalled the rules from *Wisden*, the cricketeer's bible, 'a ball must clear the boundary without touching the ground for six runs. If it runs over by way of the pitch, or bounces inside the boundary, it's four.'

'But you told me just now that the batsman has to run the length of his wicket to score a run.'

'Yes, that's right. You can do it *either* way.'

Smiling, Jude rolled his eyes. 'I think I'll stick with baseball.'

'And what's that?'

'America's favourite ball game. Only we hold our bat out to the side of us and the ball is thrown at chest height. If you hit you run for the bases. Would you like me to explain the rules?' offered the young man enthusiastically.

'I think not. In truth, Mr Mariner, your games sounds to me very much like rounders which in this country is a game most often played by girls.'

'What!'

145

May laughed deep and long before observing, 'I don't know which emotion overcame you most just then, sir. Wrath. Indignation. Disbelief . . . Maybe, in the interest of international peace, we should change the subject.'

He chuckled, 'Maybe you're right. I'd hate for us to have our first quarrel so soon.'

May tapped him on the arm with her parasol and sniffed haughtily in mild rebuke of such forwardness. 'I hardly know you well enough for us to quarrel. Such things are for husbands and wives or . . . ' The word 'lovers' had been in her mind but suddenly it embarrassed May too greatly to utter such a word, especially to him. 'Quarrels are for grown-ups,' she amended.

'And how old might you be, mysterious jewel?'

'Old enough to know flattery when I hear it,' she tittered.

'But what else would you have me call you in your name's stead? It suits, you must admit.'

'My name is May Bird,' he was told, her attention having left Jude to fall with concern upon Obediah. 'I do believe he's hurt himself. Oh dear.'

Jude followed behind her, cursing the fat man for his intrusion, however blameless, upon their conversation. He'd forgotten all about him, presumed he'd regained his feet and some of his dignity and gone back to fielding in that ridiculous cricket match.

Obediah sat unsteadily with a hand to his crown, one or two other players already enquiring as to his health and offering assistance as May quickened her stride.

'Please, miss, will you tell me where we can meet?' pressed Jude, panicking inside at the sight of her retreating back, yet knowing this not to be the time or place to continue with their conversation. The fat man was, it appeared, the one she had called 'guardian' earlier and, although he didn't look to be seriously hurt, Jude didn't like to intrude, nor, for that matter, carry on his courtship under such adversely distracting circumstances.

She knelt, her indigo skirts billowing out about her like some richly coloured powder puff, feeling the growing lump on Obediah's head, yet taking time to turn and smile at the seriously attentive young man hovering behind her. 'Tomorrow at the drawbridge,' she suggested, bringing a sigh from his chest and ending his indecision and suspense.

He nodded, then left her in peace to play ministering angel, smiling as he strode across the abandoned pitch. He'd forgotten to ask what time, but that didn't matter. If need be, he'd stand sentinel at the iron railinged structure which separated Broad Quay from Narrow Quay all day long. And at each step he took, Jude said her name in idiotic repetition, enjoying it and consigning it forever to memory. May Bird, May Bird, May Bird . . . He guessed with certainty that this was it, Love, and with cheery intoxication and a maniacal outburst of laughter, he gave himself up to the irrepressible pull of emotion, happily enslaved.

CHAPTER 17

Despite his bump on the head Obediah went to work as normal the next morning, approaching each new week in business, as usual, as a fresh challenge. Anne was doing charity work for the parish and Jasper was off to school, leaving only May and Mrs Veysey at Number 8 Beaufort Rise. It had been planned that they would take the horse omnibus to Broadmead and do the family shopping for the week, Bertha partaking of an illicit tot of gin at The Greyhound as was her habit when not under the watchful eye of her teetotal employer. But May, with persistence guaranteed to wear at the housekeeper's patience, had got around the persuadable woman to give her unconditional liberty for the day. Bertha might have doubted the wisdom of such a concession but she couldn't say 'no' to May, counselling her only to 'behave' as she waved her off down the chequered tiled steps at the front of the house.

May took to the street as if her heels were suddenly winged in mythological fashion, using every suitable shortcut to lessen the time and distance between the edge of Clifton Down and the city centre. Descending Denmark Street, she began to wonder whether she'd chosen the right dress, bonnet and shoes. She'd taken such care, but still she wasn't certain. May wanted Mr Mariner – Jude – to be impressed, but she dreaded overdoing it. After all, he was only a lowly seaman with, doubtless, few good articles of clothing to his wardrobe. To over-dress herself might make him feel self-conscious about his own material short-comings. Men could be so touchy about that sort of thing.

She wore a striped peppermint and white cotton skirt over several starched petticoats, her calves in thin, grey woollen stockings, and feet in sturdy black ankle boots, betraying her child's status, and causing May to frown at thought of them. She hated the thought that young Mr Mariner might think of her merely as a *girl*. Her blouse was white and crisp, a dozen tuck pleats ironed with precision down over each breast, which stood proud with youthful thrust, a fine, plain shawl of untreated cream wool draped about her arms in case of chill weather. Though the likelihood of that was remote, for the pressure in Obediah's barometer had been rising steadily for days and showed no sign of fall or deterioration into thunder storms. And lastly, upon her head and saving her fair skin – and more especially her nose – from freckling too badly, she plonked a straw bonnet lined with deep green satin and trimmed with wax cherries and emerald ribbons, the latter also acting as a fastening beneath May's chin.

They were not her best clothes, nor her most elegant, but she knew them to have a certain charm and captivating quality. Neither would she have to spend all her time worrying about trying to keep them spotless, for they were easy to launder and unlikely to cause Mrs Veysey apoplexy, as had almost happened when May ruined that costly white lace hand-me-down of Anne's last summer with grass stains.

At the bottom of the hill where the adjoining street runs parallel with Broad Quay, May stopped on the corner opposite Thornley's Hat and Cap Shop and breathlessly surveyed the drawbridge, immediately spotting Jude leaning against the watchman's box positioned on the end of the bridge nearer her.

He had changed, to her surprise, out of yesterday's clean yet tattered sailor's garb, into lightweight flannel trousers and frockcoat of a fawn hue, the white, high collared shirt beneath tied flamboyantly at his throat with a silken paisley neckcloth of many blues. His jet locks were combed back

149

off his face and gleamed from a recent washing, and his feet were shod in leather that glowed dimly, bespeaking quality, though by no means newness.

Heart hammering, as the picture of him stamped itself appreciatively on her brain, May checked her own appearance in the shop window behind her and then crossed the road to him, so intent upon smiling when she had caught Jude's eye that she had to jump out of the path of a dray from George's Brewery or be trampled under the hooves of the powerfully built horses.

Jude took her hand and clasped it, not in a handshake, because he sensed that they had gone far beyond that point already, but with tender possessiveness, making it apparent that he didn't care to relinquish it again. May felt liquefied as he touched her and looked at her, and couldn't even remember the greeting she had been rehearsing all the way there.

'Thanks for coming,' said Jude, putting her hand through the crook in his arm and leading May across the drawbridge.

'How could I not? I hope you haven't been waiting long?'

'Since seven this morning,' he laughed. 'I didn't know when you'd come and couldn't abide the thought of missing you. How long do we have?'

'All day.'

'Wonderful. Well let's find a cab, Miss Bird, and get away from all this bustle forthwith.'

'And where, might I ask, do you intend taking me?'

'To the seaside.'

'*Where*?'

'My captain's been to Bristol before and he told me that there's a dandy place called Weston-something-or-other, and that we can get there on a branch line off the Exeter Railway.'

'You mean Weston-Super-Mare,' May supplied, dumbfounded by the suggestion.

'That's it,' he affirmed. 'Well, are you game?'

Afraid at the prospect, yet excited too, and somehow assured by the knowledge that he would be with her, May nodded, tentatively at first, then eventually with vigour. 'I'm game, though pray indulge me patiently if I give in to terror of such a diabolical means of transportation. I shall try, but I cannot guarantee to keep control of myself. After all, not even out of deep affection for Mr Brunel have I ever been even remotely tempted to take to the railways, despite his countless offers of hospitality in his private car.'

'Then, miss, I must count myself truly honoured to have been so swiftly persuasive,' commented Jude lightly, as he handed May up into the first cab in line at the cabstand, the driver, who leant against a hoarding advertising the Public Baths folding his newspaper and climbing aboard to take the reins.

They crossed the Frome again at Bristol Bridge, a Georgian structure of three elegant arches with balustraded parapets, the smell of hops from the nearby brewery over-sweet to the senses, the shipping crammed into Welsh Back giving the occupants of the cab material for desultory conversation as they strove to come to terms with the wholly captivating presence of the other.

Once at Temple Meads Mr Mariner helped May down to the cobbles before the mock Tudor façade which hid ticket office, boardroom and passenger access, and paid the cab driver, before taking her arm and hurrying May along. The clock, set between turrets and battlements in the arched gateways, showed only seven minutes before the hour of nine o'clock.

'We must hurry,' coaxed Jude urgently, eyes alert for the ticket office the moment they had entered the inner precincts of the terminus.

Breathlessly May kept up with him, too aware of the necessity for speed to be petrified by the close proximity of broadgauge Flyers that hissed and whistled in noisy, novel manner inclined to endear them to most of the enthusiastic passengers.

'Two second class returns to Weston-Super-Mare, please,' Jude instructed the man behind the little arched glass window, searching for crowns and shillings amongst the dimes and cents in his pockets.

151

May waited nearby, watching a train go out heading for Paddington, London, with none of its passengers showing the expected signs of fear or panic as she glimpsed them through the windows of their carriages. Only those in third class, who were obliged to suffer the spartan planked seats and open topped carriages just behind the smoke belching engine, didn't appear to smile overmuch. May had always thought Isambard harsh for insisting that third class passengers suffer the elements of weather *and* flying cinders as a kind of perverse punishment for not being rich enough to enjoy his railway as he had intended it should be. Catering for the poor was not his style and tended – he often remarked without a scrap of compassion or hint of remorse – to mar the overall effect he was striving to create.

As May was thinking this, none other than Mr Brunel himself walked towards her along the platform, having descended from a meeting of the Board in the rooms above the ticket office. His intention was to have 'the hearse' coupled up to the next train to Swansea in Wales where he was expected for dinner shortly after noon.

'May Bird, as God is my witness, what are *you* doing here, and willingly too, by the look of it.'

'I'm being taken to Weston,' May told him, so glad she looked fearless for him.

'Is Obediah convalescing by the seaside then after that knock on the head yesterday?' he wondered, mildly amused.

'No. I am going with a young gentleman. You may have seen him yesterday, at the cricket match.'

'A young man? Ah, Birdy, it seems you're growing up before my very eyes. And where is this young man now?'

'He's coming now, with our tickets. And I fear, sir, that we'll have to dash or else miss our train,' apologized May.

'Miss your train? I should say not! You know me better than that, May, surely?' And laughing low and hoarsely as a result of smoking too many cigars at his last meeting, the black clad, top-hatted figure of Isambard strolled up the platform and had words with the flag-holding guard. The guard nodded, replaced the red flag back within the confines of his dark wool uniform and shrugged his shoulders helplessly at the driver the other end of the train, who was leaning out of his Flyer and demanding, in a short-tempered shout, to know what the hell was happening.

Jude reached May at about the same time that Isambard did, the two men gauging each other with unabashed interest and then nodding unconsciously with approval, so unwittingly amusing that May could have laughed.

'Mister Brunel, sir, I am honoured to make your acquaintance,' vowed Jude genuinely, as he clasped the hand extended and gave it a vigorous shake which almost had the diminutive Isambard wincing. Compared to Jude Mariner he had the stature of an undeveloped boy, and found himself having to look up to a young man who, he mused with awe, might not even yet have finished growing!

'Heavens above – a yankee! What might one be doing in Bristol?' he enquired, laughing. 'May, does Obediah know you are consorting with colonial rebels? I somehow doubt it.'

'No, dear I K, he doesn't. Our meeting was hurriedly arranged, leaving scant time to go through formal channels in order to obtain approval. Mr Mariner is only a visitor to our port, his time limited.'

'Then don't let me detain you a moment longer, child,' urged Isambard, chuckling. 'I tentatively give young Mr Mariner my approval, and do, in Obediah's stead, grant you permission to be abroad with him, May. Though I trust you will do me the courtesy of returning home at a decent hour before this day is done?'

'Of course, sir,' agreed Jude obligingly. 'I shall see Miss Bird home safely.'

'One moment, May. Here, take half-a-crown for a donkey ride or a dish of cockles. Be certain you keep it safe in your pocket. Right; now off! The driver looks to be building up more steam than his engine, and I'm loath to let the railway's reputation for punctuality flounder because of my misuse of power. Have a happy day, the pair of you.'

'We shall, sir,' called Jude without doubt, propelling May forward at a run along the platform, then up into one

153

of the second class carriages in the middle of the train. The door slammed shut, Isambard lifted his hat and nodded to the questioning guard, and then the red flag appeared once more, raised, then fell to clear the train for departure.

Two heads appeared side by side out of the window, arms waving excitedly to the stylishly moded figure poised on the platform. May's childishly shouted 'goodbye' echoed around the vast covered terminus that was roofed like a banqueting hall, its iron girded roof craftily fashioned to simulate hammer-beaming. The train lurching into motion and the ensuing noise was not half as terrible as she had imagined, especially when Mr Mariner stood so close, taking her mind off all other thoughts save those of himself.

Out of the station and with Isambard lost to sight, May and Jude found a bench seat and focused their avid gazes on the scenery going past the window. Soot blackened buildings thinned surprisingly quickly, giving way to farms and estates once they'd crossed the Avon. May remarked, with a voice higher than normal due to excitement, 'Travelling by train is the most wonderful treat.'

Jude nodded in agreement, relieved to discover that to be so, and confessed, 'I must say, Miss Bird, that before we boarded I was a mite worried too. You see this is the first time *I've* ever travelled by such means. But I didn't dare tell you that, not when you might be needing me to give encouragement and support.'

'Such dishonesty was chivalrous, sir,' laughed May, watching the smile playing on his mouth and wishing that sometime those lips might join with hers.

Turning and walking away down the platform to intercept the station master and query the delay in readying his private car, Isambard was smiling, the sunny day and recent encounter cheering him. He could remember what it was like to be that age, to feel the first stirrings of complex adult feelings, to go through days in a daze of tortured anxiety. Poor things; he wished them well.

Still, the American seemed to be a nice young man, and was certainly handsome, which was not unexpected if he was to be a good match for the beauteous May. And then it struck Isambard that he knew nothing about the man, not even his name, and had allowed May to go off on a train with a perfect stranger! Could she look after herself? Or had he made a grave error, lulled by a handsome, trustworthy looking face? Would the American behave as befitted a gentleman when continually presented with a delectable woman's body ruled by the head of a precocious child?

When the station master reached him, doffing his cap deferentially, it was to find Mr Brunel's black eyebrows almost touching in a deep frown.

CHAPTER 18

The tide was full in by the close of morning, sweeping, in brown tidal waves, across the mud and sand flats of Weston-super-Mare, the breeze that accompanied it riotous with the smells of salt, seaweed and the essence of the Bristol Channel.

At first May had tried to act with the sort of demure propriety which came naturally to Anne Goodbody, but such pretences soon crumbled at sight of the sand and sea. Her delight in those erstwhile unknown quantities was wholly girlish, her squeals as she removed stockings and boots and lifted her skirts to paddle without a qualm for propriety, bringing forth a throaty chuckle from Jude. He followed suit, no more able to resist the drawing power of the water than May, his socks stuffed in shoes and thrown farther up the beach where the tide should not ruin them, his flannel trousers rolled up as far as he could force them, leaving calves bare. His, alone of all the male bodies on the beach, possessed a healthy tan from his outdoor existence.

'You'd think, would you not, that spending most of my life afloat I'd be disinclined to take to the water unless it was quite necessary. I find myself doing many things I normally wouldn't countenance, merely because of you. Your influence is alarming.'

'It's not me,' vowed May, bending to pick up a broken piece of shell that shone with a precious delicacy which belied its humble mother-of-pearl. 'It's the seaside. It's

affecting everyone the same, haven't you noticed? Look at
them. They were all prim and proper when they alighted
from the train with us. But now the ladies are riding donkeys,
playing bat and ball and paddling – all with abandon. At
home in their drawing rooms they'd be horrified at the
thought of anyone even so much as glimpsing their ankles.
Whereas here, having given themselves up to the undeniable
pleasure of the place, they're showing their legs off up to
the *knees*, if you please, and thinking nothing of it.'

'Yes, you're right, and so are you, come to that, Miss
Bird – showing your legs off, I mean – and they are the
shapeliest, most enchanting on the beach, I do declare.'

'Mr Mariner, you're nothing but a smooth tongued
yankee!' laughed May, shaking her head and wagging a
finger disapprovingly. 'The gentlemanly thing would be for
you to cease looking upon me as a female. Rise above such
things and enter into the spirit of the occasion.'

They strode along the waterline, May's petticoats and
skirts and Mr Mariner's trouser legs getting progressively
wetter as their splashings and larking increased. When the
tide receded again, they went with it, as if reluctant to see it
go, and giving way to mud beneath their feet as they walked
further out into the great estuary. Behind them the figures
on the beach were small, distant shapes, the men in those
unmistakable stovepipe type top hats and the women in full
crinolines. But May and Jude, to all intents and purposes,
were alone, only the noise of the ebbing water keeping them
company, the mud strangely pleasant as it oozed through
their wiggling toes and sucked noisily at their ankles as if it
would have liked to hold them there for all time.

May eventually found it difficult to walk unaided and
clung to Jude's proffered arm with squeals of delight, their
turning, in order to retrace their steps – in the interest of
prudence – a pantomime the outcome of which was really
quite inevitable. May lost her balance, couldn't free her foot
in order to regain it and lunged for Jude as her last hope of
remaining upright. He, in the same instance, had bent
absently to investigate a blow hole in the mud where a crab
or lugworm might be residing, so that May's toppling into

him took the sailor by surprise and sent him violently down onto his hands and knees in the odorous silt of the estuary. May landed on top of him, the accident only making her giggle the louder, then rolled off sideways to embed herself in the mud beside Jude.

The effort to move was too much initially, so they stayed put, she looking up and he looking down, their roaring laughing at the misfortune befallen them so acute that May had to hold her midriff as if in pain and Jude collapsed sideways in an undignified, muddy heap, quite helpless.

'Oh, heavens!' he groaned, emotion momentarily spent and eyes shedding tears of mirth. 'Whatever shall we do?'

Gasping and breaking down with laughter as she tried to climb to her feet, May took some time to answer and then made little sense. 'I don't know . . . Oh my, just look at me! This is awful . . . *Awful*! I'm covered, right the way . . . ' she giggled beyond caring. 'Right the way down my back! And look at you!'

Together, for support, hands transmitting more mud, they came to their feet, eyes surveying the damage sustained by the other, concern at their predicament completely overshadowed by hilarity.

'Miss Bird,' Jude commiserated, finding it hard to keep a straight face, as his gaze went over clogged bonnet and ringlets at her nape, her indistinguishable blouse and skirts so saturated with mud that they were dragged by their own weight down to the ground behind her. 'I'm afraid your very fetching outfit is ruined.'

She nodded, trying to find the pocket in the side panels of her skirt and produce a handkerchief in order to wipe her splatted face, but giving up in frustration when all she found was mud. 'And so is your suit, sir. You look like a mudlark,' she pointed out, thinking to regain some of her dignity by chipping away at his.

'Yes indeed,' he agreed cheerfully, spreading his legs and flinging wide his arms, then crashing headlong backwards into the mud.

May gaped at him, bursting into peals of laughter even as she thought him mad and crouched over him precariously, her head swooping down and lips covering his before she had time to think and stifle the impulse.

He sighed in gratitude, muddy hands holding her captive about the shoulders for several moments while he tasted that inexperienced, lusciously red mouth.

She pulled away and straightened up, startled by her own forwardness, then proceeded to lay the blame on Jude with her haughtily gasped, 'Mr Mariner!'

'Miss Bird!' he mimicked in the same vein, standing up to survey the splendidly clear impression he had left in the mud. 'I find it hard to comprehend your present show of indignant coolness when it was *you* who kissed *me* and not vice-versa.'

'Ooh.' He was right, of course, and May simmered down again almost immediately, assured of losing any argument entered into with him. Instead she smiled and came up close against him, smearing him inadvertently with mud as she commanded, 'Well, in that case, Jude, kiss me again.'

Muddy hands caught about her waist and shoulders, squeezing the air from her deliciously with a man's strength, and his mouth played over hers with equal passion, the gentle pleasure setting his body aflame with emotion that was barely in control.

He was hard against her, firm and assured, and the feeling of being possessed within the forged circle of those arms set May's heart thumping and insides churning with some wonderful, terrible emotion. She felt weak and without will, a being awakened to the existence of desire. It was only many moments after the kiss ended, when they were trudging back through the mud to the beach, hands clasped in an unspoken, almost primeval acknowledgement of bonding, that May found she could once again smile, the mounting tension of wanting and longing having eased and lightness returned.

The moustachioed and mutton-chop whiskered man behind the counter of a gaily awned stall upon the promenade stared agog as Jude stepped forward to be served in a head to toe coating of mud, the tiny companion at his heels in a

159

similar state of woe and squirming with the embarrassment of being stared at by so many.

'An' whaat wood ee be whan-tin', me deeer fella?' he wondered, his Somerset accent so thick that it might just as well have been a foreign language for all the sense Jude could make of it.

The young American shrugged, turning to May for an interpretation. She muttered back, hopefully anonymous under the concealing brim of her bonnet, her head bowed, 'He's asking what you want.'

'Oh! Of course. What else *would* he ask?' laughed Jude. 'I should like to purchase one of those brightly coloured pails, thank you, sir. The ones stacked here. Yes, that's them. The ones the children use for building sandcastles. And that will be . . . ?'

'Buckets'll be sigspunce an' two farvin's to ee,' supplied the stall minder.

May translated while Jude surveyed a handful of change from his trouser pocket, everything he touched thereafter muddied.

'I've found a sixpence but which are the farthings?'

'They've got a bird on the tail side.'

'I don't seem to have any of those.'

'Then give him a penny and he'll give you two farthings change,' urged May, growing a little short of patience now, as her prolonged presence in so prominent a spot attracted an ever-growing crowd of amused promenaders. She couldn't remember ever having been so acutely embarrassed and couldn't begin to think what Mr Mariner wanted with a small, fancy bucket suitable only as a child's plaything.

She felt bound to tell him, as Jude took her arm and guided her down the steps from the sea wall onto the sands again, that she had, 'No intention of sitting about to be gawped at while you indulge a whim and build sandcastles.'

Jude laughed, stalling her by the standpipe at the bottom of the steps, where those wishing to rinse their feet before replacing their shoes – thus foregoing the discomfort of sand in their socks and stockings – could do so, courtesy of the Sanitary Department of the Town Hall.

'Tell me, Miss Bird, would you rather be muddy or just plain wet?'

Comprehension dawned, and with it a look of horror. It was logical, she couldn't deny, and May could only admire the simplicity with which he dealt with matters, and the sensible solutions he arrived at, but . . .

'Mr Mariner, I could not, really. Just think of everyone laughing and staring.'

'But aren't they doing that already?' he queried, the truth of his words undeniable as they both looked about and found themselves once again drawing attention of an amused variety. Even the donkeys and Punch and Judy theatre were forsaken as the children came to stare at this much more interesting mucky pair.

'Tell you what,' laughed Jude, who, it seemed, was unperturbed at being so unusual a spectacle, 'you can drench me first and see if you can't pluck up courage in the process.'

May looked sheepish.

'Here, take the bucket and get to work. I exonerate you of all that follows. How's that?'

She took a deep breath and held the bucket beneath the fast running tap. 'Ready? You're going to have to stoop a little or I'll never be able to rinse higher than your shoulders.'

'Sure. Like this?' And he hunched his shoulders and bent his knees comically, causing every boy within close proximity to indulge in orang utang impressions, crying out in surprised hilarity as the first chilled water was emptied over his head. He spluttered, laughed and made an exaggerated show of suffering from the cold. 'Shucks! Brr, Miss Bird, that came as a danged shock, I can tell you.'

'Shall I continue then?' she wondered, seeing that only his head was once again 'clean', though unlikely to stand up to close inspection. It was going to take more than a mere bucket or so of water each to get them back to normal.

'Continue miss. If I grit my teeth real tight I think I can just about stand it. Hey, you youngsters, instead of just standing about laughing at me and this unfortunate young lady, why don't you fill your buckets, too, and help us get cleaned up? The guard won't let us board the train home if we arrive at the station all muddied, and you wouldn't want to see us stranded here through no fault of our own, now would you?'

Eager children, thrilled by his request and with devilish glints in their eyes, looked to their parents for approval, all hell breaking loose when the adults – amused by this free, wholly absorbing source of entertainment – gave them the nod.

Water flew in all directions, dozens of small, gaily painted tin buckets having their contents hurled about with energetic zeal by sailor-suited boys and pantalooned and lace pinafored girls who needed only the slightest excuse to become totally unruly and extremely noisy.

May tried to keep out of the way at first, to put Jude's broad frame between herself and the chilly crystal abundance of tapped Mendip water. But one bucket eventually caught her, then another and after her initial shrieks of shock and humiliation May gave up, even removing her bonnet and unpinning her hair to make the 'little dears'' task the easier.

She clung to Jude, laughing and choking as children, armed like a firing squad with buckets at the ready, threw the contents at her *en masse*, the usually dignified parents urging their offspring on with hearty 'Hoorahs' and less restrained, 'Go on, dear, *drench them*!'

The mud sluiced away eventually, Jude held up his hands to calm and quiet the hyperactive, laughing crowd encircling May and himself, thanking everyone jovially for the service that they had kindly done. 'My friend, a fellow native of yours, and I, a son of the colonies of old, cannot thank you enough for helping us out of our predicament. Sir. Yes, you sir, in the stovepipe hat, and sporting that enviably well knotted neckcloth. Can I entrust half-a-crown to you – as an obvious gentleman of quiet authority and natural organizational abilities – so that these children might each be rewarded with a candy bar?'

'Why yes, young man, I dare say I can honour such a request. But by "candy" do you mean "rock"?'

162

'Shucks, sir, I don't rightly know. I thought candy was candy the world over.'

'Not in England, young man,' corrected the promenader with faint superiority of manner. 'Here we have "sweets". Never fear, though. Trust to my discretion and I think all present will be satisfied. There isn't a child alive who doesn't appreciate the qualities in a stick of seaside rock.'

'As you think best, sir. All that my friend and I ask of you and the rest is that we be allowed to just walk off and melt into the crowds, to find somewhere to dry out with dignity,' bargained Jude with a roguish grin.

Hands shook theirs and people called out cheery farewells, all the usual starchy airs and graces seeming to have absented themselves on this excursion day.

CHAPTER 19

Damp, but in no other way out of the ordinary now, May and Jude caused no more curiosity at the seaside, any second glances cast their way due to the fascinating beauty of May's unbound, flaming hair, hanging snarled and dripping down her back.

They found a quiet stretch of sand and lay out prone so that the afternoon sun might dry them a little, watching the gulls at the tide line and discussing the possibility of the estuary's islands, Flat Holm and Steep Holm, being inhabited. A brass band marched up and down the sea front at intervals, playing the popular tunes with just enough gusto to keep the drowsy hordes on the beach from dropping off to sleep.

Jude rolled over, leaning on his elbows with his jaw cupped in his palms to look down at May.

She sighed, eyelids flickering against the powerful rays of the sun, her small, lightly freckled nose beginning to turn pink. He stooped, lips brushing hers with an elusively swift kiss. Her eyes opened, their brilliance exposed fully to Jude for the first time, and it was his turn to sigh, to drown in the feeling of well-being her warm smile evoked.

'Lie there much longer and you'll get blisters on your nose.'

'Umm . . . It's just so . . . lovely . . . ' she breathed, raising her hands over her head and stretching with pleasure like a cat. 'Let's go and find a tea shop then. I'm so hungry

I could eat a dozen currant buns and drink a gallon of tea.'

'Good idea. That's one English custom I haven't sampled yet.'

'Haven't you? Don't Americans drink tea?'

'Some families may do. But mostly they prefer coffee.'

'Mr Goodbody likes coffee sometimes. Mrs Veysey and I go once a month to buy his favourite American blend at Carwardines. I must say I like the smell that drifts out of that shop, prefer it, in fact, to the taste of the actual coffee.'

So they found a small tea shop in a side street where there was a table free, and Jude left the ordering to May, glancing around surreptitiously at the genteel classes partaking of their ritual afternoon cup with all the gravity of addicts in an opium den.

They sat at small round tables covered in cotton damask cloths and with a flower posy as centrepiece, pouring the piping hot amber liquid from china teapots decorated with roses or geraniums, sipping, talking and licking crumbs of custard slices, buns and pastries from the sides of their mouths. They must have been aware of the other customers in the cramped little parlour, yet it was as if each table was bordered by some invisible barrier, keeping each separate and cultivating perpetually the Englishman and woman's possessive regard for privacy, even in a crowd.

A waitress in a brown cotton dress with white cuffs and collar, her hair neatly hidden beneath a fussy cap atop her head and her front swathed in an elaborately frilled pinafore brought the tray of tea and cakes, bobbed politely then was off to a nearby table where a female, with the stuffy dignity of a dowager duchess, was wagging her finger aloft to signify her need for immediate attention.

'Help yourself to the cakes, Jude, while I pour the tea. It's had plenty of time for brewing now and consumption should be almost immediate afterwards. Would you like sugar?'

'I'm not partial,' Jude said, holding a custard slice – a confection of flaky pastry topped with icing and filled with cold, set custard – and eyeing it warily. One false move and there would be a disaster.

May laughed at his predicament, then took pity. 'Put it down sideways onto your tea plate, sir, then take your knife to it. It's much more manageable in smaller slices. Now, here's your tea, without sugar, and just a dash of milk so that the temperature isn't allowed to drop too greatly. Tea must always be hot and fresh to the eye. Never murky or over-brewed, which is called "stewing".'

'Miss Bird, I do believe you British are more fanatical about the drink even than the Chinese.'

'You're probably right. Doubtless the British Empire would crumble if the armies were denied their tiffin and we females our afternoon repast. Mr Goodbody tells me that the economies of several countries rely on the tea that they export to us – China, Ceylon and India. It's almost our *duty* to keep drinking.'

They both laughed at that, low and discreetly as befitted their surroundings, and Jude savoured the brew with exaggeratedly thoughtful expression, not of a mind to give his verdict until he had tasted his second cup and May had sent the waitress off to refill the pot.

'You must be favourably disposed or you wouldn't have downed so much with such speed,' she surmised, while he swallowed the last of the custard slice with a murmur of delight and then considered the bakewell tart.

'I must say I found the tea pleasant. Better, certainly, than I had expected. In fact I can't remember ever having enjoyed something so much in all my life as sitting here now, eating delicious cakes, taking tea and looking at you.'

May glowed, believing him implicitly.

His hand, large and work-roughened, callouses ingrained with paint – from ship maintenance May supposed – coursed amongst the plates, milk jug and sugar bowl until it had reached May's poised fingers and covered them. Their eyes met, each gaze unmistakable in the message it gave out to the other, and their fingers laced and squeezed with tender regard, leaving both very much aware of the monumental stage reached in their relationship.

'I've no way of knowing, yet I'm sure, Miss May Bird, that I'm in love with you,' whispered Jude bashfully, eyes flickering uncertainly between her and the currant bun on his plate.

'Are you? Heavens! I don't know how I'm supposed to react to that news,' chuckled May, her cheeks pinkening with pleasure. 'For all that I appear full grown and used to the company of adults, I've never before been faced with such a declaration. If I were Anne very likely I'd be overwhelmed – might even faint. Some women, I know, would hide behind a fan and enjoy the experience privately, torturing the gentleman concerned with a merciless disregard for his feelings. Etiquette probably has rules about this kind of thing and how to deal with it. But I must trust to my instincts. It fills me with joy, Jude, to know your feelings, and also makes it easier for me to reveal mine. Though I think you must guess them; I feel myself to be transparent. Ever since I laid eyes on you and you looked at me with those blue eyes of yours, I've been unsettled just as if I were struck by some malady. But that cannot be, for I never get ill. Therefore it has to be this "love" thing you were talking about. I've never, in all my born days, come across anything quite so powerful. Have you?'

'Well . . . there was a typhoon once, due north of Java,' quipped Jude.

'Don't joke. This is much too serious!' he was admonished.

'I know. But I thought a little light relief might help. I need something to distract me from you. You're so beautiful, you know, that all I keep thinking is how much I want to kiss you.'

May drew herself up, dragging her hand from his grasp as she went on her guard, her smiles warm in answer to his compliments. 'Control yourself, do. Can you imagine the horror you would cause these gentle folk if you gave in to impulse? Being in love is as much about suffering as it is pleasure. You will have to grow accustomed to both.'

'I shall suffer only till the end of tea. Then I shall spirit you into some shop doorway where the shadows are deep and kiss you long and thoroughly,' vowed Jude, his third 'cuppa' tackled with swift confidence.

167

'Then by all means let us make haste,' urged May in amused undertones, her feelings much akin to his own.

Their kiss, when they found the longed-for shop doorway, was not without interruption and, after suffering a tongue-lashing from one irate old woman whose path to buy cockles from the seafood stall was blocked, they moved hurriedly, laughing at the mischief and holding hands again as if touch was now as important as breathing.

They passed a shop where books old and new were shelved ready for sale, and another where tempting sweets filled glass jars in the bowed, multi-paned window frontage. Five minutes were spent there, selecting quarters of sugared almonds and fudge, bars of Fry's newest confection, chocolate, with the intention of keeping such treats for the return journey by train. But only sugared almonds still remained undevoured by the time the couple had reached the end of the street and paused to look over the jeweller's wares in his barred shop window.

'Well looky there,' said Jude, pointing at a silver brooch from which dripped three emerald tears, with the central one larger than those flanking it. 'It's the very colour of your eyes. Let me buy it for you.'

Thrilled at the thought, still May shook her head negatively. 'No, I couldn't let you.'

'Why not?'

'I don't know. It's just what people always say in like situations. And they must have good reason.'

'Name one. Go on, I insist,' laughed Jude.

He was always laughing, May thought, sidetracked by his flashing teeth and exuberant charm. Never had she met anyone so full of the joy of just living, someone who derived such pleasure from things so unremarked upon and simple. Her chest swelled with emotion and May's arms encircled and hugged him, thrills running through her at the contact. And Jude, loving her nearness, hugged her back, tighter, capturing her arms within his own and holding her long enough to steal a very hurried, playful kiss.

'Ooh!' was all May could think of in the way of admonishment, then she came up with one of those reasons he'd been so set on receiving before accepting her refusal.

'And I cannot accept a gift from you because I've no money to spend on one for you in return – having spent most of my half crown on sweets – and therefore it just wouldn't be fair.'

'What nonsense! If that's the best you can do, Miss Bird, then I shall just go ahead and get it for you anyhow. You can continue with your arguments then, if you wish.'

'But it's too much,' she insisted, reading 4s/6d on the little white cardboard price tag cottoned on to it. 'Four shillings and sixpence must be at least a month's wages for you, Jude. No, I *can't* let you buy it.'

But laughingly he told her with much blandishment, 'I've kept a portion of Blackbeard's treasure, which I found last year in the Caribbean, on my person this day with the sole intention of furnishing you with a token of my love. You *can't* deny me that right, unless, of course, you'd have me doubt the intensity of your feelings?'

In consternation she shook her head at his clever manipulation of things, and watched him saunter into the shop with a broad grin on his face.

Soon the silver piece he'd taken a liking to was being lifted from the window, to emerge within a minute on a bed of cotton wool inside a tiny lidded box bearing the black lettered engraving Thos Priddy & Sons for Precious & Semi-Precious Stones, Gold, Silver and Fine quality chiming clocks. Browsers welcomed. Repairs also undertaken. Est: 1776.

Jude took up the trinket and pinned it at May's breast as if it was a medal, vowing solemnly, 'This is a token of our love, which shall endure for far longer than Thomas Priddy and his sons and their sons and so on, or even the United States of America, which enjoy the distinction of having been established equally as long.' May giggled, and he kissed her whilst holding her firmly by the shoulders, lips making noisy contact with each of May's cheeks, like some General in the French Foreign Legion bestowing the *Croix de Guerre* for some exceedingly heroic act.

Their laughter at nothing in particular dying eventually,

they reached the station at Weston-super-Mare in thoughtful silence. 'Had I better speak with your guardian soon? How do they do such things over here?' Jude wondered aloud.

'The first thing is for me to sound Mr Goodbody out on the matter, Jude. Perhaps I could see that you are invited home for tea.'

He frowned. 'The conventional way is too slow, darn it!'

'But there is no other way, is there? Can you imagine, if I tell Mr Goodbody that I've been kissed for the first time and fallen madly and instantly in love as a consequence, that he'll be entirely convinced? He'll say I'm too young, don't know my own mind, have no idea what love truly is and need to spend my time in more worthwhile pursuits, like Anne. He'll give me a hundred good reasons why I can't be in love, and listen to none from me which might lend credence to my declaration. Mostly he'll go on about "women's fancies". He always does whenever Anne gets a bee in her bonnet which doesn't altogether meet with his approval.'

'Then perhaps I should tackle him. I might be better able to persuade.'

'Let me smooth the way first, Jude. It'll only take a little time.'

'We have very little of that,' she was reminded.

A shiver ran through her. 'Don't speak of sailing away, please. Not today. It's been so lovely. I want nothing to spoil it. We'll work things out.'

'Suddenly I find the situation vaguely worrying,' mumbled Jude. 'What lies between us will be looked on by others as insubstantial.'

'Yes, that's what I feel too, don't you see? I cannot go to Mr Goodbody yet and tell him I love you. He wouldn't believe me, would become protective and possibly even hostile towards you, and from that could emerge all manner of problems. What *shall* we do? As you say, we do not have time on our side . . . not for anything. Ideally I'd take you home first as a friend whom my guardian could come to

170

know and like, then later, subtly, you could begin to pay me court and, when Mr Goodbody deemed me old enough, make your proposal in the proper manner.'

'Then run away with me,' suggested Jude, not entirely joking, his smile no longer so apparent. 'If your guardian cannot accept the possibility of love at first sight as we do, let us run away and get married elsewhere.'

'We cannot. I am a minor and need Mr Goodbody's consent. Because of my very lack of years and his fatherly concern for me, nothing I can think of would make him agree to our match at this moment in time,' surmised May, woefully resigned.

'Then all is hopeless,' growled Jude, his shoulders sagging and face devoid of smile.

'Not hopeless. We still have the days until you sail, after all. And, although we cannot be together for always just as quickly as we would like, we can build our relationship by writing to each other and being together whenever you come back to Bristol. It may be painful – I don't know, but I think it probably will be – losing you when I love you so assuredly, but one day, not too far into the future, you will sail in and stop a while and Mr Goodbody will readily consent to our being wed and everything will be wonderful.'

'It's all very well being brave while we're still together, May. The reality of our parting will be quite a different matter,' Jude told her, words laden with prophetic doom that ultimately brought smiles to their young, still far from careworn countenances.

'Don't worry. Fate will be kind, I'm sure, presented with such a true and deserving love,' opined May, popping an almond into his mouth then selecting a pink coated one for herself. She was keeping deliberately light of mood, as if that in itself would ward off ill-fortune, determined that no dark clouds should descend upon so marvellous a day. She smiled at Jude as, arm in arm, they strolled down the platform to await the arrival of their train. Her eyes widened and mouth opened to issue words which never took form, as a train, with a black private car attached to the rear, backed down upon the station, the gentleman at the rear door –

171

which was foremost to them – lifting his fashionable top hat and smiling with satisfaction at the couple's surprise.

'Isn't that Mr Brunel?' Jude queried.

'Yes, indeed it is,' marvelled May. 'I could have sworn he said he was scheduled to attend a meeting in Swansea.'

'He did,' confirmed Jude.

'Then what is he doing here?'

'Why don't you ask him? It's evident from the look on his face that we are the reason for this appearance. Maybe he thought you needed a chaperone.'

'Yes. Knowing Mr Brunel he probably thinks you guilty of abduction and has come down here to escort me home and save you from yourself.'

'Greetings,' called Mr Brunel, his smile as wily as any fox's. 'My meeting finished early and I thought, "Wouldn't it be nice to give May and her young gentleman friend a ride in the Hearse". And having nothing better to do this afternoon, here I am. Come aboard. Here's my hand, May, to assist you up the steps. Careful with those skirts. That's it. You, Mr Mariner, look too agile to be needing such help.'

'Quite so, sir,' agreed Jude, taking hold of the handrail and leaping up onto the iron platform beside them.

'Do go in,' ushered the man, bringing up the rear. 'Did my touch deceive me or *are* you indeed wet, May?'

She nodded, tittering amusedly as she remembered. 'Oh yes, I'm wet, though not *as* wet as I was. Mr Mariner and I had an accident in the mud.'

'It was necessary, sir, for us to be washed down with buckets of water,' Jude explained.

'Heaven preserve us,' breathed Isambard. 'Well, we'd better find some blankets to wrap you both in and see if a hot drink of some kind can be procured.'

'Really, sir, there's no need to go to all that trouble on my account. I'm almost dry and disinclined to take chills. You get immune to bad weather and drenchings when you're a sailor.'

'Mr Mariner,' Isambard correctly him wryly, forthwith, 'the blankets are to protect the velveteen seats in this saloon, not to afford you warmth!'

172

May giggled again, very much at home with that side of Isambard's character.

In cut-glass, stained-glass, and inlaid wooden splendour, where windows on changing scenery were draped with velvet and inscribed boldly GWR, the seats and tables of woods from South America, upholstered in horsehair stuffed plushness, sat May, Jude and Isambard Kingdom Brunel as the last train of the day took them home to Bristol.

CHAPTER 20

Sometimes, especially on days like this when the whole male-dominated world seemed to rear up before her, steadfastly quoting the law and thereby thwarting her, Aurelia wished that she had allowed herself to be better educated when younger. But like so many others she had gone along with her parents' doctrine and assumed there to be no good reason to learn aught else save reading, and arithmetic enough to be able to accomplish household accounts with competence.

Now today, and not for the first time since Courtney's death, she was forced to employ – unsuccessfully – her feminine wiles on the family solicitors of Craddock, Mountjoy and Dyce to secure a larger allowance from her late husband's estate. The fact that Courtney's solicitor had also been her father's did not seem to favour her. Somehow they seemed to know her to be grasping and spendthrift and accordingly, were wary whilst solicitous. A senior, and therefore highly experienced, member of the firm dished out tea and sympathy but little else besides. Her wiles were as nothing when pitched against his superior intellect and sage-like knowledge. In not so many words Aurelia was told yet again to tighten her strings in the financial sense and wait patiently until such time as poor Courtney could legally be declared dead. Had she realized, on that night long ago when she'd assisted her husband – with the violent force of a cruel heel – into the waters of the Floating Harbour, that disposing of him thus would lead to such financial difficulties, maybe she would have thought twice before murder. But she hadn't had cause to be versed in the law to that extent, and had assumed that if everyone knew him to be dead – with or without a body – that she and Larry would inherit forthwith. Stupid, irritating Courtney! Even in death he still managed to be less than her ideal. She was forced to wait seven years, no better off than before, drat it, before she might legally benefit in any way from his will!

Her mood, therefore, as the family coach – in need of a refurbishing which she could not afford – transported her home, was vile; her countenance, as she stared blank and unseeing out upon Castle Street, as hostile as winter weather from the north-east. She blamed herself not at all, but vented her temper on all about her, starting off with her driver when they reached Number 6 Beaufort Rise and found that Avon had taken Larry out for the morning to look over the bonded warehouses and offices on Broad Quay owned by the Midwinters. It was hardly the driver's fault that they had made the detour in order to collect Larry for nothing, but Aurelia lashed him with her tongue even so and dismissed the unfortunate man from her service with a venomous dialogue before he'd completed his drive around the corner to her own home.

Avon did not take kindly to being pressed into service as a baby-sitter by Aurelia and had only relented when she pleaded desperation, having an appointment with the family solicitors but unable to call on the child's nurse to perform her duties because she was in bed, on doctor's orders, with a mysterious abdominal malaise. Food poisoning was suspected but Aurelia's cook had gone instantly on the defensive and hotly denied that she could be in any way to blame.

Anyhow, Avon found himself lumbered with the timid, irksome Lawrence and had decided that the best way to keep the child occupied was to take him to the office with him that morning. Given a large window to look out of, Larry would quite happily sit there all morning watching the goings-on at the docks, and in no way be a nuisance to his uncle. He knew better than that. Larry had learnt, even at the tender age of four, that the best way to survive, to enjoy a relatively trauma-free existence, was to make himself virtually invisible in the company of adults, and never to show spirit or voice a difference of opinion. His mama – when she deigned to allow his presence in her parlour on those afternoons when she would show him off to visitors come to take tea – expected him to be well behaved to the extreme, to sit like a boy doll in his best, freshly laundered sailor suit and say just the right, sweet things when spoken to by his mother's acquaintances. Otherwise he was to remain silent. These rules he adhered to obediently, intimidated to the extent that he had a permanent stoop, and a head that seemed to have shrunk down warily into frail shoulders and lodged there. Once he'd stammered, but Aurelia had knocked that nervous habit out of him along with his thumb sucking. Now the only outlet for this child's fears was in a shrinking of limbs and ceaseless trembling that caused outsiders to think, quite in-accurately, that the 'little chap' suffered from the cold inordinately. In truth what he suffered from was Aurelia. She made no effort to hide the contempt and disappoint-ment she felt for her offspring and he, wanting so much to be loved and gentled, hugged and adored like most other boys of his age, suffered in silence the anguish of knowing himself unloved, a failure at four.

Avon neither liked nor disliked Larry. As far as he was concerned the child was one long yawn, devoid of sparkle or endearing qualities. Aurelia had cowed him into some-thing as insipid and spineless as Courtney had been before him, such a specimen guaranteed to arouse Avon's dislike rather than pity.

When Avon's scant tasks at the office had been dealt with satisfactorily, he handed Larry his cap and coat, tapped on his own mid-grey top hat which matched precisely his impeccable three piece suit, and ushered the boy down onto Broad Quay.

Not overly tall and carrying not a spare ounce of fat upon his frame, Avon Midwinter was an imposing figure even so. Much of it had to do with the way in which he carried himself, a kind of athletic arrogance packaged in sartorial know-how. Note was taken whenever he stepped out on Broad Quay, and many were those who acknowledged him with politely respectful nods and forelock touching.

'I've some paying on the nail to be done around at Corn Street, then, young man, maybe we'll take a break from business and visit a coffee house. Ever been to one before?'

'Oh no, Uncle Avon!' gasped Larry, quivering with delight and terror combined at the prospect. 'D-do you think it'll be all right?'

'Will your mama object, do you mean? I doubt it,' said Avon, flatly dismissing the possibility. Aurelia really wouldn't concern herself about Larry unless *not* to do so affected *her* adversely. 'Maybe we'll have lunch too. I know a dining room where they serve up the most delicious oyster pie or steak and kidney pudding if you'd prefer it, with trifle for dessert.'

'Ooh yum!' drooled Larry, eyes bright at the mere mention. Throughout his short life he may have been kept short of affection, save the professional variety dished out by his nurse, but Larry had never been starved of food, and these days it was his greatest, perhaps *only* pleasure in life.

Avon looked around for a cab, saw one just pulling up at the stand by the drawbridge and took Larry's clammy hand, disdainful of the touch. He'd never known a child yet who possessed a smooth, pleasantly dry palm.

'There's our transport,' he said briskly, striding forward with erect carriage, his swiftness making no concessions for the tiny four-year-old almost running to keep up beside him. 'Do hurry, Larry.'

177

'Someone's already getting into the cab, uncle,' the child observed.

'Oh blast it! Then we'll have to wait for the next,' mumbled the man, glowering at the couple climbing up into the dark blue liveried conveyance, the young man pausing with one foot on the step to give the driver directions.

Avon knew him instantly and hardly needed to speculate on the identity of the female who had preceded him in an anonymously fast blur. 'May!' he hissed low under his breath. 'And that bounder from the cricket match!'

'Uncle Avon?' wondered Larry worriedly, not knowing what had changed the man's mood so drastically for the worse.

The cab drew away and came towards them, Avon dropping Larry's hand and dashing out into the melée of the busy thoroughfare without mind to his safety amongst the drays and carts, his face thunderous and intent, governed by emotion rather than common sense. What he wanted, Avon couldn't truly say, save to put an end to the growing rapport evident between them and, just maybe, give the interloper a fist-full of knuckles smack dab on his nose! Any man handsome enough to make his jaded sister sit up and take notice was certainly a threat. Avon couldn't abide the thought of May being with him, and vowed that she was destined only to be his.

A cart blocked his path just as they passed by, the horse picking up speed, and although he could see them laughing and sitting close, simpering like a pair of fools in the hold of obvious pleasure, Avon couldn't make his shouted demands heard above the everyday din of the city centre. 'May Bird, how dare you! Come back this instance!'

His sole achievement was to make himself look a trifle silly, and knowing that didn't please him much either. Taking a deep breath to calm himself, the man regained his dignified mannerisms and crossed back to the bemused and worried Larry.

178

'Uncle Avon, are you all right? Who were the people in the cab?'

'Nobody of import,' Avon forced himself to say calmly, his heart twisted and crushed by the sight of her laughing and smiling with another as she never had with him. But there would come a day . . . Yes, one day he would *make* her laugh, he vowed illogically, as if force could make all things possible.

'Here comes another cab now. Give me your hand and I'll help you aboard,' he instructed quietly, though with a chilling undercurrent that made Larry feel unsure and just a little afraid.

Old Market Street, off the Bristol Centre, ran into the Stapleton Road, which headed north-east. Travelling up it in their hired cab were May and Jude, he laughing over a signpost that declared Fishponds to be four and a half miles in the same general direction.

'Fishponds? I don't believe it!'

'It's true. But I bet there are plenty of odd place names in New York, too, if only you'll stop making fun and think.'

'All right, I admit it. There's Yonkers for a start. Or how about the Bronx?'

'Blimey!' laughed May. 'Where do they come from?'

'The Dutch back in the seventeenth century, I suppose.'

'D'you know, besides the suburb of Fishponds there's also a Kingswood. Mr Goodbody told me that once it was a real king's wood – the place where he used to take his supporters hunting.'

'That figures, I suppose. Any idea which king?'

May nodded. 'Bad King John. Mr Goodbody says that hundreds and hundreds of years ago this same King John lived in the castle fortress in the middle of Bristol City.'

'I've not seen any castle,' pondered Jude.

'It got knocked down just after the Charles-whose-father-got-his-head-chopped-off became king.'

'We were taught something about that when I was at school. Charles' father – who was also a Charles – and

179

his cavaliers, fought against Oliver Cromwell and the Roundheads. Cromwell won and Charles lost his head, then several years later, by popular demand, his son Charles II was restored to the throne.'

'If you say so, Jude. I'm not too attentive when it comes to history lessons.'

'Seems to me that the weather's going to be just as good today as it was yesterday,' he mused.

'Yes. But today, Mr Mariner, I must be returned home safe *and dry*. Do you understand? It took a great deal of explaining yesterday.'

'I shall do my best, miss, And are you going to tell me where you're taking me? Those instructions you bade me give the driver weren't very enlightening. And you are being very mysterious.'

'I thought we'd have a picnic. Nothing special, mind you. Just bread, cheese and pickled onions which Mrs Veysey readied for me, and a bottle of ginger beer. There's a place – Stapleton Glen – where the family come sometimes when the weather's good. I thought you might like to see it also.'

'Sure.'

'I think it's one of the prettiest places I know. Anne says it's "picturesque".'

'I don't care where we are just so long as I'm with you, May,' breathed Jude, his face bright, and that light, jovial manner of his prevalent as usual.

May giggled, snuggling up close as his arm trailed about her shoulders. 'Tell me more, sir. I'm not so naive that I'll believe it totally, but even so it's very enjoyable.'

'A jester I may appear, but when I tell you I love you I'm wholly sincere.'

His Persian blue eyes smouldered and May softened in his grasp, undone by his serious sweetness and the unintentional silliness of the rhyme.

The cab halted and May straightened up primly, staring out and sighing, to find that they had arrived. 'Our destination is reached and once again I've been saved from myself.'

180

'What do you mean?'

'You make me forget – rules, responsibilities, propriety. Since I met and fell in love with you – two whole days! – I've been in a daze. It's wonderful. A most glorious feeling, but I sense, too, that dangers lurk. And I think that you, Jude Mariner, are the greatest danger of all.'

'Dangerous? *Me*? How?'

'Because I cannot resist you. Promise me that you will try, as shall I, to act with restraint.'

'I promise to comply with your wishes at all times, to do only that which pleases you.'

'That is not quite what I mean. In fact to do that would be *very* dangerous.'

'What it boils down to is that we have a difference of opinion over whether I am or am not dangerous. I don't know where you got so foolish a notion, but I vehemently deny it, of course. In fact this whole conversation is foolish and I'm going to kiss you May, before we alight from this cab, to take your mind off it forthwith.'

He cornered her and covered her laughing red mouth with hungry kisses, lips wholly persuasive in their pressure, his large calloused hands snaring her waist and shoulders and dragging her close.

'Oi,' complained the driver, opening the door to hasten their alighting, 'that sort o' feeng ain't decent in broad daylight. Let 'er be, lad. Youm like the Big Bard Wuf wi' li'l Red Ridin' 'ood.'

'You see what I mean,' admonished May, as she pulled free and could breathe freely once more. 'You make me forget.'

'But you have exactly the same effect upon me,' pointed out Jude, uniting them further with so oddly shared a problem. 'And I'm not complaining.'

CHAPTER 21

Stapleton Glen was a small section of tree-flanked valley down through which a sprightly River Frome ran, powering mills and coursing over the weirs in its path.

There were two mills: the smaller Whitwood Mill and, upstream, Witherlays Mill, which was known to all and sundry as Snuffy Jack's Mill on account of the miller who worked there having such a nicotine habit. The latter building was a sprawling, rubblestone affair much added to over the years, until it seemed naught but a conglomeration of angles and eaves, gables and irregular aspects, the whole gaining a modicum of uniformity from a coat of fading whitewash. Beside it, crossing the Frome, ran a high weir behind which the waters deepened, the wooden paddles of the sizeable wheel ever turning to keep other wheels – unseen within the building – in motion.

Off the track, through woods of alder and water-loving willow, and ivy-choked slopes leading down to the water, where gentlemen of leisure strolled with pretty females on their arms, the young lovers laid out the coarse-spun blanket brought along by a practical May, and placed the wicker hamper on top, much of the food quickly devoured amidst spluttered, mouth-filled conversation. May, freed from the scrutiny of adults, foresook her table manners completely and ate with unseemly gusto,

Jude relaxing accordingly as her mood affected him. Their talk was desultory to the point of trivia while the food was consumed, but afterwards family somehow encroached, and was discussed in general terms, as if young man and girl did so on sufferance, resenting the time spent.

May learned of the cruelty of Jude's father and the unhappy existence of his mother and sister, told him in turn of Cedric, Jasper, Anne and Obediah, and how her darling Jon had died three years before but was still, and maybe ever would be, a clear, bittersweet memory in her head. But she did not tell him about the Birds . . . about Teddy selling her on the cobbles before a public house and her never-ending humiliation at the mere thought. Nobody would ever willingly know that secret from her lips. Besides, it was so long ago, most people who *did* know had nearly forgotten, time clouding the facts. May Bird had always seemed to be at Beaufort Rise, adopted like some poor relation into the household, and that was how everybody pictured her. She was, but for an unfortunate birth, a Goodbody.

So she told Jude, plainly, and felt it *was* so in her heart, 'My parents are dead. And it all happened so long ago that I cannot recall them with clarity. Obediah Goodbody gave me a home and has been a good father to me ever since. He is a kindly man, so gentle in his ways that it would be difficult for anyone who knows him well not to love him.'

'And what will he think of me, can you guess? Will he, who undoubtedly dotes on you, find me worthy of his ward?'

'Of course. Do not forget that I am adopted and *not* his true daughter. My father was no man of substance such as Mr Goodbody. I come not from the merchant classes, though it is my good fortune to move within such exalted circles now. A sailor will do well enough for his girl.'

'A sailor for the time being only. But one day . . . Well, who knows. The more I am with you, the less charm does the sea hold for me,' he said, smoothing the burnished crown of her head which was freed – now that they lingered unobserved – from the confines of a bronze tafetta bonnet which matched her dress and very nearly, in the subdued light beneath the trees, merged with her hair in hue. 'But I've come to see the sense in doing nothing brash where courting and winning you is concerned. It must be done properly and that of necessity will take time. Winning the respect of your guardian cannot be accomplished in a week. I am resigned, therefore, to losing you temporarily, to sailing away and keeping in touch, for the time being, only through letters. The pull of the sea is still strong enough, you see, May, but even more than that I desire to present myself to your guardian as a captain rather than humble sailor. Even *I* shall feel worthy of you when I carry a Master's certificate.'

'That's sensible. And for such a plan you have my blessing. We are young, after all, with a whole lifetime stretching before us. I must finish growing up and you must become a captain. We'll come back together then and nothing but *nothing* will ever keep us apart again. That will be our pact,' said May gaily, sounding far more mature and agreeable than she actually felt. Losing him – and she must, she realized – was going to hurt a great deal even if it was ultimately for the best. Having spent every moment away from him over the last few days wishing only for his presence again, made the prospect of months on end of deprivation a dreadful prospect. An hour was too long without him – a day, a week or month might prove to be beyond endurance.

'Kiss me, Jude, please do,' she instructed, almost pleadingly. 'Kiss me so that I forget everything, especially your leaving me. We cannot be seen from the footpath and are, for the time being, wonderfully alone.'

There was something to the timbre of her voice, some new quality of huskiness that came to Jude's ear and sent a wave of emotion coursing through him in response. Without lengthy coquettish invitation, but merely by asking for that kiss, May Bird somehow offered him all, her green eyes filling his mind with their beauty. To look into them was to think of the undergrowth in which they lay upon the blanket, and the trees and deep, dammed waters behind the weir. Her eyes mirrored life in its most marvellous guise. And her hair, that mass of unruly waves which a multitude of pins found hard to control, was the sun.

She was quirking an eyebrow at him, her deep red mouth curling in amusement. 'Why are you looking at me that way? Didn't you hear me? I want a kiss.'

'What way?' he wondered aloud, reluctant to be forced back from his mental adoration of her.

'Your eyes changed while I was watching you. They went strange . . . dark and sort of clouded.'

He smiled, not of a mind to laugh as he might normally have done, increasingly aware of the spark, kindled in his belly just now, beginning to flame with the agony of wanting, his loins throbbing in a sweetly painful manner.

She ran her eyes pleasurably over the imposing size of him; over shoulders broad and legs lengthy and muscular, recalled the tautness of buttocks and felt an odd, quite unknown emotion stirring within her, causing her inner thighs to tingle sensitively.

'Kiss me,' she breathed, kneeling before him with such appeal that Jude was soon lost to all reason and came up against her with hard violence, his desire without doubt as her belly pressed to his loins and the turgid flesh pulsed and reared delightedly at the contact between them.

May felt the bruising force of him pressing at her, while his hands clutched her behind to keep her close, and she issued a sigh of deepest delight against his harsh mouth. She felt herself being levered down onto the blanket, felt his hands fumbling with her clothing. She knew what might happen, had been given an elementary no-nonsense education in the facts of life by Anne, but everything was now happening too fast, so fast that she knew not her own mind. They mustn't, shouldn't . . . But she loved him so assuredly, wanted to . . .

Her bodice was unlaced and chemise tugged down,

exposing small rounded breasts with deep pink crests to his gaze, then his mouth, and May could only lie gasping at the unexpected deliciousness of sensation which that caused.

'We mustn't . . . daren't,' she told him falteringly, her whole body arching with erstwhile undreamt of desire as his large, warm hands found the curls between her legs for the very first time and probed deeply there. '*Lordy*! Stop now. Don't Jude.'

He'd got free of his trousers and at the sight of him fully aroused May took fright and began to move agitatedly, her senses split between longing and fear. '*Don't*!'

He moved on top of her, that bruising, intruding part of him insinuating itself between her stiff legs, his head softly shaking in denial of her pleaded request. He covered her mouth with his own, his savage kiss muting her protests, a hand forcing her legs wide enough for him to make a swift entry.

He closed his eyes against the tears welling in hers and gloried lustfully in the knowing of a female's body for the first time, the exquisitely frail beauty of May driving him immediately headlong to a climax, his manhood pulsing and releasing forth its ecstatic flow.

'Oh God . . . God . . . ' he growled amongst the tumble of flaming hair at her shoulders, holding on to May so tightly she was left gasping for breath. Then, even as he staggered to his feet, dazed by the explosion of new feelings which had overwhelmed him, Jude shook his head wretchedly, the ravaged girl upon the blanket causing him guilt and shame.

'Can you forgive me? I'm sorry – *so* sorry. I completely forgot myself, lost control. I've never been with a woman before,' he admitted, as if that could explain his actions, 'got carried away by events.'

May, having drawn her legs together and pulled down her skirts for decency's sake, looked tiny and wounded, her face grave and her voice, when she spoke, an accusing kind of whisper. 'You hurt me,' was all she would say, as if she hadn't suspected he was capable of such. 'I never thought it would be like that.'

He knelt before her in abject misery. 'Please say you'll

forgive me! Oh my God, you're bleeding! What have I done? What shall I do? Here, I have a handkerchief. Let me help you.'

May smiled then, touched by his concern and rather amusing ignorance. 'Virgins sometimes bleed, Jude. But I shall suffer no permanent damage.'

'Two clumsy, naive virgins we are. What a disaster this has been. Forgive me for being so inept, so thoughtless. I should have listened to you and never acted as I did, then maybe I'd still have your respect . . . and love.'

May came from a sitting position onto her knees, her still naked breasts warming him sensually through the thin cotton of his shirt, her arms circling and clutching at him, touching his thick neck and raking through the wiry jet locks that nestled on his collar.

His maniacal hunger was gone, but at her contact Jude felt his manhood firm, hardening to a lengthy shaft of desire once more and betraying blatantly his continuous need. He sighed, embarrassed by the lack of control he seemed to have over that particular part of his anatomy, then gasped as her slender fingers fastened about the lenghth of him. He thought her quite amazing, for despite what he had done to her it was obvious she wished to try again, to find pleasure the second time rather than hurt.

'Oh, May!' he breathed, mouth swooping down to cover hers, his body twitching from the sensations her artful little hands evoked, a groan sounding in his throat. He unbuttoned his shirt and flung it aside, laying back and bringing the girl with him, his hands roving up beneath her skirts as she continued to toy with him.

'I will do nothing that is not to your liking. You can be in control, whatever happens depending on you . . . your wants. You can ride me,' he told her with a sigh, as her hands cupped and very gently squeezed the delicate sack at the base of his rearing hardness.

May nodded, smoothing her cheek against the black curls on his impressively broad, bronzed chest, her insides trembling and sex moistening from the pleasure of touching him. Her hurt had been short lived and now she was curious enough to want to explore the possibilities of lovemaking properly.

His hands were light, tantalizingly so as they stroked May's silkiness and slid into her depths and soon, in a way she had never known before, she wanted desperately to feel him within her, to be speared upon him and glory in him to the limits, desire seemingly boundless.

She moved over him, her body gliding down over Jude's and thus impaling itself upon that awesome instrument of pleasure, her breath hot and belaboured at the young man's throat as she strove by instinct alone to give him pleasure whilst finding gratification herself. She drew herself up, rearing and tightening about him, then slid down again, taking him to the hilt, and, when she had reached that gasping, groaning point of no return, it was Jude who manipulated her trembling body with hands on her hips working her upon the upwards thrusting shaft of desire.

May whimpered, quivered and throbbed about him, his stabbing relentless then until he, too, reached that sublime, quite indescribable moment of purest joy.

At length May slid off his sated body and lay down by his side, an arm lying languidly across his torso.

There were no words for what they felt, no adequate sentiments that might match what had gone before, and so they roused in dreamy silence, dressed each other with accompanying smiles both knowing and shy, and took the blanket down to the Frome's edge to wash the tell-tale blood from it.

There were horse omnibuses and cabs available, but they preferred their own company still, and decided that they'd walk, for a while at least, their hands clasped tightly and lips meeting when the urge to steal a kiss became too much of a temptation.

Along the way there was a small church outside which they paused, maybe thinking of a future wedding day, but not voicing their thoughts. Idly they read the Gothic arched gravestones. In Loving Memory. Greatly Missed. Forever in Our Thoughts. Beloved Husband. Dear Wife.

'Let's move on,' pressed May, feeling out of place

amongst tombstones and untended graves. 'I don't want anything to do with death to come spoil this afternoon.'

'But churches are happy places too, don't forget. Most of these people were in love once, newly wed and as awkward with each other as we are. Don't think of them as ancient bones, but young lovers, beings vibrant with the longing to know all of delight. Come inside with me and let us make our vows before God,' suggested Jude, affected by the quiet, neglectful beauty of the place.

But May shook her head, scandalized by the suggestion. What he'd said had sounded vaguely improper. She didn't regret for a moment love in the grass, but somehow she didn't feel right about entering God's house. Women in the bible who did as she had earlier usually landed up being stoned or suchlike by the righteous ones. Could she say without doubt that God wouldn't strike her down with some retributional thunderbolt for her wanton display of earthly pleasure with a man?

'Please,' coaxed Jude. 'It's been a long time since I did any praying. Captain Jack's supposed to hold Sunday service aboard ship but he's always a bit lax about that sort of thing. I'd like to declare my love for you before God, and ask for His blessing.'

Always, when he wanted something badly enough, she had noticed, Jude Mariner turned on the charm like a little boy, his white teeth flashing and uplifted features topped by dark curls and dominated overall by those devastatingly beautiful eyes, guaranteed to win him favour.

'All right. But don't let go of my hand. And, if I get struck by lightning, please see that I'm transported home with a modicum of dignity for burial.'

He laughed. 'Don't talk daft. You're going to live to be a hundred, just so's you can keep me company in my old age.'

Inside it was gloomy, the light coming in through stained-glass windows behind the altar and leaded lights in the nave, the tiny altar beyond the rood screen draped with royal blue brocade and bedecked with candlesticks and plate, crucifix and candlesnuffers of heavily wrought silver.

189

No thunderbolt descended through the leaded, oak beamed roof and very quietly May accompanied Jude to the front pew, kneeling and praying mechanically as she ever did in churches, then sitting back and glancing about whitewashed walls that maybe once had been resplendant with the primitively crude paintings of demons and devils, dragons from the Underworld and the clergy's favourite – gargoyles. Such things, however, had proved too much for the delicate middle-class sensibilities of the average Victorian congregations, and the Ecclesiastically artistic foresights of what might await the wicked in hell were obliterated by stark pure coats of limewash.

Jude, seated beside her in a grass-stained suit much crumpled from their earlier intimacies, straightened up from his silent prayer and beamed a smile at May. His hands, which carried the lingering scent of her, grasped and squeezed hers between large palms, his strong fingers almost crushing in the intensity of their embrace.

'Let us swear before God that no matter what, no matter how long, and even without the bonds of true marriage, we shall keep ourselves only to ourselves. No matter what shall transpire in the future, that we shall love each other regardless unto eternity.'

'How very solemn you are,' observed May, bringing a little lightness to what was becoming almost too serious a religious ceremony. 'I swear. Now let's get out of here. It's cool, damp and smells musty. And I prefer the sun.'

'I am solemn because you mean so very much to me. Oh how I love you, May, can't you see? So much so that it almost hurts.'

'Come.' She took his hand and led him forth, pausing when they were beyond the gabled porch and hence no longer in God's house to plant a kiss tenderly on his mouth and stare with reverence into his eyes. 'That which I could not with propriety do in church surely tells you better than words what my feelings be?'

'Aye. And none of this is going to make giving you up any the easier. Maybe wanting to be a captain wasn't so marvellous an idea. After all, how could I want to be away at sea while you're here? I look at you and I think of babies, of settling down and sharing every waking moment with you. All the plans I made no longer seem so appealing, the course I had plotted potentially the wrong one. I don't want to go away any longer if it means losing you.'

Knowing the depth of his feeling warmed May pleasantly, dispelling the chill which lingered from the church visit, but she cautioned him. 'Say no more now, my love. Think of these things long and hard and make no decisions in heat or haste. Even loving and wanting you as I do, I wouldn't want you to stay now if in the future you came to regret your lost opportunities for achievement. But only you can decide, Jude. I'll abide by your decision.'

'In so blissful a state as I presently am, I don't think myself capable of anything more decisive than buying two omnibus tickets home!'

CHAPTER 22

In tall mahogany, glass-fronted dressers on the four walls of the Goodbody dining room was amassed the family silver and china. Coalport and Spode, Wedgwood and Derby glowing pale, while silver salts, salvers, rosebowls and candlesticks twinkled as testimony to Mrs Veysey's meticulous and frequent cleaning.

Partaking of breakfast on a morning when the curtains had been drawn back to reveal uncertain weather were the children and patriarch. Mrs Veysey and Wendy the maid hovered over them with porridge and kippers, fat, succulent sausages and trays of lightly grilled love apples which were beginning to become more widely known as tomatoes.

Anne munched toast and marmalade, checking over a neatly columned sheet of writing that was her itinerary for the day. Obediah scanned the morning paper folded beside his plate, scoffing in derision at some reports, whilst nodding vaguely in agreement with others, the odd fork-full of golden-brown smoked kipper finding its way between his lips. Jasper gulped down the food set before him, his unseemly haste somehow sacriligious when Mrs Veysey's food was involved. Hers were the type of culinary delectations that deserved to be savoured with sedate relish.

'Stop gobbling like a turkey,' she scolded, and snatched the school cap from his head while she was about it. 'And there'll be no hats at my breakfast table me lad. Whatever next!'

'Sorry,' apologized Jasper automatically, as if he was obliged to do so with such frequency that it had become second nature.

'And do 'urry up or youm gunna be late fer school.'

'Yes, Mrs Veysey. But if I hurry you're likely to accuse me of gobbling like a turkey again.'

She narrowed her eyes at him. 'Don't you be gettin' smart!'

'Jasper!' snapped Obediah, looking up with a severe expression. 'That will be quite enough. I'll have less talking and more eating, thank you.'

'Sorry, papa,' muttered Jasper contritely. Then he tightened his lips at May who, with her head lowered so that none could clearly see her countenance, was grinning at his fall from grace. He kicked her on the shin beneath the table, extracting an 'Ouch!' of pained surprise from her.

Obediah's eyes raised from the newspaper again. '*Now* what is going on?'

'She's laughing,' betrayed the boy.

'But he kicked me,' she countered.

'Really! You two are beyond a joke first thing in the morning. Jasper, get yourself off to school or you'll be late for the bell and risk a caning. May, eat your breakfast. You've hardly touched it.'

'She's lost her appetite because she's in love,' jeered Jasper, satisfied by the look of alarm which swept her face, and the embarrassed heightening of colour that accompanied it.

'Stuff and nonsense. What's he on about, May? Perhaps you'd care to explain?'

'It's that baby-faced yankee at the cricket match. He's turned her head,' supplied the boy before issuing a gleeful 'Cheerio' and extricating himself from any adverse consequences which his loose-tongued disclosures might have brought about.

The next time she saw Jasper, May promised herself, she would strangle him with her own hands, so help her she would. But in the meantime, Anne and Obediah had paused to stare at her with curiosity abounding.

193

'Jasper exaggerates, as always,' she laughed, trying to make light and little of the matter. 'I've merely been showing Mr Mariner the sights of Bristol while he's in port.'

She cast down her eyes, blushing, Obediah's enquiring eyes disquieting after what had taken place between Jude and herself yesterday. Could he tell, God forbid, by some physical sign she had failed to notice and obliterate, what they had done? She felt transparent and knew not only guilt but fear of discovery. He, who had lavished such care and fondness upon her, who had truly made her what she was, would be *so* thoroughly ashamed, that she was made wretched by the thought.

But he saw nothing, and doubtless trustingly thought her incapable of something so wicked, and merely smiled indulgently at her discomfiture and suggested, 'Surely it's about time then that you brought this young man home for tea?'

May rose and, going to her guardian, lapped her arms about his neck and hugged, her lips planting a smacking kiss on his smooth, bald head. 'I shall ask him. Thank you. And I'm certain he will accept the invitation.'

'Considering your delight at the prospect and having observed that no other youth thus far has ever had quite such an effect, am I to deduce that this young man – what did you say his name was?'

'Jude Mariner.'

'That this Jude fellow is altogether something much more special than the norm?'

'Oh yes.'

'I suppose he'd have to be in order to stand a chance with you. I look forward to meeting him then.'

'And he you, dear Mr Goodbody. Do you think I might be allowed to forego breakfast? Only I've promised to meet him and take him to the zoological gardens and I'm so up in the air that I'll be late unless I pull myself together soon.'

'Yes, run along child, and enjoy yourself. Only remember, you are as a daughter to me and I expect your standards to remain high accordingly, and thus maintain the Goodbody honour.'

She tried to be as light and jocular as he. 'Of course. Not for anything would I willingly displease you.'

'Well, well,' observed Anne with wry good humour, when May had departed, taking Mrs Veysey along with her to see her properly attired on departure, 'So little May has been smitten for the first time. How novel. I'll admit I suspected nothing, unlike my observant brother who so accurately pin-pointed her emotional state. I have heard tell, though maybe thankfully have never experienced such, that these girlish crushes can be quite heart-rendingly acute, but given time, are survivable. I should, I suppose, be a trifle sorry for her, but I'm not. Would that such an experience could be mine.'

And Anne sighed wistfully, putting a brave, unfortunately plain face on things, and mustered a smile when Obediah soothed, 'Have heart, dear daughter, for you are but twenty years and time is still on your side.'

Victoria Square was the newest and grandest yet of the fashionable addresses to appear in Clifton. The pale stone villas of four storeys or more looked out upon a contrived garden, fenced off for safety's sake behind wrought iron railings, where smartly painted green bench seats formed ideal spots for idle perusal of shrubs and ornamental fountains, courtesy of the Merchant Venturers who owned the site. Here, or rather on the thoroughfare which ran around the square, the two lovers had assigned as their meeting place.

There was, like an island in the middle of the road, a monumental gas lamp of four clusters on wrought spars on top of a classical column, the whole resembling, to May's mind, a giant's candelabra. Around it, no doubt to deter any young rascals who had it in mind to try and scale the monstrosity, was a circular balustrade fence in local stone similar to that employed in the overlooking villas' construction.

Jude was already there, watching earnestly the road off the square down which May would come, his graveness of countenance forewarning her of ill tidings. She waited for a cab to pass and pull over against the inordinately high pavement to let down its fare, then crossed to him, holding him urgently, as he did her, and begging of him, 'Tell me what it is.'

'Captain Jack says we leave tomorrow, all being well and finalized, on the early evening ebbtide.'

'Oh.' She had nothing to say. She had been expecting this, after all, yet even so was non-plussed and knocked aback by an overwhelming feeling of despair.

'Let us walk,' coaxed Jude, taking her arm and leading them in the general direction of Clifton Down. 'My reluctance to go is strong indeed.'

'Then *don't*. Stay. Your Captain will surely understand? We'll go and see Mr Goodbody. He's already professed a wish to become acquainted. We'll find some way of remaining together. I don't think I can stand to lose you, Jude.'

'No. I know. Our feelings are closely akin. I cannot settle things in my mind. And when I'm with you it's difficult to be objective. We must try and come to some decision agreeable to us both.'

But, as he'd said, once with her, holding her hand and somehow intoxicated by her nearness, serious talk fell by the wayside and the looming crisis was pushed stubbornly to the backs of their minds, its unwelcomed existence manifest only in the unnaturally moody quietness of the pair.

The animals of the zoo, caged amongst fine botanical gardens, did, for a time, take their minds down happier paths, but always lurking just one step ahead, it seemed, lay that fatalistic moment, and no matter how they tried to hold back, to postpone it, that step would have to be taken and decisions made.

They circumvented the perimeter of the monkey temple where the small, agile rhesus monkeys scurried amongst pseudo Hindu architecture on an island at the centre of a sheer sided pit, watching the antics of adults and young absorbed in the task of communal grooming; tiny, almost human hands, picking about in the fur of their neighbours. Through the minds of the adolescent observers poised at the wall which guarded one species from the other, ran a momentary feeling of envy at the simplicity with which the other was able to conduct its life. They ate, fought, cleaned and slept, their rules for life simple and their main aim apparently to do little else save procreate.

The lovers, when they felt themselves to be not of interest to the rest of the sauntering crowds, touched tenderly and with glances that transmitted their feelings. They wandered almost aimlessly towards crisis point, very much in love and yet incapable of feeling any of the animal hunger of yesterday, so miserable were they, the day passing unwillingly from their grasp until eventually Jude had to relinquish her, promising a meeting on the morrow beneath the gas lamp in Victoria Square, there and then to inform her of his intentions.

Never again would an evening seem so long to May. She could not face supper and, to save herself from the pain which mere mention of Jude's name could wreak, had to avoid the concerned and interested Obediah when possible.

'But . . . ' His voice had died away in the face of her obvious distress.

'I fear, sir, that he will leave tomorrow and that I shall not be able to bear the loneliness that losing him will cause,' she had moaned, mounting the stairs to her bedroom on the third floor, the quicker to evade her guardian's questions.

He stared after her, face perplexed and eyes kindly, trying to soothe her by reminding her, 'But I've invited him here. Will he come? Maybe there will be time tomorrow before his hour of sailing and try to arrange things so that they are at once satisfactory and not too distressing for you and your young man? If I find him to be of sound family background and good natured mayhap I'll give blessing to his courtship. Is that what you want? Are things *that* serious? Only remember, you are still tender in years and no woman yet, despite your blossoming done too soon. Does this Jude fellow appreciate that?'

'Yes, the obstacles are many and well known. Yet what matters his courtship, when all is said and done, dear Mr Goodbody? For I know in my heart that his going away will

197

separate us by oceans,' choked May, having paused on the landing to answer, before fleeing to her room with a wail.

Obediah expelled his breath in a noisy sigh, before turning to Anne in the doorway to the dining room. 'Oh dear. You are unfortunately right, dear daughter, when you make comment on the torment of first love. May is going to need all our help and understanding over the next weeks if she is to get over this yankee without undue pain of loss.'

'The poor, foolish girl,' lamented Anne, as she dished out haddock pie with duchess potatoes and petit pois, and cast an eagle eye over Jasper's hands to ascertain their state of cleanliness. 'She's had the pick of every young man in Clifton. And they've all been pleasing to look upon and well connected to boot. Yet she falls for a sailor, a *yankee* furthermore, whose background is sketchy to say the least. If only she could have chosen a little better, this night she might not be so wretched.'

'Correct. Still, she is very young and not, I think, quite capable of being certain of her own feelings yet. Doubtless we'll have a week or two of misery, days when she will not eat and the like. I know, because, don't forget, your mama once put me through the most appalling misery during our days of courtship before finally consenting to become my wife. We must be understanding and gentle, and you, Jasper, will most definitely *not* taunt her with the fact that her love is lost to her. If I hear that you have been so unkind I shall personally see to your chastisement.'

'Yes, papa,' agreed Jasper, knowing that his father, when he used *that* tone of voice, issued no hollow threat.

'Now let us be at our supper before it cools. I do so detest cold fish. Tell me of your charity work today, Anne. And you, Jasper; what did you at school?'

May Bird had long since ceased sleeping in the attic like a servant. She had a bedroom next to Anne's nowadays, furnished with mellowed pine which sported brass furniture. Not as fine as the mahogany or satinwood in Anne's room, but far better than anything allocated to Wendy, the housemaid. At the windows there were blinds and half

198

curtains of ivory lace upon brass poles, and drapes of fine chintz that paired with the bedcovers to lend the room uniformity. And on the waxed, hardwood boards, were scattered the rag rugs which May and Bertha Veysey made in their spare time as a means of keeping idle hands busy. It was a pretty, homely room given over to handicrafts, with cushions in patchwork and seat covers in petit point, and May preferred it, though with regard to taste she supposed she shouldn't, to the impersonal elegance of Anne's sleeping quarters.

She undressed and then donned her nightgown, sitting at the poorly silvered mirror of her dressing table to undo braids and brush her hair, ignoring the same body which last night she had studied with curiosity in the mirror, the nightgown discarded then in some kind of brazen show of defiance towards the conventions. Last night she had been glowing, still alive with the pleasant memory of his hands upon her flesh, the heat of his mouth and mystery of his body during the final, wondrous intimacies. Last night she had looked herself over, wondering what it was about her budding body which might most have pleased him, and touching where he had touched, only to find, disappointingly, that she could not evoke any of the overwhelming sensations that his strong fingers had. Tonight, her nakedness gowned as if it displeased her, she stared into her own green, pain-blanked eyes and sighed once, then again, a depressed shudder setting her whole body trembling. She couldn't remember ever having been so unhappy.

Her sleep was fitful and each time she woke May thought of the morning to follow and knew, deep in her heart, that he was going to go. He loved her, very much, she had no doubt, but he could not in honour claim her until, in his own mind, he was worthy of her. Men were such infuriating fools!

She hoped tomorrow would never come, and yet, paradoxically, she could hardly wait to be with him again even knowing it would be the last time for a long time.

As if Jude had brought the sun with him and had now packed it away ready for departure, May awoke to a blustery grey day that had all the trees skirting the street bowing and in danger of losing their leaves. She refused breakfast, though did sip unenthusiastically at the Earl Grey tea which Mrs Veysey insisted she drank before being allowed to depart for her rendezvous.

Her dress – a deep blue-grey – somehow matched her mood, and about her shoulders was a black woollen shawl which paired with her severe Sunday best bonnet. In her reticule she carried a sheet of folded paper from Obediah's study, upon which she had painstakingly printed her address, her neatness and care borne of a disproportionate fear that Jude might misspell it otherwise and hence his longed for future letters be posted other than to herself.

Obediah let her go without comment or counsel, certain in his own mind that time only could determine what should be. This present chaos of emotions would either peter out like so many adolescent crushes, or else develop into something deeper. He should have liked to meet this Mariner fellow, but sensed that this day the sweethearts would give his request no thought, their time jealously squandered upon themselves.

May went down the geometrically tiled steps and along the pavement past Number 6, her pace quickening noticeably as Avon Midwinter appeared at his front door. He was a model gentleman in a grey business suit, its perfectly cut frockcoat collared in sapphire velvet and waistcoat adorned with a costly gold fob watch pocketed and chained at his waist. Black patent leather shoes click-clicked down over the steps and then May, speeding on, heard him call out to a cab that happened by, anticipating, at that hour, just such a fare down to the centre. He hadn't seen her, she could tell, as she compulsively cast back a wary glance, and breathed easier, though did not slow her pace. Today of all days she could well do without a pestering from him.

Clifton, a district built solely with the comfort and ease of the affluent middle-classes in mind, believed in adopting every modern convenience. They had gas, water on tap, paved streets and flagstoned pavements on which to saunter without fear of encounter with anything as unsavoury as gutters. Most of the new streets off Sion Hill and Victoria

Square had the added convenience too of raised pavements which stood proud of the cobbled roads by at least a foot (even two feet in many cases due to the hillside location), thus making a lady's alighting from her carriage – in one of those fashionable yet totally unwieldy crinolines – much easier. She no longer had to step down, negotiating steps which she couldn't see because of voluminous, all concealing skirts, but just stepped out onto firm ground raised permanently for her convenience.

Hurrying and maybe careless, with her mind on Jude just two streets away by then, May forgot about the kerb depth and didn't seem to look where she was going at all. She stepped off the pavement in her headlong endeavour to be the quicker with the man she loved, and was lucky not to get herself crushed beneath the wheels of a passing carriage which managed to veer wide of her floundering form.

A female of genteel breeding squealed and nearly swooned at the accident befallen the passerby right next to her. The carriage stopped, brakes applied, and the driver jumped down, trying to assist the dazed May, while his fare – a bespectacled wine taster for Harvey's the wine merchants – wondered with concern, 'Deary me! Is she all right?'

'Miss, be ee all right?' echoed the driver.

'I really don't know. Heavens, I feel so silly,' groaned the embarrassed May as, crumpled and grimy, she was helped to her feet. She yelped then with pain and quickly seated herself on the kerb with assistance from those about her, her ankle hurting so that she felt sure it was fractured or perhaps even broken clean.

'Maybe she needs a sherry,' offered the man in the carriage who always carried a silver flask on his person.

'No, no,' corrected the woman who had squealed earlier, 'Brandy is the thing for shock. Does anyone have any?'

'Please,' May insisted, while everyone went on talking over her head. 'I'm not in shock. I just landed awkward, jarred some bones and twisted my ankle, I'm certain.'

'You shouldn't take any chances, and certainly shouldn't try walking on it again until a doctor's taken a look,' decided the woman who was now examining the rapidly swelling ankle and grazed flesh through the tears in May's stockings.

'But I have to be somewhere else. I'm supposed to be meeting someone,' said May desperately, gasping as the woman's no-nonsense handling of her ankle caused extreme pain.

'Yer meetin'll 'ave to wait,' the cab driver told her, bringing nods of agreement from the others as he decided, 'I fink we oughta getcha down to the infeermry wivout delay.'

'I can't! There isn't time!' cried May, but even while she continued to protest, the driver was lifting her into the carriage and placing her beside a concerned fare who was a trifle alarmed at the prospect of maybe having to play nurse on the journey.

'Please take me to Victoria Square instead. *Please*!'

CHAPTER 23

He paced, dark brows converging in a deepening frown, then whiled away another minute or so by strolling around the circular stone wall balustrade which fenced off the gas lamp in Victoria Square, his worried blue gaze continually on the avenue from which she usually appeared. He took the silver-cased watch from his pocket once more and checked the position of the hands for the third time in an hour. What was keeping her? The time left to them dissolved fruitlessly before his eyes. This wasn't like May.

Another hour passed. He took the small box from his waistcoat pocket and reassured himself needlessly that the emerald ring he'd bought to give her – as a token of their secret engagement – was still nestling on its contrasting tiny red velvet cushion, then snapped the box shut again.

How could she do this; be deliberately late on their last day together? For she had known, he could tell when he'd left her yesterday, that he *was* going to leave her, that today would be for their goodbyes and, more importantly, an exchange of addresses. But even as he thought it he couldn't imagine her doing it deliberately. Something had caused her to be delayed unavoidably, surely? Human nature being what it was, Jude then automatically indulged in alarming thoughts, considering the possibility of an accident having befallen her, or maybe some malady which, God forbid, kept her confined to her bed and unable to meet as they had planned. No, no, it was nothing like that. There was a much simpler, far less fearful explanation for her non-appearance so far, he told himself. Being a female it was more than likely that she lingered still in her bedroom, undecided upon the choice of apparel for so solemn an occasion. Yes, he would rather think along those lines. They were far more comforting. For, after all, hadn't he taken great care with his shaving and dressing that morning, selecting a casually styled, though expensively tailored suit with which to impress her on their final time together? Jude wanted her last picture of him, the memory of which she would carry until they next met, to be one that pleased and touched a chord of fondness which would endure.

Another hour and more came and went and Jude's agitation and worry mounted. She had to come – had to. If she didn't . . . It didn't bear thinking about, but he did. He might very well lose her forever because he had no way of finding her, had never, because of the initial secretiveness of their association, escorted her boldly up to her own front door. She *had* to come. And it would have to be soon.

The tides were good and high Jack had informed him knowingly; almost as good, in fact, as in spring and autumn when they came with enough power to cause a Bore. Captain Mitchell had decided that they'd leave on tonight's ebb of tide and that was that, his word final and brooking no argument. Jude hadn't even bothered trying to persuade him into a later departure, therefore, and had listened attentively to one of the captain's impromptu educational anecdotes of a nautical nature, which might, after all, just conceivably prove of value to him as a would-be master in the future. He learnt that the River Severn, with its awesome tidal power, once or twice a year produced a freak wave which started life as an insignificant ripple in the wide mouth estuary parallel with the mouth of the Avon. The wave then built steadily as it travelled up the river towards Gloucester, separating English kindgom and Welsh principality, the giant, solitary breaker heralding a tidal mass of churned brown water which habitually flooded the low lying meadowland of the Severn Valley, and doubtless frightened the grazing livestock witless.

Damn the Severn Bore, Jude cursed in his mind, shaking

it from his thoughts irritably and focusing his attention once more on the avenue down which May failed to come.

Perhaps she couldn't face saying goodbye, poor, sweet thing. Or just maybe she had schemed and manufactured this absence, thinking to appear when the tide had retreated and he (presuming that she believed he couldn't countenance leaving without seeing her first) had stayed behind and allowed the *Celestial Piper* to sail without him. He shook his head vaguely, disinclined to believe that. Such calculating wiliness wasn't in her character. She was a serious, mature young lady not given to such foolish games.

It rained, and with collar pulled up about his ears and hands thrust into pockets, Jude stiffened against the elements, hardly aware of the weather as he watched and waited, hoping, yet somehow knowing – though there was no reason to be sure – that May Bird was not going to appear. He'd sensed it in his bones, the fatalistic feeling of depression heightened by the unpleasant chill of the rain as it plastered his jet hair in cow licks about his face, and trickled down the back of his neck even with his tight collar acting as a barrier. Black eyebrows drew together and to his eyes, replacing a lively, loving sparkle, there came a hurt that stung, and despised tears to glisten on his lashes. They did not stay there long, however, for Jude quickly dashed them away, taking a deep breath or two to restore his equilibrium. He would spare her another half hour, but if she hadn't come by then he would have to leave. Yes, he *would*, he was adamant.

He watched the hands of his time piece, watched the avenue, then, when time had run out, stood in an indecisive dither with acute desperation.

There was an old woman huddled on the far side of the island which housed the gas lamp, calling out feebly in the hope that some of those using the busy thoroughfare might buy the fresh lavender sprigs she hawked. Jude went round to her, ignoring the blue headed stems, which she immediately produced from her basket in abundance, and begged loudly above the noise of rain and traffic, 'Ma'am, if a young girl with red hair should come after I depart, do you think you could give her this address which I've written down?'

She squinted and thrust the lavender at him more insistently, scowling when he shook his head in exasperation.

'I don't want your flowers. I want you to give this to a young lady,' he barked plainly, holding forth the folded sheet of paper.

'Eh?' she squawked, completely bemused, and it was then that Jude's suspicion of her deafness was unhappily confirmed.

He shook his head, his words low and miserably mumbled as he moved away. 'Nothing. Forget it, ma'am. It was a dumb idea, anyhow.'

Jude wandered back around the stone balustraded circle to that spot where yesterday they had so eagerly fallen into each other's arms and kissed in greeting, and stared helplessly at his feet. His hand deposited the folded paper into a crevice between neighbouring slabs of stone which topped the balusters, though he was hardly aware of the absent action to relieve himself of something that henceforth was useless, doing it like a mourner laying flowers at a shrine to lost love.

He had lost her, though the enormity of that fact would take a while to strike home with true devastation, and if he didn't go now he'd likely miss his sailing, too. So he turned and retreated towards the road which led down to the docks, though pausing and silently pleading with fate, as he was about to put Victoria Square out of sight for good and all, that when he turned for a final look she would be there, running down the avenue frantically to keep their rendezvous. That's how it was in books, when the hero wished real hard and had suffered just enough for you to feel sorry for him, Jude thought, crazily. Yet his sweeping, desperate scrutiny of the avenue was without reward. But then, he'd known it would be, for real life *was* like that – a mish-mash of loose ends and untidy episodes that trailed one after the other with none of the clever intricacies of fiction that led, most times, reassuringly towards a happy ending.

A young ragamuffin brought May's brief, worrisome notelet to Obediah's office on Prince's Wharf, and he read it and at once called upon his subordinate, Mr Wedlock, to take charge of the itinerary draft for the *Southern Star* which was even then having her cargo of South American timber winched onto the quay by a crew of stevedores.

'An accident has befallen me,' she had written, her brief, exasperatingly vague text due to the meagreness of the scrap of paper which she had managed to procure and upon which her words were hurriedly scratched.

Obediah, adoring May and alarmed merely by the knowledge that misfortune that day had been hers, took a cab to the hospital immediately and found her sobbing and greatly distressed, her badly sprained – and now bandaged – ankle bothering her not half as much as the knowledge that the accident had prevented her meeting with Jude.

She wept disconsolately, soon saturating the handkerchief which Obediah had proffered, and no soothing on his part had the capacity to render her less distraught.

'Oh, dear dear dear,' he bemoaned, his double chins quivering. 'Oh dear me, what a calamity.'

He saw her settled without too much discomfort into his hired cab, then requested the driver to take them with all speed to Victoria Square, her spluttered story having touched him with pity. This Mariner fellow was sailing today, going away for a lengthy spell at sea in all likelihood. That was bad enough a contemplation for two young people who thought themselves in love, but when one of them never showed . . . That was pure tragedy.

May's eyes scanned Victoria Square with a bleak, resigned stare of misery, as Obediah ordered the cab to stop and climbed out to circumvent the island in the thoroughfare upon which the gas lamp stood supreme. He felt helpless, inadequate, and avoided the tearful green gaze of the girl staring from the window of the cab.

Mr Mariner, it would appear, had tired of waiting and had to rush off in order to catch the evening tide, leaving a very unhappy female behind him. Obediah passed the old woman selling lavender and climbed back into the cab, apologetic as he told May, 'Sorry, dearest, but there's no sign of him.'

She squeezed her eyes shut against the gas lamp and its associated memories, acknowledging the expected with a faint nod of the head.

'Let's get you home,' coaxed Obediah tenderly. 'We'll think about what's to be done then. There's always the American Consulate in Queens Square, after all. Maybe they'll be able to trace him.'

May held on to that thread of hope like a drowning person, her eyes lingering on the windswept square as the cab pulled away, heading for Beaufort Rise. She did not notice – and why should she? – one particularly violent gust of wind that lifted a scrap of paper from its niche in the balustrade and carried it forth, airborne, to dance on the cobbles of the thoroughfare before being trampled under hoof by some gainfully employed beast of burden pulling a means of public conveyance.

Patriarch, housekeeper and the Christian-hearted Anne, fussed and hovered for the next day and more, striving to make May comfortable and thus lessen her physical pain, whilst steadfastly avoiding all reference to the young man she had lost and the mental anguish that was causing. Even Jasper had been instructed to mind his sometimes inappropriate, always pointed remarks on the matter. Mr Mariner and all pertaining to him was, henceforth, taboo. That was the Goodbody way of dealing with such things, and had come into play before, as when Jon and Jessie died. Memory was pain. And while grief remained acute and memories still far too sharp, they would not allow themselves to think, kept the pain at bay as best they could until they felt stronger and, therefore, better equipped to deal with it.

But May's memories overwhelmed her, were so dominated by an overdeveloped young man with eyes as blue as a Persian cat's and hair black and waving, that she thought initially she'd go mad with the pain of grief.

People around her were kind and understanding, but

May knew the workings of their minds. They thought she needed a week or two of cosseting and sympathy and that then she'd be over him and able to look ahead with cheer, some other young man eventually taking his place in importance.

Yet May knew in her heart that there would never come a time when she'd be *over* Mr Mariner emotionally, that her love and remembrance would be for ever.

She looked up from the book she had been gazing at with a total lack of concentration or interest and found herself being scrutinized by a harsh-faced Avon from the other side of the garden fence. Immediately May stiffened amongst the cushions on the wicker chaise longue which had been set outside beyond the French windows so that she might recuperate in a warm and pleasant garden, drawing herself up to face the adversary, though she had nought but his expression to guide her actions. Her chin rose aggressively and her eyes instinctively narrowed to stare down her nose at him.

He sneered, eyelids closing momentarily with dismissive disdain over cool grey eyes, his words calculatingly hissed. 'Your mien is both unimpressive and out of place, Miss Bird. You see, *I* know what you've been up to. Your act of haughty innocence fools me not at all. I saw you with him!'

May blanched. What had he seen and when? That awful, chilling smile of Avon's and the confidence of him completely undid her, a pink flush of guilt rushing up over her face. She muttered back at him defensively, 'It's none of your business and I'll discuss it not with you, sir.'

Had the sprain not kept her helplessly immobilized she would have taken herself off immediately within doors, but as it was there was nothing for it but to recline there stiffly and listen as his voice came again, low and seething with anger, and his neck above stiff white collar suffused with wrathful colour.

'Slut! Did you have to betray your lowly origins by bedding down with the first common sailor to catch your eye? Truly, Miss Bird, I am disappointed in you. You were worthy of better.'

Angry then, May would have forgotten caution and spoken her mind, telling the arrogant Midwinter exactly what she thought of his unwanted opinions and innuendo, but he gave her no chance, taking off in swift, highly charged fashion and disappearing through his French windows.

He had had to withdraw in order to check the surge of anger that had overcome him at the realization of her infidelity. Up until that point where her face turned red with guilt and embarrassment, he had never been certain, his suspicions merely something without substance which had tormented him. But now he knew, even without verbal confession from her, that she *had* been with that yank, giving away the virginity which Avon had always somehow thought of as his own – a prize to be claimed at a later date.

He had had to leave her company or else give in to an urge to vault the fence and strangle her for betrayal. Slut! She was his and some day soon he would make her realize that, and make her pay, too, for the misery this day's revelation inflicted upon him.

By subtle degrees the picture in his mind changed. No longer was she the sweet, bright fairy princess of his erotic fantasies. She changed; becoming tawdry. In place of innocence came licentiousness, instead of the child lover he had craved for so long, there was a gaudy slut with orange hair, teasing him as unmercifully as her predecessor had, and laughing at him, too.

So he promised himself that one day he would have her, tame and cow her and wipe away that smile of deceitful pleasure once and for all, erase that other lover from mind and brand her for ever his.

CHAPTER 24

Tucked out of the way in a tiny cobbled cul-de-sac off Boyces Avenue, near Clifton's Mall, was a public house of Georgian origins named The Albion. It was not patronized perhaps so greatly as some of the pubs in the city centre, but the landlord never complained even so, for his regulars from the Clifton middle-classes were ever eager to reach into their pockets for the purchase price of his ale, served almost on their doorsteps. Convenience had made The Albion popular.

Built around a cobbled yard where trestles and benches were set near the central doorway, it was an odd stuccoed building with shallow roof, tall upstairs windows and broad, multi-paned ones downstairs that flanked the central door. At the sides there were barrel stores and stabling and, beneath the hanging, noisily sawing sign set out near the road to attract attention and thereby custom, a trough where a rider's mount might take refreshment whilst its owner downed a tankard or two inside.

Ned Bland – having been forcibly ejected from The Rummer and The Hatchet after proving himself undesirable by brawling, causing much damage and also losing the landlords their custom – had climbed the hill to Clifton via Park Street two days before and been drinking there heavily ever since, his welcome now wearing thin. There was just something about Ned Bland that automatically made most people withdraw from him in disdain – an unwholesomeness in both manner and appearance.

He'd found the atmosphere inside The Albion chilly –
though maybe he was lucky to get served at all after last
night's rowdyism – so this midday he'd purchased his pint
in a pewter tankard and taken himself outside to down it,
keeping his own odorous company, though he, long ago,
had become so accustomed to the sweaty staleness of himself that it no longer even registered in his nostrils.

He gulped then wiped a grimy hand across his frothy
curled lips, snarling then kicking out at a cur which came
closer than was prudent to take a furtive sniff at such a
decaying delight.

'Git!' Ned warned, the steel-enforced toe of his hob-
nailed boot missing the fleet of paw animal by a hair's
breadth.

The dog vanished and Ned leant heavily onto the trestle
table before him, watching the pedestrians strolling past the
gap just beyond the cobbled yard, his solitary brown eye
narrowing calculatingly as he weighed up the possibilities
for pocket picking. He'd have to do something, for sure, for
he'd naught but a farthing in his pocket and that wouldn't
even buy him half a pint. And his thirst was far from being
quenched. He should do all right, he decided, for there
seemed to be more dandified gents and ladies per square
mile in Clifton than in any other district of Bristol. Every
style and fashion sauntered by to tantalize his greedy eye;
true gentlemen in suits of black or grey broadcloth and
stovepipe hats, gents in canary yellow waistcoats and green
redingotes, sombre frockcoats, top hats, bowlers, tartan
trews, fine jersey wool trousers cut indecently tight . . . Ned
watched them with a snarl of hatred and envy for their
material means, downed the dregs of his pint, then took off
to mingle with them in search of easy pickings.

Had he been cleaner maybe the pedestrians amongst
whom he tried to go surreptitiously might not have given
him so wide a berth. As it was his very smell made all wary,
and several ladies of delicate sensibilities were seen to hold
flimsy handkerchiefs to their nostrils in an attempt to save
themselves from the unpleasantness of inhaling.

After an hour Ned had spirited away two half-crowns and

one shilling from their rightful owners. Then he turned and strolled back the way he had come, of a mind to return to The Albion and partake of another pint and maybe even a snifter of rum before time was called. But something very peculiar distracted him.

Ned wasn't the type to notice particular smells, for his own dire odour overpowered all others. But as he ambled along, tossing a coin and anticipating the coming beverage with a grin, a distinct perfume wafted to his nostrils and immediately triggered something in his brain. His interest was thoroughly arrested. He knew the smell well, instantly able to call the owner to mind. His grin broadened, but as he turned, looking back to the woman he had just over-taken, he was confused to find that she bore not the slightest resemblance to Red from The Dolls' House. Yet he had been so sure.

He walked parallel with the dainty slippered, satin gowned and cloaked figure with blonde ringlets peeping from white crepe bonnet, and gave her a thorough, quite insolent looking-over, his frown deepening. The smell, like a cottage garden on a summer evening, was definitely Red, but the woman who now glowered and quickened her pace, wasn't, not by any stretch of the imagination. She was sweet, pale and definitely the simpering kind given over to the affected pretensions of the middle-classes. Ned detested her instinctively, matching her snarl for snarl and scowl for scowl before he fell back and allowed her to continue with her hurried walking, out of sight but very much in mind. For the first time in several days his mind was wondering about something other than obtaining money to buy the demon drink.

The encounter with Ned Bland had a disquieting effect upon Aurelia. She had never expected him to wander as far afield as Clifton, but had always thought him far too lazy for so strenuous a walk in search of richer pickings. She wondered whether it mightn't be safest if she never went to The Dolls' House again, but she doubted she could long forego the pleasure of bedding with so memorable a fellow.

213

And if she didn't go for a while, through a sense of unease, then any suspicions he had might be confirmed. She had to go as usual, tomorrow, and act her usual self, for Ned, though powerful of body and blessed with sexual prowess, had never been over-bright, and *she*, surely, could quieten any suspicions of his? The risk was worth it, Aurelia judged, just so long as she might keep Ned as her lover.

Ned, contrary to Aurelia's disparaging generalization about his lack of intelligence, played out their next meeting with a deviousness which matched her own. She never guessed the extent of his suspicions, and he never let on, treating her, as ever, like his slave, a gorgeously licentious female put solely – it seemed – upon this earth to gratify his basest needs. They forgot themselves in pleasure, unmindful of the squalor about them and filthy bed beneath which crawled life minute, ever striving greedily to take all and more than the other had to offer.

'Ah, Ned,' she groaned, at his mercy, her manicured nails scoring his dirt-engrained back.

He grunted and grinned, his humour pleasant because now he was certain about the real Red and could see a profit to be made from a neat and juicy piece of blackmail. Take away the red hair, red mouth and heavy make-up about the eyes and there, if you please, was that simpering female of the upper-classes he'd seen yesterday. Jubilantly he forced her legs wider and ground away at her, much to the woman's delight, thinking that, maybe, next time *he'd* charge *her*, and handsomely too, for the sake of keeping her secret solely between the two of them.

Had she guessed at his criminal thoughts, doubtless Aurelia would have been more cautious, but he really did give a good performance, sending her off home content physically and relieved of worry. She hadn't, therefore, expected him to do something as wily as follow furtively behind her, keeping to the shadows and eventually making note of the address where she stopped, dismounting there in the moonlight and removing that flaming wig to disclose locks pinned close to her head as pale as the moon whose light betrayed her.

214

Ned nodded to himself with satisfaction then and watched her quietly walk her horse on the grass to the rear of her enormous, ostentatious mansion, avoiding the gravel drive which might have made noise enough to rouse the servants. When she was lost to sight he strolled out into the beam from a gas lamp on the corner of the street and rummaged in his pockets for pipe and tobacco, leaning there for a while to smoke contentedly and survey a possible source of wealth the likes of which he'd never, until then, dreamt of, his one eye closing against the sting of tobacco smoke like some heinous parody of a wink.

It was two nights later when they came face to face again.

Avon had come to keep Aurelia company at dinner, the pair of them – never given to holding much in the way of conversation – partaking liberally of the pre-dinner sherry, the wine which accompanied the meal, and afterwards, brandy and port as they played a hand of bridge without real enthusiasm.

Avon left soon after and Aurelia, clutching the decanter of fine old ruby port and her glass, took herself off to her study, to pore over the housekeeper's monthly accounts. She was certain that the old witch was fiddling the figures and pilfering, but as yet had been unable to amass any real proof.

The room was there for effect – to impress callers mostly – and served no real purpose, its shelves crammed with finely bound volumes, having been bought as a job lot from a local bookshop at a mere fraction of their true worth. Aurelia had never so much as glanced at a book, let alone lifted one from the shelves for examination. And she rarely used the room, save for pay days when she fancied that sitting behind the leather-topped, mahogany desk lent her an extra air of authority. She liked to intimidate her servants, taking special delight in handing forth their wages with one hand, only to demand back so much in penalties incurred with the other, citing the broken china, the shoddy laundry and mending, and the tasks which, she insisted, had been entirely neglected. Many were the young, inexperienced maids who, out of an overriding fear of their employer, found themselves working for next to nothing.

The entries in the ledger seemed accurate, mathematically at least, and Aurelia knew that she must look deeper, perhaps even painstakingly check through every apparent purchase that the housekeeper had made over the last month, demanding, if necessary, that the articles be physically produced on the morrow as proof of purchase and all monies paid out thus accounted for. Having grown suspicious of the woman's honesty and worth, her employer was now determined to single-mindedly pursue and expose the truth; the downfall of any who would dare to try and cheat her an obsession to Aurelia.

Fanatically she checked the laundry list, ready to pounce on any discrepancy. Let there be one more dress or nightgown listed than there should be, Aurelia vowed silently, and the housekeeper would be dismissed without a reference, her departure likely speeded along by a pointed-toed boot aimed at her posterior!

Lady Spicer smiled at the prospect, then visibly jumped as, out of the blue, a rat-a-tat-tat was gently played on a glass pane in the French windows.

She swung around, startled and fearful, the possibility of burglars automatically coming to mind, then disappearing as swiftly as Ned Bland's face, grinning and winking, came close to the glass, his large, open-pored red nose squashing against the pane to appear truly enormous.

'Aren't you goin' to let me in, Red?' he asked, chuckling.

'Ssh!' Aurelia snarled, dreading that one of the servants might discover him and thus cause a great deal of awkwardness.

He was clever. Too damned clever! He had really fooled her into thinking that she was safe, and knowing that she had been duped so made Aurelia exceedingly angry. Coolly she took a deep breath, composed herself and opened the door to him, even managing a rather superior smile and offering congratulations.

'Well done, Ned. I really am surprised. How come you recognized me that day on The Mall? After all, I bore no resemblance to Red, but was, as I am now, very much myself.'

'Yuh overlooked yer perfume, me dur. I noo it straight off. Ta tell the troof, I was surprised when ee turned up at The Dolls' 'ouse t'other night. That was a brave gamble on yer part. But foolish too.'

'Evidently, seeing as how you then followed me back here and found out where I lived. What else do you know? That I'm a reasonably wealthy widow formerly married to a knight of the realm, that at all costs I will hold on to my reputation and position?'

'Aye, summat like that. We know each other well, Red; well enurf t'come t'some sorta arrangement. Now I was finking that it 'ould be a right terrible shame if we two fell out. I mean, I do so like our lill bitsa fun. Only, now that I do know about ee, I'm wundrin' whether ee shun't be apayin' me fer yer pleasure. Tha's fair, ain't it? I ain't greedy an' so me silence ain't gunna cost ee any gert sum. 'Ow do a shillin' a week sound to ee?'

'It sounds very reasonable, Ned,' she agreed, leaning calmly back against the desk where moments before she had been working. Her hand trailed over the leather top, out of sight of Ned, by-passing the ink well and quill, the blotter and pen-knife, then pausing when it felt the knife-like letter opener.

'Only,' she continued with a shake of her head and a frown, 'I'm not prepared to be blackmailed, no matter for how piffling a sum or whether or not I can easily afford it. You've spoilt everything, you fool, don't you see? Things can never be the same again. Thanks to you Red can no longer exist. You've betrayed my trust and cooked your own goose. Do you honestly think that I would allow you to get away with this?'

'I din't 'spect ee to be such a bad loser, that's fer sure,' Ned conceded, frowning.

'I'm sorry, but . . . ' Aurelia's voice trailed away as she stepped calmly forward. In fact her unperturbed manner was such that poor Ned Bland, a lowly, wily opportunist if ever there was one, was taken completely by surprise and

217

had no idea what Aurelia was about until, smiling insincerely, she clapped him to her like a comrade brother-in-arms and plunged the long, serated blade of Sheffield steel deep into his back.

He gasped, his eyes rolling in shocked realization as he fell, his head clunking against the corner of the desk and maybe even causing the fatal injury.

Belly down he lay, issuing one grunt before giving up the ghost, his head bleeding profusely for a while, blood meandering with thick sluggishness amongst the thin, filthy grey locks on his head.

Calm regained totally, Aurelia stood over him for a while making certain in her mind about the best course of action to take. Falsehoods accumulated, forming a story in her head which eventually seemed satisfactory.

He was an unknown intruder, who, having stolen in while she worked alone and unprotected in her study, had demanded money, jewellery and, God forbid, her *favour*, in return for the promised safety of her son, Lawrence. The letter-opener had come to hand and, reluctantly – because she was gentle and unused to any sort of violence – she had had to stab him to save herself from a fate worse than death. She only hoped that the gentlemen at the Bridewell would understand her need for such action and might quickly wind their investigations up without too much unpleasantness. And it was as she wished.

Her anguished scream had brought the servants running, her study suddenly invaded by concerned employees in nightcaps and gowns, hands holding candles and lamps, and females shrilling hysterically at the sight of blood. Then the butler – having soothed and calmed the noisily distraught Aurelia from her weeping long enough to glean her version of what dastardly deed had taken place – sent the odd job boy down to the Bridewell for police assistance.

The officers were business-like but considerate as they gently put their questions to her and reached the same conclusion as the butler – namely that Lady Spicer had been the victim of a straightforward burglary and assault.

She was known to them, of course, from the tragic time

some years before when her slightly inebriated husband had apparently fallen into the Floating Harbour and drowned, and, as they left, taking the stretchered and discreetly covered body of Ned Bland with them, their senior officer patted her hand sympathetically and tried to lessen her sobs with a few tactfully issued words. After all, there had never been, surely, so unfortunate a lady as she? Bad luck did seem to plague her in quite grievously large doses.

Aurelia sobbed on, downing the sedative which the doctor insisted she take after examining her, but quieting not all. In bed, with people hovering dutifully concerned about her, the crying continued, her body racked by real shudders of despair. She was acting for no one's benefit, each tear quite genuine, though not from shock at a most awful experience as everyone else would assume, but from grief.

Ned Bland was the only person whom she had ever allowed to get close to her, whom she had come, in her own deplorable fashion, to love. Killing him hadn't been easy. If only he hadn't been so untrustworthy and greedy at the end she wouldn't have had to kill him at all. They'd still have each other, indefinitely, into the future.

In her mind she cursed him and groaned against the pain of his loss, while outwardly she cried on, desolate, those about her destined never to truly know why.

And her mourning lasted for some time, though secretively of necessity, Ned's demise causing a sorrow the likes of which the deaths of her drowned parents and husband never had; this black period in her life was slow to be over-ridden by the more dominant, cold and warped facets of her character.

CHAPTER 25

Jack Mitchell reluctantly swallowed the cold, gritty coffee already in his mouth, then slung the rest to starboard, where the fierce wind took it up and sent it overboard.

'In God's name, what do you call that?' he thundered at Jude, who was skulking back towards the companionway and the warmth of the galley. 'For two weeks now the crew and I have been forced to eat and drink the bilge you absently throw together. Snap out of this mood, lad, and get your mind back on the tasks allotted you. I'll not stand for one more mug of cold coffee, so help me I won't.'

'Sorry, cap'n,' sighed Jude, barely listening, his body merely pausing in deference to the other's authority before he set his feet moving again. He was mechanical and dreary, unaware even of the brisk beauty of the Atlantic on that fine summer morning.

'Take the wheel for me, Dougie,' barked Jack to the nearest seaman, thrusting his empty mug against the man's chest with exasperation and contempt for the unpleasant brew it had lately contained.

Able Seaman Douglas McInnes juggled with the tin mug, then got a firm grip on it, his other meaty palm closing about the Celestial Piper's turned and carved, brass reinforced wheel. 'Aye, aye, cap'n.'

Jack – never a patient man – stalked off with purposeful steps in pursuit of the now disappearing back of Jude, his face red with anger, and contrasting brilliantly with the white-blond of his hair. 'Hold your horses, lad, for I tell you now I'm disinclined to accept yet another of your muttered "sorry's".'

Jude slowed, realizing that Jack was speaking to him, and the captain came abreast of him in the narrow and gloomy passage below deck. Face to face, Jude's eyebrows raised just a little in puzzlement at Jack's raging features. The captain grabbed at his elbow painfully and dug in a thumb and two steely fingers, holding on and tightening like a crab until Jude felt bound to issue a surprised complaint.

'What's up with you, cap'n Jack? Let go!'

'What's the matter with me? Ha! You can ask that, walking about this vessel, as you are, like some blank-faced zombie popped out of a Louisiana swamp. Tis you who needs to sort yourself out. You're mooning like an idiot over a piece of fancy skirt who's likely got herself another man already. You've got to learn not to take this loving lark too seriously, lad, can't you see? Your trouble is, you're too naive. Kiss a girl once and you think that's it, a life-long commitment. You're a fool, your only defence being your lack of experience. Forget her like she has you and look ahead to the next port and the next girl. You're a handsome lad, Jude, and many are the girls who'll throw themselves at you just like that easy piece back at Bristol. You can't love 'em all so intensely or you'll not last the course. She's only special because she's your first, and I can understand that, but don't be a complete ass.'

At first Jude was unattentive, barely listening to that which Jack had levelled at him, for he'd heard it more than once since their sailing from Bristol. But eventually some of the captain's words became irksome and the young man bristled, not liking what Jack insinuated. He spoke of Jude's beloved May as if she were no better than some gin-swigging doxy selling her favours on the waterfront. Bursting with indignation, he launched himself at Jack with fists flailing, attacking like some chivalrous knight bent on avenging honour besmirched.

The first blow took Jack completely by surprise and left his nose gushing blood and swelling by the second.

'Why you . . . !' Jack drew in a deep breath of outrage,

dodged the next blow and floored young Jude with an upper-cut that connected cleanly with his chin.

The crash and thud 'of Jude hitting the floor in the passageway brought the off-duty members of crew from all directions, to hover just out of harm's way and watch this set-to which many felt had been on the cards for weeks.

Jude grabbed the leg of one man and used it to help haul himself upright. But he wasn't on his feet for long. He staggered, swayed, swung an ungainly, unlikely punch, then succumbed to a one-two from Jack, the first fist hitting him smack in the eye and the second smashing into his face somewhere between the angular downward sweep of his jawline and his ear. There was an explosion in his head, a terrific pain in the region of his ear, then Jude knew no more.

Jude lay, conscious now and still, silently mourning the incident that had put him to bed with a face that felt as though some rogue elephant had stamped on it. And his heart was heavy on two accounts. He'd lost May and knew the constant pain of that, and now, damn it all, he'd alienated the stalwart Jack.

He should never have been so quick to lose his temper, knew Jack's rude, abrasive manner to be innocent and absent of all malice. Jack treated all women, whether governesses or chambermaids, in the same irreverent fashion, seeing them merely as potential bedmates and propositioning them as such. Women, to him, were for robust bouts of lewdness between bedsheets, to pleasure and be pleasured by, but he'd never have thought to apply romance or tenderness to such a procedure. There was sex for Jack, but love just didn't exist.

Had *he* then, Jude wondered, trying to analyse it all and be rational and fair, deliberately used Jack's rough and ready manner as an excuse for picking a fight? If he had, he thought wryly, with a wince as his fingertips probed his sore jaw, then he had definitely picked the wrong opponent, and must subconsciously have *wanted* to be knocked senseless! Had he? Maybe he had. He'd heard somewhere that the easiest way to end pain was to set about incurring another hurt far worse to take the mind off it. Jude laughed throatily in ridicule, for if that was so, it hadn't worked at all. Nothing was ever going to lessen the hurt of losing May Bird. His laugh petered out falteringly and Jude clapped an arm over his eyes, his weeping quiet and discomfiting, his rough linen shirt soaking up the unmanly, tell-tale tears he felt he shouldn't be crying but couldn't contain any longer.

By the time they docked in New York with the stevedores seeing to the unloading of Derby and Worcester china and Sheffield cutlery, Jude and Jack had shaken hands and resumed their very special friendship. Jack promised to keep his opinions of Miss Bird to himself in exchange for Jude's renewed efforts to cheer up and start functioning again satisfactorily in the galley. Maybe the young man's heart *was* broken and his feeling of despondency not quickly overcome, but did the rest of the crew have to fear daily that they'd be accidentally poisoned by his absently careless hands? Jack had asked, displaying a jovial sense of diplomacy.

Jude had conceded and thereafter his mind was kept determinedly free of thoughts of May while he assisted cook in the galley.

As usual he stayed at Jack's place, a solid four-storeyed brownstone on the lower east side of Manhattan, which was upkept for the captain by an exceedingly efficient, though unfortunately bossy housekeeper called Mrs Vernon.

Jude deposited his lowly wages as a seaman and considerable commission as a painter in the bank as usual, bought a small trinket for Thirza in a vain attempt at carrying on as normal, and met her from the young ladies' seminary she now attended on Lafayette Street.

At sight of him she gushed with her usual enthusiasm, slotting her arm through the crook in his and strolling until they had reached Prince Street and slowed before the city's modest Roman Catholic Cathedral* which had been built

* *It burnt down in 1866 and the present cathedral now stands on Fifth Avenue.*

223

back in 1815 by one Joseph Mangin, a Frenchman, who was also responsible for the elegant façade of City Hall.

'You've grown some more,' Thirza said admiringly, giggling. 'Soon you'll be clunking your head in drawing room doorways.'

'I haven't had to contend with too many of those. On ship it's far worse, believe me. There's not the vessel been built to take a man with comfort if he be more than five and a half feet tall.' Jude tried to sound light and carefree, but weighed down by sorrow and faced now with the sad sight of a once pretty sister turned into a pale and wobbly dumpling, he felt a weary wave of depression wash over him. She was bloated and ungainly, a delicate silver ring he had bought for her not long ago now cutting noticeably into the finger on which she wore it.

'Your appearances out of the blue sustain me, you know. How long will you be in New York this time?' Thirza wondered, allowing herself to be led to the busy thoroughfare beyond the church precincts.

'For quite some time. We'll be seeing each other again, have no fear. And, Thirza, if you ever need to get in touch, you can leave a message at Captain Mitchell's house on Christie Street. It may, if I'm at sea, take time to reach me, obviously, but I'll get it in the end.'

'I'll remember.'

CHAPTER 26

The following afternoon Jude had been waiting, as Thirza had hoped, at the wrought iron gates of the seminary, his presence causing several other pert young ladies to correct their posture and pass him by with shoulders back and modestly covered breasts thrusting forward, their eyes devouring the overwhelmingly handsome male whilst at the same time issuing flirtatious invitations with lashes aflutter. He smiled absently, politely, but hardly saw them; females – especially those approximately the same age as his sister – rousing no interest in him at all. They were all such babies at fifteen, simpering and suchlike fit to infuriate a sensible young man like himself. And then he was thinking of May again, remembering that her simperings had been few and far between and wholly pleasant, most of her adolescent experiments in the art of flirtation doubtless carried out on such willing victims as Mr Brunel, Daniel Gooch and that pot-bellied guardian of hers. So that when she came to him, their courtship was not marred by a surfeit of childish silliness. How *old* had May been? Jude had wondered of a sudden, realizing he had never been privy to that information and had never thought to ask. Certainly she must be two years older than Thirza at least, for she acted with such maturity. And then he pushed her and the pain she caused steadfastly from his mind and concentrated on Thirza and the discomfiture she displayed whilst asking if there was possibility of a meeting between mama and himself. She felt that the request pressurized him, putting him in an awkward position and appealing to his sense of duty more than was fair.

Yet he had jumped at the chance, nodding enthusiastically and uttering in a voice that seemed to sing, 'Oh yes, yes; oh yes.' Then his sudden burst of joy at the thought died, as he put voice to his fears; 'But how? Thirza, I have thought so often about seeing her, but to do so would surely place her in danger. My terror is for her lest papa find out. If he knew I had visited the house in his absence, he would likely act the beast.'

'Then let us come to you, if your captain will oblige by making his front parlour available. Tomorrow?'

'Why not?' agreed Jude, laughing, seeing no good reason for disinclination towards the suggestion; a meeting at Jack's meant no problems as far as he could see.

'It being Saturday tomorrow, mama and I will use the excuse of a visit to the milliners and haberdashers to absent ourselves from home in the afternoon.'

'I shall be expecting you, whatever the hour.'

'There is just one thing though, Jude.' Thirza felt compelled to forewarn him in preparation.

'Yes?'

'Mama may seem a little different – absent of manner and not as alert as she used to be. I hardly need ask you, I know, but be patient. You see, she fell down the stairs and did some damage to her head which the doctors can't rightly put name to. She's not mad or stupid, you need not fear. But she can be introverted and ponderous.'

'God in heaven, Thirza, why haven't you told me this before?' wondered Jude sharply, his mother's welfare always of great concern to him.

'I knew you'd only worry. And what good would that have done? Tearing your hair out and fretting can't change things.'

'Then tell me how it happened, this accident,' he demanded to know, catching her wrist and bringing Thirza to a halt on the sidewalk so that she was forced to face him.

'It was no accident, Jude,' she told him calmly. 'I never saw it happen; found her at the bottom of the stairs and him

226

bending over her and shaking her without hint of compassion. But I *know* he pushed her.'

Jude knew his father too, his capacity for any cruelty, and doubted not the truth of Thirza's words. He hovered there in a pause of horror, oblivious momentarily to all that went on around him on Lafayette Street and imagining sickly, over and over, the hefty weight of Morgan Somerton pushing the placid and weak Mary-Anne down the long, steep flight of stairs.

Thirza grasped his hands and chafed them concernedly, her gaze full of worry. 'Are you all right?'

In truth he felt quite ill, feeling the prickling of cold sweat on his forehead and the unpleasant beginnings of churning in his stomach. If he didn't gain control and quickly, he just might do something he hadn't since childhood and be physically sick.

Getting into a white-hot rage would help no one, after all. Only calm and rational would he be able to decide what was best for mama and Thirza. So Jude overcame his feelings of revulsion and made the effort to resume his easy-paced walking. His mind, however, was not so quick to toe the line, and continued to curse like some unholy litany; how could he, the evil dog, how could he?

Up the steps to Captain Mitchell's house climbed Mary-Anne and Thirza, the daughter lending a steadying hand at her mama's elbow. The door opened even before they'd put their toes to the top step and there, reaching out and grasping the prematurely aged woman to him with a tear-laden travesty of a cheerful welcome, was an immaculately tailored Jude, Jack and Mrs Vernon hovering behind and waiting their turns to be introduced.

Once in the parlour the conversation remained desultory for a while, Jack and Jude, Mary-Anne and Thirza happy to allow the talkative housekeeper to lead them from one light topic to the next, while they ate cake and drank tea, made comment, grew familiar with their surroundings and got acquainted.

Mary-Anne chattered, but her eyes kept going back

lovingly to Jude, marvelling at his height and broadness of shoulder and delighting in his fine, almost beautiful rather than handsome features. Jack sat and ate, remaining, as ever, sparing with his words and simply enjoying the novelty of a family about him. And Thirza, having brought Jude and mama together as promised, allowed herself to relax and luxuriate in the comfortable homeliness of the house on Christie Street.

It was a friendly house, she could tell, just by looking around. Her house was a residence, a stone and mortar testament to her father's wealth, but this was a home, complete with threadbare carpets upon which you didn't feel obliged to tip-toe reverently; and pile upon pile of gentlemanly muddle which Mrs Vernon had evidently foresaken trying to eradicate after years of vain attempts at total order. There were books crammed untidily upon shelves in no particular order, alongside windows curtained in thick white lace and draped over mellowly in tassle-edged brown velvet that undeniably bore the look of Mrs Vernon's handiwork. There were shelves for ships in glass cases and hanging upon the walls mementos of exotic voyages which doubtless provoked inquisitive questions from many a caller. What was the story behind the four-cornered Chinese hat and pointed slippers? How came they by the ceremonial headdress of a warrior chief from a tiny island off the coral atoll of Mururoa? Such belongings probably caused endless conversations liberally spiced with embellished anecdotes.

Mother and son perched facing each other upon the sofa, reaching out and touching hands often as six years were sketched in, Jude's account of them almost dismissive and far from compensating his mother for having unfortunately missed them.

'I intend being a captain also, mama,' he told her, 'Just like cap'n Jack. And one day, if I'm worthy – and I pray it's so – I shall be master of his ship the *Celestial Piper*.'

'That will be wonderful, dear. And when you are in New York, as now, you *must* let me know so that Thirza and I can meet you and I can assure myself that you are truly well.'

'Yes, mama. But what of you? How, when I am at sea or elsewhere am I to be certain of your safety and know peace of mind? Thirza has told me about your *accident*. Yes, I know, you see, and I'm fearful of what the future holds.'

'Jude dear,' his mother soothed, wanting to make little of the problem and thereby cause him the minimum anguish, 'you must not worry for me. Look after yourself.'

'How can I not worry?' he growled impatiently. 'There is no end to his brutality and well you know it. Be sensible, for Thirza's sake as well as your own and let me find you somewhere else to live – somewhere safe. Leave home like I did and start to live; it's your only hope.'

'Son, despite your size, still you are a boy at heart. Everything is so simple to your mind. But the reality is much more complicated. I cannot leave Morgan. I would be reneging upon the duties I vowed to undertake before God in church. I cannot – will not – for my pride will not allow it. I'll not have others, wickedly tongued, say that I left him, deserted my position. They'll not have the satisfaction,' she said slowly, much thought going into the words.

'But that's suicide. Will you let your own pride kill you?' he raged, angry with her then.

'There was a time, Jude, long before you were born, when drinking for your father meant merely a social glass of sherry or wine, when I truly loved him and he was not the unkind man he is today. I cannot entirely forget those times or my feelings then. These things also keep me loyal to my husband.'

'He's undeserving of such loyalty. Mama, please, reconsider. I have money and am well able to afford a small house or apartment rooms for you and my sister. I have continued to paint, you see, papa's objections as ever ignored, and it is from that – painting the sights all around me when I'm on some voyage or other – that I have accumulated no small amount of wealth. I am becoming quite famous, even in New York, as Mariner the marine painter.'

'Oh, I *am* proud. I always knew such a talent couldn't entirely be quashed. But what is this about *Mariner?* Have you changed your name?'

'Only for the purpose of painting and making a living, mama. I thought it prudent, now that my work is sought and higher prices continually being paid, to guard against detection by papa. You see, many of my paintings hang in the New York galleries and the name Somerton might draw attention. Someone might see it and mention it to papa, and it's unlikely that he wouldn't reach the correct conclusion. I have no wish to be tracked down by him and forced back home because I have not, technically, reached the age of maturity. And I fear he *would* do such out of spite.'

Mary-Anne sought to maintain this new lightness of mood, steering the conversation bit by bit away from the possibility of her leaving Morgan, which was so tempting but quite impossible. She was his wife. And that meant for life. 'I can see that I shall have to show a little more interest in the finer things of life from now on, and shall go more frequently to the galleries to keep up with your progress and, just maybe, buy one or two paintings. Oh, the thought makes me dizzy with wicked pleasure! Can you imagine paintings of yours hanging at home right under your father's nose without him being aware of it? How irresistible.'

Her laughter was infectious and Jude couldn't help but mildly follow suit, grinning and rumbling deep in his throat at her admirable show of spirit.

She had learnt to be clever over the years in order to survive the outrages of her drunkard husband, so out-manoeuvering Jude presented no real challenge at all. Drastic talk of running away from home was forgotten and the final minutes of the visit were spent in discussing art. Thirza joined in again, enthralled by her brother's captivating description of the joy he had felt the first time he had ever truly captured the force and violence of a broiling sea upon a humble canvas, there to trap it for all time.

Mary-Anne listened and smiled too, appearing to her off-spring to be absent but otherwise almost unchanged, happy beyond words to have rediscovered her son and taking great comfort from the fact that between voyages he would be near, and henceforth she would know it. She conceded little, her only promise made on the steps before the front door when their carriage arrived to take them home.

She caught his arm and held it possessively with gloved fingers, smoothing away that troubled look from his creased brow with her sensible words. 'Know, dear boy, that I shall not hesitate to seek help from you should I feel I truly need it. Just *knowing* where you are has given me new strength. And you are not to worry, do you hear? I forbid it. Get on with your own life and, so that we do not risk losing touch, from time to time you can invite me for tea.'

There were kisses on the cheeks, hugs, and then he was handing them into the hired carriage, his mind a muddled picture of mama, Thirza and May, who surfaced to be painfully remembered. His frown was deep when he closed the front door on the outside world.

CHAPTER 27

Once, long ago, there had been a castle at Bristol, with the rivers Avon and Frome acting as a natural form of defence about it. Since the demolition of the Norman fortress during the seventeenth century, however, parts of the river Frome had been built over, so that it flowed mostly underground by the nineteenth century, emerging to form Broad Quay near St Augustines Reach. But the island-like accumulation of acres remained, mostly surrounded by water, and retained its regal placenames of the past too. Beyond Prince Street was Queen's Square, an elegant location with fine Georgian and Regency town houses surrounding a green, tree-covered expanse. Here the American Consulate – one of the first to be set up in Europe – occupied premises at Number 37.

On several occasions in the weeks following the American sailor's departure, Obediah Goodbody was to escort an ever greatly despairing May there to seek news in vain, then see her home again past the hated King Street which never failed to bring back the horror of incidents long done, and thus add to her distress. For there, six years since, she had been sold by her father outside The Llandoger Trow. It seemed to May to have taken place a hundred years ago, so much had happened since, yet she remembered it as vividly as ever, her stomach churning with the abhorrence of it all. Obediah would hold her hand tightly on those necessary occasions when old, evocative paths had to be crossed and there was, anyhow, always the greater trauma of the present to pale such things to a lesser importance. What cared she that in the past her father had so callously sold her, compared to the unbearable possibility of losing Jude Mariner? What was done, she had come to terms with, but that in no way applied to present events. She *wouldn't* believe that she would never see him again.

But those at the Consulate, despite their helpful attitude and diligence on May's behalf behind the scenes, found their efforts unrewarded. They indulged her, charmed by so alarmingly pretty a maid, but she knew that secretly they derived amusement from her plight. To those grown gentlemen of diplomatic bent, she was naught but a silly chit suffering the pangs of first, though far from meaningful love.

Also, to May's frustrated rage, the amount of information she had been able to give them to help in their search had been pitifully small.

'What is his occupation?' she had been asked. Simply, she had said, 'Seaman.'

'On which ship?'

'I'm afraid I don't know.'

The bewhiskered man behind the desk, who wrote down her answers with quill on paper, and several other men at similar desks behind him, looked up at that with eyes widening, and May had felt obliged to explain, 'I never had cause to ask. We did not meet close to the quays for it was my assumption that Mr Mariner did not wish me exposed to such a rough area. I know only that his ship was docked on Broad Quay and that they sailed out on the second Thursday of last month.'

'Well, that's *something*, I suppose. It may just help narrow down the possibilities. There weren't many American ships docked on that stretch during June.'

'I'm sorry I can't be more helpful but, you see, we had little time to get to know each other really well.'

'Might one ask *how long*?'

'Three days.'

Everyone present raised their eyebrows at that and somebody even chuckled in amusement, causing May to stiffen with offence. Obediah laid a calming arm about her shoulder and became even more supportive than usual.

'Gentlemen, please, it ill becomes you to scoff. Who can say how long it takes for people to fall in love, after all? Would any of you care to make a precise estimate? Nay, it's impossible, is it not?' Obediah chided them.

'Point taken, sir. And my apologies, miss, for having derived amusement from your plight.'

She smiled wanly in forgiveness and brought pleasure to all. For this young lady they would move heaven and earth, even if it meant tracking down this young patriot of theirs only to find that she, more than likely, had had a change of heart and found that she didn't love him so completely after all. For there wasn't, to their minds, the contrary female alive who knew her own mind with certainty from one day to the next.

The questions had then resumed, May proving to be more helpful on certain of those points.

'Can you say where he came from – a city or suchlike?'

'I can do better than that. Mr Mariner lived in New York, on Wall Street near Broadway. I'm sure it was something like that. He told me so and the names have stuck in my mind.'

'Oh, well in that case there should be no trouble tracing him at all.'

'There is just one slight problem. You see he no longer lives at home and there is bad feeling between him and his father. A great deal of discretion would be needed when making enquiries.'

There had been more sighs from the Americans at that. 'Well, that complicates things, miss. If your beau left his home when there was bad feeling, chances are he wouldn't have bothered giving his father his present address.'

'There is a mother and sister though, whom he is very fond of. They might be able to tell you, *if* you could make your approach unbeknownst to the father.'

'Maybe. Leave this with us, then. It'll take some time, obviously, to make enquiries, shipping always subject to the whims of weather etcetera. Give us a month and a half – maybe two – and then perhaps we'll have something for you, miss. Be assured that we shall be doing all in our power.'

She had taken the proffered meaty hand with thick blond hair on the back and shaken it with her own more delicate, white cotton-gloved hand, smiling her grateful thanks at the promise, whilst Obediah made short of the polite formalities of leave-taking. 'My thanks to you, gentlemen, on the young lady's behalf, *and* my own. And now we'll bid you good-day. I'm sure you have other important business which is equally deserving of your attention.'

But, despite the politeness, helpfulness and general optimism exhibited that day by the hovering officials present at 37 Queen's Square, Jude Mariner could not be found. There was no family called Mariner on Wall Street or any avenue adjoining, the Consulate's man in Manhattan had informed them, and, searching deeper, the only one he had knowledge of in the vicinity was an artist who was then enjoying a rise in popularity and favour amongst the rich folk on Millionares Row in The Bowery. Could that be him? they had wondered.

Oh, how she wished it was. But how could it possibly be? Jude was a humble sailor not a painter, the gulf between the circumstances of the two so enormous and unlikely that she had to shake her head and come to terms with the fact that the investigations by the Consulate would naturally wind down, Jude Mariner, to them at least, as good as dead.

Weeks passed for May in a morose withdrawal from all that pertained to the social aspects of life. By day she moped and caused the patience of many about her to waver, their sharp words kept in check only by self-will of commendable proportions, and at night she lay on her bed and thought of nothing but him and love lost and cried tears that left her green eyes ugly with red swelling. Others placed their hope on time to do the healing, and if not to eradicate, then to soften and dull May's hurt by progressive degrees.

But for May time did not so much heal as add to her sorrow with fresh misery.

Anne it had been who, when necessity arose in years past, appraised May of the facts heralding womanhood; her no-nonsense approach to the subject, despite her pink-faced discomfort, greatly impressing May and leading her to regard the prim young woman as something akin to advisor and mentor. But now she suspected something that turned her secretive and wary, something which she knew she would be unable to discuss with Anne. So one night she waited until all was dark and quiet, then crept below to the library by the tawny light of a fancy mantled oil lamp held in her tense, grasping fingers.

She knew even before she entered Obediah's snug, well used domain – its walls lined with books, whose cloth or leather spines were frayed and cracked from continual use, whose desk bore the accidental scars of age and leather chair mounted upon castors beneath, in the knee hole, was in need of re-upholstery for the umpteenth time – that the very worst had been brought about by her whole-hearted, yet foolhardy encounter with the American and that she was nurturing the beginnings of his child within her.

Just thinking of it sent a thrill of terror and awe coursing through her spine. She sought the thick, faded volume on medical topics solely to confirm her dreadful suspicion, then had to take her courage in her hands to actually open it at the relevant page. Frightened, and only then becoming aware of the dire consequences of a pregnancy, she wished with all her heart that by ignoring the facts the problem would just go away. She thought of having to confess her immorality to dear, trusting Obediah and quaked at the thought. He'd be within his rights to open his front door and direct her down the steps with rigid disapproval, and she, cast off and thus publicly put to shame, would lose all those who had been her friends, who had put their faith and energies into making her a better human being than the pathetic waif who had come into their lives so long ago. A lump came into her throat and she thought about the people whom she had betrayed and for a while her concentration on the pages of the book faltered and she lost herself to silent, distraught and frightened weeping, unable to comprehend a life where Obediah, Jasper, Anne and her dearest Isambard had no place. Surely she would die from all this hurting? Within the space of two months and more, her whole world seemed to have turned upside down and inside out and then fallen completely apart.

She found it, the confirmation she did not want, and read it through carefully, digesting as much as possible so that nothing which happened in the months ahead should surprise or frighten her unduly, nodding reluctantly as she found an undeniable coinciding of symptoms. Yes, she had been aware for weeks of odd physical changes, had felt *different* though had no explanation, had experienced bodices that were suddenly uncomfortably restricting about her breasts and a general loss of equilibrium. She was not physically sick but then neither did she feel at her best, her appetite suffering from strange new quirks of preference, and at times seeming to desert her completely.

May put back the book, rolled the chair back under the desk and left the library with silent tread, her mind so full of fear and problems that sleep, when she climbed between the sheets, was impossible.

How long did she have before the child became apparent and she had to confess? The book had been vague on that, concentrating more fully on the development of the child in the womb than the outward appearance of the mother. Maybe she still had several months if she could rely on the unchanging fashion for extremely full skirts and tightly laced bodices. But what did it matter how long she went without shame detected? There was, after all, only one outcome and it would leave her world in ruins. She might, she supposed, trying to be practical, use the time to plan some kind of future for herself and the baby, for it could be so easy to give oneself up and end up at the mercy of some butchering midwife in the poorhouse. Even in so wretched a state, May had the spirit to vow that such would not befall her. She would save every piffling penny from then on and squander nothing on frivolities. She could easily go without her ribbons and lace, her chocolates and penny novelettes. And then, when the awful day came and she was alone and of necessity fending for herself, she could at least forego the added burden upon wit and spirit of being without financial means.

In her heart she wished the child's existence away, unable to foresee future joy for the pain and devastation that would doubtless be the initial consequence. But even then, in perhaps her worst moments of despair, May was able to feel and think of the child as her only testament to that great love which she had felt for its father. For that reason, if no other, a spasm of possessive delight flushed her being then was as quickly gone. For Jude, whom she would never believe had gone from her for ever, and for herself as proof of their undying love, she therefore resigned herself to bringing the child into the world and providing it with a decent life, no matter what unforeseen hardships that might entail.

She might have wanted to stay safe and pampered, snug and secure for ever, basking in the warmth of a happy home where friends abounded, and remaining a child for the indulgent Isambard to spoil, but she knew now, with a baby to change circumstances drastically for all time, that she must change or else be unable to cope with the responsibilities which were going to come in a flood. At fourteen, and long before she had anticipated a real need to, May Bird was going to have to grow up.

Any odd behaviour exhibited by May in the days following her clandestine confirmation of pregnancy was attributed by those about her to lingering traces of melancholia. Quiet and withdrawn she was, they had decided, showing all the classic symptoms of someone with a broken heart, and so they indulged her, humouring her sometimes anti-social tendencies.

Some days she appeared quite normal and, if not buoyant and chirpy, then at least pleasant enough company for Anne who persuaded her to lend a hand in her charitable endeavours. But on other days she seemed to detach herself from everything and leave her earthly husk in languid repose about the house on Beaufort Rise, her spirit having vacated the body. Thus she seemed to cope with Jude Mariner's sailing away tolerably well and to blank it and the future steadfastly from mind.

And there were yet other days when she couldn't stand to be confined to the house and its gardens and took herself, in shawl and bonnet, down over the forty-nine steps flanked by half-timbered shops and lit by gas lamps at night, which Bristolians had long ago curiously named the Christmas Steps, emerging by St Bartholomew's Hospital at the foot of this cobbled and novel thoroughfare, to look over the confined stretch of water within Broad Quay.

Maybe she went there in the vain hope that a black-haired, blue-eyed sailor would find life without her impossible and sail in to search for and claim her. Maybe she went there to watch the waters which had taken him, feeling a little nearer by doing such. Or maybe, for at this time of crisis May felt that she lived one day at a time never knowing what might happen next, watching the tall ships with their masts naked of all save rigging, their hulls riding gently, restrained by mooring lines, offered her some undefined form of comfort.

CHAPTER 28

There came a time, after the worst of the mourning period had been survived, when Aurelia felt compelled to go abroad once more at night in search of a man. Loss and pain had dulled her appetites for a while, but now the old, familiar stirrings at her greedy loins had returned, and stimulating and finding release at her own hand could no longer bring true or lasting satisfaction.

The trouble was, however, a lack of selfless, generous manhood in the city public houses. With Ned gone and Aurelia too afraid of exposure to frequent The Dolls' House, she found procuring men difficult indeed. In the pubs the men put their thirsts and any alcoholic dependency first; a fancy piece of skirt with a painted face and a new, realistic black wig, no matter how agreeable to the eye, having to patiently bide her time and work hard to catch a man's eye and cause him to think seriously about possible fornication. Sober, they were wary, dubious of coquettish persuasion, and ever mindful of the fearful possibility of being discovered by some rolling pin wielding spouse. Drunk they were more amenable but incapable of performing up to the kind of standard Aurelia had come to take for granted after her pleasurable years as Ned Bland's plaything.

Many were the times lately that Aurelia had no sooner raised her skirts accommodatingly than she was flinging them down again with a frustrated curse, and throwing the money contemptuously back into the customer's face. Lord, what she would have given for a good lover!

Then one night, to her infinite relief, she found one, quite by chance, who was to prove irreplaceable.

Disguised and cloaked, Aurelia had left her house on foot, thinking of seeking company closer to home than was normal for the sake of convenience, but at the first inn she entered she came face to face with one of the partners in the firm of family solicitors, Mr Craddock, and had had to make a tactical retreat. Pretty soon she had wended her way down through the crescents of Clifton and found herself at the bottom of Merchants Road in Hotwells, undecided then as to which direction to take. To her left lay the heart of the docks, reached by way of Mardyke and Canon's Marsh. To her right lay the Cumberland Basin and the quiet of the Gorge. She sighed and then sauntered down Nova Scotia Place instead, drawn towards the turn of the century hostelry by its welcoming lamp which beamed light far out onto the waterfront. It was a strange place, notably quaint and picturesque amongst the bustling grime of the docks; its small, isle-like ground taken up by the pub and a row of cottages built there by the Port Authority for their retired workers. The pub, which was called The Nova Scotia, had been named in honour of the 1713 Treaty of Utrecht which had been arranged by John Robinson, the Bishop of Bristol, and had caused France to cede Nova Scotia to the British.

Earlier, though fading fast now from her mind, a glance back during her walk had brought the striding form of a tall man cloaked in all-concealing dark brown to her curious attention. She had wondered whether he took her for a street walker and was, perhaps, of a mind to proposition her, and so she had slowed, almost stopping, so that he might catch up with her if he was of a mind. But he had not. Instead, and causing her instant alarm, he had stopped dead and made no move again until she did. She didn't like that, instantly on her guard and wondered for what reason he so obviously trailed her.

She would have liked to turn boldly and march up to him, demanding to know what he was about, but she was, in truth, frightened by the mysterious individial. One was always reading accounts of prostitutes being beaten up or done to death and discarded in the murky waters of the Avon by monsters who outwardly appeared sane and normal.

So it was that Aurelia had taken to her heels, dashing down one street, then another and taking so crazy a downhill course that she had been confident of losing her unwelcomed stalker. And indeed she had, her pause upon the junction of Merchants Road and Cumberland Road showing her to be quite alone once more. Still, she was not entirely happy until she found herself in the relatively safe light from The Nova Scotia's lamp, and spied a solitary, friendly looking, healthily robust stevedore leaning on the wrought iron railing at the water's edge.

Mystery and murder faded from her mind as she came slowly by with a swagger and sway of hips that made her skirts swirl, smiling in answer to his beckoning wink. Here was a man, Aurelia felt sure, who was looking for a good woman rather than the easy pleasure of beer or rum.

Encouraged by a quick perusal of his work-hardened frame, she paused and leant her back into the rail a little way off, though she was careful to remain within talking distance.

She hitched her cloak back over her shoulder vampishly so that he might see her slim body and, more especially, her all but naked breasts rising enticingly above the cotton of her scantily cut blouse. Then she smiled and licked her lips, a deep breath causing those breasts, which had caught and now held his attention, to thrust forward, nipples hard and plain to see against the material which confined them.

He sucked in his breath and grinned with appreciation. 'Now thar be a sight ta cause a gert swellin' in a 'ealthy man's trowsas, I can tell ee.'

Aurelia giggled and changed position, turning and leaning over the rail supposedly to gaze out over the waters, but in truth it was merely a devious means of exposing her breasts completely as her blouse gaped open, and thus assure herself of his full attention. Not that the man seemed to need much blatant prompting to make improper advances.

He came nearer, his rough, nasal tones lowering accordingly as he voiced his thoughts aloud. 'What I 'ouldn't give, deary, ta get me 'ands on those *an'* more. 'Ow much do ee charge fer allowing a good bloke ta get friendly? I've nowt but me night's beer money but youm welcome ta that.'

'If you'll but give me true pleasure, I'll charge you only a token penny,' Aurelia bargained, her breathing already laboured and juices running.

'A penny be it? Gaw! Then I be yer man, dur,' he chortled, coming close then and wasting no time in sliding a large, plump-fingered hand down her blouse to squeeze her pendulously positioned breasts. 'Ooh, my,' he sighed, his loins rubbing urgently at her buttocks and setting Aurelia atremble.

'Do you know a place where we can go?' she wondered impatiently.

'Waz wrong wi' 'ere? No one'll see; light be too poor. We be astandin' 'ere enjoying the view. Least ways others'll fink so.'

'But . . . ' She forgot her protest as his other hand gingerly found its way beneath her skirts and went straight to that place which seemed to dominate her existence so. She arched with pleasure and pushed her buttocks demandingly against the hardness straining at his loins, all caution gone as desire ran white hot.

Her skirts were surreptitiously lifted and bunched conveniently about her rump, then she felt the cool hardness of him prodding and held her breath in anticipation, gurgling ecstatically as he thrust home.

She had known, sensed, that he wouldn't be a disappointment. There had been something about him; an authoritative manner and Aurelia gave herself up to his dominating approach and received pleasure the likes of which she'd been craving for so long.

Bent over the rail with her rump presented to him, she allowed him all liberties, gasping and squealing with unimaginable delight at his hard and hurtful, sustained and masterful usage.

At buttocks, waist, breasts and twitching flesh between

her legs, his fingers delved and probed, stroking and sometimes even scratching until Aurelia sobbed out her pleasure and turned limp in his arms.

Spent and delighted by so accommodating a female, the man rearranged his clothing and gave her another wink as she slapped down her skirts and turned to him breathless and appreciatively smiling.

'If ee be wantin' more o' the same, I be 'ere most nights ta take a draught afore goin' 'ome for supper.'

'I'll remember that,' breathed Aurelia, before brazenly walking away as if nothing had happened, to turn just once at the end of Nova Scotia Place to watch the man enter the pub.

So dreamy was her mood that she didn't see the man in the shadow of the buildings on the far side of the road, the eyes that watched her eclipsed by the hood of an enveloping brown cloak.

There was no reason for Avon Midwinter to spend much time at his business premises on Broad Quay, but even so he did. A veritable army of clerks and dogsbodies were at his disposal, buying cotton from America's southern states, eastern spices and rum from the Indies, yet it offered some amusement to the bored gentleman to be involved when it suited him.

He liked to turn up out of the blue and create havoc in the pathetic, servile lives of his staff, dishing out instant dismissals as if he were some cruel, all powerful deity, with never a thought for the destitution such merciless behaviour would cause. He sat at a grand desk of burr walnut, surrounded by roll-top bureau, secretaire and bonheur du jour, the walls, with their dramatic scarlet flock paper, liberally dotted with grimy oil paintings of several past generations of Midwinters. The actual amount of work which he did was negligible and suspect, usually lacking a sound foundation, so that, when he had thankfully departed, his highest placed employees had discreetly to doctor and fiddle his written dictates in order that business be done in the best interests of everyone. The future livelihoods of all concerned shouldn't be dependent upon the ill-judged whims of the delinquent Mr Midwinter, who, like his father before him, was but a pale imitation of the grandfather, Victor, who had built the business up and created the family wealth and status from far humbler beginnings.

Today though, to the relief of those in the outer, far less plush offices, he had so far done no work at all, but reclined in a chair pulled close to the window so that he could watch May Bird perched with desolate air upon a cotton bale on the far side of the quay. Twice this week she had done the same, much to Avon's perplexity, sitting there like some ghostly apparition – so pale and distant did she appear – to unwittingly irritate and obsess him.

Was she going mad, he wondered, thinking it possible considering her lowly origins, or was she out to pick up another sailor to replace the last one who had shipped out? He had no way of being sure, knowing only that he didn't like her presence there – he could find no peace of mind. Even in broad daylight the busy quay was a male domain to be avoided whenever possible, and Avon himself preferred to use transport in the vicinity rather than go about on foot and risk being rumpled and robbed by the dockland ruffians. What could Obediah be thinking of to indulge her so? She needed a firmer hand to keep her under control.

As he watched, thinking that Anne Goodbody's grey satin hand-me-down dress suited May's exquisite form not at all, a scruffy, grinning worker of humble demeanour directed a casual remark her way, which was, Avon didn't doubt, a coarse form of compliment. His hackles rose and he stood up, and snatched his hat and great coat from their stand on his way out of the door.

She was going home, so help him, she was, even if he had to manhandle her into a carriage and get her there by force. He'd not sit idly by and be forced to watch any Tom, Dick or Harry make passes at her that way. She'd wounded him deeply enough with her consorting with that yankee interloper, and he certainly wasn't going to stand for any repeat performances with new partners. Whether she knew it or not, she *was* his and it was, he felt, his prerogative to save her from herself until such time as he cared to claim her and take over such responsibilities.

Avon climbing down from a hired cab and walking towards her through a scattering of mooring lines coiled like snakes, baled tobacco and crates which omitted the heady aroma of coffee, gave May power to rouse her from her lethargic mopings which the stevedore's lightly flirtatious remark of minutes before had failed to do.

His grey eyes, flanking his straight, sharp nose, were livid and bright, his hand upon her shoulder hurtfully aggressive, so that May twisted away from the contact and came to her feet the quicker to lose any disadvantage she had.

'Wha . . . what do you think you're doing!' she said loudly, with angry puzzlement, causing those unloading *The Roebuck* to pause, their eyes lingering upon the unexpected scene being played out on the quay.

'Miss Bird, I really *must* insist that you go home immediately, before you bring trouble down upon yourself,' Avon ordered, his manner superior and bossy enough to fuel further May's developing temper.

'You are not my keeper to be telling me what to do. When will you ever learn to mind your own business?'

'When you begin to act responsibly. Anyone would think that you relish the thought of being attacked by these low types, the way you continually hang around here of late.'

She snarled, sure that she would burst with outrage, spluttering, 'Why you low, dirty-minded . . . Of all the nerve . . . !'

But then other bodies insinuated themselves between her and Avon and she realized that the dock workers had been listening too, and were as indignant at his insulting slur of a statement as she was.

Four burly fellows with plenty of muscle gained from their daily toil on the Bristol waterfront made themselves into a human wall which blocked her view of Avon, while one of them bade her, 'Get off wiv ee, litlun, an' leave this moufy gert lummux to me an' me mates.'

246

May didn't need telling twice. The last of the dreary lethargy which had gripped her shaken off, she ran fleet of foot, not pausing even to look back once for the sake of curiosity. After all, she knew without doubt that Avon was going to take a licking and could derive as much satisfaction from the thought as from the spectacle.

Avon drew himself up haughtily in the face of such imposing adversity and issued a cold threat as his last means of defence. 'Lay so much as a hand on me and I'll see you all out of jobs, so help me I will. You'll none of you work these docks again.'

'Ha! Ee down't scare me an' me mates, Mr Fancy Dresser. No, indeed ee down't. I ain't no weak wench o' tender yurs.' And so saying, the curly, black-headed, swarthy skinned stevedore, backed up eagerly by his accomplices, launched himself at Avon, who – although he stood his ground with an arrogant foolhardiness – went down without too great a delay beneath a combination of blows, and then had the good sense to stay put – however undignified and infuriating that might be for one so proud – until they had sauntered off, honour satisfied, and gone back about their work.

He dragged himself up, grimacing once at the filth on his clothes and again at the pain in his jaw which felt as though knocked out of place by several wooden mallets. Then, becoming erect like some grenadier on parade, he repaired to his cab and ordered the driver away with calm authority, as if the fracas had never been. The driver was left to wonder whether the man was to be reviled as a fool or admired for his unfailing self-discipline.

May had slowed by the time she reached the Christmas Steps and began to climb past a hotch-potch of terraced, bow-windowed, multi-paned and sometimes leaded Victorian and Regency shop fronts, her breath coming in painful gasps, and still confused by Avon's unexpected behaviour. His strange, possessive nature concerning herself was disquieting to May, and this latest example sent unpleasant chills up her spine. Why wouldn't he leave her alone? The trouble was that her rebuffs didn't seem to register at all. He ignored and dismissed them almost as if they had no importance, as if his wants and wishes came before all else – especially the wishes of others. And now too, adding to her distress, he had obtained an extra form of ammunition; he could use his knowledge of her unsanctified union with Jude to coerce her into greater amenability. There seemed no escape, whichever way she looked at things. Sooner or later she was set for a fall.

She climbed the final, forty-ninth step onto the pavement at the top, and was about to cross the road outside of the almshouses and chapel of the Three Kings of Cologne, when Avon Midwinter stepped before her from nowhere yet again and snatched successfully for her wrist. Forcefully, and ignoring her vociferous protests, he manhandled her towards his cab, as singularly determined as ever that his wishes be carried out.

'I *will* see you home, Miss Bird.'

'But I prefer to walk!' she spat, catching his shin with a well aimed stab of her pointed-toed boot as he swung her up into the front opening of the hansom, then jumped up beside her before she might escape, holding her there imprisoned in her seat.

Black lacquered, low-level doors closed in about their legs and then the cab was under way, Avon calling up behind him to the driver, 'Beaufort Rise, cabbie.'

May ceased her useless struggling and sat stiffly, seething quietly while he smirked beside her, her eyes steadfastly focused on the road seen ahead through the upstanding ears of the horse which pulled them.

'I'll not stand for much more of your current attitude, Mr Midwinter, I warn you. I'll tell Mr Goodbody,' she told him coolly, trying hard to keep calm, and regain her dignity.

But he smiled sneeringly, his grey eyes narrow and slanting and full of contempt for her feeble threat. 'I don't think you will. Because if you did I might just have to mention to him about you and that yankee.'

'Just *what* do you know about me and Jude, I'd like to know?' she demanded.

'Ah, now that would be telling. My ace remains my secret, and thereby I retain the advantage.'

'But blackmail is useless. I have nothing with which to buy your silence.'

His laugh was superior; a low, acid rumble in his throat. 'You have yourself, and that is the price I shall ask. But not just yet. Oh, dear, sweet May, don't look so stricken. I'll not demand you hoist your skirts here and now, have no fear. I tell you only that you may grow accustomed to the idea and resigned to the fact.'

May shook her head vehemently, her mouth twisting in disgust. 'No! I'd rather go to Mr Goodbody myself and confess all.'

'Acting the martyr doesn't altogether suit you,' he opined cynically. 'I caution you to do nothing in haste. Anyhow, you angelic looking slut, as I've said, I'm not yet of a mind to collect any debt. You may have time to consider while I am occupied in America at the Charleston branch of my business. I've taken it upon myself to go to inspect my colonial counterparts in person to assure myself that they run things as profitably as is possible. So you are reprieved.'

'It matters not how long I have to consider. My answer will not alter.'

Avon shrugged, unconvinced by May's show of noble integrity, then caught her to him and forced a kiss upon her furiously spluttering mouth.

Released, she wiped the back of her hand across her lips, as if the touch of him were poisonous, and lashed out in an attempt to slap his face.

As ungentle as ever, he thwarted the attempt with a steely grasp of fingers about her wrist and cautioned; 'Careful. Don't you see that we've arrived home? Act normally or your guardian may ask awkward questions.'

She snarled wordlessly at his abundant confidence and nerve and even had to suffer his helping her down onto the pavement for fear that their arrival might be watched and conduct noted.

'Good-day, Miss Bird,' Avon wished her insincerely, his

voice sarcastic to the extreme as he showed her to the steps of her home.

'I sincerely hope that your ship sinks!' she hissed hatefully to him under her breath whilst sporting a fixed smile.

CHAPTER 29

Secretly at night, when she was supposed to be in bed, May unpicked the seams of her dresses by candlelight and let them out to their limits, her greatest fear being that she would betray herself by so suddenly growing out of all her garments.

But the changes were subtle, and her bodice coped with womanly breasts and waistband merely slipped upwards as corsets were meanly loosened. Obediah commented on her plump, healthy appearance in complimentary vein, and that, it seemed, was all the note that anyone gave to an outward appearance that so completely and convincingly concealed the drastic changes within.

No one guessed. But then, why should they? Could Obediah be expected even to contemplate his dearest charge doing anything so disgraceful as falling pregnant? Of course not! She was still only fourteen, a child in his eye who had but lately taken her first exploratory steps towards the threshold of womanhood. He could never have so much as *thought* of her capacity for such wickedness.

Because they trusted her so, she was never suspected. And, while May took comfort from the fact, it somehow also heightened her shame.

The uncertainties and side effects May also suffered alone, steadfastly not allowing herself to exhibit a sickly appearance, and shirking none of the heavier household chores it had ever been her lot to help Mrs Veysey with.

Whatever discomfort she might feel she suffered silently, there being no one with whom she might safely share her troubles, and eventually the sickness went of its own accord and she felt almost well, her strong constitution standing her in good stead.

One day she looked from her bedroom window and watched as Avon Midwinter departed, his travelling cloak fashionably cut from blue wool with velvet frogged collar, his collapsible 'Gibus' top-hat held gracefully in his hand as he climbed aboard a luggage-laden coach. And then, not only did May feel well, but the cloud which had most darkened her existence of late departed too, leaving her feeling that despite her treachery and the resulting calamitous sadness, she might, if fate continued to be kind, survive this awful time in her life without harming others and herself too greatly.

Optimism abounded around that time when she first felt a flutter of life within her, the baby's quickening lending new substance to the manner in which he existed in May's head. She, on an emotional high, romanticizing the future, visualized Jude returning to wed her and give a name to a son who would be just like him, only in miniature. And she would call her son Jon after her dearly remembered playmate of yesteryear and Obediah, coming to love Jude as much as she did, would forgive them their sinning and bless their union vowed in Church.

Oh, *if only*, she was to lament more than once, dreams *could* become reality.

Months, then whole seasons passed, the festivities of Christmas seemed to rush by in a colourful, gay moment of elusive pleasure; then the coldest, most uncharitable months of bad weather, until – although May wished with dread that time would stand still – the month of March was upon her, when, she had calculated, she would be delivered of the child. All time, from then on, was borrowed.

She had saved enough money so that at least during her confinement she could afford food and help. Afterwards she would have to work, maybe farm labouring or suchlike. May contemplated the possibility without relish, but knowing that such employment would almost certainly guarantee that she could keep her child with her. Many were the babies who found themselves strapped to their mothers' backs as they worked on the land through the summer months. Thus she envisaged the future; neither over-optimistic, nor too gloomy either, seeing herself accommodated in some humble tied property upon the domain of an unspecified landed gentleman of the upper-classes.

She would not give in to fear of a far more accurate picture; she would not acknowledge the possibility of landing up on the streets. She knew of such things after all, for wasn't Anne always returning home with woeful tales of those unfortunates she helped with her charity work? The cities were full of waifs and beggars who couldn't get jobs through lack of education or lack of seasonal demand, full, too, of young women who had come originally from good, though impoverished homes, who had, for differing reasons, ended up homeless and so desperate that they then sold the use of their bodies. According to Anne – who lent a sympathetic ear to their tragic retellings of fatefully unhappy and sordid pasts – the cause of their fall was often a child born out of wedlock and a father who then shirked his responsibilities. There was more than one governess in Bristol who had been impregnated by her employer then put out on the street to fend for herself, usually taking up the only kind of work left to her as an outcast from society – prostitution.

Such things May *wouldn't* think about. A whole summer lay ahead before she must face her first winter alone, and she felt certain that she would find a stable situation that, even if they were impoverished, would keep her from contemplation of starvation and prostitution alike.

Besides the money hidden at the back of one of the drawers in her pine tallboy, May had also amassed a selection of baby linens. The tiny silk embroidered gowns and caps, stockings and undervests had been Jon's, and it pricked May's conscience to spirit them away from the trunk in the old nursery where they had been neatly folded and stored, presumably for the next generation. But, counter-acting against her guilt at having committed theft, was a feeling – which came, not just from within her, she was certain – that Jon would have been, indeed *was*, pleased to have her use his layette for her baby.

So much time was spent in hiding and worrying about the physical changes which pregnancy brought, that May never really had a chance to enjoy the wonders of the experience. When he kicked or thrust out a limb, seemingly irate at the merciless confining imposed by her bodices, May had, of necessity, to try to act as if nothing had occurred, to smile through the shock of the infant's assault upon the walls of his prison. There was nothing more ludicrous or nerve-racking than trying coolly to beat Obediah at cards – to deal, concentrate, calculate and still hope to win – whilst feeling as if one's abdomen housed a giant, constantly working churn!

May longed constantly for the retiring hours, when she could close her bedroom door and uncase her over-active, protesting body which seemed now to be ever at the mercy of the tiny being within it. It was so strong, its shoving elbows and knees so often causing May to hold her breath and visibly wince, that she never doubted it would be a boy, and took a measure of comfort from the fact. He would continue to be strong after birth, she imagined, and would grow to be a healthy boy well able to look after himself. The stigma of his birth would forever be a burden but if he was strong and proud despite it and she gave him love and plenty of support, May believed that they could manage and build some sort of life for themselves that had quality.

The dreaded day arrived looking no different than any other, the weather hesitant about taking on too many spring-like characteristics just yet. The wind was keen and sun weak, barely lifting the temperature to a comfortable level above freezing, and, when the family assembled for breakfast that particular morning, cottons were forsaken yet again for snugger woollen garments.

To May the lingering cold weather was in part a blessing, for it gave her an excuse to keep swathing herself in shawls and lace neckerchiefs which camouflaged her shape. Unfortunately her pallor was not so easily overlooked and Obediah noted it as he glanced down the pristine white-clothed length of table to her position on the right beside Anne.

'Are you quite well, dear girl?'

May moved a kidney about her plate without appetite, her eyes dull beneath drooping lids from lack of sleep. All night she had moved restlessly upon her bed, in no pain but certainly uncomfortable, her mind so active and full of garbled thought-dreams that it was impossible to settle and completely drift away.

'Yes, I'm well,' she reassured, smiling for his benefit. 'I couldn't sleep; that's all.'

'You look peaky to me, despite the encouragingly robust changes to your person of late. I hope you're not going down with something. Try using a warming pan tonight. There's nothing like warm sheeting, I find, for speeding one off to sleep. We can't have you being ill, especially with the weather still so uncooperative. Health problems always seem to manifest themselves in bad weather and be worsened by it.'

May could read him like a book at times and knew that he was thinking about Jon who had perished during another spring's approach. And she was quick to allay his fears, though guilt at the spoken falsehoods stained her cheeks pink. 'I'm never sick, that's a fact. And I don't intend being so in the foreseeable future. Really, there is no need for worry. I'm much more concerned about what you call my robust appearance. Mrs Veysey must take the blame in part. Her desserts and puddings of late have proven irresistible and I confess to having over-indulged on several occasions.'

'Then what you need is exercise,' Jasper opined. 'You should take up tennis or suchlike.'

'Will you teach me?'

'Good grief, no! I'd never live it down. You'll have to join a club. There are some now that do not object to female members, though of course they're still banned from the club houses.'

Anne snorted. 'It really is *too* bad that women are continually treated so. Why, in heaven's name, shouldn't they be allowed into the club houses?'

'Oh, come now, Anne,' Obediah reasoned on the lesser experienced Jasper's behalf, his words greatly resembling those of a hundred generations of males before him when presented with such female argument. 'We gentlemen simply must have our exclusive male preserves – it's tradition.'

'Tradition indeed!' she riled derisively. 'Cloaking it in grandiose terms hides not the true nature of your words. Tyranny perpetuated by the male of the species against the female is what it really is.'

'Anne, dear, don't raise your voice so. It's quite unseemly.'

'I beg your pardon, papa. But these matters concern me deeply.'

'But I don't see why. Can you not simply accept that men are stronger, wiser and therefore superior?'

'No, papa, *I cannot*!'

'You're just jealous because you're inferior!' jeered Jasper.

'Now, son, there is no need to be unkind,' his father admonished, though Anne and May – bristling with united indignation – noted that he didn't contradict the youth.

Anne expelled her breath with a huff and attacked her bacon rasher angrily, realizing the futility of further argument. Start talking sense and men automatically closed ranks, she had found.

So breakfast passed and May came through it undetected, Anne and Jasper's bickering unwittingly acting as a diversion. The baby had stopped moving and a calm, quite unnerving peace had descended on May, warning her, so that she was able to rise from the dining table when the first weak and unalarming waves of labour coursed her abdomen, and ascend to her bedroom as if nothing were happening.

Anne came out into the hall and called up the stairs after her. 'Shall I have your company today at the church hall?

I've a ton of old donated clothes to sort through for the needy.'

To her own ears May's excuse sounded rather poor, but it seemed to satisfy the goodly Anne. 'Do you mind if I don't? Only I want to finish *David Copperfield* today.'

Anne laughed. 'A book by other than Mr Dickens and I'd not be so accommodating. Yes, stay home, May, and enjoy the final pages, just as I remember doing.'

'Say no more, Anne. If you tell me how the story ends I'll never forgive you!'

Anne's tittering faded as she returned to the dining room to help Mrs Veysey clear the silver from the sideboard, and May started across the landing, pausing and gazing through the open door into her guardian's room. He seemed to have returned there to find his favourite muffler, and stood before his cheval mirror as he wrapped the fine woollen garment about his stiffly collared and bow-tied throat.

Then May passed on, not wishing to disturb him, carrying that familiar picture of him with her and smiling. He and Jasper could be so typically male, so boorish and unfair, but nothing that Anne said in hot temper was ever going to change them. Obediah sincerely believed – because that was what every other male before him had ever been taught – that he *was* superior, and that women were weaker. And that was how he liked to think of them. A woman with too much of a mind of her own would have scared him. But to think of women as weak and frail, defenceless and in need of protection, well suited his chivalrous concepts. Women, to him, were for cherishing and saving. After all, it was because of his biased attitude, inbred from centuries of male domination, that May Bird had been delivered up from the clutches of evil and placed in his loving care. She had been too small and weak to look out for herself and so he had taken charge, dealing with all in a strong, just manner.

Oh, how she wished she had courage enough to go to him now, to be the young, frightened child again – which indeed was how she felt inwardly – and have him take charge. He'd know what to do, how to solve this terrible problem. Obediah, a large, ungainly man, with balding pate, squarelensed spectacles and a rotund form that ill suited his elegantly cut clothes, would have all the answers, and she could be a child again, could cry and be wretched, casting off the problems along with the tears shed on her guardian's shoulder.

But May lacked that sort of courage. Or maybe it was love of the man which stalled the impulse. He was too good and kind to be laden with such a problem. She didn't have the *right* to do that to him, must see this thing through on her own if she was ever to be a responsible adult in the future.

When Anne departed for the church hall beneath the parcelled weight of more clothing for the needy, and Jasper dawdled along the pavement on his way to school, rolling his beloved glass marbles before him. May began to fill her wicker shopping basket with all those things she had been hoarding over the last months. At nine o'clock Obediah's hired cab arrived to transport him to work and just before half-past Mrs Veysey called up the stairs to inform May that she was off shopping and wouldn't be back until it was time to cook dinner at midday.

Half an hour later May was gone. She wore her thickest woollen dress with her thickest woollen shawl and cloak on the top, and upon her head was her Sunday best bonnet, her arm through the handle of a basket crammed with those of her worldly possessions she most felt there would be future need of.

She looked back when she had reached the end of Beaufort Rise, hating to go yet seeing no real alternative, tears welling then flowing down pale cheeks as she wandered away, her diminutive, black figure stiffening with fear against the discomfort which had now taken a relentless hold.

The horse-omnibus – which travelled out to the rural communities in the suburbs – was full, the other passengers taking little note of the quiet, discreetly cloaked girl crammed in their midst. They passed farms and travelled lanes whose hedgerows of hawthorn had been laid out to form boundaries back in the days of the Norman Conquest. Not far away either, near the Avon's mouth, and more than a thousand years before, the invading Romans had taken to landing at and using Shirehampton as a west country port, building their mosaic decorated villas further inland at King's Weston. But nobody this day gave a thought for the history which lay all about them. Such things of familiarity and abundance they took very much for granted.

They made conversation with their neighbours concerning the business of the day, talked of visiting, going to market or, in the case of one linen-smocked labourer, of searching for a job upon the land, his former employer having laid him off to save on wages through the dormant winter months. He looked desperate and pessimistic, the poor-house looming as a dreadful prospect for his family, for even now they were surviving on charity and that couldn't last much longer. It seemed that there weren't enough fields to keep all would-be hedgers and ditchers gainfully employed this season.

May listened absently to the tale of woe, of wife and children facing eviction from their tied cottage, but she could muster up scant response in support. Her own dilemma was much too serious and presently critical to be bothering herself with his. And, when they halted by the large stone cross in the middle of some market town (which might have been Westbury-on-Trym, though muddled by pain, May wasn't entirely sure) she was relieved to be able to alight and then dismiss him entirely from her mind.

For a long while she stayed there, in the midst of a traffic circus with no clear idea of what to do next, watching the scattering of people going about their business in the small, though busy community. At the dinner hour shops shut and pub filled, and May trudged off with no clear plan in mind. She had thought to beg the help of some kindly looking woman or other and get herself safely to a midwife, but her discomfort was now such that decisive thought became difficult. She wandered, too fearful and ashamed to make the initial approach, thinking all the starched, proper looking women whom she passed in the streets to be too goodly to have any sympathy for a creature such as herself and willingly give the help May might beg.

Distressed and just a little disoriented by the mounting pain that had control of her body, she climbed the hilly path before her with slow, belaboured movements, half contemplating a rest at the top and formation of some sort of plan. But once there, beyond the clustered houses, events overtook her completely. Her labour became so intense that no longer could she truly lend her mind to anything else. She needed help but she was no longer capable physically of summoning it. Brows knit in a frown of pain, May laid cradling hands beneath her belly and walked falteringly, and sometimes stumbled as her body sagged and skirt hem tangled about ponderously treading feet. Leaving the path, she sought refuge within the discreet cover of a hillside copse to spare herself the horrendous possibility of giving birth on the edge of footpath.

The grey sky turned dark and, between her bouts of torment, May was aware of the night noises – of badgers leaving their sets and owls vacating their barns to soar white and eerie against the night sky, then perch aloft to hoot out their messages. Amongst the grass and nettles something stirred with a soft rustling and May could do little else save lie and worry, giving a startled gasp, then a sigh of relief, as a young rabbit hopped into the broken moonlight then out again.

Like an animal she gave herself up to instinct; howling mournfully when the experience reached a level not easily borne, and weeping at the unrelieved, cruel pain. Her body burned, a liquid stickiness and cramping, horrendous pain devouring her lower body, while her forehead was frosty cool, the perspiration which dulled her glorious hair, plastering it wetly against her brow, unpleasantly and unnaturally chilled.

After the pain there were moments of infinite relief and the realization that she had somehow survived the ordeal. Then came the emptiness and the fearful, terrible certainty that the baby had been born dead.

Weakly May struggled to sit up, her hands feeling about

tentatively in the all-consuming darkness, groping with terror amongst the blood and expelled tissue, searching by touch in the absence of the earlier silver moonlight, until her frantic fingers touched a tiny, still limb.

She lifted the cold, wet form reverently and clutched it to herself, her body racked by shuddering sobs of sublime pain. Her baby was dead and that, to May, was a cruelty worse than anything which had recently been exacted.

In the dark, with one sense denied her, the others became sharper, their acuteness only serving to make her torment worse. She could smell the blood, feel it and the rest upon her legs and on the grass which was her bed, could feel a tiny head and torso and bunched-up limbs. She pictured the infant in her mind, giving it features which the dark denied, and then sobbed the harder.

For minutes, maybe longer – for time was not easily judged and neither had it much importance for May, lost as she was in her misery – she rocked, stiff with pain, holding the baby to her, crying for herself and the final part of Jude now lost to her for ever. Then she seemed to rouse herself slightly, and in a pain induced haze, mechanically go about the necessary business of attending to the child.

She could not bear the thought of scratching some sort of grave for it amongst the trees, and instead cut and tied its cord with scissors and thread from her basket, wiped it clean as best she could and adorned it in one of Jon's baby night-gowns.

She would go back the way she had come, May told herself. There had been a church on the road into the town, a church with a vicarage. If she wrote a note on paper torn from her diary, begging the assistance of God's appointed servant on earth, surely the man, finding the sad little corpse upon his doorstep with the coin upon it to pay for his services, would see that it, innocent being that it was, was properly lain to rest?

Forced by circumstance to be rational, May came to her feet unsteadily and endured the long dark walk back into the town, her petticoats tied haphazardly about her legs to try contain the bleeding, and her possessions removed from her basket and bundled now into her shawl which she had knotted and slung over her shoulder. The baby she had placed in her basket, lying it, wrapped in a fine woollen blanket, upon a bed of clothing it would never need, like a fledgling in a nest, then draping a final, concealing shawl of fringed cashmere over the basket.

Devastated and weak, May could think no further than that. Once she had placed the infant safely into God's hands there wasn't, surely, *anything* to follow? It had ended, for her, when the reason for being – life itself – faded and died, cheating her of its existence. She didn't want to go on any longer.

CHAPTER 30

When May – absent all day without even the vaguest of reasons – failed to arrive home in time for supper on the evening of March 12th, Obediah began to pace uneasily, beside himself with concern. He questioned family and housekeeper yet again, begging them to own up without fear of punishment if they were covering for the mischievous absentee. But they truly had no idea where she might be or why, and were, in truth, as fearful as himself despite uttered assurances to the contrary.

'She's likely called in somewhere for tea and been talked into staying for supper as well.'

'Yes. After all, she is *very* popular,' Jasper added. 'Or maybe she joined one of the neighbourhood tennis clubs like I suggested and is taking all night to finish her first game. I doubt her play'll be up to much, not if her talent for tennis is anything like it was for ping-pong. She was useless!'

'Yes, maybe,' hoped Obediah, though he seemed unconvinced by the suggestion. 'But it's so unlike her to be late home without letting me know. She's always so considerate – loath to have me worry on her behalf.'

By ten o'clock the poor man could stand it no longer and had contacted the police down at the city Bridewell, taking little comfort from the fact that they were able to assure him that nobody answering her description had yet found its way to the mortuary off York Street.

No one slept that night and Mrs Veysey, giving in to the occasional tear of worry, brewed one pot of tea after another and prepared plates of cucumber sandwiches which no one had appetite enough to eat.

Dawn had come and found Obediah alternately scouring the nearest streets in the hope of spotting her on her way home, or else prowling with much snorting of helplessness about the house. What could he do? Where should they start looking? God, he prayed, calling on the Almighty – despite his former lack of religious faith – in a bid to leave no possibility overlooked, please God, bring her home safe and sound to the family who so mightily love her. If Birdy were taken, gone to join Jessie and Jon – God forbid! It was unbearable even to think of it; Obediah doubted he could live through the pain. She meant as much as his own children, was the bright spark who warmed and cheered them all, filling the whole house with her bountiful, unbegrudged wealth of spirit.

Obediah couldn't face work and was understanding when Jasper begged to be excused school. Together they stood in the elegant bay window and watched the road both ways, while Anne and Bertha Veysey tried to do simple, undemanding chores such as the dusting – a Meissen figurine falling victim to their absentminded clumsiness. Dashed to smithereens upon the marble hearth, the expensive china piece was consigned to the dustpan by Bertha, its loss as nothing compared to the present woefully dire situation. She wasn't about to lament the destruction of a mere material possession when the very life of someone she held dear might be in jeopardy or already lost, though God forbid, she too was loath to think about that.

Noon had come and gone, with no one much interested in dinner, when Bertha, positioned at the bay window, watched without great interest the progress of a cart coming down Beaufort Rise. Only when it stopped unexpectedly before the steps of the Goodbody household was her curiosity truly roused. And then she stiffened, gasped dreadfully and banged on the window pane to alert Obediah who was standing farther down the street on the corner, his eyes darting hopefully in all directions, longing for the sight of a well-known figure with young and sprightly step.

When her frantic knocking failed to alert him, Bertha thrust up the sash window violently and yelled without mind for such unseemliness before her neighbours, pointing at the cart, and then he came at a run which turned his face red with the exertion, his chestnut eyes full of fear.

The children, brought running from other rooms in the house by the housekeeper's outburst, ran behind her down the steps to the cart, their father arriving breathlessly gasping only a moment later.

The carter, dressed in corduroy and homespun much patched and mended, with a felt hat pulled down over his ears and moth-eaten scarf knotted about his neck in a vain attempt at retaining some body warmth, gave them but a cursory glance as he let down the tailgate and afforded them their first glimpse of May. They had known – sensed – that she was on the cart, but they were unprepared for the terrible vision that met their eyes.

Lying on a bed of parsnips and potatoes which presumably were destined for some market, was her unconscious form and a lumpy bundle beside it, her face quite grey and skirts stained black with her own blood.

Bertha squealed with horror and drew away, her collar feeling too tight and air intake somehow suddenly inadequate as a faint threatened.

'Oh, good grief!' cried Obediah, leaping forward and clutching May to him, thankful beyond belief to find her warm still and alive, *just*.

'Poor May!' Anne gasped, fighting back her emotions.

And Jasper, fretting and completely bewildered, wondered aloud, 'What's happened to her?'

The carter wasted not his attention on one so young and insignificant, turning instead to a distraught Obediah who knew she must be moved but feared that doing so was going to cause her more suffering.

'I take it ee do know this wench then?'

'Yes, oh yes,' acknowledged Obediah.

'Good. I din't know fer sure whether bringing 'er 'ere

265

were the right fing ta do. I found 'er crumpled at side'a road t'other side'a Westb'ry wiv a few fings tied up in a shawl. There were nuffin ta tell I who she be save this 'ere book wiv the writin' in front. Me schoolin' ain't too good but I knew the word Clifton frum sign posts an' when I reached this 'ere district did show the writin' to a copper an' explain bout findin' the wench. Ee give I good instructin' bout 'owta git 'ere.'

'I am eternally grateful,' Obediah thanked him, tearful with sincerity.

'It be me duty as a God-fearin' cit'zun. Now I'll give ee a 'and inside wiv 'er if ee like, then be on me way. Market'll be over afore I do git thur otherwise,' said the carter, calmly and sensibly.

'You are a good fellow. Yes, if you could carry her forth I'd be so obliged, for I am not, despite my girth, a man of much strength.'

'And in the meantime, Jasper, you run to the church hall and get the doctor. He's not the family doctor, I know, but he's nearer and, I think, better suited to deal with May,' instructed Anne, deciding what was best.

Obediah worried, in a dither of fear and uncertainty, following the capable carter up the stairs, the lolling form of May moaning unconsciously from time to time in the man's strong arms.

It was the carter's opinion that, 'She do look vury much like she miscarried or the like. Least ways what ails 'er be summut along them lines.'

And Obediah digested that possibility in shocked silence, hardly able to credit it, save for the evidence of his own eyes and the lurking knowledge that it would have had to be a reason *that* serious to have forced May away from the home where she had always been so happy. He felt the tears come and was still crying mournfully when the doctor arrived and carter had been paid for his time and trouble and allowed to go on his way, reluctant to accept Obediah's coin and mumbling to the effect that it felt wrong to profit from an unfortunate female's misfortune. But Obediah insisted, glad above all else to have her back. A harder, more callous

266

man with neither time to spare nor another being's welfare uppermost in mind, might merely have dumped May at the nearest poor house or even, perish the thought, have left her to her fate at the side of the road! A handful of silver was little enough payment for the carter's goodness.

For an hour he paced on the landing outside her door, while the doctor and Anne cleaned her up and tended to her, anxiously waiting to know if she would live or die. And when, at length the doctor appeared to assure him that she would, with care, recover completely, Obediah gave himself up to tears again and was advised by the doctor to have a liberal measure of brandy.

Obediah gave a declining shake of the head and smiled weakly, not wishing for the dulling effects of alcohol on his already shock-numbed wits. He saw the doctor down the stairs to the front door, leaving Anne to sit with the still unconscious casualty, and bumbled his way through a series of embarrassing questions.

'What happened to her, doctor?'-

'One can't be certain, and we'll know better when she comes to and is able to tell us herself. But from my examination I'd say she delivered a full term baby. Had you no idea?'

'No,' said Obediah, nonplussed and feeling a shade ridiculous at such an admission, his head indulging, of its own volition, in a series of slow disbelieving shakes. 'There were no signs at all. Nothing. I thought only that perhaps she was getting a little plump.'

The doctor shook his head. 'There is not an ounce of spare fat upon her frame, Mr Goodbody. She must have ate very sparingly indeed in order to gain only the minimum necessary weight. I presume the baby died at birth. Infant mortality is usually the outcome in such circumstances. Without the assistance of a midwife there is little hope. You really should have that drink; you look pale and in some distress. This is not the first case of concealed pregnancy I have dealt with and neither is it as uncommon as you might think. Your daughter and I work closely together on community health and welfare projects, usually giving free medical attention to the sick who are too poor to pay. She has requested that I, as a friend, should not probe too deeply into this case. Is that your wish also?'

'I . . . Yes, I suppose it is. In truth I haven't given the legal aspects of this too much thought. I'm so . . . so upset, I cannot think. Everything is becoming too much for me to cope with.'

'Then I should leave it to Anne. She is a very sensible, competent person. Concern yourself only with nursing Miss Bird back to health and the rest will of its own accord just fade away and be thus resolved without being made the knowledge of all.'

'Indeed that is sensible, doctor, and I thank you for being so understanding. Ruining her reputation on top of everything else can serve no good purpose at all. Much better not to seek the truth.'

'Quite. Good-day, sir. I shall call again tomorrow to see Miss Bird, though if it is more convenient for you to do so, you are at liberty to say it is a social visit and that I have come to see Anne. We have discussed it and she is agreeable. Neighbours can, I know, be exceedingly nosy when it comes to the mystery illnesses of others and will ask all manner of prying, tricky questions without compunction.'

'Thank heavens for a wise daughter and compassionate doctor. What should I have done without you both? More than likely succumbed to feminine hysterics, I think.'

The doctor laughed with soft politeness as he passed through the doorway and started down the steps to the street.

May raised her eyelids and saw with surprise Anne seated beside her in her own familiar bedroom. How came she to be back home again? Then again, did it matter how? She was happy it was so, should like to die in her own bed with the people she had loved about her. Her body weak and mind bathed in grief, she relived again those awful hours in the cold darkness of the wood where her baby had been born, though, why oh why, not alive!

And it had all been for nothing, the lying, concealment

and deceit, for here she was mysteriously brought home and now she would have to die knowing that the truth was known to all and that she would be remembered always with shame. She sobbed wretchedly at the thought and wished herself back walking dazedly like a drunkard along some road which led she had known not where.

Anne caught her hand and rubbed it while her voice came to May's ears, urgent and enquiring. 'May? May, can you hear me?'

'Sorry,' was all the girl on the bed could find it in her to say; her lips – not their usual inviting red but pale and bloodless looking – trembling as she tried to keep control over a mass of shattered senses.

Anne ran from the room, then almost immediately returned with Obediah, allowing him to come forward and staying back herself to hover, in case she was needed, near the foot of the bed.

It wrenched at May's heart the harder to see her own anguish and pain mirrored on his tear-crumpled face and again all she could say, even though she knew it to be totally inadequate was, 'Sorry.'

'It doesn't matter. My sweetest child we're only glad to have you back – to know that you will be well again.'

'I will?' she wondered weakly, the thought, at that moment in time, giving her no real cause for joy.

'Yes, the doctor has assured us. With care you will be well again. But *why* did you go? We were so worried, so afraid for your safety.'

Her voice was feeble. 'I couldn't face you. You would be so disappointed. So ashamed of me. Running away seemed best. That way there was only my shame.'

'Oh, Birdy, if you'd been truly lost to us it would have broken all our hearts. No matter what you did we would still love you. You poor, silly girl, don't you understand? You should never have felt that you had to face this terrible ordeal alone. *Never.* I blame myself. Maybe you felt that I expected too much of you. But . . . Oh, *if only* you'd come to see me, told me! You're not yet fifteen and should never . . . Goodness, gracious . . . !'

He broke down, burying his face in the patchwork quilt as he sat beside the bed, and sobbing noisily, his whole, large body quivering with misery.

May could do little else save smooth the sparse hair on his head and beg him, 'Please don't. I cannot stand it. Your hurt is because of me and only adds to my shame.'

'I don't mean to make you feel more wretched. But I cannot help thinking, picturing you alone and frightened giving birth,' sniffed Obediah, sitting up again and striving, for her sake, to regain control.

'I wanted the baby so, despite all. But it was still and quiet at the birth and I knew in my heart that it was dead. It's best so, many would say, I know, yet the pain of that loss is almost too much to be borne,' sobbed May.

Anne, listening discreetly, wept into her handkerchief, but made no move to intrude upon their outpouring of grief. Obediah, who also knew first-hand the terrible desolation of losing a child, was, she felt, best qualified of them all to offer what little comfort there was.

The Reverend Redvers Partridge took a degree of delight in the solitude of his bachelor evenings that was, he often thought with a chuckle of secretive mirth, quite wicked and inappropriate in a man of the cloth. After days spent visiting parishioners, writing sermons and deep theological examination of thought, there was nothing to equal the pleasure of lounging before one's own cheery hearth with a glass of whisky or sherry and a clay pipe packed with a favoured brand of tobacco. He didn't have to be polite or remember to honour the collar about his neck and all that it stood for. He could be himself and, oh, that was such a relief at times! If he wanted, he might have one whisky or sherry *too* many and actually get tiddly, or play a tune unlikely to find favour with his stuffy congregation on his pianoforte in the privacy of his own parlour, his dog Snarler howling along in accompaniment.

The women of the parish threw their virginal daughters at him still, despite his forty years and a plain countenance, in the hope that eventually he must, surely, succumb to the charms of one and go traipsing down the aisle. Yet so far he had eluded them, finding little in any to make him want their company without foreseeable end. The only one he truly appreciated was Ethel Burton and that because she cooked the best Dundee Cake he was ever likely to taste, but she was already married and Redvers was glad, being quite content to forego any temptation.

On the evening of March 12th, 1850 he was seated at his small writing desk in the parlour making his latest entry in the parish register. He always worked that way, preferring to take home the paperwork during the early months of the year when the church vestry was chilly to say the least and greatly to be avoided.

Poor old Jackie Dean, dying before his time after labouring all his life on the land, had been buried that afternoon, the grave-digger having much trouble breaking through the frozen ground even with a pick-axe. Redvers had conducted the service, hurrying more than usual through the words from the Good Book so that he and the mourners could the sooner find warmth indoors, confident that no one had noticed. Certainly Jackie, who had had little time for the church during his life, was unlikely to have been much bothered by the less than thorough observance of Christian homage paid at his burial.

Redvers made the entry in a right-hand slanting scroll, then closed the heavy, leather and metal enforced binding of documents with a snap of finality, thinking that, for what it was worth, there had passed another life and that man seen against a universal background, was truly of scant significance. Everything went to dust and was eventually forgotten. He sighed, then smiled at Snarler who had come to sit beside him and take up a plaintive, insistent spate of whining.

'What's up with you then, boy?' Redvers wondered, intrigued by such uncharacteristic behaviour.

Snarler, a cross breed of dubious parentage, who mildly resembled one of those long-eared springer spaniels head-on, but was, when viewed from behind, more like a typical black and white border collie, left the parlour and went

271

along the passage with its threadbare carpet runner, to the front door, where he stood and barked, repeating the ritual twice more and with doubtless frustration, until Redvers took the hint and followed to investigate.

'Oh, *what* is it, Snarler, old boy? It's much too inclement to go out walking if that's what you're after,' the vicar told the dog shortly.

Snarler, whose name was the only truly vicious thing about him, woof-woofed insistently by way of reply. And then, in the hushed lull which followed, the man heard something and looked from dog to door then back again, smiling. 'I do believe you were trying to tell me that someone is out there. You're far cleverer than I sometimes give you credit for, aren't you?'

The Reverend Partridge opened the door and looked out only to find no one on his garden path, as he'd been expecting, but then he looked down to his front step where a wicker basket stood from which issued forth a protesting, faint mew-like noise.

'Well, bless my soul, what have we here? A kitten perhaps? Back, Snarler and behave. I know you've no liking for cats.'

He took hold of the handle and lifted the basket, a fine woollen shawl sliding off one side under the force of its own weight to reveal, to the man's utter astonishment, the tiny oval of a baby's face peeping from its swathe of blanket.

'Saints preserve us, a baby! Get out of the way, dog, weaving about under my feet like that. You're liable to trip me. Let's get this unexpected, extraordinary little visitor in by the fire. Now where do you suppose it came from?'

Back in the parlour with Snarler staying close and ever curious about the strange sounds which the baby made, Redvers Partridge contemplated picking it up and rocking it in hope of quieting its crying, but then thought better of it. He'd never been much good with babies, always exhibiting a nervous awkwardness at christenings when he was required to take them up and drip holy water on their foreheads before making the sign of the cross with accompanying intonements.

There was a pale blond, hardly visible fuzz of hair upon its crown, two tightly shut eyes, and a mouth that opened with greater frequency, now that the fire warmed its owner, to squall crossly and dominate an angry red face.

'I never thought to see the day, but it looks very much as if the pair of us have been lumbered with a foundling, Snarler. There's a note on what looks to me like the torn page of a diary, but it doesn't tell us much. How very sad for the mother one feels. All so tragically sordid. Evidently she thought the baby born dead and entreats me to give it decent burial. *So* pathetic.'

He read the words again, then aloud, their poignancy increasing in his mind the more he thought on them. 'I pray you'll bless this innocent child and see it safely into God's care, and forgive me, for wickedness was never truly in my heart.'

Redvers stood up and warmed his behind at the fire while he assessed the situation and decided what was to be done. He must be practical and not give in to sorrowing on others' behalfs. He needed immediate help for the baby and then he might deal with things in a broader context, decide on the child's future and so forth.

His sister, Dorothea, being a more practical soul than he, was his automatic choice for helper. He sent for her and she dutifully arrived shortly afterwards from the other side of town, voicing plainly her displeasure at being requested to journey abroad on so chilly a night, then setting methodically and coldly about the business of cleaning the baby and boiling cow's milk to feed it until a more satisfactory means of nourishment could be obtained.

Like himself she was unwed, devoting her life nowadays to the elementary education of the lower classes at the community school, but *her* spinster's state was not through choice but lack of male interest. She was a God-fearing, hard-working, plain-speaking, though unfortunately totally uncaptivating woman who, because of her brittle-sharp manner, touched no cord of tenderness within any man who knew her.

Moaning about the inconvenience the baby's appearance

was causing, she trickled the now cooled milk off a spoon and into its ever open mouth, scoffing (with a sneering superiority quite common in those of the teaching profession in Redvers' opinion) at his commenting on the deep blueness of the baby's eyes when they eventually cast an unseeing gaze upon the world for the first time.

'But most baby's eyes are blue, dear brother. Blue or brown. How silly that you should fail to know that,' she ridiculed.

'I've never had cause or want to be much involved with babies, sister, as you know,' he said defensively, fetching crumpets from the kitchen to toast upon the fire for want of something to do. Usually he was in bed by ten o'clock but there was scant possibility of that this night, he felt, and yawned as he wondered absently, chewing all the while on the hot buttered delicacy in his mouth, 'Is he all right – healthy, I mean, and in possession of all the appropriate bits and pieces?'

'He is a she, Redvers, and she is healthy enough to cause me little anxiety or immediate concern.'

'A *girl*? Ha, the thought never once crossed my mind. Well, well, well . . . Then, in honour of our gracious queen and her daughter, the Princess Royal, I hereby name her Victoria.'

Part 3
Jonah

CHAPTER 31

In the summer of 1850 Isambard Kingdom Brunel was invited by the Dean of Bristol to take a look at some supposed defects in the structure of the ancient cathedral which had formerly been St Augustine's Abbey. It was a minor undertaking which some may have felt did not warrant the engineer's special talents – a trifling matter that could have been left to any available and *cheaper* architect – but the Dean wanted Brunel and so he obliged, fitting a flying visit into his always tight schedule.

A snippet of his written reply to the worthy cleric read, 'shall give a couple of hours for a cursory inspection to form some opinion . . . Can be at the cathedral at 5 o'clock on Tuesday morning next, having to leave Bristol by train to Exeter, at 7.50 . . . '

Such irregular working hours were not the Dean's and he needed the aid of two alarm clocks to rouse him at such an un-Godly hour, then he trudged over the cathedral greens with half his mind still wrapped in the unreality that follows a spate of dreaming. He'd hardly reached the great Norman arch that protected the mighty doors than the engineer was striding up to shake his hand and introduce himself.

Overnight chill still lingered on that crisp bright morning as piers in the nave, the chancel, chapter house and high altar at sanctuary were looked over, and dimensions and points of stress thereof mentally noted.

The Augustinian splendour was, Mr Brunel finally

277

decided, in need of no drastic restoration and could, for another quarter century, function normally with the minimum of repairs and maintenance, and future generations would be required to put right most of time's natural ravages.

After Exeter and the satisfactory execution of business there, Mr Brunel then travelled back to Bristol and as arranged, took a late tea at the Goodbodys.

It was Mrs Brunel's idea that May should spend some time with her at Westminster, London, and Isambard, having gained Obediah's approval for such a temporary change to his ward's address, had come to collect her.

He had hardly been prepared for the change in her. A year (for it had been such since he had last seen her) had done away with all but the lingering memory of the child she had been.

This new May was quiet and careful, not ready either to lapse into easy conversation or one of her old and habitual giggling fits. He found her disquieting, her prim and properness like steel armour that kept him and everyone else at a distance. He despaired of ever finding the old Birdy again, and feared that Mary's invitation had been a mistake, for once at Duke Street, safely ensconced in the bosom of his family, with his young sons and daughter eager to be friends, she seemed to find it impossible to join in, save in a polite, detached manner.

Hours that should have been spent upon the completion of technical drawings for his engineering concerns were eaten away instead in speculation as to what had changed her. Could it be love unrequited? She was of an age to suffer from such, after all. And that American, of whom she had seemed inordinately fond, *had* sailed off and left her. It might be, yes. But then again, it wasn't like Birdy to suffer so from such natural disasters. As long as he'd known her she always bounced back, smiling bravely and taking strength from those about her. This time, though, she seemed to want nothing from anyone, enduring alone almost as if to punish herself.

If Obediah had told Isambard what had happened during that year while the engineer was absent from Bristol, then everything, naturally, would have fallen into place, and he could have understood her better and been easier in his own mind. But her secret was the Goodbodys and *their*'s alone, and they all guarded it with their lives.

Mary Horsley-Brunel's family were all notable musicians, her father and brother famous composers and pianists and she, when pressed politely, played passably well on the pianoforte, though with none of their feeling or finesse. Her overall delight came from listening to the music made by others professionally employed. Isambard was not given to such appreciation, and Mary therefore had May to accompany her instead, the young girl only truly able to relax and come alive, Brunel's wife noticed, when the rhapsody's overwhelming strains found a chink in her armour.

Mary, left very much to her own devices by a husband who channelled the greater part of his energy into work, never became resentful or accused him of neglect. She absorbed herself in the children, in music and in the social whirl. May trailed dutifully behind – and hopefully in Mary's shadow – in awe most of the time.

At a performance of yesteryear's composers Bach, Mozart and Schumann, she stood statue-like amongst the rest of the respectfully erect throng as queen and consort entered the auditorium, of a mind, it would appear, to join their humble subjects in an appreciation of sound, good music. The monarchy for May held fairytale connotations, all mystique and majesty, and she was nigh on scandalized to peep sideways only to find Mary treating the whole amazing moment with something that bordered on blasé disregard. May could only assume that seeing the queen in the flesh regularly, and moving in such exalted circles, were everyday occurrences to Mrs Brunel and thus to be thought little of.

Such was the constant excitement that May was to some extent bombarded out of the gloom which had so thoroughly afflicted her, and she could see that Obediah had been wise to accept the Brunels' invitation despite her objections. It wasn't that she hadn't wanted to see Isambard. Of course she did. Rather she felt bad and sullied, a miserable creature not fit to keep their company and deserving of all the woes that had befallen her. She was wicked. *Wicked*. And that was why everything had been taken from her, even the baby which had been proof of her sinful, unworthy ways.

But one could only think along those foolish, destructive lines for so long. Obediah said she wasn't bad and even got angry with her when she insisted it was true. Now, with the pain dulling and the episode fading with time, she was beginning to realize that it was dead and gone and really should be buried. It would ever be there in her mind, but she should start anew for the sake of the others if nothing else. She owed it to them. Having inflicted her treachery upon them she really shouldn't saddle them with her misery as well.

Bit by bit, therefore, May returned to something that more greatly resembled her former self, and those about her sighed with relief and were once again at their ease and willingly enthralled all over again.

Mary's brother, John, played Chopin (whose black framed memorial tin-type had pride of place on the wall above her piano, the 'master' having died at the end of the previous decade), Liszt, Mozart and Schubert, but for the rest – the operas and the like – they haunted Covent Garden and missed few of the performances, some mutual favourites being Donizetti's operatic *Lucia di Lammermoor* and anything by that erstwhile wonder of the violin, Paganini. His music made them cry, so superb were the beautiful compositions. Those who strove to duplicate his delight in sound had their work cut out, his genius a frustration to all others, and Mary and May could see in part, why those terrible stories about him had first taken form. Maybe he *had* sold his soul to the devil in exchange for the beauteous sounds emanating from his strings and bow. Many said so. Whatever, for five years after the poor Paganini's death, the Church refused to allow his burial on consecrated ground!

'For myself,' Mary would sigh, almost brusquely dismissive of such superstitious idiocy, 'I think rather that his music had more to do with heaven than hell and that those who would have us believe otherwise are asses!' And May had wholly agreed.

1851 came around quickly, time seeming, as ever, to rush on when there was so much to occupy it. It was the year of the Great Exhibition, with the Empire preening itself before an impressed world, all that was best about Britain displayed in an iron, glass-faced palace designed by Joseph Paxton which would later inspire Brunel the engineer in his planning of a new passenger station at Paddington. Isambard was involved in an advisory capacity as a committee member, along with Prince Albert, exhibits for the machine section display there only on his say-so. Thus it was no real surprise to find his friend, Daniel Gooch's latest and greatest broad-gauge Flyer *Lord of the Isles* given pride of place on a plinth at the very centre of the exhibits. Exponents of the narrow-gauge system could only fume in silence, completely out-manoeuvered. Yet it was the sparrows trapped within the structure who initially stole the show, putting the whole exhibition in jeopardy and capturing the nation's interest. The story carried on for weeks in *The Illustrated News*, the queen herself eventually voicing misgivings about building a glass structure around a tree full of lesser birds. Something had to be done. And quite right too, Isambard had thought wryly. One couldn't have one's monarch covered in sparrow droppings come the day of the grand opening. What a sight that would have been . . . what a humiliation! She and Albert, with their representatives, lording it over the visiting foreign dignitaries and businessmen looking for new marketing outlets, and the whole thing overshadowed by a twittering mass of bowel emptying sparrows!

And then, and somewhat to Isambard's disappointment, the Iron Duke, old Wellington, came to the queen's rescue with what would ever be his most famous directive of unwarlike nature, 'Get sparrowhawks, ma'am.'

Unwelcome residents quickly annihilated by such birds of prey, the Great Exhibition opened on time without hitch or embarrassment. The Brunels went, of course, feeling it their duty to partake in such a once-in-a-lifetime spate of flag-waving jingoism. Mary and May took charge of young Isambard, Henry Marc and Florence, treating them to several visits to the sweet stand that sold confection from the four corners of the empire, while their father sauntered, his expression giving nothing away, around the engineering stands of foreign competitors. He was well-known; his fame, it seemed, had spread across all the major continents. And people – engineers like himself – came to shake his hand and pay their respects, many voicing their open admiration and own inadequacies in comparison. He listened to all, politely dismissive of their praises yet never-the-less greatly satisfied by the experience.

By the spring of 1852 letters alone could no longer keep the Goodbody household satisfied. They wanted May to come home, writing to her individually and applying their own unique brands of emotional blackmail. May and the Brunels succumbed to the pressure and reluctantly they relinquished her, though only on the understanding that she was to spend a summer holiday with them the following year.

When May's carriage pulled away from the forecourt of Temple Meads Station on its way to Clifton and got caught in a traffic jam within sight of the terminus, she was to find herself – amazed by the coincidence – beside a hackney carrying Avon Midwinter. Like the proverbial Bad Penny, he seemed to be forever turning up.

Evidently, during her absence in London, he had returned from his business trip to America, older (he was then twenty-five), immaculate as always in his dress, and showing but faint signs of debauchery. He was good at concealing his inner self from others. Only the lines of dissipation around his mouth and eyes were more apparent than they had been when last May had been unfortunate enough to be forced into an encounter with him.

She thought about turning her head the other way, of unfurling her parasol, perhaps, and shielding her face from him, but then she shook her head, no longer of a mind to be intimidated by him. After all, she wasn't now the uncertain fourteen-year-old he used to think he could bully and black-mail. Three years had passed since then and she felt stronger in her self, certainly able to face him, for, most importantly, he no longer had a hold over her, any attempts at blackmail futile. And, of a sudden, she couldn't wait to tell him so.

She called to her driver to stop and then called to the passenger in the coach now parallel with her carriage, 'Why, Avon Midwinter! How was your trip to America?'

Her appearance, so near and so beautiful in amber velvet coat and muff, with a crepe and petersham trimmed bonnet to match, took him by surprise and for a moment there was unmasked delight upon his face. He barked to his driver to halt also and set his sharp-nosed features into an habitual, thoroughly insincere smile, his thin lips barely achieving a curve.

'Ah, Miss Bird, it's such a pleasure to see you after so long. The girl has become a woman, and a delightful one too.'

'Your tongue is as smooth as ever, sir.'

'And yours as cruel. Tell me, do you remember our last conversation?'

'Oh, but of course,' trilled May gaily, her whole being somehow buoyant and mirthful at the thought of outwitting him. 'You thought to blackmail me. Isn't that correct?'

'Well . . . I wouldn't have put it quite *that* way. Persuade is a better word, I think,' he drawled, leaning nonchalantly on the sill of his coach's open window.

'Whatever, it really doesn't matter, because, you see, it won't work. Mr Goodbody knows all about me and the American,' informed May, smiling, green eyes bright.

Avon raised a quizzical eyebrow, his impressed look and words far from genuine. 'Does he, indeed? Well, well, Miss Bird, I'd never have thought you had it in you to come clean and confess.'

She hadn't, of course, but she wasn't about to tell him that. 'So in future I'd be obliged if you'd leave me alone. I'll not tolerate your pesterings now that there's no longer a good reason to endure them. Your hold on me is broken, Avon.'

His smile was lazy. 'Is it? We shall see. Having lost the means to force you into my bed, I'll merely have to try something new. Maybe I should offer you marriage now,' he mused.

She gawped, incredulous. 'Ha! Your gall is unbelievable. I wouldn't marry you if . . . '

'If I was the last man on earth. Yes, I know,' he cut in, yawning as if bored by the cliché. 'But perhaps for you, dearest May, I *shall* be. What happens if I make it common knowledge that Mr Goodbody's ward – a waif of unknown background to begin with – is no virgin either? Those families who in the past acted liberally and indulged their sons by allowing them to pay court, would pretty soon bring their boys to heel and forbid them your company. Who will marry you without a reputation? Few men would want you knowing another had been there before. But *I* would because I want you *that* much.'

May was hot with anger and embarrassment, his indelicacy shaming her. Such talk before coachmen was unforgiveable. 'Then ruin me,' she challenged him angrily. 'See to it that no man will ever marry me. But even then I shall never marry you. *Never*!'

'Never say never. It's so humiliating when one has to eat one's words.'

'Oh . . . bah!' May spluttered, lost for a final cutting word. 'Coachman, drive on.'

It would serve him right, the arrogant, beastly man, if she *did* marry him, for then she would truly make his life a misery; make him pay for each and every discomfiting moment he had ever caused her; take her revenge by placing her lowly, tarnished self in his stuffy, class-conscious, oh-so perfect household as a permanent reminder of his baser instincts and desires.

She was the dark side of Avon Midwinter's aspirations and, were she to marry him, everyone henceforth would know it and the chink in his armour would be fully exposed and he would become vulnerable.

It was preposterous, of course, for she had no intention of doing anything so foolish, but even so, once the thought was there in her mind, she could not shift it.

CHAPTER 32

1852 – the year when Brunel's plans for a suspension bridge across the Avon were finally dropped because of the drying up of funds, and the year when the Iron Duke died – was also the year when young Mr Cedric Goodbody returned home from his inordinately long Grand Tour, with a mind, it was assumed, to settling down and taking his place as heir apparent in the family business.

A debonair twenty-seven-year-old with basic good looks and exceedingly good prospects, he immediately aroused Aurelia's interest and, soon after he had got back into the mundane routine of working life, she had decided upon an informal garden party at her home, which would be her own, very special way of saying 'welcome back'.

Seddy – though he frowned nowadays when anyone used the old childhood form of address – had been happy enough to accept her generous gesture, yet, having lived next door to her for most of his formative years and feeling no great affection for her, he was even so, very much on his guard. Seddy was a man of the world now, or at least he liked to think so, and he felt he knew what devious thoughts ran through her head. The Widow Spicer – low on funds because of the crafty way in which the family solicitors had been instructed to execute matters on behalf of her late husband – doubtless saw him as a potential source of easy wealth. Cedric's spine tingled at the mere thought. She was like some praying mantis eager to devour, or – despite her pale delicate appearance – a fearful spider hiding beside her carefully spun web. Well, he had no intention of playing the part of hapless fly.

With his family he attended her garden party, thinking there safety in numbers and remembering to act as a gentleman and be polite and gallant towards his hostess, but striving to make certain that she didn't manipulate him into any situation that might lend her advantage. He partnered May, his honoured and blushing adopted sister delighting in such a position, and thus Seddy felt easier and at liberty to unwind just a little and even enjoy himself. With a female attached to his arm all afternoon it would be nigh on impossible for Lady Spicer to accuse him of compromising *her*! He remembered well the insidious coquettish tactics she had employed upon Courtney to secure marriage and wasn't about to be tricked thus. A hint of impropriety from her and Obediah Goodbody would feel duty bound to order his son to marry her to rectify matters. Just as the full blown roses in Aurelia's garden hid their wickedly sharp thorns, so the apparently pleasant afternoon gathering was rife with invisible pitfalls.

The hostess wore icy blue and wielded a fringed parasol daintily. The men's suits were stylish in flannels of dove grey, steel blue and formal black, lightweight to be practical on so pleasantly warm a day. At their necks cravats were knotted *à la* Byron, *à la* Prince Albert, or L'Irelandaise and L'Orientale; and on top of their heads, and raised often in respectful greeting of fellow promenaders, were their hats, both stovepipe and topper. When the ladies came close, by accident or to share some tidbit of gossip, their crinolines collided and were forced out and up, thus affording any gentleman lucky enough to be at hand a glimpse of neatly shoed or booted feet and trim, silk-stockinged ankles amidst a froth of petticoat flounces. Ah, such forbidden delights!

May wore Eau-de-Nil, the afternoon dress simple and modest in poplin over lawn petticoats and hoops, its decolletage and three-quarter sleeves trimmed with peppermint lace and bows. She was veritably melting in the heat, the two illicit glasses of wine – which Seddy had procured mischievously – doing nothing to cool her, but outwardly she looked cool and crisp, the pale green extremely deceptive.

They walked round the crescent-shaped bed of headily perfumed roses that was bordered by regimentally precise rows of dwarf marigolds and candy tufts, amusing themselves by remarking somewhat disparagingly, though without true malice, upon Aurelia's other, very grand, though exceedingly stuffy guests, until Avon appeared and, without asking, joined them.

'Come, come, Cedric, you can't keep May to yourself *all* afternoon. It just isn't fair. Her presence in your home day in, day out would be quite sufficient to keep you happy, I should have thought. Why don't you let some other eager gentleman stroll her around the garden for a while, and stop being so possessive,' Avon admonished, good-humouredly, nigh on snatching the girl out of Cedric's hands before he could attempt to start even mildly objecting. He was two years Avon's senior but he very much lacked Midwinter's inbred tyranical bent and smooth arrogance, and allowed May to be whisked away with a frown settling on her pretty face, his shoulders shrugging helplessly. In truth Cedric was worrying more about an encounter with Aurelia now that he was alone and vulnerable to her wiles, than whether May could cope with the overbearing Avon.

'Poor May, your hand is so hot,' her abductor cooed in obvious false lamentation. 'I think we should confiscate a tray of champagne from one of those ridiculously grand-looking waiters my sister hired for the afternoon, and take ourselves off to the cool of the summer-house down by the fishpond.'

'I think not,' said May firmly.

'Oh, don't be so prickly! Why ever not, pray? I'm hardly likely to rape you in broad daylight with so many people sauntering about, now am I? Don't be so stubborn always. You really *do* look frightfully hot and in need of a shady spot in which to regain your composure. But if you insist on braving the heat and any subsequent consequences, take comfort from the fact that if you faint I shall be at hand to personally loosen your bodice.'

That possibility stopped May in her tracks, and she shot him a narrowed, green glance that was quite unfriendly.

'Come on.' He locked his arm about hers and led the way through the scattered guests towards the less formal, rather more shrubbery-secluded lower half of the garden, relieving a waiter of his glass-laden tray on the way. He was so quick to take charge that May was allowed scant time to think.

The summerhouse was a hexagonal structure of half timber and herringbone patterned red brick, topped by a quaint conical thatched roof. Its north walls were solid and windowless, and inside a bench seat had been built where people might rest a while and enjoy the view south through arched doorway and generous windows. From the bottom of Aurelia's garden one could see right the way down to the river at Hotwells, along to Mardyke and even across to Gas Ferry Road by the *SS Great Britain*'s former dry dock.

But May, seated beside Avon, was hardly aware of the view. She sipped at the wine he'd insisted she should drink, made uncomfortable by being so close to him. And he didn't seem inclined – deliberately, May felt sure – to lessen her discomfort by indulging in polite conversation, but stayed as silent as she, staring straight ahead with an indolent air. For want of something with which to occupy herself, May was soon sipping at another glass and casting surreptitious glances sideways to watch his lazy, grey-eyed profile.

And then, at length, he stretched out his grey jersey trousered legs before him with a barely audible purr like a cat and crossed them at the ankles, wondering aloud, 'Have you given our last conversation together any further thought?'

'Hardly,' she sneered, relieved that at last they were speaking. Sparring with words she understood and could cope with, her tongue just capable of holding its own against Avon. But unknown tactics, the likes of which he'd employed just now, were wholly disquieting.

'You'll not get a better offer, you know. I'll honour you with marriage, position, wealth. And I'll overlook your shortcomings – your *used* status and humble origins. I

288

doubt you could do better elsewhere. I am, though I detest boasting, one of the richest men in the city.'

'Again, Avon, I can only say that you are wasting your time.'

'I think maybe not. I'm not your beautiful blue-eyed yankee, I know, nor do I expect you to feel for me what you obviously did for him. But face it, May, he's gone for good, while I'm here and willing.'

'But I don't love you. Surely you must care about that? What sort of sham would such a marriage be knowing that?'

'You don't love me. Nor I you. So what? We could have ourselves a marriage beneficial to us both despite a lack of romantic fervour. I don't believe in love anyhow.'

May was in the process of mulling that over when other voices invaded their quiet place in the garden; Cedric's pitched higher than normal with nervousness and Aurelia's honey-sweet and utterly persuasive.

'Why, dearest Cedric, I do believe you're trembling. Your hand in mine is trembling just like a captive bird. *How* sweet! I chose this path down which to stroll with you on purpose, dear, so that we could be alone. I wanted us to be together for a while without all the others. One can't be one's self under the prying gazes of so many. And I've *so* been wanting to welcome you home, to steal a kiss of greeting . . .'

'Lady Aurelia!' Cedric squeaked, scandalized by such forward, even brazen, behaviour.

'Kiss me, Seddy.'

The two in the summerhouse looked at each other wide-eyed with amused surprise and strove to stifle their mirth.

There were the sounds of a brief struggle, a sigh of surrender from Cedric, then low animal whimperings as their embrace became increasingly empassioned.

Poor Seddy, May worried, thinking that the very thing he had dreaded was now befalling him. And then, surprisingly, Avon took her arm and brought her to her feet, gallantly offering to save the gentleman from his sister's wily clutches. 'I think perhaps it's time we made our presence

289

known. To allow things to continue longer may cause everyone a great deal of embarrassment.'

Avon made much of coughing and clearing his throat, then embarked upon a loud description of the view, supposedly for May's benefit, but actually to alert the disarranged couple behind the summerhouse to the fact that they weren't, after all, alone.

'Well, Miss Bird,' drawled Avon, amused greatly by the situation, and taking no small measure of satisfaction from having thwarted the jaded Aurelia in her devious plans, 'I think we should start back towards the house now. Otherwise your guardian might worry and I'll be in his black book.'

She took the arm he crooked and slotted hers through it, more at ease now that she knew Seddy to be near, and they strolled back the way they had come, looking convincingly surprised when they encountered a red-faced Seddy and tight-lipped Aurelia in a flustered state to the rear of the summerhouse.

'Fancy meeting you two here,' Avon said pleasantly.

'Yes, fancy,' muttered Aurelia, who never was too good at masking displeasure when she felt it.

'Showing Cedric the latest shrubs are you?'

'Y-yes. That's right.'

'May and I were just admiring the view.'

'I heard, dear brother. Though being able to see it every day of your lives, I should have thought the pair of you would have tired of it by now.'

'Such a panorama is never likely to pale either in memory or reality,' Avon eulogized mockingly. 'Shall we all stroll back to the lawns together? I think you've neglected your other guests long enough, sister dear. And you mustn't monopolize Cedric so, either. *Everyone* wants to welcome him home, you know.'

'Thank you, Avon dear, but I do not need reminding,' snapped his greatly irritated elder sister.

May and Cedric both survived the remainder of the afternoon without further incident, the pair of them sticking together like glue for mutual protection against the Midwinters, and Seddy sighing more than once, reflecting, 'Thank God you and Avon turned up when you did. I truly believe Aurelia would have ravished me in the undergrowth otherwise!'

Aurelia felt that she had lost her chance with Seddy after that fumbled attempt at her garden party. Hungry kisses and a bold hand at the bulge of his crutch had testified to his healthy response to her advances, but even then he had seemed to hold back, reluctant to accept that which she had so blatantly offered. She had hoped to sweep him off his feet, to seduce and win him before the poor fool knew what had happened, but Avon and that freckle-faced May Bird had had to stick their noses in where they were not wanted and Cedric, shocked out of his lustful bout of abandon, had had time to collect his thoughts and wits apace and retreat.

Damn and blast them all! she cursed in her mind, drinking to their purgatory with an enthusiasm that sent her bitter ale sloshing over the rim of her tankard.

But what the hell, she consoled herself, smiling contentedly across the chipped oak trestle towards her companion. She still had Artie Fear, the dock worker she'd met that night by The Nova Scotia. He was good at soothing away her anger and resentment towards life in general, making her forget all for a time, save himself and the wondrous torture of delight he could inflict upon a submissive body.

In a scarlet dress that sported neither hoops nor petticoats beneath, and with her pale face subtly altered by dramatic make-up and dark wig, she felt bold enough to go about the docks whenever the urge took her, confident that no one in such lowly surroundings could have even the remotest reason for knowing her true, other self. To them she was just a slut; a mite better looking and more wholesome smelling than some of the regular ones who haunted the docks, and with all her teeth surprising sound in her mouth, but a slut still for all that.

Artie downed the dregs of his pint and got to his feet, aware that he had had just enough, and that to indulge the beer further would put the physical performance expected

291

of him faintly in jeopardy. He'd have been aggrieved not to have given his best, especially for the eager, unimaginably accommodating Nest (as Aurelia now called herself). Her kind, with extremes of desire which far outdid his own, was a rare breed, by crikey, and he was well aware of his good fortune. Nowadays when his wife complained of a headache or a woman's ailments as a means of denying him his husbandly rights, Artie didn't take his strap to her angrily as he would once have done. If his wife was reluctant, he simply used that unspent lust upon the appreciative Nest when they next met as planned.

'Be ee ready?'

'Yes,' replied Aurelia, finishing her beer and following him out the door of The Ostrich onto the cobbled waterfront in Lower Guinea Street. 'Have you anywhere planned for us?'

'Well, it were a mite tricky t'night. I had ta borrow a mate's row boat. T'ain't none too clean but at least we'll 'ave a bita privacy.'

'And where's the boat?'

'This way, Nest, me luv.'

He took her arm and guided her down stone steps made slimy by the last tide, then helped her into the filthy carcass of a small rowing boat. Oars splashed sloppily through the black waters and soon they were floating in the middle of the lamplit Bathurst Basin, their only company the ducks which lived amongst the reeds edging the fields opposite. Plans were underway to build a grand new general hospital overlooking the basin but as yet the proposed site was still being grazed by cattle.

Once they were drifting far away from the lights ashore and the moored shipping that thrust up skeletal rigging against the dark night sky, Artie pulled a tarpaulin over them both and fell upon the sprawling Nest who waited hungrily.

What did it matter if Cedric Goodbody had taken it upon himself to flee from her advances to Gloucester under the pretext of visiting an elderly and much loved relation? His loss seemed piffling compared to the utter delight that Artie could cause between her trembling thighs. She would be magnanimous and let Cedric go like small fry, for in retrospect he was likely as worthy of her contempt as Courtney had been before him. And as she thought of Courtney, resenting his intrusion upon her intimacy, and groaning involuntarily as Artie thrust deep within her, she remembered he was down there somewhere, maybe even right beneath her! A rotten, bloated corpse trapped amongst the debris of this or some other stretch of inland water! Her face screwed up at the thought and her passion dwindled, much to her consternation, but Artie never noticed so caught up was he in the overwhelming and elusive emotions of the moment. He ground away, forcing her legs wider so that he could go ever deeper, his climax violent and drawing a guttural shout of appreciation from him.

Less than satisfied and angry with Courtney's ghost and Artie's premature achieving of fulfilment, Aurelia sighed with disappointment and sat up, shoving aside the tarpaulin to find, somewhat in surprise, that they had drifted out of the basin and were now beneath the footbridge which crossed the waters at Princes Street, the huge bulk of Bush House – Acraman, Bush, Castle & Co's warehouse for storing their China tea – looming ahead to her right.

'I think you'd best get us ashore, Artie, before we drift all the way to the Cumberland Basin,' she told him tersely.

Still puffing breathlessly from the exertion of his pure and simple brand of rutting, Artie Fear buttoned his trousers up and did as asked, aware, from her prickly manner, that she hadn't got quite as much out of his performance as she usually did.

The rowing boat hit the stone steps in the shadow of Tucker and Hoskins Wharf, but Artie laid a stalling hand on her shoulders, his mood jovial and conciliatory. 'Be ee still 'ungry, Nest?'

'Hungry?' Sullenly she pretended she didn't know to what he referred.

He cupped a hand proudly about the lumpy mass in his trousers. 'Fer the likes o' this.'

'You're very perceptive,' she admitted.

He grinned and lifted her skirts, hands moving lily white legs apart to expose her fully to his whim. He wasn't up to riding her again just yet, though given ten minutes or so in which to fully recover that mightn't be the case, but Artie knew another simple means of making her smile return, and for so good a girl as Nest he was prepared to take the time and trouble. He opened her and then attacked, his tongue thrilling her almost immediately to a state of mindless bliss.

CHAPTER 33

On a July evening so warm that all the houses in Beaufort Rise had their tall sash windows pushed up so that lace window panels were set fluttering, Avon Midwinter came to call, expressing a wish to talk alone with Obediah. It was not long after May's seventeenth birthday.

Anne, Jasper and May (Cedric was still hiding in Gloucester) knew nothing of the visit until they returned from playing cricket on the Downs, the caller passing them on the tiled front steps and pausing briefly to touch his hat formally to the young women.

'Miss Anne, Miss May, good evening.'

'Good evening, Mr Midwinter,' they replied almost in unison.

And then he was gone – ignoring Jasper who carried his cricket bat slung over his shoulder – his suave, good-looking face wearing the faintest hint of a smile.

'I wonder what he wanted,' wondered May, watching him involuntarily as he strode next door and climbed his own front steps.

'Maybe he's been doing business with papa,' guessed Anne. 'It wouldn't be the first time.'

'Who cares one way or the other,' dismissed Jasper, pushing ahead of the dallying females and dropping bat, ball and stumps thoughtlessly in the hall. 'All I care about right this moment is my supper. Hitting all those sixes has given me the most ginormous appetite.'

'Me too,' said the like minded Anne, while May nodded, an expectant look on her face as she tried to guess what they would be eating.

But Obediah stalled them all, appearing from the study and instructing, 'Anne and Jasper, off with you and wash up before you go to table. And you, May, would you spare me a minute or two in my study?'

'Me? Yes, of course,' she said, mildly puzzled.

'Don't look so worried, child. You've done nothing wrong and need fear no lecture.'

Jasper and Anne, intrigued as much as May, lingered a moment or two whilst exchanging quizzical glances, then, mindful of Obediah's wishes, dutifully trudged upstairs to rid themselves of all evidence of grass staining and dirt.

Obediah foresook an authoritative pose behind his desk in favour of informality at the fireside, gesturing for May to take the Queen Anne chair opposite his own, then smiling at her. 'Sorry about the air of subterfuge, Birdy, but I thought you'd like this matter kept private for the time being, if not *always*.' He coughed, then continued, 'You may have seen Avon leaving just now . . . '

'Yes, I did.'

'He came here this evening knowing that he would be assured of time alone with me, so that he might discuss marriage. It seems, my dear, that the man is smitten and has, consequently, asked me for your hand.'

'What!' May's mouth fell open and she blinked incredulously. 'His impertinence and audacity never cease to amaze me.'

'Not half as much as they amaze me, Birdy, I can tell you.'

'You should have thrown him out. Or at the very least demanded that he leave immediately,' declared May, shaking her head at the preposterousness of the situation. 'That man just will not give up.'

'No, it appears not. I take it you have no intention of accepting?'

May shook her head and sighed helplessly, very much in a quandary. 'He's pestering me so that I'm at my wits end.

And he's *so* determined. He *insists* that we shall be married – and no amount of rejection seems to deter him from his aims.'

'Were I you, Birdy, I think I'd be vaguely flattered by that.'

'Yes, well . . . ' May rose and went to stare out of the window, thinking of the persistent Avon who, even during her years of puberty, had invisibly stamped her as his property. Maybe she should feel flattered, and perhaps she *was*, just a little. The young man was, if nothing else, consistent in his wanting of her, even knowing her to be – to use his word – *used*.

'Shall I politely decline on your behalf?' her guardian prompted, thinking that there would be an end to the matter.

'Yes . . . No . . . Oh, I don't know! What did he say to you, might I ask?'

'His propsal was formal – business-like even. He would offer you marriage without dowry, a reasonable allowance and complete control of his domestic affairs. In other words the household would be yours to run as you desired. I thought it a good offer. But none of that matters if you have no feelings for the man. Is it that you cannot feel tenderly disposed towards him because of lingering feelings for your American?'

Mention of Jude out of the blue unsettled May further and she steadfastly refused to think too deeply on that subject, shaking her head. 'No, I'd be a complete fool to go on wanting that which I know to be lost.'

'Then is it that you fear Mr Midwinter's reaction when he finds that you are not a . . . a virgin bride?' bumbled Obediah, going red with embarrassment at having to speak such a word in feminine company.

May felt bound to tell him then. 'Mr Midwinter knows about my liaison with the American. I know not how, but he does. Though he has no knowledge of the child born of it.'

'And so shall it remain, pray God. Poor Birdy, now your former brightness is quite gone. Talk on one subject necessitates raking up all manner of unhappiness from the past, doesn't it? I'm sorry. Let us conclude this business as soon as possible and then go take supper. Mrs Veysey's cooking and the light conversation at the dining table will cheer you again.'

'I do not love Avon,' May stated, as if somehow that explained all.

'Many are the successful marriages which have no such emotion at their foundation, though,' pointed out Obediah, rising and heading for the door. 'I'll tell him "no" then, shall I?'

'No, wait. What is your personal opinion of the man, sir? And how would you look upon such a marriage?'

'Base not your eventual decision upon any opinion of mine, Birdy. You alone know what will be. As for Avon as a catch: I doubt you could do better. Gentlemen at his level usually seek their wives from the titled upper-classes, their wealth paying for the introduction of blue blood into the family and for the aristocratic pretentions. One cannot doubt, therefore, the strength or depth of Avon's feelings towards you. Yet, as for Avon the man, I know little, maybe even less than you do on that score. He's a dark horse who seems to invite rumour and speculation.'

May nodded faintly in agreement, voicing her thoughts aloud. 'He loves me no more than I do him, and opinion seems against him in the matter of reputation. Yet still instinct tempts me, marriage to such a man a tantalizing prospect. I'm going to need some time, dear Obediah, before I finally decide.'

'That's probably wise. In the meantime, though, we have to join the others for supper and try to outwit their combined talents for wheedling out the truth of what we've been discussing here.'

Aurelia's first instinct when she found herself pregnant was to go and murder Artie Fear for having put her in such a state, then, when she had overcome her shock and was a shade more rational, anger gave way to demands for his help in rectifying matters. And Artie, once he knew that no

298

financial burden was to fall on him, turned out to be helpful enough, supplying Aurelia with the address of the best abortionist available and making all the necessary arrangements for a nocturnal visit. Aurelia had told him it would have to be done at night, and he hadn't pried, trying to find out why. Everyone was entitled to their secrets, after all, and he wasn't too curious about his girl's true circumstances just so long as she went on being as nice to him as she was in the early days of their strange and very basic affair. Sometimes he speculated on her being a servant or governess by day, but most times he couldn't be bothered to waste effort in trying to fathom her out. He was just a simple man who was happy with his lot. Many were the men who would have envied him, Artie didn't doubt, having at his disposal a female of insatiable sexual appetite.

The midwife-cum-abortionist-cum-herbalist and sometime witch lived on a lane in the truncated shadow of St Mary Redcliffe, her shuttered abode sparse, plain and none too clean, her manner brusque to the extreme. Whether delivering babies or helping females rid themselves of unwanted infants, she went about her work in a coldly detached, methodical manner, in the business for no other reason than to make easy money at a minimal risk.

Aurelia didn't take too kindly to being ordered around by this unwholesome, officious baggage of indeterminate middle years, but there was no alternative.

Legs wide and knees up, she offered her sex to the butcher woman's instruments, teeth gritted against expected pain. Larry had been such a disappointment and so *surplus* somehow, that the mere thought of another child had ever filled her with distaste. She wanted no more brats. And, besides, how could she? Her husband had been dead for six years! It would be difficult to explain away her baby under such circumstances and, she thought acidly, she doubted her contemporaries' credulity would stretch to a virgin birth!

Nauseous and weak-limbed, Aurelia let Artie lead her to a cab after she'd been fixed up and the startings of a child within her doomed to drain from her body in a stream of blood. He took her to another place – a friend's place, he told her – and there, making some pathetic excuse about having to be elsewhere by ten o'clock, he left her alone to see herself through the following hours of crisis. What good would he have been, after all? These types of problems were, he reasoned, for the women involved to sort out. He'd done his bit by seeing her 'fixed up' and was going to spend the rest of the night in The Greyhound well away from any unpleasantness.

The night was a lonely horror for Aurelia and she wondered, when dawn began to send faint grey light through the dirty side-street window and the blood showed chilling red all over the lower half of the straw pallet on which she lay groaning, whether she wasn't bleeding to death.

Artie – probably drunk, she didn't doubt – hadn't returned and panicking, she dragged herself out of the hovel and onto a nearby thoroughfare where she flagged down a cab, needing the driver's assistance to climb aboard. He likely thought her drunk too, but when she paid him in advance he was at once discreet and efficient, getting her up the hill to Clifton before the early summer sun was truly up and brightening the skies over St Werburghs and St Pauls.

She waved aside his offer of assistance once he had dropped her off on the corner of her street, insisting, 'I'll be fine, believe me. Good morning.' Then, when he had driven out of sight, she cast furtive glances about to assure herself that no early risers or milkmaids were out and about and removed her wig, hiding it in her bundled up shawl.

The hundred yards to her house seemed the longest she had ever walked and she nigh on collapsed with relief when her stable hand – the one person who had an inkling as to her nocturnal female philanderings – silently opened the rear door to let her in. As ever it was his duty to await her return when she went abroad at night, to keep her comings and goings secret from the rest of the household and also look after the horse she used sometimes for such assignations. In return Aurelia remained silent and indulgent concerning his rapist tendencies and turned a blind eye to his unsavoury, feared attentions bestowed on the lower maids.

By bullying, coercion and sheer menace he had had them all; deflowering the virgins without a care and finding gratification in the debasement and humiliation of every one. Lady Spicer pretended she had no idea of what was going on under her own roof and appeared to keep herself far above anything so sullied and ostensibly lower-class. Though that didn't stop her playing the voyeur when her stable hand took some hapless female servant down the garden to the potting shed, there to ravish her amongst potted geraniums and seed trays. Aurelia, on seeing him heading in that direction, had often taken herself up to her bedroom, from where she could see directly down through the glass roofed structure and assess his every violent performance.

His known presence about the lower floors of the house at night kept everyone else as far away as possible for safety's sake, and this dawn Aurelia was to be very thankful for that fact. Sycophantically efficient, he handed over a candlestick as usual and set about locking the doors while she took the servants' staircase – the quickest route – up to her own floor. Her accomplice, with his sub-intelligent mind not easily applied to anything save thoughts of pleasure in the inflicting of pain on pretty things, grunted a respectful 'goodnight', but seemed quite unaware of her far from normal physical state.

She dragged herself up the bare-boarded newel, her pain overwhelming, then had to use the walls to steady herself as she moved along the corridor to her suite of rooms. Once inside she shut and locked the door then sank with a sob of relief to the floor, feeling safe at last. Why did her fun always seem to cost so, and in more than monetary terms? It just *wasn't* fair! Were she the gambling kind she'd have put money on her making a complete recovery and being able, damn it all, to fall pregnant countless more times in the future! She'd not be one of the *lucky* ones left conveniently barren by such a dreadful experience. No, because life for her just wasn't fair.

After a while she felt strong enough to clean her face of its tell-tale make-up, unlock her door and put herself to bed on top of a thick pile of sheeting to soak up her bleeding. Later, when she'd had a fire lit in the grate to cheer her while she stayed in bed with an imaginary cold, she would burn the bloody linens there and no one would ever be any the wiser.

Genuinely wan and with a handkerchief poised to dab at her nose, she greeted her maid with her usual polite and starchy indifference. 'I'll be staying in bed today, Birchwood, so you needn't pull back the curtains. I seem to have developed a summer cold. Such a nuisance.'

'Oh dear, ma'am, I am sorry to hear that. Is there anything I can get you – a toddy or cough syrup?'

'No, it's all right. I'll just sleep. Have it known that I do not wish to be disturbed,' said Aurelia, wearily, sinking lower into her soft mattresses with a wince and thinking cynically that it would take more than a draught or two of porter to restore the colour to her cheeks. She closed her eyes and gave herself up hopefully to sleep, relying on that to put her wounded and exhausted body to rights, and cursing as wholly unfair her clandestine lifestyle that was slowly wearing her out before her time.

Always, when May needed to be alone, or to think, she took herself to the garden and sat herself down upon the white wrought iron bench seat near the patio, shaded by exotic, tall yuccas and the wispy swaying of asparagus grass.

Time trudged on, yet still she had come to no firm decision concerning Mr Midwinter's proposal, all her reasons for equally matched by those against.

In his favour was his position and wealth, his tendency to overlook her past indiscretion and his general good looks. Had she seriously been contemplating marriage, he could not have been a better choice. He was lenient to the extreme, considering the fact that she was little better than a fallen woman, and thus May was forced reluctantly to think of him in warmer terms.

Putting aside Avon's proposal she tried logically to picture her future, to see life as it would probably be. Would she marry? She'd never thought twice of that possibility, her heart, as ever, ensnared by the memory of three days one never-to-be-forgotten summer. No, she couldn't imagine marriage, felt that the Goodbody household offered her all she needed in the way of love and companionship. Yet was that a fair outlook? Did she have the right to their hospitality indefinitely, a spinster, like Anne, relying on the hardworking and ever benevolent Obediah to provide the food for her mouth? She had never given it thoughtful examination until then, and May was alarmed. She really had *no* right, despite knowing her guardian more than willing to be so used by those he loved, to go on without responsibility or true purpose into the future, like some pampered parasite. But Obediah liked it that way, she reminded herself, knowing how he loved to spoil her and Anne, indulge his sons and show kindness in abundance to Mrs Veysey and Wendy, the housemaid. Though even knowing that didn't make it right. She *owed* it to Obediah, after all he had done, to make a good marriage. Then he would feel, she knew, that his endeavours on her behalf had been worthwhile.

Having decided, therefore, that she *should* marry, was Avon truly a suitable choice?

There was no denying his ardour, for his pursuance of May had ever been single-minded – some would say maniacal! Yet there lingered that area of doubt in her mind, that, perhaps irrational, unease. In her mind, when younger he had personified the Big Bad Wolf, and for some illogical reason that association still persisted. She had never felt that she could trust Avon. There was an undeniable dark side to him that automatically made him appear less dependable.

Over and over she had thought along similar lines, her contemplations resolving nought. Then, this day, with the sun setting in the sky above Somerset on the far side of the Avon, that young man of like name came from the back of his house to lean on the fence languidly and arrest May's attention with a lazy query.

'How much longer, pray, Miss Bird, do you intend to keep me dangling before you deign to give me an answer?'

She rose from her seat, pink-cheeked of a sudden with the embarrassment of being disturbed from thoughts of his own good self, scrunching her hands at the folds of her flame and white striped cambric skirts in a furtive bid to dry them. 'Believe me, sir, your proposal is ever in my mind. A decision is, however, proving difficult to reach.'

'Are there questions you would ask of me? Certain points that trouble you?'

She shook her head, looking him over shyly as if appraising him anew, taking in nose, grey eyes, pale hair and meagerly lipped mouth of a full-blooded red. Could she stand his arms about her and his kisses, his body having certified and legal ownership and dominance of her own? Maybe *those* were the questions she should have asked herself.

An eyebrow raised in indolently quizzical manner to form a sweeping arch over a steely eye as Avon wondered, amused by her glazed, far-away expression, 'What are you thinking about? And why do I get the overwhelming impression that I figure in your musings?'

May roused herself and, not bothering to try and reply, took a deep breath and asked him boldly, 'Would you humour me by bestowing a kiss? It's forward I know, but . . .'

'*Please*, there's no need to try and justify your request. I'm more than willing,' laughed Avon, neither nonplussed nor discomfited in the slightest by her forwardness. He seemed to guess that the kiss was part of some idiotic female test, contrived by her for God only knew what contrary reason. Even so, he indulged her, making certain she wouldn't forget the experience in a hurry, either.

The moment she stepped close and leant accommodatingly just a little further over the fence towards him, Avon enfolded her with arms about her waist and shoulders and held her to the firm, lean length of him, his mouth swooping and crushing hers with an ardent kiss that had Mrs Veysey gawping scandalized from an upstairs window.

His mouth was harsh and breath sweet, lips moving hungrily upon May's in a not unpleasant manner, their contact dry and stirringly warm. And when he released her gently and held her a moment about the arms to instinctively steady her, May had to admit to positive rather than negative surprise. No, she didn't mind his arms about her, or his kisses. He was confident and accomplished, handling her with all the arrogant self-assurance of some Latin gigolo and, for a moment or two May succumbed to his charm.

'Was it satisfactory?' Avon asked, his voice heavy with the drawl of conceit. 'Or maybe you'd care for another?'

'No thank you. One kiss told me all I needed to know.'

'Really?'

'Yes. If your offer still stands, sir, then I shall be pleased to be your wife,' May said softly, the enormity of the decision lost amidst a new wave of self-consciousness that made her cast her eyes down to the flagstones of the patio.

Had she seen his face May would have been surprised further, for there was genuine delight on the sparsely fleshed face. His voice was buoyant, with laughter touching it, 'Well done, Miss Bird. I'm so glad you've come to your senses at last.'

'Only time will tell,' breathed May with the teeniest twinge of doubt.

'I'll post the banns, begin arranging matters. Have you any preference as to marriage date?'

'No. Though having decided, I think we might just as well finalize things as soon as possible.'

'I'm all in favour of that. Heavens, your acceptance has taken me so by surprise that I've neglected to obtain a ring. We must do things properly, no matter that the engagement will be a short one. May I choose it, or would you rather we shopped together?'

'I'll leave the choice to you, Avon. You have such good taste.'

'Yes,' he agreed, as pleasant then as she was ever likely to see him. 'And now that we are affianced, might I presume to ask for another kiss?'

'You may, though I think you'd best restrict it to the back of my hand in view of the number of faces I can feel spying on us from overlooking windows,' said May, primly.

She held out her hand, but once he had hold of it Avon

305

was no longer satisfied, drawing her close then with a violent urgency that made May blush, and kissing her thoroughly and deliberately, in a manner calculated to make all peeping spectators gasp in genteel shock.

CHAPTER 34

At twenty-two years of age and for the last twelve months of them stationary at a height of six feet four inches, Jude Mariner had, in Jack's relieved opinion, finally finished growing. His impressive stature ill-suited ship life and many were the lumpy, bruised foreheads acquired from omitting, through forgetfulness, to stoop when negotiating doorways below deck.

The spring of 1852 found him aboard the *Celestial Piper* shipping out of San Francisco, skirting South America and the daunting prospect of the Horn ahead.

They had picked up a cargo of nitrate from Valparaiso on the Chilean coast, then sailed the southern trades until the most southerly tip of the continent of America, Tierra Del Fuego, and the straits of Le Maire beckoned. Then the sea became hostile, a broiling black, spewing, foaming cavernous monster, intent on devouring man and ship. It was a passage which Jude had done more than once before, but he never became blasé about it, nor swaggered about port when he'd completed a successful voyage to boast of the exploit. The Horn was a subduer of men. It had made him realize time and again how very feeble and small he was when pitched against the awesome forces of nature. To take Drake's Passage took courage, but to survive it depended completely on the will of the sea gods.

The worsening weather heralding winter in the hemisphere which had the Antarctic for an underbelly, meant a rough sailing around the cape, Captain Jack having to steer a course for Port Stanley in the Falkland Islands so that damage to the barque's foremast could be given temporary repair. There they had spent a miserable fortnight and more, having to buy garments of sheepskin to keep themselves remotely warm from crofters of British stock who had colonized the bleak landscape years before and raised equally British sheep as their means of existence. After a fortnight of basic hospitality – from islanders who had seen enough wrecked and crippled ships limp into their coves to no longer find them novel – the fractious crew of the *Celestial Piper* were all heartily sick to death of mutton stew and chops, and leg and shoulder roast, and even looked forward, perversely, to shipboard fare. At least their cook dished up slop that could be said to be of an interesting variety. They were unprepared, therefore, and greatly disappointed to find that *he* had bought several sheeps' carcasses and that the unrelieved boredom of mutton, for the sake of fresh and nutritious meat, would continue for yet more weeks to come!

In mid-ocean, with never a sighting of Argentina or Brazil, the forgotten island of Tristan da Cunha or for that matter St Helena, Ascension Island or the coast of West Africa, the *Celestial Piper* escaped the doldrums and began to make up time in the northeast trade winds, a summer docking in Falmouth still very much a possibility. And then, two days north of the Azores, with the Scilly Isles off the south-west tip of England their next expected sighting, the majestic lines of the *SS Great Britain* swept into view and the *Celestial Piper*'s thirty strong crew amassed on deck to take a look at the famed vessel passing.

From her twin funnels plumes of white smoke trailed behind her like ribbons against the cool blue sky, and on her six masts canvas was crammed and wind-filled, keeping the gleaming black iron hull swiftly cutting through the water, its sombre colour broken by the use of Nelson chequers in a becoming stripe along her side.

She cut the water with grace, bowsprit dipping then rising from the foam and spray, the unicorn figureheads flanking a crown-adorned shield that bore the arms of Bristol.

'Well I never,' Jack sighed, thoroughly impressed, 'there's a sight to behold. She's the queen of the seas and no doubting.'

'But what's she doing in these waters? She never usually comes this far south on her Atlantic crossings,' Jude queried.

'I did hear it said, last time we were in New York, that she had been sold to Gibbs, Bright and Company of Liverpool to do their Australian run. Now that would account for her position.'

'Aye. Well, good luck to her. She's in need of some.'

Jack laughed. 'You ever were a pushover for a beautiful lady.'

And Jude smiled wistfully, watching the liner and returning her passengers' excited wavings until they had grown too small to be clearly seen.

No, he was still only a pushover for *one particular lady*, Jude mentally corrected Jack, despite all the other's endeavours to turn him into a carefree womanizer like his own good self. Jude had succumbed, but only in part, sleeping with Amy Becket back at San Francisco quite simply as a means of releasing sexual tension. Afterwards, when relief had proven only fleeting and her services apparently unable to bring him permanent peace, he had been sorry for the indulgence. Sex was in the head, Jude was of the opinion, the natural urges relatively easy to ignore if one put one's mind to it; the ministerings of a woman by no means crucial. After all, monks seemed to manage without resorting to the ease of fornication. Jude supposed he had bedded her to please Jack rather than himself, to give the father-figure in his life peace of mind by somehow proving that his 'sòn' was normal in all basic respects. Only by appearing to have recovered from his broken heart, to be back on an even keel – as Jack liked to phrase it – did he escape the captain's affectionately bullying tactics.

Amy Becket had been a fetching harlot, though not yet so long in the business that she'd lost completely her charming air of naivety. Compared to her contemporaries she was still fresh and appealing, and, of greater importance to Jude – if he must poke her for appearances' sake – clear as yet from all those fearful transmittable ailments which were the additional hazards of whoring about. Jack had contracted more than one dose of the unmentionable in his time, and seemed to accept his lot philosophically as the price paid for pleasure without the complication of relationships. But Jude had no wish to be similarly afflicted.

He leant his body into the handrail and rested on his elbows, giving an unconscious frown of disappointment at the lifestyle of his mentor, his black locks – grown down to his shoulders in crinkly, neglected waves – catching in the stiff Atlantic breeze and sweeping back from his tanned face. As a sailor Jude thought Jack admirable, yet in other aspects of his life he offered an appalling example to young, impressionable minds. Jude guessed that it was only the strength of his own character which had saved him from turning into a rather poor replica of the older, exceedingly worldly man before now.

Far in the distance to the south, where the horizon separating turquoise sky and sea was hard to discern and the sun touched a million wave crests with a silver artistic stroke, *Great Britain* was now a hazy dark spot growing ever smaller; then she was gone, only a white-grey trail of smoke marking the sky.

Jude thought, with admiration anew, of the illustrious engineer Mr Brunel, and felt a certain pride in being able to say that once he had met that very man and shaken his hand. His mind went back to that Monday train ride, back to Weston-super-Mare and the mud of the Bristol Channel, to dwell on May Bird and all the quaint settings that had enhanced her loveliness that day and branded her forever in his memory.

And then the thought struck and Jude stood up erect, his face expressing the amazement of discovery.

Mr Brunel would know where to find her, wouldn't he? Of course he would! They were acquaintances of old – more than that – they were friends. *God*, why hadn't he thought of it before!

Jude wanted to whoop for joy, to launch himself into the

air with a yell. He controlled himself, however, indulging only in a low and endless, merry chuckle.

'What's tickled your fancy?' wondered Jack, cocking a dark eyebrow that was at variance with his white blond locks.

But Jude only shook his head and issued a hearty, 'Nothing.' For what Jack didn't know wouldn't cause him unnecessary disquiet.

England lay not too far away and there waited his love – his May – and this time he *would* find her. This trip would not be soured by bitter-sweet agony and frustration at knowing her near yet beyond reach. This trip the joy of seeing her again would be his. He willed the ship to go faster through the waves, energy and enthusiasm suddenly boundless as he answered Jack's command with an, 'Aye, cap'n,' and scrambled up through the rigging ahead of the others, to unfurl more sail so as to capitalize on the freshening northeasterly driving them ever towards port. She was only days away, yet even that amount of time seemed suddenly unbearable.

May had taken it for granted that the wedding would be held at the Clifton parish church of St Andrews. However, Avon quashed such assumptions almost immediately, his thoughts on the matter far more grandiose. He considered St Mary Redcliffe, that parish church being the most beautiful in the city, if not the land; then the solid old Norman cathedral of St Augustine off Narrow Quay; and finally decided on the city church of St Stephen. May breathed a sigh of relief, for a cathedral wedding would have terrified her, and though her personal preference was for St Andrews, where she had always dutifully worshipped with the Goodbodys, she bowed down before Avon's choice, not so devout that she felt the issue warranted argument. But the business of the venue made her realize one thing; Avon, as ever, very much suited himself, unmindful of the wishes and thoughts of others.

The banns were read, the choir hired and the organist rehearsed her Mendelssohn, whilst the servants at Number 6 Beaufort Rise were put to creating the most expensive and elaborate wedding breakfast that Clifton society had seen all summer. It was to be the wedding of the year; Avon would not have it otherwise.

May, caught in a whirl of trousseau purchasing and gown fittings, paid for by the immensely proud and ever generous Obediah, remembered little of the hectic weeks leading to her wedding, save one unexpected and totally out-of-character concession on Avon's part. All the scullery, parlour and laundry maids who had ever shared his bed or enjoyed his sexual favours in any shape or form, had been dismissed and hastily replaced by good plain girls hand picked by Mrs Butler on his instructions and behalf. This he had told May, expressing his wish that they start married life with no clouds of doubt lingering overhead. She had appreciated the gesture, the esteem in which she held her fiancé enjoying an upsurge for a while.

White was not thought greatly suitable for the brides of Victorian England, it being used then more often for burials, and the nearest that fashion and etiquette permitted the bridal hue to transgress towards the *blanc* was ivory or magnolia. Most brides, however, shied away from white anyhow, for it smacked too greatly of coming out balls and the naivety of first seasons. To be sophisticated and apparently grown-up, they plumped for pastel blues and pinks, lemon and Eau-de-Nil, or the ultra chic écru (though not if one was of a sallow complexion).

May hummed and hawed for a long time in uncertainty concerning the right colour for *her* and was eventually persuaded by Anne towards a peachy-magnolia satin that had overskirts of blond gauze with tambour work all about the vast hem like a never-ending garland of silken lilies. Chain-stitching the design with small steel hooks took two apprentices sixteen hours a day for two weeks to complete. The finished article, though, when complimented by a circlet to adorn the hair made up of waxed lilac lilies and sweetpeas with a blond veil trailing down to the floor behind, was well worth the effort and time, and all who saw her vowed May Bird-Midwinter the most breathtakingly lovely bride of 1852.

Weddings, like funerals and christenings, were occasions of pomp, indulging in rich ceremony and procession, where there was a place for everyone and everyone knew their place. Before the church porch the carriages pulled up one after the other to unload their elegantly attired passengers, the bride arriving last as was the tradition to pause at the portal on Obediah's arm, while Anne, the maid-of-honour, straightened skirts and adjusted the fall of veil. Larry stood in the group's shadow, quaking fearfully as the enormity of acting as page in his spanking new sailor-suit hit him fully. His mama would be in there waiting – watching for his slightest mistake – and she was in an awful mood because she didn't care for his Uncle Avon marrying so low beneath him. Larry didn't altogether understand that, however, for May Bird seemed to him anything but low. He liked her heaps, thinking her on a par with sticky buns, gob-stoppers and humbugs, high up on his list of all-time favourite things, though still he wished she'd overlooked him for this particular role. Larry knew it would be difficult to be safely inconspicuous when he was part of the group about to receive all the attention. But Birdy had insisted, had smiled just so in that winning way of hers and told him that as far as she was concerned, he was the *only* person suitable for the job. And he had succumbed to her charm, even suffering the hated restrictions of the sailor-suit without a murmur of protest, because it was for her.

Above, on the tower face the clock hands moved with a mechanical clunk around to five past ten, and Obediah laid a soft kiss upon May's lightly powdered cheek.

'Are we all ready?' he enquired.

The murmured reply was in the affirmative, and they moved forward into the gloomy interior, seeing neither aisle, nave or arched Gothic windows, the enduring medieval masonry forgotten as occasion took a hold and humbled them to nervousness.

Avon, somehow dominating the sea of admiring faces, watched her approach from the front pew, his insolent gaze fastened upon the splendour of her hair which had been swept back and coiled into a chignon beneath the stylized floral wreath. His morning-suit was dove grey, the waistcoat – just peeping from beneath – a dashingly gay canary yellow to suit the assumed joyousness of the occasion. He always knew precisely how to dress for every occasion, even the knot of his cravat carefully tied to be in keeping.

Hymns were sung and the vicar indulged in some lengthy sermonizing as to the meaning of a truly Christian marriage, then came the vows, maybe too quickly done, it seemed to May, to be properly understood or appreciated. In truth the whole service had something of an unreal quality. She opened her mouth and repeated that which was required, neither elated nor sad. Numb, rather. If any should ask her in a week's time for her recollections of the happy event, she felt she'd be unable to accommodate them.

Avon, with his warm, dry, manicured fingers, slipped the gold band onto her finger beside the engagement ring of an oval ruby in a setting of lesser diamonds, and gave a vague smile, almost – May felt – in self-congratulation. Yes, well he'd got what he wanted, hadn't he? Why, therefore, shouldn't he look pleased, and why should it disconcert her? Maybe it was because the smile wasn't wholly pleasant, because it had elements of hunter and prey or cat and canary to it. It was an untrustworthy smile and May's insides succumbed to a nervous flutter.

However, she wasn't about to quake just yet, she told herself, firmly. She was no innocent virgin to be devastated by or tremble at his victor's show of prowess. To build him up so in her mind was quite ridiculous, for he was, after all, only a man; a harsh man, granted, but still only a man and human for all that. She really shouldn't allow herself to be daunted so.

He had wanted her badly enough to marry her, even knowing her used, and she should be grateful, she knew, for that. She might love Jude Mariner now and for ever but that was so futile and pointless. As a second choice Avon was not so bad. Indeed she knew of many women – besides his dismissed housemaids – who had been thoroughly charmed by the handsome gentleman with something of a reputation. May was not, nor had ever been, so easily won over, but she would admit to finding him physically attractive, and viewed the coming intimacies of the marriage bed without maidenly trepidation. A little experience, especially when dealing with the tried and, frankly, jaded Avon, mightn't be such a bad thing. If not greatly knowledgeable then at least not entirely ignorant, May thought that she could cope with him and perform her wifely duties well enough to keep him happy. Leastways if he acted in a proper, gentlemanly manner he would not find her unyielding or unresponsive.

Jude crept into her mind once, to mar her day with the never-ending sorrow of his loss, but she shook him from her thoughts and their ill-fated child with him, making herself mentally close that chapter of her life for all time. She owed it to Avon to forget that which had gone before.

With loud organ blasts of melody proclaiming the deed done, she took Avon's arm and went back down the aisle, smiling at all those beaming faces both familiar and strange, who were present to add their goodwill to the proceedings.

Outside, before the porch with its notice board advertizing a forthcoming discussion on the 'Irish Problem', they arranged themselves *en masse* for a pupil of Mr Fox Talbot who was going to take the official photographs to mark the occasion.

May and Avon were the central figures, with the bridesmaid and page posed before them on a low bench, then beside Avon was his best man, Mr Dyce, the solicitor, Aurelia, and a somewhat reluctant Cedric with the Gloucestershire Goodbodys with whom he'd taken refuge squeezed in to the side. Fortunately, however, the spider seemed to have lost interest in her fly. Beside May was Obediah, and next to him Mr Brunel, Mary and the children. Behind were the crowded, jostling secondary guests, spouses and offspring, all eager and excited at the prospect of immortality on photographic paper. Jasper was forgotten throughout the following technical procedures, as the guests were instructed to painstakingly hold their poses for a lengthy exposure time, and not until the printed photographs were presented – with a bill for payment – to the newlyweds some weeks later and they browsed with mild interest over the assembled figures and faces, did they spot the youngest Goodbody. He had shinned up a lamp standard and was there, hanging for posterity like a monkey from the horizontally protruding ladder supports, with a wicked mischievous grin splitting his face!

The heady scent of roses wafted up about bride and groom as the landau – pulled by two matching dapple-greys – drove leisurely back up the hill to Clifton. Bystanders turned to watch their progress, smiling at the outstandingly lovely bride and the arrogantly proud man beside her. Yes, Avon Midwinter had good reason to feel pleased with himself, his male contemporaries felt, and they envied him the coming night, a little heady at the erotic pictures that instantly sprang to mind. The women looked at May, noted her gown in all its costly perfection and doubtless remembered their own wedding days wistfully. Their dreams had still been intact then, the future before them all bright and rosy.

Avon half turned to May, breathed in deeply and possessively her soft, understated perfume. From him it was somehow an oddly affectionate gesture. Quite out of character and unlikely to be repeated again in a hurry.

'You know,' he said musingly, as if the possibility took him totally by surprise, 'we really *could* be happy together.'

May nodded, smiling. 'It has occurred to me also. Let us promise here and now, Avon, to try our very best.'

He took her white-gloved hand in response, holding it firmly as he regarded her, his hungry eyes intent. 'I promise.'

SEEDS OF LOVE

Valerie Georgeson

In turn-of-the-century Tyneside, money doesn't grow on trees. With Ma dead, Da often at sea and sister Fanny getting into trouble with the lads, June Ridley's life isn't easy.

Beautiful, innocent, uncertain of the future, Jane wants more than marriage and countless children. So she takes a job in George Beattie's flower shop, cared for by his gentle wife Adeline. Torn between affection for the shy Ronnie Wilson, and the more exciting advances of Jack Purvis, Jane is forced to grow up overnight when the conflict ends in tragedy.

Then Adeline dies in childbirth. George's dependence on Jane and her feelings for him slowly change to love. But marriage to George is no bed of roses. Dark passions reappear to haunt them, and only her brother Robert's return from India gives her solace. But finally, Jane finds happiness, learning that the seeds of love must be firmly rooted if they are to grow into a flourishing plant . . .

Also from Futura by
Valerie Georgeson
THE TURNING TIDES

FUTURA PUBLICATIONS
FICTION/SAGA
0 7088 3272 5

HEARTS AND FARTHINGS

Beryl Kingston

London in the 1890s . . . a foggy city bustling with
activity and bubbling with Cockney repartee.

To this alien world comes Alberto Pelucci, an early
immigrant from distant Italy, dreaming of adventure and
romance. Adventure enough is the verminous room of his
first night's stay in London, but romance seems more
rewarding when the shy Alice accepts his hand. Only on
their wedding night does he realise that his bride will
never share his passion for physical pleasures.

And so when Alberto meets Queenie Dawson –
exuberant, sensuous star of the music halls – his ordered
new life is flung into turmoil . . .

HEARTS AND FARTHINGS: the heart-warming saga
of a man torn between two women, and of children born
in the last, bittersweet days before the war that should
have ended all wars.

FUTURA PUBLICATIONS
FICTION/SAGA
0 7088 2976 7

NO WORK TODAY

Flora Pearce

Set in a Midlands mining village in 1908, where work is
scarce and hardship a way of life, NO WORK TODAY is
the moving portrait of one family and the love and loyalty
that sustain it.

Mary Ann, courageous and spirited, single-handedly
provides for her children when deserted by her selfish
and philandering husband, Raish.

Katy, her vivacious and captivating daughter, seeks
financial security in marriage. But she can never forget
the handsome, charming man who first loved her.

Paul, hardworking and ambitious, dreams of mine
ownership and prosperity. But too late he learns the high
cost of success . . .

And Ben. A fighter for miners' rights, hot headed and
impetuous, he covets his brother's wife.

Above all of them hangs the shadow of their drunken and
domineering father – the man they all have reason to hate
and the man their adored mother has never stopped
loving . . .

FUTURA PUBLICATIONS
FICTION
0 7088 3589 9

All Futura Books are available at your bookshop or
newsagent, or can be ordered from the following address:
Futura Books, Cash Sales Department,
P.O. Box 11, Falmouth, Cornwall TR10 9EN.

Please send cheque or postal order (no currency), and
allow 60p for postage and packing for the first book
plus 25p for the second book and 15p for each additional
book ordered up to a maximum charge of £1.90 in U.K.

B.F.P.O. customers please allow 60p for
the first book, 25p for the second book plus 15p per
copy for the next 7 books, thereafter 9p per book

Overseas customers, including Eire, please allow £1.25
for postage and packing for the first book, 75p for the
second book and 28p for each subsequent title ordered.